The Rose and the Thorn

A Beauty and the Beast Retelling

Katherine Macdonald

"Beauty and the Beast"

Original story by Gabrielle-Suzanne Barbot de Villeneuve, published in 1740 in La Jeune Américaine et les contes marins (The Young American and Marine Tales)

Illustration 1907 by Hazel Frazee

Cover design by: Lydia V Russell
Rose Motif by: Katherine Meyrick
Chapter headings: Nicole Scarano
Dividers: Elisa Bugg

Follow on Twitter @KateMacAuthor

Contents

Author's Note

The story of Beauty and the Beast has always captivated me. It's partly the fault of Disney's 1991 animated masterpiece; who could not fall in love with such witty dialogue, gorgeous animation, and brilliant score? But at its heart was a simpler story: the story of a girl who saved a beast.

There were precious few fairytales that depicted women as the heroine, and while the original Beauty of Villenueve's tale may have had little agency in her own story, it was nevertheless unique at the time.

There were, however, a few things I found problematic about the tale, namely that Beauty comes to love the person keeping her prisoner, and that her father traded her freedom for his own.

I had no plans to rewrite the tale myself until I had a dream of a girl wandering into a meadow filled with flowers, only to find herself a few moments later in a desolate castle, inhabited only by a beast. She became trapped not by him, but the laws of the land. It was a relationship founded on far more equal footing. That image formed the opening of what became The Rose and the Thorn, that, and the horrifying nightmare element of the dream: a pale face in the mirrors.

I hope you enjoy reading it, as much as I enjoyed writing it.

Dedications:

To Kirsty,

This is perhaps not the first story you and I had in mind, but regardless, you will always be my first and greatest fan.

And to Theo,

Who taught me both the meaning of fear, and the meaning of courage. I will one day return the favour. You have been warned.

Part One: Winter

In the bleak midwinter, frosty wind made moan,
Earth stood hard as iron, water like a stone;
Snow had fallen, snow on snow, snow on snow,
In the bleak midwinter, long ago.

--Christina Rossetti--

Chapter One

A Rose In Winter

Winter has haunted me since the year I turned nine, the year my mother died. The memories I have of that night are suspended in a snow globe of emotion, sharp and tangible as glass.

I was watching the snow fall thicker and thicker outside the window, falling so quickly and viciously it slid like volleys of arrows. My younger sister Hope had fallen asleep in my older sister's arms, and Honour, despite her best attempts, had drifted off too. Firelight flickered against their sleeping faces, two primrose cheeks pressed against each other, still, calm, immobile. Only Freedom and I were still awake, our ears pricked for the next of our mother's moans, Papa's reassuring words, Nanny's soft voice.

There were no reassuring words now, no soft, soothing voice of Nanny's. No moans, and no crying. An awful, penetrating silence, as sharp and hard as the cold north wind that kicked and screamed against every crevice.

The memory of that bitter, dark hour is so etched into my mind that I swear I can remember each knot in the floorboards beneath Freedom's pacing feet, each flake as it seared against the glass. I can count each time the fire dared to crackle.

Even now, as my breath ekes out in misty spurts, I see it hit that window pane, obscuring the icy tundra outside the window of the little house. I see the little girl reflected in the glass, who would be irrevocably altered before the night was over.

Since that day, winter has been my enemy. I have never been able to enjoy the first flakes of the season, build snowmen with my younger siblings. For years, I refused to even open the curtains on snowy days, would kick and scream whenever Nanny suggested a walk. I wanted to shut it out, forget it existed, forget the empty chair beside the fireplace, the hollow dip in the other side of Papa's bed. If I shut my eyes tight enough, buried my face deep into my pillow, I could hear Mama singing in the kitchen, see the autumn wreath glowing in her golden hair. Winter had never come, never claimed her.

Eight years later, the screaming has turned to grumbling, perhaps more today because Freedom is bossing me about and I shouldn't even be here. It was Honour's turn to gather with the hunting party, but she wasn't feeling well and so I took her place. "Call it an early wedding present," I snipped, a little harder than I meant to. Honour looked up at me gratefully nonetheless, and then proceeded to start retching again. Nanny wandered past our door and muttered something about "wedding nerves" rather gleefully.

I know Honour can't help being ill, but that doesn't lift my mood. The cold claws at every naked inch of me as I ferret about the bushes, searching for the few pickings we haven't managed to scavenge. It is a bleak midwinter, the woods lie almost barren, and our stores do not fare much better. Poor Honour, who had dreamt so long of a spring wedding. It would be a meagre affair at this rate, all nuts and sour, salted meat. Freedom said she brought it on herself, "Who gets married in *winter*?" but she and Charles had said they simply could not wait any longer.

"Deer, deer!"

Something leaps out of the bushes; a dark, impish shape. I throw myself backwards, upsetting my basket, as a doe comes springing through the mist. There is a sudden streak of silver and a short, sharp whistle.

The doe slumps to the ground, a bolt straight through its neck. The rest of the party arrives moments later, with a bout of boyish cheer.

"Brilliant shot, Freed!" says Charles LePrince, stooping to admire his handiwork.

"Thanks. Fancy a pelt as a wedding present?"

"I should be the one to be presenting you with gifts," Charles gushes, breaking into a grin, "for allowing me to marry your beautiful sister–"

Charles is one of perhaps a handful of people outside of my family that I actually like, as well as James Saintclair, another member of our party. Charles is one of those people it's very difficult not to like. He is effortlessly cheerful and kind and always looking for ways to make people happy. His affable nature is matched only by Honour's.

"Oh, hush," Freedom scoffs, "she's not all that–"

While the rest of the boys launch into an overly-detailed description of why my sister is, in fact, "all that" James Saintclair stops to help me up. My eyes are still rooted on the doe. I am no stranger to dead creatures, but there is something haunting about the splash of colour in this forest of black and white, the steaming spread of blood in the snow.

"Are you all right?" James asks. He picks up my empty basket, then frets with the berries awkwardly, picking them up one by one.

"Quite fine," I reply. I brush the snow off my shoulders, more from habit than vanity, then help him with the berries. I scoop up big handfuls of snow in the process.

"Rose?" Freedom notices me standing under the tree, and scowls. "Were you there the whole time?"

"Um, I suppose so, yes?"

"You should have stayed on the path! I could have shot you—"

It had not occurred to me until that moment how close the deer had been to me; a few feet between us was all. Another hunter might have missed.

Another hunter.

"What are you talking about, Freed? You, miss? In what world?" Charles claps his shoulder, but his gaze on me doesn't waver.

"Stay on the path, Rose!"

I glare back at him, and stop narrowly short of stamping my foot. "Shoot forward, Freedom!"

His scowl darkens, as it always does when people use his full name, but he turns nonetheless and heads back onto the path. The rest of the party follows suit. Even James Saint-clair leaves my side to lift the deer. He is a big, strong fellow, but almost as gentlemanly as Charles. We grew up together, and many like to imagine us more than friends. They are not without reason, yet despite what happened between us at the Mayor's winter party a few days ago, I have never really thought much about it, or James' feelings on the subject.

Is that wrong of me? I wonder, picking up my basket. Do I owe him an explanation? Does he want one? Do I want one? I am not like Honour, dreaming of love and marriage. I find myself torn between longing for a life of peace and solitude or questing for adventure, but I do not know what James wants. I am too afraid to ask, and he is too polite to.

I sigh, pushing the thought away, and take two steps forward.

That's when I see it.

A glimmer of stark whiteness amidst the muddy grey, shining like a drop of starlight, at the foot of a tree just a little further from the path. A snowdrop.

It ought to be impossible. We are in the middle of winter. Spring is months away. It cannot be and yet... here it is.

I have to pluck it. I have to take it back to show Beau and my sisters. Or perhaps I can press it, make it part of a wedding present for Honour. I feel a tiny, pin-prickle of excitement rustle through me as I bend down to take it, stowing it safely in my basket.

Then I notice something else, something much more miraculous and completely impossible. Through the gap in the trees is glorious colour, a myriad of pink and yellow and orange, a sunset pressing through the gloom in the middle of the day.

I am too afraid to scrub my eyes, too fearful it might vanish. Instead, I push forwards, climbing through the branches, until my feet crunch against the floor of the field my mother used to take us to in summertime, to play in the stream that divided the land.

The field beyond the stream –which but yesterday had been a dark, grey slab in the landscape– has been transformed into a blossoming meadow.

I have to be dreaming, or it is some kind of mirage. It is so clear, so perfect. Soundlessly, I move through the snow-covered field and down towards the stream, expecting it to shimmer away any second, but the meadow just grows closer. There are daisies, buttercups, cowslips... long poppy stems, brushing blue skies. Blue skies overhead!

"It's not possible," I murmur, moving down to the water's edge.

There was a saying, in our village. "Do not cross the stream at the end of the meadow." There were multiple stories for why this was the case. Some said that fairies would come and snatch you away. Others said that something bad had happened to a child who strayed beyond the borders. Most people agreed it was probably a warning from the last war. There had been a battle, not far from here, and enemy soldiers had once camped beyond the stream in the woodland that used to live there. Or so the people said.

Even Papa heeded the warnings. He used to scold Mama for

taking us there, but she promised to keep us away from the stream. We were allowed to play in it, but not over it. Of course, the minute her back was turned, Freedom and I both rushed up the side and down again, giggling. Honour gasped and fretted for days, but she did not tell Mama. Perhaps she was afraid we would not be allowed there again.

The first day of spring after Mama died, I hopped over the stream once more. That time, I wanted it to snatch me away. I wanted it to take me to a faraway place, a place where Mama was still alive, or, if it couldn't do that, to take me to a place where it didn't hurt any more to miss her.

The pursuit of something equally impossible is why I am crossing it this day.

I gather up my skirts, tucking them into my belt, and swing my cloak over my shoulder. Securing my basket in the crook of my arm, I hop onto one of the large, flat stones in the riverbed. I move quickly, wishing my clothes weren't so heavy.

I haul myself up on the other side.

A part of me expects to find the mirage over, but it is still here; the tall, glistening meadow, the flowers swaying in the breeze. I laugh, overcome with giddiness, and run. My skirts and cape come loose and flare out behind me. Petals dance in the breeze, warm sun kisses my skin, and a soft spring wind plays with my hair. The sweet scent of–

I stop immediately. The flowers don't smell. All around me is pristine beauty, but all I inhale is cold, colourless, wintry air. I reach out, inching my fingers towards the petals of a poppy.

Mist rolls in. The sun vanishes. A cold chill sweeps across the meadow. The grass around me turns yellow and brittle, and the flowers crumble like ashes. If a scream escapes me, it is lost under the roar of the wind. My basket is pulled from my grasp. I start to run, back towards the stream, but I can barely see two feet in front of me. The fog grows thicker and denser, and fastens around my throat like a rope.

Where is the stream?

It was here moments ago. It was right here. I... I must have been turned around. I've lost my bearings in the fog. I stop, trying to slow my breathing, when my eyes fix on something in the distance. Dark, arrow-like tips slice through the cold haze. A building? There is nothing in the woods, nothing for miles. It must be a tree, although I can't remember one being there before. But what else could it be?

I creep closer, and the dark, looming shape rises far above the mist. Not a tree. Not a tree at all.

It is a castle, but not like any I have ever seen before. It is carved out of something much smoother than stone, barely visible behind the black tangles of brambles. It should be a shell, but as the fog dissipates, I can see windows, doors, tall, solid walls. No ruin, although I have never seen anything in such a fixed state of complete disregard. The garden is a graveyard, both overgrown and utterly lifeless. It is a mass of thorns; all is black and grey. Once powerful fists of ivy cling to cold lumps of colourless stone. Statues, although of what, it is impossible to tell.

What on earth is a castle doing here?

The wind howls, and thunder claps across the sky. Rain slams against the stones. There is nothing for it; I race up the steps to the front of the castle, pausing only for a second at the door. It should be rotten or covered with barren ivy like the rest of the building, but although it is old and weathered, the ivy has snapped off around the frame, as if it has been opened recently.

The thunder claps again, and I wrench open the door and slip inside.

Light protrudes into this dark and dismal place through the remains of the shattered windows. Shards of coloured glass are scattered over the marble floor, tiny fragments of amber and blue amongst the swathes of leaves. I have never seen coloured glass like this before. When I lean down to take a piece in my hand, it is surprisingly sturdy despite how thin and fine it is, and almost seems to shimmer, more like crystal than glass.

Screens of deserted spiders' webs coat the rest of the room, shielding a great deal of it from view. I can make out faint tapestries, pieces of furniture, but little else. Great pillars rise out of their trappings. They seem too narrow to hold the weight of this ceiling, and are carved with impossible precision, as if plucked from the mind of a painter. Ivy tumbles into the room, making it seem more tomb than palace.

Was this place some vestige from the war? Perhaps it had some silly tale attached to it too, like the stream, and the villagers had been told to be wary of it. But why they wouldn't mention it is beyond me.

Or, perhaps... perhaps the tales weren't silly at all.

I drift over to a table in the corner. There is a small ivory-faced clock there, its hands frozen in motion, and a golden candlestick. A little drawer reveals a handful of matches. A few seconds later, and a gloomy light flickers into motion, illuminating the faded tapestries hanging from the walls. Great chunks of them are missing, threads dangling like shredded flesh. Bits of the woodwork are damaged too, but not by time. They look like they've been clawed, or even... bitten.

Thunder cracks against the sky. I jolt involuntarily, backing into a nearby bust. It crashes to the floor.

Somewhere, above me, another crash echoes out.

"Hello?" I call. "Is someone there?"

There is no reply, but the silence reverberates down the empty hallways.

I set my candle aside and pick up the bust. It is of an old, warty man, who frankly looks a little better without his bulbous nose. My concerns at ruining the piece of art are limited. It is clearly not the likeness of a person; his ears are webbed like a fish. A fanciful creation of an imaginative sculptor. I leave it where it lies and retrieve the candle.

"Hello?" I call up the stairs. Nothing but my own voice bounces back. For a second, just a split second, I think I hear a voice, softer than the wind and even less substantial.

Welcome, welcome, welcome...

I am clearly imagining things, just like I must have imagined the field of flowers. Perhaps I tripped somewhere, banged my head–

Another crash, a scrambling. Something big moving about.

"Hello?" I creep up the steps, trying not to sound afraid.

Something, a dark, shadowy thing, runs from one door to another. Inside the other room, there is another crash, a low moan, like the sound of an animal.

Whatever it is, it is not human.

But it is also afraid of me.

The dust in the air seems to breathe, and swirls about the space like a ribbon caught in a breeze. There are footprints in the dust, huge, massive paws, as wide as a bear's, long as a wolf's. What creature lurks behind that door?

Freedom's voice resonates in my head, telling me to be cautious. I can see him drawing an arrow, but I ignore him. I remember my Mama telling me, when I was frightened by a stray dog as a little child, that he was more frightened of me than I was of him. I saw the way he cowered under the horse cart, the way his brows furrowed and his eyes widened, and I knew she was right.

I step into the room.

The creature paws at the door in the back of the room, half-hidden by shadows and a large wing-back chair. A massive, bear-like paw scrapes at the wood, and a long, wolfish tail sweeps the floor. The rest is just a black shape.

I set down my candle, eyeing the poker near the fireplace just in case.

"It's all right," I say, as calmly as I can muster, "I won't hurt you."

The creature stops pawing at the door almost immediately. For a second, I think I hear it whimper, or sigh, but I must be mistaken. The sounds I'm imagining are too human for whatever this is.

It turns towards the chair between us, grasping at the arms, and I catch a brief flash of its face. A single blue eye stares at me through a hole in the back of the chair.

The huge paws have nails like talons. My fingers itch, involuntarily, for the poker. I pray it cannot see that fear in me.

"I won't hurt you," I repeat. "Come on... come out from behind there. Let me see you."

The creature groans and shakes its head. No, I *thought* it shook its head. It is an animal, and animals cannot shake their heads in reply.

I act as if they can. "I'm not afraid," I say, "and you shouldn't be either. Won't you come out?"

The creature lets out another sigh, makes a motion almost like a shrug of defeat. Its gaze screws to the floor, looking down almost... almost as if it is ashamed. Then it steps out into the murky light and rises to its full height.

It is as tall as a bear, broad and wide, covered from head to toe in black fur. It is slimmer than a bear though, with rear legs like wolf's. Its face... it has such a strange, twisted face. Part lion, part wolf, with a flat snout and nostrils, and a thick mane sprouting at its neck. Two small horns loom over two massive eyes, shadowed by wild eyebrows. I could not have dreamt up such a creature. No, creature is not the word. Creatures can be animals, be fairies, be beautiful and wondrous. No, this thing is a beast.

"Oh, crickets." My voice feels numb in my mouth. It is like I am looking down on the scene from afar, watching someone else speak for me. I have no idea where the courage comes to speak my next few words. "You're certainly a strange-looking fellow."

The beast sighs and sags, returning to its hiding place behind the chair. It is wearing a red cape, fastened around its neck with a clasp. What kind of beast wears clothing?

The blue eye spies me from the hole. "I've had worse said," it returns.

A sudden squeak escapes me, and I knock back into the wall, clasping my hand to my mouth. I slide to the floor, spitting out curses and taking fitful snatches of air.

"You... you can *talk!*"

"Quite well, so I'm told."

"You can *talk!* You're talking!"

"Yes."

"But... but... but..." As I stumble on my buts, it occurs to me that stranger things have happened in the past... hour? I have lost track of time. "What are you?" I ask finally. "What... what is this place? Where am I? *Who are you?*"

The Beast sighs. "I am... only what you see," he says. His voice is deep, and rumbles like the thunder still churning across the skies. "As for this place... it is hard to describe. It is a hidden place, a place of... of a power all but faded. It appears in your world but twice a year, and then vanishes into the ether."

"I was in the field," I splutter. "I was... in the woods, and then I saw this place, over the stream... You can't... you can't move a *castle.*"

"And you cannot make a beast speak, yet here I am."

"This... this isn't possible! This is the sort of thing from... from *stories.*" I had spent all of my life with my head half in the clouds, half in-between the pages of the books I devoured, and for many of those years, I believed that I believed in the tales they told. It was only now, in this moment, I realise I was wrong. I never believed, not truly.

"Stories," the Beast replies, "must come from somewhere."

This is too much. I sink my head into my hands and breathe deeply. *In, out, in, out.* I try to count, to steady the heart beating frantically against my chest. I pinch my temples, feel the short, sharp pain. I am awake. I am not dreaming.

"I'd like to go home now," I say eventually, my voice a faint whisper.

The Beast lowers himself to the ground, and shrinks back into the shadows by the empty fireplace. "I am so sorry," he says. "Truly, I am. For your sake. You will not be able to return tonight."

"What?" My insides freeze. *No, no, no...*

"Why not?"

13

"The portal." His voice is low. "The gateway between my world and yours. It has shut."

"When... when will it open again?" I try to keep my voice steady, but I am afraid of his answer. I am afraid because I already know.

"The portal opens but twice a year," he replies, and fixes me with his cool, blue eyes. "I am sorry."

"No!" I shout. "No, you're wrong!"

Panic grips me. I stare at him, waiting for him to change his words, to make them not true. I cannot be stuck here. I will not be.

His expression –what little I can discern from it– does not waver, and the truth hits me like a punch to the gut.

"No," I say numbly. "*No!*"

I turn on my heels and flee the room, paying no heed to whatever he calls after me. I shriek at him, yell at him to leave me alone. He doesn't. I can hear him behind me as I race back down the stairs and out into the full-blown storm.

Rain pummels my face, sharp winds pulling at my clothes and hair. I have to wrestle with my skirts just to get down the steps. The sound is enormous. Grey clouds arch like waves, the thunder roars. The landscape is shrouded in a dark, moving haze. I can see so little, but I don't care. This place will not keep me.

I find myself in the empty field and keep on running. Undergrowth snaps at my heels. Overhead, there is a flash of lightning. The drums of thunder follow, so strong that the earth beneath me shudders and convulses.

I race further into the field. The skies are so dark it could be night. The rain sears against my skin, the cold burns my throat. I want to scream, but there's no breath left in me.

Where am I?

Lightning strikes the ground a few paces ahead. I let out a soundless shriek, toppling into a nearby bramble patch. I fight against the thorns, shredding my fingers, but it strikes again before I can move, closing in on me like some kind of predator.

Can lightning do this?

The castle has been swallowed up by blackness, but so has everything else. I can't see anything. No path, no escape, no way out. I spin around hopelessly, searching for something to guide me, to pull me out. A part of me expects Freedom to appear out of nowhere and drag me to safety, but another, larger part of me knows, with absolute certainty, that he is not coming. No one is.

I call out his name, anyway. I call for Papa, and Honour, and Hope, and Beau... I even call for Mama. Praying that she will take me.

The clouds clash overhead, the lightning cracks, the thunder booms, and for a minute, I think I might be dying. My breath stills, my eyes drift, and all thoughts seem to dribble away.

Chapter Two

The Beast

It is dark when I wake. All is quiet now, all still. I am warm and clean and dry.

I sit up slowly, rubbing my face. My skin feels rubbery, as if it belongs to someone else. For a moment, I think I might be sick. I feel dizzy, lost, hazy. I must be at home. Honour has swaddled me up in blankets, tucked me in bed–

But this bed is too cold to be mine, and when the feeling returns to my skin, I feel silk.

This isn't real. This isn't happening.

I roll onto my right, reaching out a hand, searching for Hope. Her bed has been but a few inches from mine all of her life.

But no hand clutches mine, only air.

I'm still in the castle.

I lie back and breathe, carefully, counting every breath, hoping that this will keep my mind from drifting. My hands have been neatly bandaged. I touch my fingers cautiously, but there's only a slight, fuzzy pain underneath the gauze.

As my eyes adjust, little portions of the room open up. I am lying in a large, four-poster bed, under a soft quilt and layers of silk, but they smell a little musty, as if they have lain dormant for a long time. Thick rugs carpet the floor, rich drapes hang over the windows. It is clearly an elegant, sumptuous place, but it all looks grey and lifeless. I am not used to the silence. My whole life, I have shared a room with my sisters. The night is always filled with the sounds of breathing, of other people shuffling under their covers. I have always liked the rare few moments of the day when I could be alone in my bedroom, curled up behind the curtains, lost in a book. I have always liked solitude.

Until now, that is. This solitude is unnatural in its endlessness, its completeness. Silence engulfs me.

My feet find their way into a pair of soft slippers. I stand up and go to open the curtains. Dawn, or something like it, has started to break over the far-off mountains, illuminating the same pale, barren garden I walked through the day before.

Those are my mountains, I realise. They are the same mountains I can see from my room back home. How can it be that I cannot reach them?

A chill prickles across my skin. I move towards the fireplace and pull a new log into the grate. Tiny, faint embers from last night's fire remain. I prod at them with the poker, expecting the job of re-lighting it to take some time, but there is a sharp click and all at once there is a roaring fire before me.

I jump back.

Really, a fire that makes itself shouldn't be too much of a surprise, seeing as I appear to have stumbled into some kind of abandoned fairy realm, inhabited by a mysterious talking beast. A self-maintaining fire should be easy magic compared to that.

The Beast.

Was he the one who brought me up here, bandaged my hands, removed my wet clothes? His paws did not look capable of such deft actions, yet I was sure he was alone here. Who else could have done such a thing?

The pearl-faced clock on the mantelpiece chimes softly. Seven o'clock. People would be stirring at home by now, lighting fires, starting breakfast. Freedom would probably be preparing for another expedition into the forest.

Or would he be? He had probably been up all night, scouring the forest in search of me, forming a party, organising a hunt. Papa would have gone with him. Honour would have stayed behind, comforting Beau and Hope, only letting her own fears show once Freedom and Charles returned and told her they had had no luck.

I can see Honour's face breaking, shattering like a piece of glass. I can see her falling into Papa's arms, and Freedom wrapping himself around both of them. They would have sobbed, and worried, and fallen into fitful sleep. My heart clenches at such a thought.

"I'm so sorry," I say aloud, as if my voice can somehow travel where I cannot. I stare into the embers, wishing I could send a message from this hearth to theirs. *I'm all right. Don't worry. I will be home. I'm safe.*

Am I? I had not felt safe during that violent storm, the one that seemed to chase me like a cat did a mouse. I am trapped in this place, after all, trapped with only a monster for company, albeit a seemingly well-meaning one.

I am not sure I want to see him again. I would prefer to stay in this room and sleep away my troubles, sleep away the time I have to spend here. Had he really said the portal only opens twice a year? Was this place to be my home for the next six months?

I stare around my chamber, wishing away the gaudy, alien furnishings.

No, not my home. My prison.

I sit in the room as the weak sun rises, and the flames flicker and hum, the warmth never quite reaching me. It is a good hour before I move again. My clothes have disappeared somewhere, so I am dressed only in my undergarments and the thin pair of slippers. The dresser houses little but a small array of nightclothes and underthings, but the wardrobe has three large, rather ridiculous gowns.

I have never been the sort to be vain, but these puffy dresses are hopelessly outdated; the sort of thing that would have been fashionable some twenty years ago. They are all quite inappropriate. None of them match my mood. I just want something familiar, or plain, but that doesn't seem to be an option.

Finally, I pick the least offensive of the gowns and, with some difficulty, wrestle into it. It is a poor fit, impossible to lace properly on your own. Luckily, my boots are sitting beside the fire. I must look quite the picture, with my unkempt hair, well-worn boots, and a fine gown, but I don't give it much thought. Even if I was ever the sort to care much for my appearance, there is no one here to see me.

A cold chill sweeps down the corridor as I step outside my door. Dim lights flicker into half-life, casting shadows along the walls. Portraits of long-ago people, tapestries of ancient times, landscapes of forgotten moments in history all stare down at me.

The occupants of the paintings look strange. At first, I cannot put my finger on it, until I gaze upon one so unusual I at first take it for a fantasy landscape. It is a picnic between a large group of creatures. There are small, stout wrinkled little men, tall, elegant women with sharp features, tiny beings with wings or horns. Not human, no matter how delightful.

But the castle in the background is this one.

At first, I take it just for something fanciful, imaginary, but after this one I notice the features of the others. So many of the subjects have wings, or unusual eyes or noses or ears. In fact, the more I look, the more I wonder if any of these people are human at all.

There are several ruined statues with missing arms or legs, some busts lying in scrambled heaps, the occasional painting marred by deep tears in the canvas. So many signs of a battle.

But why was this place not plundered afterwards? And if, by some unlikely chance, both sides destroyed each other– where are the bodies? Dust, dirt, leaves, and crumbled stone coat the floor– but not a single bloodstain, or a hint of bone.

A shiver runs through me, and I quicken my pace. I half expect to come across some dusty skeleton, some faint, eerie remnant of life, but the place is utterly deserted– no signs of life past or present.

I reach the entrance of the castle. Light streams in through the painted glass, casting the first colour I have truly seen on the hard marble floors. Hardly knowing where I am going, I turn left down another short corridor, and find myself in an armoury. It is well-stocked, but neglected. Back in the village, General Beaumont was known to have the best armoury for miles around, yet his collection pales in comparison to this. There must be thousands of weapons; bows, blades, spears, clubs... no muskets though, and a great portion of the cache is unfamiliar to me. There are instruments I cannot name, can barely describe, and even those I know seem different some-how. The detail on some of the blades is as exquisite as it is alien.

I pluck one of the crossbows from the wall, and Freedom's voice swells in my ear. He compliments the weight, the feel, the design, and criticises the condition, the badly-maintained string. The voice grows so loud that I abandon the weapon, slamming it back into the bracket, and seize a sword instead. It is far lighter than any of General Beaumont's swords that he used to let me hold, much lighter than any of Freedom's practise swords. Freedom never let me use his real one, but for years we would chase each other round the garden with weighty wooden blades, until Beau was old enough to hold one and Freedom decided he didn't need a brother substitute any more.

I thrust the blade into a nearby dummy, cursing his name, but the voice inside just grows even more vocal.

You'll have to hit harder than that. Raise your elbows,

straighten your wrist—

Stop it.

Faster, Rosie. You'll never keep up at this rate—

I attack the dummy, slashing away at the layers of cloth and leather.

You're not strong enough. Come on. Do some real damage.

My cuts get more and more wild. Sand pools onto the stone in tiny trickles.

Harder! I won't always be around to fight your battles, you know—

I let out a scream, raise the sword above my head, and swing it into the dummy's neck. The blade sticks fast. I lack the strength to remove it, so I kick it in its makeshift stomach instead, and keep kicking and punching until my hands ache and it starts to bend on its stand. It hangs there, a mess of rags and straw and sand, the blade still protruding out of its neck.

"My, remind me never to anger you," says a voice from the doorway.

I startle. The Beast is standing in the arch, his huge hind legs treading the threshold.

"Good morning," he says cheerfully, and then casts his eyes towards the dummy. I wonder if he wants me to apologise for damaging his property. "Has the world outside changed so much that all young ladies are now schooled in sword fighting?"

Only the ones with older brothers to teach them, is the first thought that rises to my mind, but this would mean giving him something about me, and I don't want to give him anything right now. I don't want to give him anything ever.

"No," I say shortly.

The Beast stares at me for a few seconds, perhaps disappointed in my response, but quickly recovers. "Then you must be a rare maiden indeed to... decimate a dummy so."

I cannot think of anything to say to this, so I remain mute. My stomach decides to fill the silence for me.

"You are hungry," the Beast says regretfully. He steps away

from the door, giving me a wide berth. "Allow me to offer you breakfast, at least."

The *at least* hangs there for a little while, and I have the merest notion of the distress I am causing him in my bluntness. But I quickly quell it. I care nothing for his distress when my own presses against my every crevice. Instead, I nod, desiring food above bitterness, and allow him to lead me to a grand dining room. Our entire cottage could have fitted neatly inside of it. The table is the length of our garden. It is impossibly, monstrously big.

This room is better kept than some of the others. It is damp and dusty, but without the troves of cobwebs, and is decked in gold and white. There are only two place settings, but the rest of the table bulges with enough silver to suit a royal guest.

The Beast pulls out a chair clumsily and gestures for me to sit before springing away, letting me push it in myself. He hovers by the side of the room.

"You'll find food readily available here, whenever you want it," he explains. "I do not know quite how it works, but it keeps me alive, so..."

Cautiously, I lift the lid from my tray. A simple, glorious smell races up to greet me. A hearty porridge, filled with nuts and dates, fresh milk, a little pot of honey. Undoubtedly what Nanny has produced for everyone else this morning. The smell makes me want to cry. The taste is even worse. The flavour dissolves into paste as I struggle to swallow, my body craving sustenance over grief.

"You may go or do whatever you like here," the Beast says. "The castle is your..."

He means to say "home" but he stops himself just in time, perhaps anticipating the venom he would receive from me if he dared make such a declaration.

"Yours to explore," he continues. "That being said, the chamber at the end of western corridor. The one with the gold door. Please refrain from going in there."

"Why?" I ask. "What's in there?"

There is the merest twitch of a smile in the corner of his jaw. He's got me; I asked a question. "The bodies of my former brides," he says matter-of-factly.

He waits for me to startle, or laugh, but I do neither. "Well, I can understand you wanting to keep that hidden," I reply, just as calmly. I do not repeat the question. Limiting my prison by a single room makes little difference to me, whatever the reason.

"It's a... a personal request," he adds. "I would keep it to myself."

I force myself to swallow another mouthful to avoid looking at him, and avoid continuing the conversation.

"Your name," the Beast says eventually, "what is it?"

I don't see how I can avoid giving him this. "Rose," I say quietly. "De Villenueve."

Now it is my turn to wait. I wait for him to say "that is a lovely name" or something else equally boring, but he does not. His eyes rise a little to my hair, perhaps noticing the red sheen to it, and he nods a little, as if to say *it suits you.* Instead, he says, a touch forlornly, "You may call me Beast, for that is what I am."

We part ways, almost silently, after I have finished a few more mouthfuls. My gaoler, the Beast, my unwitting host – whatever he may be– hovers in my trail long after I have departed. I see him lurking in the shadows as I ascend the main staircase. I know he must be thinking of following me, perhaps offering me a tour, but thinks the better of it. Good, he is learning. Learning that there is no point in trying to befriend me. Maybe he believes my resolve will soften over time, but he does not know me. There were days, weeks even, after Mama's death, where the only sounds I uttered were sobs. I spoke to no one. I can retreat into my grief like a shell, emerging only when I see it is safe to. When the way opens to go home.

I have no need of a friend. No need of anyone. I am perfectly fine by myself.

This is the mantra I repeat to myself as I explore the castle.

It is hard to put to words the precise state of the decay and desolation etched into the walls of this forgotten place. There is a pale, penetrating loneliness chiselled into every statue. A kind of loneliness made living. It haunts every rock and stone, every sinew of every room. A whispering, blistery loneliness. In a breath's moment, I swear I can hear voices, and at the exact same time, all I can hear is the deafening sound of utter nothingness.

The gardens are a desolate wasteland, a graveyard of trees and statues. A seasonless, flavourless, hollow place. Nothing but dust and dirt, the shrapnel of nature, coats the dry ground. The trees are as thin as bones. They hang like skeletons, and when I reach out to grab a low-hanging branch, it snaps in my hand and dissolves into shards of brittle bark. I have never seen a place outside of a picture book containing so many shades of grey and brown.

The base of the castle is home to several ruined outbuildings and follies, empty stables, a deserted coach house, a plethora of lifeless residences of stone and mortar. Any plant life I come across mirrors death too, although when I examine one of the rose bushes and dig down to the wick, there is a slight flash of green. Not quite dead, then, sleeping, although I have never seen sleep so still before.

There are no birds here, no insects. No sounds at all except the scrunch of stone underfoot. It makes me miss the snow, and the sound of inane chatter. I have never been one for noise, vastly preferring the company of books to people, but crave noise now. I long for any kind of sound. Is this what it feels to be a ghost, alone in some kind of half world?

A large stretch of water lies at the edge of the castle grounds, sheathed in mist. The water, what little of it I can see, is crystal clear, but it is a void, empty of life. The surface is taut, like the skin of a drum, but looks hard and shiny as glass.

The bottom is robed with rocks and pebbles and dirt. Not even weeds will grow in this place. My foot catches on a stone as I try to turn away. I pick it up, thumb it gingerly, then hurl it into the waters. Ripples shatter the surface and glide outwards. I hear the sound of it sink to the floor, and a bubble breaks to the top. The sound is as blissful as it is haunting.

I wander as far as the endless meadow, and haunt the edge for some time, staring out at the rolling mists and knowing they shield nothing. It takes but perhaps some thirty minutes at a good pace from my door to the stream where I crossed into this place. How can that thirty minutes have turned into six months?

A few feet ahead of me, before the mist truly expands, a tiny spot of colour catches my eye. A little glint of red. For a second, I know I must be imagining it. There is no colour here. I close my eyes and wait for it to go away. But it's still there.

Tentatively, I creep forward, certain that it will vanish before I reach it. It doesn't. The mist even appears to roll back, revealing the cause; my basket, half-filled with berries from the last hunt, and my single, solitary snowdrop.

I do not know what I intend to do with them, but I am glad to have the basket returned to me. It is of no particular value, sentimental or otherwise, but it is mine, and I have so little of that here, that I scoop up the basket and its contents eagerly, and head back the way I came.

It is now about midday. I tire of the gardens. There is still plenty to explore, but it does not interest me anymore. Clutching my basket tightly, I head back up the castle via the kitchen entrance. The ruins of a once great herb garden front the doors. It reminds me longingly of my garden at home, although mine was nowhere near this size. Gardening is my second love, after literature. It pains me to see such devastation.

Hardly knowing why, I drop down on my knees, scrabble about in the dirt, and bury my little horde. There is no hope in me that they will grow, but perhaps I need to believe that something good can live in such a place.

Getting back to my room is difficult. I take several wrong turns through the winding corridors before finding my way to the entrance hall. I remember to turn right at the top of the stairs, but I have no idea which door is mine. I don't even know what mine means. What does it matter which room I go to? There's nothing of mine in there. But I want something that I have used before, if only for a few hours.

I fling back each door I come to, taking no note of the contents, searching into the gloom for the right place. Finally, I find my door. My clothes have been brought back, and I immediately shed my gaudy trappings, shredding away the frills and layers with such force that it begins to tear.

I find a plate of bread and cheese, some dried fruit, and a pot of lukewarm tea waiting for me. Did the Beast bring it up, or... the castle? He said to go to the dining room for food, didn't he? Either way, I'm barely hungry. I pick at it a little and sip at the tea.

I don't feel like doing any more exploring, so I try to find something in the room to occupy myself with. There are three books on the dresser; a sentimental book of poetry –the sort Mama would have liked – a book on fairy tales, and a well-thumbed adventure romance. I think I've read the last one before, and it offers me a small home comfort despite its tedious prose. There must be a better selection somewhere in this castle, but I lack the energy to search for it and don't want to ask the Beast. I wrap myself in a blanket, settle down by the fire, and lose a good three hours in it.

The clock ticks too loudly, and I am incredibly aware of how slow time is passing. *Hurry,* I urge it, *please.*

By the day's end, I have read half of my available material and am not keen to resort to the sentimental drivel. Neither do

I want to leave the room. A great, claw-footed tub sits beside the fire. I draw myself a bath and get to work untangling my curls and scrubbing away the dirt, a task I make last as long as possible. Then I comb it out and sit beside the fire. There's a small sewing box to the left of the hearth. It feels out of place in such a grand room –would not the previous occupant have had servants to manage such tasks?– but it is a welcome find. I can set to work fixing the damage I did to the dress earlier.

One of the sleeves is hanging on by a thread, a seam is split, and some of the fabric has frayed as a result. I never much cared for puffy sleeves anyway, so I turn them into cap sleeves instead. I'd ripped several of the frilly layers in my haste too, so I decide to take those off entirely, slimming the dress down considerably.

I work for most of the night, unpicking needless embroidery, trimming layers, disposing of ribbons and gauze. My fingers start to ache, and I realise that the strange, fuzzy pain from the brambles has gone. I unwrap my hands.

There is not a blemish on them.

Castle of Thorns

T here is no routine to the next few days. The only consistency is that each hour is spent trying not to count the hours. I breakfast alone in my room, then pick up my sewing, attempting to make something comfortable from the gaudy gowns. I re-read the books, or borrow one from another of the bedrooms. Sometimes I wander the gardens, but I always seem to find myself in the gloomiest of places and this does nothing to improve my mood. Occasionally, I drift into the armoury. Target practise offers some release, but I get little enjoyment from sword play. I keep hearing Freedom's condescending voice in my ear and even though I want to use the blade to spite him, the mere memory makes me ill. I wouldn't be here if I'd listened to him and stayed on the path.

After the first few evenings, the castle shows signs of learning my habits. The fire is always made up when I want it, and a bath is prepared every evening. I eke out a little joy from this, experimenting with the basket of potions and concoctions that sits beside it. One turns the water golden and makes my skin smell of honey, another glitters like starlight. A third turns the bubbles into fresh flowers, that sadly only last until the water cools.

I think of Honour, with the last one, and the dress she had made for her wedding. How badly she wanted flowers for it. How badly I want to be there. A girl who grows up in a sleepy village with her head in a book should be glad of the opportunity for adventure, but although the castle is expansive, I feel its walls shrinking against me. No matter how far I can wander, I know the place is still a cage. I can't deny that my curiosity heightens with each passing day, however. I do want to know the history of this prison, how it became one.

The Beast remains a stranger to me during this time. Sometimes I see him, lurking in the shadows nearby, or glancing at me from an upstairs window. I pay him no heed, hoping that he'll vanish altogether if I ignore him for long enough.

I explore a few rooms of the castle each day. I take my time in this, for once I have seen all the rooms I will know the true limits of my cage.

Every morning, I open a door, and examine the contents inch by inch, like a prisoner stroking the bars of his cell. I am methodical in my approach, picking one floor, one corridor. Once inside, I run my fingers over each surface, disturbing dust inches thick. Years of dirt are scraped away. Many of the rooms house nicer objects than mine; mine is too gaudy, the furniture large and clunky. These venerable places are sparsely but beautifully decorated; dressers as slim as silver birch branches, curtains as finely-woven as spider's silk, paintings that look as if a fairy's breath was captured on a canvas. Everything is delicate and dainty and as perishable as a cloud. And yet, somehow, has endured the ages.

When I am feeling a little more daring, or searching for some amusement, I raid the rooms for books, trinkets, and items of clothing. I am richly rewarded, finding beautiful dresses, soft slippers, tomes of lore, fur coats. I feel like a pirate, taking my spoils back to my chamber and ferreting them away.

One morning, I come across a little bedroom not far from

the kitchens. A servant's room. It is just as prettily decorated as some of the finer chambers. Like all of them, it is covered in cobwebs, but it lacks the neatness of the others. There is a book half-open on the bedside table, an empty cup and saucer, papers over the desk, a half-worn candle. The bed is not pristinely made, the covers are crumpled, and the hairbrush on the dresser still has several fine, white-gold hairs clinging to the bristles. This is a room that was used and loved, and then, quite suddenly, abandoned.

I admire some of the fine, floaty gowns in the wardrobe. The material is so light it is almost insubstantial. But for some reason, I do not want to take any of them. There is still a feeling that they belong to someone.

A little glint of sunlight twinkles in the corner of the mirror. I glance up, but it has already disappeared. There is no sunlight here, I remind myself. It was probably only a reflection.

A week after my arrival, when I have explored all the ground floor rooms to the left side of the castle's entrance, the turn comes to enter the grand doors to the right. My breath immediately rises out of my chest and explodes into the vast space before me.

It is a ball room, ancient and otherworldly. Even in its abandoned state, its grace and elegance persevere. It is white, shimmering, ethereal place. Great cascades of ivy pool into the room from the shattered crystal ceiling, and twist up from the balcony, meeting somewhere in the middle to spill onto the marble floor.

At the end of the room, in a melted heap, sits what looks like the remains of a seat. No, not a seat; a throne. This is a throne room. This fits, for I feel like I have stumbled upon the archaic celestial home of some great forgotten god.

Behind the throne is a large portrait, but it is scorched beyond recognition. I can make out little but the graceful sweeping robes of a woman, and the figure of a broad-shouldered man. She is touching the back of his hand lightly, a touch that should be reserved but somehow conveys the impression of warmth. It is staring up at this ruin that curiosity finally overcomes me.

"What happened here?" I ask aloud.

It takes him a while to respond, peering out from behind the pillar. "I'm sorry, are you talking to me?"

"Is there anyone else here for me to talk to?" I ask pointedly.

He hangs his head. "No," he says quietly, "I suppose not."

"You suppose?"

"The magic that sustains this place... what little there is left of it... it was alive once. I do not believe it is, any more."

I think of the twinkle in the mirror, and my wish-fulfilling room, and wonder if it's as dead as he believes it to be. I repeat my original question.

"A great battle was fought," he explains, "between light and darkness."

"Who won?"

"Neither. In the end, both parties destroyed one another, and this place along with it."

"Why does it appear in my meadow twice a year?"

"It doesn't," he replies. "It can appear in many places, all over the world. It's just by chance it appeared to you."

"Then why does it appear at all?"

The Beast tilts his head. This next reply takes time. "Old magic," he says. "It has rules that must be followed. Every curse cast must have a chance of being broken."

"Every curse?" My interest is now truly piqued. "This place is under a spell?"

"It is not merely a castle."

"What else is it?"

"A prison."

I swallow, because I realise, for the first time, he is not just talking about me. This is his prison too. I wonder what he did to deserve it. I wonder if he did anything at all. I wonder if he, like me, is dying to be free.

"How... how long have you been here?" I ask.

"My entire life," his voice is very light. "I know no other home but this."

"But if the way opens twice a year–"

"Somehow I do not think I would be too warmly received in your world."

Guilt, regret, sympathy –some faint pang of emotion– rises in my throat. "You have not been alone here all this time?"

He shakes his head. "There were survivors, after the war. Loyal servants. They were my constant companions for many years. Then the magic that sustains this place began to wane. They sacrificed themselves to ensure it didn't fade completely, becoming part of the very walls."

"Have you been alone since then, or have other people found their way in?"

He nods. "Seven, including you. But not one for almost three years."

Three years of this utter solitude. How can he bear it? The question falls to the tip of my tongue but I catch it just in time. *Don't let him think you care.*

But why does it matter if he does? What do I possibly have to lose by making a friend of him? He doesn't seem to have any say in me being here, and I can't deny that I am... intrigued by him. And in our short conversation so far, I have stopped counting the minutes.

"What do you do?"

He startles a bit, looking like a cat might after sneezing. "I'm sorry?"

"How do you fill your time?" I ask.

"I er, I mean, sometimes..." He flusters as if he's never been asked this before.

"I suppose I walk a lot, and I used to hunt and fish, back when there were animals, and, um, well, I read a lot."

"You read?"

"I know, it may sound–"

"No, no. I love to read. I was hoping –I'd not managed to locate it yet– but I'm supposing there's a library here some-where?"

The smallest twitch of a smile crinkles in the corner of his jaw. "A library, you say? That I can help you with."

The first thing that hits me, as I step into the darkened room, is the warm, familiar smell of dust and paper. The second thing is the tree growing right out of the centre of the floor. At first, I am entirely perplexed– a tree, in this place, in a room without light or water? But then I realise that it is a cleverly-painted sculpture. The leaves are made of fabric. They brush the high, arched ceiling, in itself a marvel. It's painted with mermaids' lagoons, dragons, pirate ships, princes and princesses, mountains and castles and desert islands, valiant steeds, sword fights... beautiful, swirling images from every story I'd ever read.

"It's beautiful," I sigh.

"Do you like it?"

I gaze around at the little balconies and spiral staircases, and the books in every colour imaginable, stacked fifty feet high. I've never seen so many books in one place before, never seen a room so tall look so cosy. I know at once that whatever other wonders the castle holds, whatever other magic inhabits its walls, nothing will please me more.

"It's perfect," I breathe, unable to stop the admiration ris-ing from me.

He nods his head. "I shall leave you then," he says. "Enjoy your reading."

He turns to leave, but before he goes, I ask, "How many have you read?"

He stops, but his words take an age to come. Is he surprised by my question, or embarrassed by his answer? "Almost every book here." His voice is very quiet.

"Almost every single one?" There must be thousands.

"Well, some of them were very dull–"

"That's so many!"

"I didn't have much else to do."

This stops the conversation for a while.

"Well, which one is your favourite?" I ask.

"My favourite?" For a moment, I think he will say he doesn't have one. Most people do not. I know of about five I could whittle it down to. "This one," he says eventually. He turns to the shelf beside the fire, right at the bottom, and delicately pulls out a tome with a single claw. It is ancient, with yellowing pages, and is covered in dust. He has not returned to it for some time. It is a story I know, albeit one I have not read for many years. I can just about remember it.

"Tromeo and Lessida?" I raise an eyebrow skeptically. "It's a love story!"

"What of it?"

"I just... I never really thought–"

"A curious choice for a monster, I suppose?"

"A curious choice for a *man*."

A sudden silence passes between us. It is not an uncomfortable one, but strange and new. Finally, he throws his head back and laughs. A deep, throaty chortle, quite alarming, really.

He stops when he sees the look on my face. "Sorry," he says quickly. "Where– where would you like to begin?"

With the history of this place.

I point towards a bust on one of the desks. It is of a curious, warty little man with pointed ears. "I cannot help but notice..." I start, "that the past occupants of this castle... don't appear fully human?"

"That is correct."

"What were they?"

"They are what is commonly referred to as the Fey."

Yes, very common... if you live in a fairy realm. I try to sound a bit more polite. "What's that?"

"A group of conscious, highly intelligent, long-living beings, including but not limited to, fairies, sprites, brownies, elves, pixies, dwarves, goblins, gnomes–"

"Those all exist?"

"You don't sound too surprised."

"Well... I do live in an enchanted castle inhabited by a talking self-proclaimed beast."

"Touché." He glances around the room. "I could find you a book on them, if you like?"

My whole body tingles at the thought. A real book on fairies. A chance to unravel the mysteries of this place. I try to quell my excitement, reveal less of myself. "Oh, yes please, if you wouldn't mind."

Without another word, he springs onto a nearby bookshelf and scuttles towards the ceiling. He pulls out a thick volume. "Can you catch?"

"Yes, but–" He flings it towards me. The force is so great that I stumble back a bit. Freed never threw so hard.

"Look out!"

He hurls down another, then leaps onto another shelf, skims through the titles, fires down more.

"You'll break the shelves!" I cry. "Or the books!"

He stops for a moment to stare down at me in what I can only assume is an incredulous manner. "Nonsense. I've been climbing these shelves for years. And I'm very careful with the books." He sounds a little hurt.

"Why not use the la–" My eyes dart around the room for a ladder, but the first one I see is missing several steps. They are snapped clean in two. The second one I see is no better off. The third is dusty and ignored. "Oh," I say, to no one in particular.

A book hits me squarely in the face.

"Oof!"

Dense pain spreads across my brow. My collection clatters

to the floor. The Beast leaps down, landing with a thud so hard that the room shudders.

"Are you all right? I'm so sorry, I didn't look before I... I'm sorry–"

"No, no, I'm all right," I insist, blinking through the pain. "I'm not bleeding, just a bruise–"

"I can get you something–"

"I'm fine–"

But he has already swept out of the room.

Keeping one hand on my injury, I pick up the books scattered across the floor and stack them on a nearby table. They are incredibly old, although reading them with just one eye is a tad tricky. The Beast returns a few minutes later with a tea cup filled with water and a hot cloth. He sets them down with shaking fingers and steps back, darting away from me like an insect from the flame.

"I really am very so–"

"You say sorry too much," I snap, taking up the cloth. The water in the cup tingles, warm in a way that defies description. My head feels instantly better the second it's applied.

"Keep it on for a few moments," he insists.

"Sounds like good advice."

He rocks guiltily on his two back paws, his tail brushing the ground, his arms folded behind his back as if he's afraid to put them anywhere else. His eyes go to my collection on the desk. "I'll take these to your room."

"You don't have to–"

"It's fine."

He is gone in an instant. The books are beside my bed when I return to my room, but my fellow captive is nowhere to be seen. I call out, "thank you" into the corridors, but there is no reply.

Chapter Four

First Flakes

"**D**on't be afraid, Rose. Don't be frightened."

Down the corridor, an infant is mewling. Finally, finally the baby is here! I dash away from Freedom's side and run to Mama's room. I see the baby. He is wrapped up in Nanny's arms, but Nanny isn't smiling and laughing like she was when Hope was born. Her face is stark white.

The rest of the room is stained with blood. There's blood on Papa, blood on the baby, blood on the chewed-up sheets. The midwife hovers at Mama's feet, which look limp and lifeless, but Mama's hands stretch out towards me.

"Don't be afraid, Rose. Don't be frightened. Be brave, my dear-heart. Be brave."

The door closes in my face.

That is the last time I ever see my mother alive.

A scream rips through the air. I awake clutching my sheets, my face wet with tears. I breathe, steadying myself, and try to focus on the ticking clock.

"I am not afraid," I repeat to myself. "Not afraid!"

There is the clattering of claws on marble, a brief moment of silence apart from my ragged breathing, and then a quiet knock at the door.

"Rose?"

My name sounds so strange coming from his lips, that I almost forget it is mine entirely.

"Yes?" I answer faintly.

"I was just... walking by and I heard... are you all right?"

It takes me a moment to answer. "Yes," I reply. "It was... just a nightmare." *A memory.*

"If you need anything–"

"I'm fine!" I snap. What does he even suppose he could do? The castle appears to be attending my whims. What else could he offer me?

There is silence on the other side of the door. "As you wish," he says with the tiny, traceable sound of a sigh. He shuffles off; his claws scratch the marble far away.

My bedsheets are hot and clammy, but a creeping cold slithers up my spine. I wrap a blanket around my shoulders and go to pour a cup of tea. The pot is usually always filled with piping hot liquid, but tonight I find it flavourless and tepid. I gulp down a few mouthfuls and sit in the window seat. Frost is gnawing at the pane.

Nightmares plague me into the morning hours. No awful memories this time, but visions of pale faces in mirrors, screaming in the hallways, and a voice telling me to run. When I finally wake, my eyes feel pasted shut. It is close to lunch time. In an attempt to energise myself, I make half an effort dressing for the day and head down to the dining room. Somebody has been polishing the silver, but it does little to elevate the gloom. I eat quickly, and head back to my chamber.

Perhaps it is the addition of the books by my bedside, but

I am suddenly wary of how the room isn't much to my taste. I decide to make good on the Beast's promise that I am to treat the place like my own, and immediately rummage around the other rooms on my floor for paintings more to my liking. I borrow cushions to furnish the bed and chairs, roll up the gaudy rug and swap it for an elegant weave, replacing the thick hangings over the bed with gossamer ones. I decide to take down the curtains and swap them as well, but before I do I become distracted with a beautiful dresser, which, despite its delicate composition, is surprisingly heavy. I can barely move it.

"A little help would be nice!" I call out to no one in particular.

The dresser shifts forward suddenly. I shriek and topple backwards. There is a flicker of something around it, like the embers of a fire.

"Um, thanks?"

Nothing else happens. I get up, brushing the dust off my clothes, and try to pull it again. It is a little better, but not much.

"Do you require some assistance?"

I leap several feet into the air. The Beast is standing behind me.

"You must stop doing that!"

"I'm sorry!" He scuttles back into the corner like a wounded dog. "I heard you moving around and thought–"

"No, it's fine, I do need some help, actually..." I say, my breathing returning to normal. "You can move *really* quietly."

"I've been told," he says, as if this is something to be ashamed of.

"Well, now that you're here..." I point to the dresser. "Would you mind?"

He nods, striding towards it and lifting it easily into his arms. He looks far too pleased with himself. "Your room?"

"My room."

We walk back to it in silence and swap over the pieces in similar fashion. He glances around at the changes. "Making this place your own, I see."

"That is the intention." I am glad he doesn't tell me that I am making it my home. This place is not my home; it never will be. The best I can hope for is a prettier cage. "Put the old dresser by the window, will you?"

"The window?"

"Yes."

His brow furrows, but he follows my instructions. Once there, I use the dresser as a platform and clamber up on top of it, standing on tip-toe to take down the old curtains.

"Are you... do you want me to do that?" he asks.

"Alas, I think this calls for defter fingers..." I say, trying not to stare at his massive paws as I take off the first curtain and throw it down to him in a flurry of dust.

He sighs. "I suppose you are right. I am just concerned you might fall..."

"Then I fall. I shall not break."

I take off the second one. "Could you pass me the ones on the bed?"

He does so. They are midnight blue with gold and silver embroidery, and remind me of starlight. I stand back to admire them and my heel slips off the dresser, but before I can scream or even fully realise that I am falling, two hard arms wrap around my back and cushion my landing.

"Are you... all right?"

I tense up. His arms are like stone, and I can feel each one of his claws pressing into my back. I cannot quite untangle my feelings; am I afraid, or more embarrassed about falling?

"Fine," I say shortly.

He does not let go, and suddenly I am gripped by discomfort. Fear, then. I am a little disappointed in myself. I swallow. "You can put me down now."

"Right. Of course."

Hastily –and incredibly gently– he slides me to my feet. He takes several steps back. How can I possibly be scared of something so awkward? Yet, all of a sudden, his towering height is all the more noticeable, his fangs more pronounced, and his black fur all the more dark. He stuffs his hands behind his back.

"The room is looking lovely," he says quickly. "Are you done with the furniture?"

"Yes," I say.

He nods, and lifts up the old dresser to take it away. I do not tell him I need it for the other window, and he does not seem to notice, or want to notice. He moves silently for the door, and I do not stop him.

I do not see him again at dinner time, so I eat another meal by myself and spend my evening sewing by the fire, not having the heart for reading. I wonder how he is spending his evening.

I feel guilty for tensing. I am certain that he sensed it, that he could see my discomfort, and I curse my instincts. Why did I do that? I should have asked him to help me finish. I should have shown him that I was not afraid–

I think about going to find him now, but I do not know what I would say. Apologise? That would almost be worse, admitting to him that what he feared I felt was true. Perhaps I should just go and... suggest we spend some time together? Doing what? I do not know what he likes to do and I do not know him well enough to ask. I have met precious few strangers in my life, and only one talking beast.

Finally, I give up on my current project and succumb to sleep. I have another awful dream, where someone is hissing at me to stay away. The shadows have eyes. It is a relief to wake.

"Rose! Rose, wake up!"

Someone is knocking at my door. For a minute, I forget where I am. The voice sounds excited, gleeful, childlike. It must be Beau, desperate to show me something. I hope it's not a worm.

"Rose!"

"Coming..."

It's only when my feet hit the rug that it comes back, but it doesn't take me too long to recover. I pull on my dressing-gown and shuffle towards the door.

"You bellowed?"

The Beast's eyes suddenly go wide, and he turns around on his back paws so quickly that he actually skids. "You're– you're not dressed."

"It is seven thirty in the morning. You woke me up."

"I–! I'm so terribly sorry. I didn't think to look at the time. I, um, apologise profusely–"

"Calm down. You can only see a spot of ankle. Honestly, you'd think I was naked."

"Sorry, I'm just not used to seeing a lady in her undergarments–"

"Well, you may have to get used to it if I am to be stuck here." We were a close family, both in terms of affection and space. We barely dressed up for the neighbours, let alone each other. How did this creature ever manage to undress me if he's so shocked by the slightest hint of skin? "Now, what's so urgent?"

"I wanted to show you..." His eyes drift round unconsciously. "I'm sorry, would you mind getting dressed?"

I groan, and close the door in his face. "Is that a no?"

"That's a 'give me a minute'." It doesn't take long to wriggle into my dress and pull on my boots. I don't trouble myself with brushing my hair. "Ready," I say, appearing in the hall.

"Excellent!" He makes a motion a bit like a jump. "This way!"

He tears off down the corridor, half on all fours. It appears, in his excitement, he's forgotten to act human. He skitters about like an excited puppy. "Come on!"

He reaches the end of the hallway and stops at a full length window, pulling at the curtains. Bright, white light pools across the floor.

"Look, look!"

At first, I wonder what he's pointing at. The gardens look just as colourless as ever. Then, suddenly, it becomes abundantly clear. The gardens are covered in a thick carpet of white.

"Snow," I say, a little disappointedly.

The Beast dances from one foot to another, his tail wagging. "*Winter*, Rose! Winter!"

"I can see that."

"Don't you know what this means?"

"No."

"We haven't had a season here for years. Years! And now you're here and–" He stops suddenly, looking like he's said something he shouldn't.

"And?"

"AND THERE'S SNOW."

"Great."

"I'm going out in it."

"I'm not."

He stops for a second and I expect to see big, hurt, puppy-dog eyes. Instead, he simply shrugs. "Suit yourself," he says, and whizzes off.

I eat my breakfast alone and then head upstairs to read in the window seat. For some reason, I find myself feeling annoyed at the Beast for racing off and leaving me here. I know this is bitterly unfair of me, since I spent several days pretending he didn't exist, so then I grow angry at my own sense of injustice.

I don't know why I'm annoyed. I like solitude. Although, I'm learning there's a difference between being alone and being lonely. I like being alone, having space to myself, time to think, room to sit however I like, be utterly me. But other people have never been far away, rarely out of earshot, and I was usually accompanied by an animal of some sort no matter where I was.

I have two dogs at home, Fifine and Azor, both large spaniels. Azor is mostly Freed's dog now– his stalwart hunting companion, brave and true, loyal to a fault. Fifine was my Mama's favourite, and after she died, Fifine seemed to redirect her lost love to her remaining babies, especially Beau. She refused to sleep downstairs in the kitchen. For almost all of Beau's infancy, she slept beside his cradle. It was only once he started to walk that she would sometimes sleep in our room. She was the sweetest, most gentlest of creatures.

Why am I speaking of her in the past tense? Fifine still *is* sweet and gentle... she's just not here.

I turn my gaze to the outside. I can just about see the Beast, frolicking in the snow just like one of the dogs, a black speck amongst the white. I can imagine him with his tongue hanging out. "Beast" is such a silly name for him, all of a sudden. He has no more fang or claw than a puppy.

"Oh, all right," I say to no one in particular, and reach over to grab my boots.

I certainly haven't missed the cold, although the crisp white snow is surprisingly pleasant. There wasn't a drop of virgin snow left in the village. I pull on my gloves as I walk, hugging my hood close to my head. The Beast doesn't look up when I arrive. He appears to be trying to pile up the snow.

"Hello!" he says. "I'm building a snowman!"

I stare sceptically at the pile. "Do you even know what a man looks like?"

The Beast stops. "I've seen pictures."

Sighing, I kneel beside the pathetic attempt and try to shape the base. "Roll a large snowball," I instruct.

"A ball?"

"Yes." It takes a little while, but eventually, our man begins to take shape. The Beast struggles with the defter jobs, so he rolls up the snow and I pat it into place. Finding branches for the arms is simple enough –he snaps them off a nearby tree with astonishing ease– and I dig into the path to find stones for the buttons and eyes. Coal would be best, but I haven't seen any here.

"This doesn't look like a man," says the Beast.

"It looks like a snowman. What were you trying to make, a marble sculpture?"

"Something like that," he admits, a little forlornly.

I untie my scarf and loop it around the snowman's neck.

"No," says the Beast, unravelling it and handing it back, "use mine."

"Won't you get cold?"

He fixes me with a quizzical look. "I'm covered in fur."

"Then why wear a scarf in the first place?"

"Because that's what people do when they go out in the cold."

"But…" I almost say *you're not people* but, while true, that's not what I mean. "Why do you care what people do?"

"It has come to my attention that most people care what other people do."

"You're not most people."

He cocks his head thoughtfully. "Apparently neither are you."

I'm not sure why he thinks this after only a few days, but I almost find myself smiling. He's the first person to say it without any kind of disdain. "Rose is very… different." People would say to Nanny, usually when complimenting my siblings. They didn't mean it in a nice way. They meant strange. Not like us. I didn't much care for their opinion, but it is never nice to know you don't belong.

"What makes you say that?" I ask.

"You don't like what other people like," he says, matter-of-factly. "You don't seem concerned about fitting in."

"Actually, that's not entirely true. It's nice to fit in. I just don't think it's worth being someone else to do it. If you have to pretend to be somebody else to feel like you belong... you don't really."

"Where did you read that?"

"That one I learned myself." It's getting close to lunch time. My stomach rumbles loudly. "Will you eat with me?" I ask.

At first, he looks like he's going to refuse. He opens his mouth, splutters a few sounds, and then swallows them. He nods quietly, and we walk back to the castle together.

"Have you got a mate back home?" he asks, quite out of the blue.

"I'm sorry?" Now it is my turn to splutter.

"You know, a sweetheart, a lover. The last visitor here had a fiancé... I felt exceptionally bad about that."

My heart stills a little. He just wants to know who is missing me. "I have a Papa, a Nanny, two brothers and two sisters," I tell him. "No young gentleman callers. Not unless..."

He raises a large, bushy eyebrow.

"Well..." My mind turns to James. I haven't told anyone yet, not even Honour, but a few weeks ago, at the Mayor's party, I kissed him.

He found me reading in a little nook in the hallway. I hadn't meant to be rude; I just scuttled away for a few moments of quiet, when I'd found a stray book lying on a chaise. I hadn't been able to resist. James found me after a few minutes, sat down beside me, asked what was going on in the story. James had never minded my curious reading habits. He was always very polite about it, asking me what was happening, what I liked about the book, etc. But I could always tell his questions were a little forced. He was just being kind. James was not exactly a wordy person, really, lovely though he was.

Is.

Anyway, James had found me there just as I was getting to a good bit. A romance scene. I had probably had a bit too much wine that night, and I suddenly found myself desperately wanting to know what it was like to be kissed.

So I kissed him.

It was very nice. Gentle. Brief. Warm. But there wasn't anything special about it. It was not the kiss that the hero and heroine of the story were about to experience.

I had asked Mama, many years ago, if the kinds of kisses in books actually existed. "You know, the earth-changing, magical, firework-causing kind."

Mama smiled at me warmly, and stroked my hair. "Only if you kiss the right person, at the right moment."

My kiss with James was not like that.

"I kissed a friend of mine a few weeks ago," I tell the Beast, "but he isn't my sweetheart."

"Oh," he stops walking for a moment, and then quickly catches up. "Not a good kiss?"

"Not enough fireworks," I conclude, and then smiling, I run on ahead.

The evening passes more quickly than any of my others. The Beast eats both lunch and dinner with me, gnawing as carefully as he can manage at a chicken bone and trying to take smallish mouthfuls. I find the sight almost comical.

Since arriving at the castle, I've had a lot of plain meals, never much in the mood for anything else. Tonight, I pray for something different, and am rewarded with a strange, softly-spiced lamb stew. There is some kind of tangy, orange fruit in it that I have never tasted before. It's sweet and tender.

After dinner, we retire to the library. I uncover an old favourite of mine, about a young noble girl who gets shipwrecked on a desert island with no one but a resourceful cabin boy for company. She has to fend off pirates and monsters, overcome her own prejudices, befriend the natives, and, naturally, falls in love with the cabin boy. Unfortunately, just as they're about to confess their love, they are rescued by her uncle and realise that the world they come from won't allow them to be together.

I've just reached the part where Evelyn has her first run-in with the pirates and manages to fell one of them with a frying pan before being rescued by Jean, when the clock chimes ten. It is getting late. We say our goodbyes and go to bed.

Tonight is the first night I cannot hear the clock ticking, and I fall into a soft and dreamless sleep.

For the next few days, we exist in a similar fashion. Each morning, we meet in the dining hall, breakfast, play in the grounds, lunch, and usually retire to the library for the afternoon. We only spend a few hours apart each day. He offers me a tour of the castle, but I prefer to wander on my own. Although he tells me he has spent his whole life here, he does not seem to know much about the place– or know much he can tell me.

It takes a good two days to visit most of the rooms in the castle –except the one forbidden to me, of course, and the Beast's– but even then I am sure I've missed a few. There is an endless supply of hallways, corridors, stairs, chambers, suites, turrets, balconies and battlements. There is such an eclectic style too. Although most of the castle has a fey kind of wildness to it, there are traditionally gaudy chambers, pieces of gilded furniture, rooms draped in patterned wallpaper with an overabundance of faux flowers and gold chandeliers. It is as if someone has picked up different parts of history and blended them together.

There is little in the castle that reveals its history to me. The rooms look as if everyone simply got up one morning and swept off without a word. The beds are made, but there are clothes in the closets, books on side-tables, the occasional hairbrush on a dresser.

Somebody, or something, is cleaning them. Layers of dust are slowly being pulled away, the screens of cobwebs disappearing. Little by little, the place is brightening. While the library remains my favourite place, on the ground floor there is a delightful round chamber housing every kind of instrument imaginable. I try the harp and the piano –always my favourites– and determine I am definitely in need of practise. I add it to my list of things to do, and think of taking up the violin as well. The room next to it is a far more sorry sight– an empty menagerie. Beautiful, empty cages, perches and tanks decorate the room, devoid of any occupants.

I have not seen a single living thing here, other than... him. Occasionally I think I see the flicker of an insect in the corner of my eye, but it always turns out to be nothing, except, perhaps, the magic of the castle made visible, for one, ephemeral second. On the third floor I discover a glorious bathroom, with a pool so deep I can swim in it, and the tallest turret has glass walls, so you can see all around you. There's a chamber full of only mirrors, and endless galleries of endless portraits. My personal favourite, next to the library, is a little roof garden, accessible only by a narrow, winding staircase. There is little there, of course –bare pots, little statuettes, a bench– but I can see what it must have been like, before. The thorns of the rose bushes remain, tumbling over the walls and roofs. It must have been magnificent in summer. There is a small fountain there too, still trickling away, and the bottom of the pool is painted gold, casting a soft glow across the stones.

I am starting to see a beauty in this place. It is a pretty pen I have found myself.

Chapter Five

The Face in the Ice

A few days later, I wake up to an excited rapping at the door. I mumble something, haul myself out of bed, and pull on a dressing-gown as I shuffle towards it. The Beast grins at me, holding up a pair of skates in his hands.

"Here," he says, "I found these for you. They should be about your size."

"What about you?" I ask.

"Oh, I really don't think they'll fit."

An embarrassing snort of laughter escapes me. Beast looks like a cat when it's just sneezed, a great big face of fluff and shock. Then he grins too, and I stop.

"Sorry," I say.

"By all means, laugh." His cheeks puff out, and he chews his lip.

"What is it?"

"Who would have thought," he sniggers, "that such a little

snort could sound so sweet."

"I do *not* snort!" I return. "Pigs snort, ladies–"

"Oh, that was a snort, but don't worry, it was a very ladylike one."

"My nanny would be so pleased... and I don't snort!"

"Do."

"Don't." I punch him in the arm, which probably hurts me more than it does him. He is as hard as a rock. This doesn't help prove my point, but it makes me feel better. He looks at me for a moment, as though I've just done something odd.

"Sorry," I say, "I shouldn't have punched you. That was mean."

"No," he says slowly, "that's not it... it's not like you can hurt me."

There is something else, I sense, but I can't think what. I seize the skates from his hands. "Shall we?"

I have never skated before. In the village, there was no flat water large enough to skate on, not even in the harshest of winters. I touch the surface tentatively. It does not move. He, meanwhile, moves straight past and glides onto the frozen lake with clumsy grace.

"Are you sure it's safe?" I ask gingerly. I have always had a fear of deep water, but this looks as solid as stone. It is difficult to imagine it is anything else, that anything lurks beneath the surface. He stops spinning around for a second to answer me.

"Mostly," he says, beaming foolishly. "Don't worry, if you fall in, I'll drag you out."

"What if you fall in?"

"Then it's going to be a very lonely one-hundred-and-seventy days for you."

"That's not funny."

"You're right. Whoever shall make you laugh if I'm not here

to amuse you?"

"Still not funny."

Laughing, he slides back out, moving from four feet to two with ease.

One-hundred-and-seventy days. He is counting, and not for the same reason I am. He is counting, because, after those days, he is going to be alone again.

Not for the first time, I find that feeling of sympathy surging inside me. But it's more than that, this time. I do not want him to be alone. It feels so much more unfair than it did a few days ago, the little puddle of sympathy swelling into a pond.

I look out at the vast, frozen lake in front of me. Will it be this large by day one-hundred-and-seventy? I pray for it to freeze inside me. I don't want to feel it anymore.

"Rose? Are you coming?"

I watch him twirling about ridiculously. I suppose if it can take his weight, it can take mine. I slide both feet onto the ice. They split in different directions and I skid to my knees with a shriek. He tries not to laugh as he glides back over.

"Are you all right?"

"Fine, fine..." I try to pull myself up, but it's difficult on the ice. Beast is holding out a hand, but timidly, as if he isn't sure he should offer it.

I remember how I tensed before when he caught me, and am determined never to do so again. I take his hand and haul myself up, grabbing hold of both of his arms to steady myself. He is solid and incredibly sturdy, more an oak in the ground, not an animal on ice. I realise he has filed down the frightening talons he brandished before.

"All right?" he asks again.

"Better."

"I'd give you some instruction, but I'm unfamiliar with skates."

"It's fine. I'm sure I'll get the hang of it."

For the better part of an hour, I experiment with my footwork, staying close to the banks so I can fall into the soft snow if I feel unsteady. Which I do, a lot. He hovers nearby to begin with, trying to catch me when I topple over. I make a bit of a game of it, sliding some distance and then launching into the bank when I feel a fall coming on.

Slowly, I get the hang of it. I begin to get more adventurous, drifting away from the bank. I am loath to go too far out. It feels safer to be nearer the solid ground– probably a good rule for a long life. He, of course, is having a whale of a time. He's picked up a good rhythm and is smoothly gliding around, one foot at a time, hands behind his back. He looks back at me often (to check that I'm all right, I think) and then promptly performs some kind of trick.

Show-off.

I try to build up some momentum, kicking my skates quickly against the surface, and sail forward several feet. The wind rushes through me, sending a quiet, pleasant chill right down to my toes. I feel light, giddy, as if I've taken flight.

Naturally, I quickly lose my footing, tumbling to the ground. I sigh, rolling over onto my back with my hair splayed out behind me, like a frost-covered cape. I trace the lines in the ice with my fingers. I had forgotten the way ice could glitter. The water rolls across the other side of the surface, brushing the ice like clouds. For a second, I think I see a flash of something silver glimmering along the pebbles. A fish? No, there are no fish in this lake.

But there was something there, I am sure of it.

I sit up, scrubbing the ice with my sleeve. There it is again– a dark, grey shape, slithering under the ice. I tap the surface, trying to see if it responds. Is it alive or not? I don't see it again.

Instead, I feel a shudder, the awful feeling of something moving underneath me. I hear a crack.

My breath stills in my throat, my heart pummelling against my chest. Sound is swiftly sucked away. I can feel the ice shifting. It is as if I am watching a spider crawl slowly up my body. I am paralysed, but I feel every trembling movement.

The cracks widen. I can't move, can't speak, can't scream–

"Rose!"

With one final, desperate look back at the Beast, I plunge into the ice.

Ice burns through my lungs, spreading to the tips of my fingers like wildfire. Cold iron grips my neck. Sharp pain ignites across my skin. I struggle, but my limbs are heavy. I want to fight. Fight against the dark and the cold, but pain in my chest is absolute. I am being torn apart.

There is something reaching for me. Someone reaching in the murk. Not to save me, to hurt me. Talons fasten around my ankles. I am being pulled down into the dark, the dark I can't see, can't fathom. The urge to scream rises but the water presses against me.

I see a terrible face, burning into the back of my eyelids. A pale, narrow, starved face, surrounded by masses of dark, swirling hair. It ought to be human, but for two long horns protruding from its skull. It is grinning at me, laughing maniacally.

No, no, no. You can't have me. I am not yours, not yours.

I kick against it. Lash out. Move. Struggle. Fight. Not giving up. Not yet...

I see something else. Something beautiful, white and gold, moving towards me. A hand reaches out. I hear words, like music, telling me to hold on.

Somebody is calling my name. I feel something grip my middle, and then blackness swallows me whole.

Wind whistles. I hear breathing. Hard, ragged breaths. I am

jostled, up and down. There's a light, yellow and red and warm. Then something is pulling off my clothes with gentle desperation.

"Help her, help her, please!"

Who is he talking to?

My head spins. Something thick and heavy falls across my shoulders. Lights dance around my eyes, and somebody strokes my hair. Mama?

I dream I see her face, and then everyone's. Everyone's that I miss.

I see the Beast's face too, and then I see a stranger's. A girl, buzzing with light. Green eyes, wild hair. I want to cry, but there is a lump of iron where my throat used to be.

"Who are you?" I whisper.

She glares at me from the mirror, her eyes daggers, her mouth open in a cruel, horrible sneer. Her teeth could be fangs. As I stare, she raises a hand towards the pane and drags a fingernail across it. The screech races down my spine. I bolt upright in a bed of furs, screaming.

"A face, a face!" I blubber. "A horrible, monstrous face! It was here– in the mirror and–"

"It's all right Rose," a calm, soothing voice says from behind me. "I won't hurt you."

In the corner of the room, about as far away from me as he can get, the Beast sits. His words catch me by surprise. "Of course you won't," I say. Then my own words circle back to me. Shame spreads across my cheeks. "Oh, oh no, I didn't mean–"

He raises to his feet, turning towards the door. "It's all right, I understand-"

"No, you don't. I'm not talking about you. I saw something in the mirror, and... and in the lake. A person, or the face of one..."

The Beast freezes. "You've gone through a shock," he says shortly. "And the isolation plays tricks on us all. You must have imagined it. There is no one else here but us."

I want to argue. It seemed so real. But then I remember a hunting trip a few years ago, when Freedom got caught in the rain for several hours, without shelter. It was freezing. By the time he returned to us, he was delirious with cold. Nanny stripped off his clothes immediately, bundled him in blankets, and sat him beside the fire. He returned to normal after a good long sleep. And yet...

"Are you sure?"

"I wish I wasn't."

I swallow painfully. My head hurts. The drowsiness is overwhelming. I urge to lie back down again, but before my cheek hits the pillow, an arm circles round my back and a teacup is pressed to my lips.

"Drink this," he instructs.

It is warm and minty. The tightness in my chest loosens. "Thank you," I whisper.

"'Tis only a drink."

"I meant for saving me."

"Oh. Well, entirely selfish of me, I assure you. Wasn't quite ready to give up the pleasure of your company."

"Pleasure? I've been beastly to you... if you'll pardon the pun."

He chuckles. "You've been lovely these past couple of days, and I cannot blame you for any initial frostiness."

"I'm sorry you thought I was talking about your face."

"It's all right. I'm used to it by now."

"That makes it worse!"

"Does it?"

"Yes!" I insist. "No one should have to get used to people being cruel to them."

He drops his head slightly. "Perhaps I felt I deserved it."

"Did you? Deserve it?"

"Are you asking... if I committed some sort of crime to be

left here, guarding this place?"

I nod my head solemnly.

"None that comes to mind. No, being here is not *my* punishment."

There is something in the way he says this that confuses me, but I cannot quite put my finger on what. "Then why would you think you deserved it?"

He swallows audibly, and for a moment, I think he is done with any explanation. Then I realise he is staring down at his hands. "For being like this," he sighs, "a monster."

The pain in his voice is palpable, and it slices me to my core. Gingerly, I reach out and slip my hands into one of his. They do not seem as large as they did a few days ago, although they dwarf mine. "I see no monster here," I say. "But then you did just save my life, so I may be riding that thought for a couple of days at least."

There is a twitch of a smile in his whiskery cheeks. "Perhaps I'll ask you again then when you've fully recovered."

"Perhaps." I lie myself back down in the furs, and turn my face towards the firelight. "The other people that came here before me. Were they... what were they like?"

"They were... apprehensive, at first. You can hardly blame them. Some... some were very afraid. One girl barely came out of her room the entire time she was here. Some were very cruel. But some were kind. One or two, I would have called friends by the time they left. None..." His voice goes very quiet.

"None what?"

He shakes his head. "It doesn't matter," he says.

I think he means to say, *none were like you*, but I'm glad he doesn't. I wouldn't know what to do with that. "Tell me a story," I ask instead.

At first, he looks a little taken aback, as if I am the first person to ever request one. "What... what would you like to hear?"

"Something true and something magical." It is the first time I have ever been able to ask for such a thing.

"Very well," he clears his throat. "Long ago, the world of

men was rampant with magic. Fairies of every kind use to roam the land, as common as cats. While some were kind and benevolent, many misused their power, until a few were as cruel as they were beautiful. Stories were spread about evil deeds, of bad deals, stolen children, curses... as if fairies were the only creatures capable of misdeeds. There was a great war, and both sides suffered terrible losses. The Queen of the Fairies decided that it was best for everyone if they withdrew from the world. She forged a new realm, one where the fairies could live in peace. But she did not wish to deny mankind their gifts altogether, and so a precious few were allowed to roam the world, only a few times a year. This arrangement seemed to suit; fairies were encouraged to be good, hoping to one day gain passage to Earth, and magic was only ever used for good purposes.

"But then a fairy with a dark heart grew jealous, and few things spoil the soul faster than festering jealousy. She thought the Queen unfair for denying them the pleasures of the Earth, and thought mankind foolish and undeserving of such a beautiful, ever-changing land, for the price of paradise is boredom. And so, a second war began, and this time there was to be no victor. The evil fairy destroyed the Queen, but destroyed herself in the process. Slowly, eventually, the land of fairies faded into nothingness, until all that remained of their deeds –good and bad– were a few simple stories."

I sigh. "Mama used to tell me a story just like that, almost word-for-word."

"You must miss her."

My head nods by its own accord. "She died when I was nine, giving birth to my little brother."

"I'm sorry to hear that." He refills my cup and encourages me to drink. "Tell... tell me about your family."

"Why?"

"Because you must miss them, and talking about them might keep them close."

So I tell him. I tell him about Nanny, our cook, caretaker

and grandmother-substitute, and her battles with the dogs and the mischief they got into. I tell him about my father. Wise, quiet and careful, who spends most of the day reading or gazing into the fire, Azor at his feet. I talk of my siblings, of Freedom, who constantly irks me, who spends all of days hunting but secretly paints in his "tool shed". I tell him of Honour, beautiful, dependable, calm and loving Honour, my closest confident, the best older sister anyone could ask for. Hope is more of a recluse than her, serious and quiet, far smarter than any of the rest of us, although not as wise as she would like to be. Yet. I tell him about Beau. I might be closest to Honour, but I have a soft spot in my heart for my little brother. We all do. He is brave and good-hearted and just wants everyone to be happy. He has a delicious, infectious laugh. The first time I smiled after Mama's death was when he smiled at me. I pause here in my story, because thinking of Beau in such a way makes me ache. I miss his chattering, his little face, the way he would creep into my bed during thunderstorms to 'protect' me. I wonder if he climbs into Honour's bed now, or Hope's.

I wonder if Honour is going through with the wedding.

"Rose?" The Beast's voice is as soft as ember. He crouches down by my side. His eyes look like diamonds, bright and gleaming. "Rose, you will see your family again, I promise."

"I know," I say, and manage to bite down the rest of my words. *But I will miss things. I will miss Honour's wedding, I will miss my father's practical tales, Freedom's silly escapades. I will miss putting Beau to bed, miss his laugh. I will miss Hope crawling into bed with me to read in silence. I will miss all of their everythings.*

I bite down on the words, but I still choke on the tears. They come fast and furiously and unstoppably. The Beast hands me a handkerchief, but it does little to stem the flood. It is not enough, not by half, so I seize the next white thing I see through the flurry of tears; his shirt. I bury my face in his chest and vibrate with grief.

Slowly, gingerly, his arms circle around me with incredible

gentleness. He says nothing, but holds me while I sob and cry for home.

Eventually, the tears start to subside. Sleep tugs at me instead, first at my eyelids, and then at my whole body. I lower myself back into my pillow. "Will you stay?" I whisper, as the darkness folds inwards.

There is a pause before he replies. "For as long as you want me."

For the first time, I do not want to be alone.

No dreams disturb my slumber, and I awake to faintest sunlight streaming across my cheek. My chest is still tight, a cold spreads through my face, but I feel lighter than the night before.

The Beast is slumped by the side of the room, but the minute my gaze settles on him, he leaps upright as if my gaze burns him.

"You're awake," he states numbly.

"You're still here."

"I'm sorry, do you wish me to go–"

"No, I just thought–"

"You asked me to stay–"

"I know, I just... have you been there all night?"

"Oh, don't worry," he gushes. "I was perfectly comfortable."

"On the floor?"

He looks down at his feet. "I usually sleep on the floor."

He is ashamed of this, of anything, I realise, that suggests he is more animal than man. He is neither to me, and perhaps that is why it bothers him– the sense being betwixt and between, belonging nowhere.

"You should eat something," he announces, before I can think of something to say in response. He brings over a tray of soup and bread.

I take up the bowl, my fingers shaking slightly. I hadn't realised how hungry I was.

"Eat up!" he urges.

I stuff my face with broth-soaked bread and chew. "You sound like Honour."

"Eat first, then talk."

"Well excuse me, Mr Manners..." I swallow, warmth spreading through my body. Not for the first time, I wonder if there's magic in the food, and not just in its ability to appear out of thin air. I take a few more mouthfuls greedily, partly hoping he will realise he doesn't have to stand on ceremony whenever we eat together.

Satisfied at my efforts, he asks, "Honour is... your older sister, yes? Hope is your younger one?"

"Correct," I say, gulping down tea.

"So Freedom, Honour, Hope and Beau? I'm noticing somewhat of a theme."

I groan. "Mother's virtuous names. It's a family thing, apparently. I think Freedom got the worst of it."

"Well, I wasn't going to say."

I giggle. "Mama thought she was having a girl, and she had her heart set on Liberty, because the war had just come to a close, but then Freedom was a boy, and so... sometimes I joke that she knew he was going to be a beast and was punishing him in advance."

"What about Rose?"

"Story goes that on the day I was born, my father bought my mother a bouquet of roses. He said they were his favourite flower, and they were *beauty personified*. He was trying to give her a hint. She was previously going to call me Beauty."

He smiles. "It would have suited you."

I pull a face. "It's a ridiculous name and you know it." My spoon falls to the bowl with a clatter. Wordlessly, my tray is cleared away. He fiddles about with stacking the crockery neatly, as if reluctant to return to my side.

"What... what happened to your family?" I ask.

He pauses for a moment, stiffening. He takes a careful breath. "My father died before I was born," he tells me slowly. "My mother... I remember her. Vividly. But more... in the way one remembers a painting."

"What happened to her?"

"She was... she left this world, when I was still very small."

He is an orphan then, all alone in the world. Not a day goes by I don't miss Mama, but to have no one, no one at all...

"What's your real name?"

"I'm sorry?"

"Your real name. You told me to call you Beast, but your mother couldn't have called you that."

"No," he replies, "she did not. But it has been so long now I can barely remember it."

It seems unlikely that he has forgotten his own name, but I sense I will not discover it. Perhaps it's very long or embarrassing. Perhaps it doesn't suit him at all. What name does, I wonder? My eyes wander over his dark, prickly body, searching for inspiration, but it is the painting of roses over his shoulder that offers it.

"Thorn," I say suddenly.

"Come again?"

"I am going to call you Thorn."

"Because... I'm a thorn in your side?" he asks skeptically. I laugh.

"No! It's because... you're a little prickly, but accompany every rose."

He tilts his head, regarding me closely with some intense expression I can't quite read. "I'd like that," he says eventually, very softly. "Thorn."

I remain in bed for the next two days, heaped under blankets and nursing a heavy cold. Thorn barely leaves my side the entire time. He entertains me by reading. He is the most animated speaker, doing accents and impressions. His company, I know, has been limited. Where did he learn how to speak like that? He breathes life into every word he reads. Worlds unfurl on his tongue.

When I'm in want of silence, he brings me my sewing and watches in amazement as I transform my bed into a dresser's shop, sniping and snitching dresses to my liking. I do insist he returns to his own room for the night, but he is back again at every sunrise with a new book for the day.

One evening, when I am left alone, I bring out a little notebook and count back the days. It has been two weeks now. Honour is getting married tomorrow. I wonder how she is, if she's going through with it without me, if anyone is staying up with her tonight. Throwing back the covers, I tip-toe out of bed, sit myself at the writing desk in the corner, and take out pen and parchment.

Dear Honour,

Tomorrow is your wedding day, a day you have dreamed of all your life, and I will not be standing by your side for it. I am so sorry, dearest sister.

I know my sudden disappearance will have been hard for everyone, and I am truly sorry for all the pain I will have put you all through. I did not mean to go. Rest assured that I am well; I am safe and unhurt, and will return to you in time. I know it sounds impossible, but it appears the rumours of stepping over the stream were true: I have been stranded in a fairy realm, in a great abandoned castle. It was a little disconcerting at first, but I find myself warming up to it. It is a bit of a grey adventure, but an adventure nonetheless.

There does not seem to be much magic left in this place, but it does have miraculous food and a rather fetching bathtub. You would love the music room, and I am very enamoured with the library. Even Hope would struggle to run out of material here!

I also appear to have made a friend. I know, me, a friend! I suppose everyone has thought my quota of those filled for years? I thought so too. He is as much a prisoner here as I am –more so, perhaps, for he has never left– and there is a loneliness inside him that he hides as well as I hid mine. We share a love of literature, although not always of the same tastes, and he makes me laugh. You know precious few have managed to do that.

I want you to know that although I miss you all terribly, I'm not miserable here. At times I am almost happy, although I cannot be truly content while I know that you all will be worrying after me. Please let everyone know that I am all right and will be home within a few months. Tell Hope to watch my garden for me, and please read Beau his favourite bedtime story in my absence. Do the voices. He likes those.

I know you will look beautiful tomorrow, and I know that Charles will treat you with every bit of the admiration you deserve. I just wish I could be there to see the look on his face when he sees you in your gown. The two of you almost make me long for romance of my own.

Please, if you can, be happy. I am trying my hardest here too.

All my love, Rose

I fold up the letter, seal it, and take it towards the fireplace. In one of Thorn's books, I heard that fairies used to send messages to each other this way.

Please, I beg, *if there is enough magic left here, let her receive my letter. Let her know that I am safe.*

I know it is a hopeless cause, and that receiving a letter out of nowhere declaring I'm trapped in a fairy castle is going to do little to elevate Honour's worry, but I still feel better watching it vanish into the embers.

That night, when I dream, it is of Honour in her dress, a wreath of holly in her hair, gliding towards the man she loves.

Part Two: Spring

I heard a thousand blended notes,
While in a grove I sate reclined,
In that sweet mood when pleasant thoughts
Bring sad thoughts to the mind.

To her fair works did Nature link
The human soul that through me ran;
And much it grieved my heart to think
What man has made of man.

Through primrose tufts, in that green bower,
The periwinkle trailed its wreaths;
And 'tis my faith that every flower
Enjoys the air it breathes.

--William Wordsworth--

Chapter Six

Sunlight and Snow Drops

The following morning, I get up and don my new dress, a floaty crimson creation with a gold bramble pattern on the bodice. I take a little time to brush my hair and braid back a few of the curls. Pleased with my appearance, I grab my coat and gloves and skip out onto the landing where I meet Thorn.

"Oh! You're up!" he says quickly.

"Why wouldn't I be?"

"I had thought you may wish to take it easy today."

I shake my head. "I've had enough of that. I'm growing restless. Shall we go for a walk?"

I head off towards the entrance hall without waiting for a reply. Something feels different about the castle this morning, but I cannot quite put my finger on what. There is an energy to the place, a lightness–

"Sunlight," Thorn stops suddenly behind me, staring out of a window at the end of a corridor. "There's sunlight– here!"

I'm about to say that there's always been light here, but

I quickly realise what he means. Whatever faint imitation of light occupied this place previously has been peeled away, and now the corridors are flooded with pure, brilliant warmth. Thorn's excitement washes into me.

Outside, sunlight paints the landscape. It is so warm I have to remove my gloves. The icicles are melting, our snowman sagging, our winter wonderland dissolving into slush. There are sounds in the gardens– the trickle of water, and something else too.

"Is that– is that a bird?"

A little robin sits in the hedgerows. Thorn and I both stare, mouths agape, as if it is the first bird we have ever seen. Then the little creature flaps its wings and soars into the sky, darting about the clouds with a partner.

"They must have come through the holes in the veil," says Thorn. "It happens every now and again."

"Birds and sunlight in one day," I say, with mock surprise. "Whatever next?"

What's next is snowdrops. Thorn comes to my room one morning, hopping about excitedly, and presents me with a tiny little bouquet of white flowers, wrapped clumsily with a lace ribbon. I barely have time to process the gift before he's seized my hand and pulled me out into the gardens. Most of the snow has gone now. Grass grows in its place.

He points to a patch in the corner of an abandoned flower-bed, where, just three weeks ago, I planted the remnants of my basket. "Look!" he grins.

Tiny, delicate white buds peer through the snow. I know what it feels like to see the first flowers of spring, I can only imagine what this must feel like to him.

"Snowdrops, Rose! Snowdrops! The garden is still alive!"

He has lost count of the years, he explains, since he last saw them.

"What's causing this?" I ask. "Why all this change? Why now?"

"I'm not fully sure," he says, calming down a little. "I was certain this place was only a year or so away from crumbling completely. And now this..." He looks at me. "It's probably you, you know."

"Me?"

"The timings match up."

"I'm not doing anything!"

"'Tis just a theory."

"A ridiculous one."

I go back to the castle and hunt for a tiny vase to place my flowers in. I have never been given flowers by anyone who wasn't related to me before, and never tied up with such a pretty ribbon. It must have taken some effort to find one, especially given how excited he was and how much he must have wanted to show me straight away. The way he grabbed my hand...

He has never touched me before, to my recollection, unless it was absolutely necessary. Not unless I touched him first. I can almost still feel the weight of his palm against mine...

I find a small vase in an abandoned chamber and take it back to mine. I unravel the ribbon, snip the ends of the stems to make the blooms last longer, and soak them in water. I put the ribbon in my hair.

That night, I ponder what Thorn has said when I reach the end of my book and lose my distraction. Am I the cause of this? I don't see how I can be. And yet...

The more I imagine this place to be beautiful –the more I want to see its beauty– the clearer it becomes. It does not seem quite so dark or empty or still any more. Even the pattern in the dining room appears to be less outlandish now.

But it can't be me. However much I might wish for it occasionally, there is nothing special about me. Nothing at all.

One night, almost a month after my arrival at the castle, Thorn declares he is not feeling himself, and abandons me curiously early. He rebuffs all offers of assistance, and departs to his own room. I read by the firelight for several hours, but I cannot get comfortable. I have a lavender bath, dress for bed, and pen another letter to Honour. The words do not come easily, but provide the distraction I was hoping for.

Dear Honour,

Our winter here has come to a sudden but beautiful end, and I am now out in the gardens where I belong. They really are quite wonderful. I wish you could see them–

A shadow ripples across the floor. There is something outside my room.

My heart freezes. Thorn? No. It can't be him. He wouldn't lurk outside my door, not at this hour.

But... But there is no one else in the castle.

The thing, whatever it is, moves. It is big, and there is the soft clink of claws on the marble. I hold my breath.

There it is again.

"Thorn?" I whisper hopefully.

There is a low, hollow growl from outside. It is not Thorn's.

I swallow. Should I stay where I am? Did it hear me speak? Does it know I'm here? My heart thumps in my ears, capsizing my thoughts. I cannot move.

The creature shuffles on.

I wait until all is silent, then scramble out of bed, lock the door, and pull the dresser in front of it. Then I hurtle back to relative safety, snuff out my light, and hide under the covers. I shake underneath them, praying for morning to come.

I wake to the sound of birdsong and slither out of bed in a half-daze, my hair sticking up all over the place. I have a faint, foggy memory of a nightmare, something horrible about a monster.

Wrapped in sheets, I pull back the curtains and let daylight spill into my room, illuminating every crevice. Two little bluebirds sit on the window ledge, twittering away. The gardens are beautifully green, little buds blossoming in the hedgerows. This side of the castle is thick with ivy.

Leaving my window open, I go to dress. It is then that I notice the dresser pulled in front of the door.

It wasn't a dream.

I rush down to breakfast. It is late but Thorn has always waited for me before. There is no one there, and no signs of anyone having eaten recently. Bread and jam is laid out, but I have no appetite for it. I head towards the library, hoping to see him curled in a ridiculous position by the fire having fallen asleep engrossed in a book. The room is deserted.

Finally, knowing I shall never be at ease until I find him, I go to Thorn's room. It is one of precious few I have never been in.

I knock politely on the door.

No answer.

I knock again, louder. Something stirs inside.

"Thorn? Are you awake? It's almost midday."

I hear something grumble and moan.

"Thorn?"

The door clicks open. Thorn appears in the gap, undressed and tousled. The room is dark behind him.

"Are you all right?" I ask, instantly forgetting why I was there.

Thorn nods sluggishly. "Forgive me," he says, his voice husky, "I did not know what time it was. I did not get the best night's sleep."

"Are you ill?" I ask. Automatically, my hand goes towards his head; to stroke his hair, or check his temperature, I am not really sure.

He jerks away. "I'm fine, Rose. I shall clean up and be down for lunch."

"If you're not up to it, I can bring you something– "

"I'm fine."

The door closes in my face.

He does not seem fine when he meets me in the dining room. Not unwell, just... not himself. He is often the quieter of the two of us, but there is a stillness to him now.

"Did... did you hear anything last night?" I ask trepidatiously.

"No."

"Only... only I thought... I was sure..." He is so snappy and sluggish that another thought occurs to me. "Did you... did you get up at all?"

"I went for a walk at one point, to try and help me sleep." He narrows his eyes, and then they slide open with realisation. "You heard me."

I nod ashamedly, fearing he can sense my thoughts. *I thought you were a monster. You frightened me.* "I called out to you," I try, "but you didn't– "

"I was half-asleep."

"If you're sure– "

"Well, who else would it be?"

No one, I realise. It is only the two of us. "Would you... like to join me for a walk?" I offer, trying to sound bright. "The maze is growing. We can probably get lost in it now."

"If you wish," he says, making it sound as if that is the worst idea in the world.

We decide to go to the library instead, where we read for a while in angry silence. Every question, every idea I have, is rebuffed.

I ask him if he will be joining me for dinner, a question I have not asked for at least a week. We eat all our meals together now, but Thorn's mood has me questioning what I have taken for granted.

"No, not tonight," he says, with no explanation.

"Why not?"

"I am not hungry."

"It's several hours away!"

I come close to losing my temper when he uses the word, "whatever."

"Fine!" I say, slamming my book closed, "Go ahead and starve!" I huff towards the door, fully intending to march out and slam it behind me.

"Rose," says Thorn quietly, stopping me in my tracks. "I'm sorry, I'm just... I'm not myself today."

We all have our grumpy days, I reason. "Is that it?" I ask, turning to face him just a fraction.

He nods slowly.

"Because... if it were anything else... I should like to know."

I expect that to be the end of the conversation. I don't really feel like making it up to him. His grumpy day is making *me* grumpy.

"Why?" he asks.

"Why what?"

"Why should you like to know if something were wrong?"

"Nobody likes to be left in the dark," I say, "and besides... if there were something I could do to help... I would want to do it."

"Would you?" Thorn takes a step closer.

"Yes."

"Why? Why would you want to help me?"

I open my mouth to tell him, quite angrily, that I am a reasonably nice person and any reasonably nice person wants to help others, but then I stop. I am not like Honour –Honour who would go out of her way to help a complete stranger–

I would never help someone without considering, however quickly, the risks and time and effort involved. I am not inclined to go above and beyond. Not for people I don't care for. But I care about Thorn.

"You are my friend," I say carefully. "And when you're not being thoroughly miserable, you are quite a good one!"

I still slam the door behind me when I leave, feeling angry and bitter as I run myself a bath and slide under the surface.

I forgive Thorn the same way I do my family: by saying absolutely nothing for a few days and eventually getting over it. It takes him a little while to realise this, however, and he cautiously darts around me for our next interactions. We do not see that much of each other for a while anyway; I have found a new distraction. Now that life has returned to the castle, it is time to resume one of my favourite pastimes– gardening. I go out bright and early one morning in search of some garden tools, finally finding some in a small store not far from the herb garden, which is to be my first project. They are old and worn, a little rusty, but sturdy enough for my purposes.

I spend the first few hours out there in the dawn, pulling up weeds, stripping out the dead plants and overgrowth. I create a huge pile of leaves and bracken. It is hard work, but I have always enjoyed it, and the rewards are reaped over a long period of time. Thorn finds me there as the clock chimes eleven.

"Good morning," he says, a little carefully. "You missed breakfast."

I wipe my forehead with the back of my hand, no doubt leaving muddy smears across my face. "I was preoccupied." I give him a smile, trying to let him know that I am not angry, not any more.

"As I see. You don't need to... dig in the dirt," he adds. "The gardens do rather have a way of... sorting themselves."

As he says this, I swear for a moment I can hear the faint tinkling of bells. I turn my head towards the sound, but he doesn't move. I must have imagined it.

"But I like digging in the dirt."

"Then... carry on. Do you need a hand?"

"Um... you could break up those twigs for me? Clear any of the rocks and branches..."

I have barely had time to re-plant the rosemary in a sunnier part of the garden before Thorn chirps, "I'm done!" and I turn around to see a neat pile of rocks, branches, twigs and leaves.

"That was quick! What did you use to break up the branches with?"

Thorn looks down sheepishly. "My hands."

"My brother would be very jealous."

He leans against the wall, half in shade. "I imagine it would be rather the other way around."

"Freedom has no need for good looks," I assure him. "His internal hideousness blinds everyone. He'd be much better off with strength. Or sense. Or intelligence."

"I'm still trying to work out if you actually like your elder brother."

"Me too," I shrug, and then I feel that familiar prick of sadness, a twinge of guilt. I'm still being mean about him, even when I miss him.

There's rustling in the bushes. I look up and see the strangest little creature under the rosemary, sweeping up loose twigs. It has a wrinkled visage, and is covered head to toe in short brown curly hair, wearing miniature mantle and hood.

"Thorn! Look!" I squeak.

Thorn scrambles in front of me, throwing out his arms as if I'm under assault. His shoulders quickly drop. "It's a brownie," he grins. "We should turn our backs."

"Is it dangerous?" It is difficult to believe, but I am learning not to judge by what I see.

"No, they just don't like being looked at..." He glances back at it anyway, mesmerised. "They're supposed to be good luck, help around the house. We should leave some food out. The others will be thrilled."

"The others?"

"The... remnants of magic. The things that clean and provide us with food."

"They're brownies?"

"No," he says forlornly. "They aren't really anything, any more."

I look back at the little creature, but it has already vanished.

I do not see any more brownies, but I keep my eyes peeled for any signs of these remnants that Thorn described. There was something in the way he spoke about them, like... like he missed them. If the brownies came back, if the garden is returning to life... I don't see why they can't come back either. They must be more than little twinkles of light, if they can materialise food out of nowhere and attend to our whims. They *must* be.

Thorn was certainly right about the gardens mostly taking care of themselves, however. The lawns rarely appear in need of trimming, and even though nobody is shearing the hedgerows, they remain at a decent length. Sometimes, I think I can hear someone shearing them, but whenever I go to investigate, I find nothing but a few heaps of leaves, which magically make their way to my compost before I can even find a broom to sweep them. I start thanking the castle whenever it does something for me, but I never get a reply.

I awake one morning to find the garden coated with a fine, white mist. Light rain, nothing like the suffocating fog that imprisons us. It looks almost magical, as if every leaf is decorated with pearls. I grab my lightest coat and go for a wander.

The foyer has emerged from its chrysalis. Cascades of ivy float in through the broken windows, ribboning down the bannisters, pooling into the hall. Wisteria winds round the pillars, fine and delicate as lace. Sunlight glitters on every surface, a myriad of colours scattered by the glass, spasms of amber and gold and honey. The wild, ethereal beauty of the palace haunts every corner, the bright, fresh aroma of spring stirring in every leaf.

The rain is feather-light, soft as silk. Tiny, shy buds begin to bloom in the hedgerows. I whisper good morning and imagine their voices. Perhaps I can finally start to identify them. There are so many that I have never seen before, do not know the name of. Thorn found me a book on Fey flowers, but the lack of petals on most of them make them hard to identify. The hedges are full of tiny buds, pink and white and orange and purple. A few look like snowdrops or poppies, but are the wrong size, the wrong colour. Nevertheless, impossibly beautiful. The lilies on the pond still lie closed, as do the roses, but slowly life is eking back into this place.

I stop for a moment under a large oak. It was raining like this when Honour told me that Charles had asked her to marry her. The two of us were out for a walk when we bumped into him. He was fumbling and awfully nervous, saying he had asked for her at the house. I think Honour knew then what he was there to ask her. I certainly did.

"I'll go on ahead," I told her.

I waited for her in the garden, despite the rain, because I was certain that she would want to tell me first. Sure enough, some twenty minutes later, Honour came skipping out of the woodland, hair, cape, ribbons flying, practically tripping over herself. She could barely catch her breath.

"He asked me to marry him, Rosie! He asked me to be his wife!"

She was shaking with happiness as we embraced, spluttering on every word as she recounted exactly what he had said, and then we went inside to repeat the story to everyone else. Nanny screamed and started to cry. Hope and Beau both rushed into her arms. Freedom clapped her on the back. Papa almost smiled. Everyone was so overcome with joy, and I was too, for a little while.

By the time that night came, the rain had thickened into a storm. I sat in my reading nook, Hope fast asleep in her bed, listening to the hushed, excited sounds of Nanny and Honour discussing arrangements. I looked at Honour's empty bed and realised that soon, that bed would be empty forever.

When Honour finally came upstairs, she didn't go to her bed or start to undress. She came to me, sat down by my side. "You should say it, dearheart," she whispered.

What I wanted to say was that I was going to miss her, that I knew we would still see each other every day, that it was silly and foolish to be afraid of change, and that I was happy for her. What came out was a rushed, sudden, and unexpectedly venomous response.

"I don't want you to marry him."

Honour just laughed, ignoring any malice in my voice, which made me mad at first. Of course, I didn't mean it, but she didn't know that. Except, of course, she did. She took me in her arms and stroked my hair.

"It's not the end of the world."

I know.

"I love him and he makes me happy."

I wouldn't let you go otherwise.

"I know you know that. It's all right to be afraid."

No, it isn't.

"You'll still see me every day."

I wanted to cry then and I want to now, but I always so detested letting other people see my tears. My eyes begin to fill. We have not seen each other in so long now, and we were never apart before, not for a day. I was so lost then. I didn't know what I would do without her. There was a reason I didn't really have any close friends; I didn't need them. I had her. I had Hope too, but the two of us were too alike. I needed someone like

Honour, who would say the things I never could, who knew what I was thinking sometimes before I thought it.

"Are you all right?" A voice prickles behind me.

I brush my tears away and pretend it was rain. "Just remembering the day my sister got engaged," I tell him. "It was raining then like it is now."

Thorn tilts his head. "Not a happy memory?"

"A very happy one," I insist. "Charles is lovely." *Do not mention the tears.*

"You sounded a little forlorn then, is all," he responds. "My mistake, I'm sure."

"I..." I swallow. *What am I doing?* "I was worried about her getting married, and moving away... even if it was only across the village. Foolish, I know."

"I don't think so," he says. "Missing someone is rarely foolish."

I wonder if he misses the other visitors, and if he misses them for them, or merely for company.

"I've never made friends easily," I confess.

I wait for him to ask why, or disagree, but all he says is, "Oh."

"Oh?" I narrow my eyes. "No, 'oh that can't possibly be true'? or, *You are far too witty to lack for company, dear Rose–*"

"Company," says Thorn, trying not to smile, "is not the same as friendship. And you said yourself that you've never tried to be someone else to get people to like you. It falls to reason that you do not make friends easily."

This is true enough.

"Honour is the closest thing I have to one," I tell him.

"What about the friend that you kissed?"

I have known James since we were children. His family used to live next door until his mother remarried and moved across town. He was the same age as me, and we loved running around and playing with swords and making up adventures together. Then we started school, and I learnt how to read. It was more comfortable to have adventures in your own head.

We were still friends, but we spent so little time together after that. I was never alone with him, we had few conversations, and although we still liked each other, we didn't know each other.

"He doesn't... he doesn't know me," I explain. "He doesn't understand me. I don't know him really, either. I think that friends usually do, don't they? It's not just a collection of what you know about them, but what you know *of* them. The sort of person they are. Whether their soul is shaped like yours."

Thorn stares at me for a long moment. I wonder if he is wondering what my soul looks like, if such a thing is possible.

"What are you thinking?" I ask after a while.

"That I am glad that you and I are friends," he says eventually, and then wordlessly walks back to the castle. It occurs to me, watching him go, that I ought to have included him.

Honour is the closest thing I have to a real friend... apart from you.

Chapter Seven

Shapes and Shadows

Time passes. The garden grows prettier, ever-so-slowly. I have never seen a garden bloom this way before. It is like it is held, suspended. A flower here stays unfurled for weeks, despite the yearning sun. I cannot understand what they are waiting for, but the place sings with expectation.

The animals continue to change and grow. Caterpillars form cocoons, emerge butterflies, which flutter around one day and are gone the next. Hedgehogs occupy the woodland, rabbits hop about the grounds. Our days start and end in bird-song.

Thorn is mesmerised. It has been so long since he has seen any kind of wildlife. While I spend hours gardening, he spends hours prowling the grounds with books on birds and forest creatures. They are all utterly unafraid of him, hopping into his lap and eating from the palms of his hands, but startle whenever I go near.

Thorn tries to teach me to fish. This is difficult, since he can do it with his bare hands and I need a net at very least. I am not the most patient of creatures, wanting to give up if I've not caught anything within a few minutes. Thorn, meanwhile, has the patience of a saint, waiting in the shallows until one almost crawls into his arms.

I teach him how to light a fire without the help of whatever magic dances about the castle walls. We roast the fish on sticks and dine by the lake, whenever the weather will let us.

Some nights, although I never tell him, I forget to cross off my days. I go almost a week, at one point, before I remember. Only four months left to go.

By the time my second month in the castle is coming to an end, the gardens are coated in daffodils. My herb garden is in full bloom. I snip buckets of them, together with the flowers, to string up around the castle or bulk in vases. Good portions of my day are swallowed by roaming the grounds, searching for new cuttings or blooms, re-planting them where I can see them more often, or making bouquets.

I do not see too much of Thorn during this time. Occasionally, he will come to join me and help with the heavier tasks, but he silently understands that gardening is one of these things I prefer to do solitary. He joins me for meal times, where we either chat amiably or read in contented silence, down by the lake or in the shade of a tree.

One day after clearing out a rose garden, I am so exhausted that I fall asleep in a little patch of sunlight and waste most of the afternoon. Thorn wakes me just before dinner, gently blowing on my face.

"Why didn't you wake me sooner?" I demand.

"You looked so peaceful sleeping. I couldn't help it."

"Well, I'm not peaceful now!"

"I can gather."

Annoyed at myself for missing so many good working hours, I retire to the music room and half-compose a piece on the piano which I title "frustration." It is largely created by slamming my fingers on the hard notes in a somewhat discordant order.

I'm more myself by dinner time, but when night rolls around, I am restless. Thorn declines my offer of a moonlit walk, perhaps annoyed by how I snapped at him earlier. We go our separate ways early.

I sleep fitfully that night. Whether it is the change in the weather, or my own temper, my bed feels far too hot. The covers twist around me, my pillow feeling hard and lumpy. I drift in and out of dreams. In one, Freedom is yelling at me. He is in the forest, painting. His hands and the canvas are entirely red. He turns and screams at me, *"This is your fault, Rose!"* and gestures to the source of the colour; a young buck with a bolt in its side.

Then I dream I'm a little girl, hiding in the meadow. Mama is searching for me, and her voice is growing frantic. I am too young to understand her panic and laugh instead. That's when she sees me.

"Rose!" she cries, half in anger, half in relief. *"Where have you been? I thought the fairies must have snatched you away..."*

Her face fades until I see my father crying over a coffin. That one's not a dream. A memory I cannot shake.

No, no, not that! Not again–

I wake, clutching the covers against my chest. I am damp with sweat, my throat parched. Something scuttles silently in the darkness, twitching around the mirrors like a spider. Not the remnants; these are shadows. The room is thick with them.

I swallow, brushing away stray tears, and breathe in deeply. *You're still dreaming.* A moment later, the room is still again, and I do what we all do when we wake from nightmares; I convince myself they're just that. *It was a long time ago*, I tell myself. *You're all right now.*

I'm not sure if years really do lessen the pain of losing a

loved one. I think maybe we just get used to the pain, like losing a limb. General Beaumont had a missing leg. He said he still felt it at times. I asked him if he missed it. He said yes, but he found ways of living without it.

It was a lot like that when Mama died. We were constantly, always aware that something was missing. Her absence was physical, larger and louder and more tangible than the sight of the empty chair by the fire. You could feel where she wasn't. There was no question of not missing her. But we found ways of living without her. We weren't given another choice.

Too hot and too bothered to sleep, I get up and open the window. Moonlight and cool air pool into the room. The moon is full tonight, and glitters over the lake. After a few moments of standing there, I am cool enough. I light the little lamp by the side of my bed, pick up the book by my bedside and flick to my last page. It is the story of a young governess in a dark castle with a dark secret. Yesterday it was positively thrilling. Tonight I am finding it a little dull.

Something slithers in the darkness. I jolt, peering out. Nothing. I must have imagined it. No, there it is again, something large and dark.

I snuff out my candle, letting my eyes soak up the gloom. It doesn't take long; the moon is large and full tonight. It ekes out corners of the graveyard.

There is a large, black shape prowling the stones, devoid of almost any other colour. When it turns its head, even at a distance, I can see two monstrous red eyes.

Eventually, it fades into shadow.

I stay awake for several more hours, waiting for it to return, convincing myself I made it up, or it was just Thorn, or a trick of the dark. Finally, sleep calls, and I fall into another uneasy dream of screams and shadows.

Emerging from sleep, I could convince myself it was a dream. The night before is always hazy in comparison to the dawn, and much can be thought a mere fancy of the moonlight. But I cannot do this. I can still feel my skin prickling at the mere thought of those dense, angry red eyes.

It was absolutely, most definitely, real.

I dress with trembling fingers, making my way to Thorn's room at little more than a snail's pace. I keep thinking I see something in the corner of my eye, imagining that the thing is going to jump out at any second. *Don't be ridiculous.* Whatever this monster is, I tell myself, it likely only comes out at night.

There is no sign of any monster now, the hallways as quiet and still as they have ever been. But there is a chill that makes me quicken my gait, and I barely even knock before shoving open the door to Thorn's room and hurrying inside.

He is lying in a heap beside the bed, curled up under piles of shredded fur. For a horrible moment, I think that he's been wounded, until I remember what he said about sleeping on the floor.

"Thorn!" I call, shaking him roughly by the shoulders. He is so heavy. A dead weight. "*Thorn!* Wake up!"

There is a low, throaty moan, and his eyes pry open. He blinks at me sluggishly. "Rose?"

"There's something here," I babble. "Or there was, at least. Last night. I thought... I was worried..."

"What do you mean, *something*?"

"Last night, there was something in the grounds. A dark shape– and do *not* tell me that there wasn't, or you were out for a walk, or anything silly like that. I know what I saw!"

Thorn swallows, and sits himself up. He hugs the furs around his waist with one arm and rubs his face with another. He doesn't look well. His hair is matted and clammy, his eyes bleary.

"There's something here, isn't there? Something other than the remnants?"

"Oh, they are remnants, all right," he says solemnly. "But of a much darker kind. When... when the great battle was fought, and the forces of darkness extinguished... a little of their essence, as it was, became trapped inside the walls of the castle."

"Like... ghosts?" I swallow. The thing last night looked too tangible to be a ghost.

"Yes. Only... they're not really dead. I hadn't seen them for so long, however, I thought perhaps they were all gone. Dried up, like the rest of the magic in this place."

"But the magic is coming back," I reason.

"They can't feed off of that," he explains. "In fact, it should have the opposite effect. But last night being a full moon... dark magic is at its peak, then. A remnant of that power was bound to show itself, sooner or later."

This makes a certain kind of sense, and I've read about the power of the full moon in one of the books from the library. But... but I have seen other things, at other times. Shadows that move of their own accord. The face in the lake.

"These things can't hurt you, Rose," Thorn insists. "I don't... I didn't want you to be afraid. You're safe here, I promise you. No harm will come to you whilst I am still breathing."

"I can take care of myself," I stand up tersely, knowing that, were I confronted with a genuine monster, this would be a complete lie. "And I'm not afraid!" I cross the room and grab the door handle. "That thing last night isn't the only thing I've seen. There have been shadows of other things. And I did see a face in the lake. I know I did."

I slam the door furiously behind me. I am growing ever more sure that the ice did not crack of its own accord. Something is lurking in this castle, something more than a shadow. Something that wants to hurt me.

I avoid Thorn for the rest of the day, either because I am

annoyed by his secrets, or fearful of my own. I spend time in the gardens, although it is a grey day, and ignore meal times. It is getting late by the time I make my way back to the castle, but I am cautious of being out after nightfall.

Turning onto my corridor, I see a thin shard of light punctuating the darkness. The door at the end of the hall –the forbidden room– is open, just a little. I teeter towards it without a second thought.

I would feel more guilty about violating his trust if I didn't feel so angry. I do not go in. Perhaps this is so I can claim I didn't break my promise. Instead, I listen.

I can hear Thorn prowling about the room, on all fours, if I'm not mistaken. I haven't seen him walk this way in a long time.

"Rose has seen her," he says.

I crane my head towards the door. Who is he talking to? As I push my head further into the gap, three tiny pinpricks of light scuttle along the floor, clear as day. They stop in front of my feet, almost expectantly. I have the strangest feeling I am being judged.

What? I mouth.

Two of them trail into the room, the third remaining just a second longer. It butts against my slipper before following the others.

"I haven't seen any hint of her or her followers for years," Thorn's voice continues. "I thought, if you were gone, then she must be too, but if she's still here... you must be as well. Am I right?"

Only silence follows.

"Where are you?"

There is the sound of something crashing. Thorn has thrown something.

"Is she in danger?" he asks quietly, the rage pulled back. He sounds sad, desperate even. "Please, just... find a way to tell me. Is she in trouble? Can I protect her?"

Another long pause.

"I am not sure I could survive losing you both." I wait a little while, but he says nothing else. As I turn to leave, I think I can hear sobbing.

A few weeks after Mama's death, Honour found me curled up under my bed, crying. The hard sobbing had stopped by then, the sobbing that came first and went on for days without ceasing, bleeding us all of tears. There were just days, days when it was all a little too much. Soon, everyone told us, it would just be moments.

Honour crouched down by the bedside. She turned her back, and I saw she had little Beau in her arms. He stared at me with large, unblinking, unashamed eyes.

"Would you like to hear a story?"

In my little nest of blankets under the mattress, I nodded.

Honour is not good at stories as a rule, but she was good at this one. So much so, that Hope appeared out of nowhere and scurried under my arm, and a pair of feet in the doorway showed that Freedom was listening too.

"On the day of Mama and Papa's wedding day, the first true flowers of spring bloomed in the woods. Mama couldn't stand the thought of not having any to decorate her simple dress with, so she strolled off to find some in the early hours of the morning.

"When it came to breakfast time, and she did not return, no one worried too much. Mama did love the woods so; she was probably distracted by their beauty this time of year. And it was the morning of her wedding– perhaps she needed a little time on her own.

"But then another hour went by, and then another. The wedding was to be in a few hour's time, and the bride was still missing. So, her mother sent her sisters into the woods to search, and the rest of the party carried on readying the village for the wedding as if nothing were amiss.

"Hours ticked by, and still no Mama came. The woods had been searched; not a leaf was left unturned. The church bells tolled and the villagers assembled. Still no Mama. The groom's family twittered and fussed, and Grandmama kept on excusing and dithering– 'there's a hole in her dress' 'they're just fixing her hair' 'the cart has thrown a wheel'– until there were no excuses left. Finally, Papa stormed out of the Church and demanded to know of his would-be-mother-in-law where exactly Mama was.

"'Oh, dear Henry, I wish that I could say! Alas, dear Grace, she is–'

"And then, as if swept in by the clouds, Mama appeared in the village square in a shower of rose petals. She was wearing the most beautiful gown that anyone had ever seen, silk and gossamer, and embroidered with such delicate needlework that spiders themselves couldn't have spun it. She was covered in flowers, head to toe, and never a more radiant bride had the village ever seen.

"To this day, no-one knows where Mama went during those missing hours, or how she came by such a beautiful gown. The petals eventually faded, as did the radiance of the fabric, and some who came across it later said that apart from the stitching, there was little special about it. But the villagers could never forget her beauty that day, nor the way she kissed her bride-groom at the church, with such passion they thought for a second that she might be a fairy changeling herself."

By the close of the story, Freedom had slipped into the room and put his arm around Honour, and reached his hand under the bed and grabbed mine. I did not know what he meant by this at the time, but looking back, his actions spoke louder than Honour's words. But they were both saying the same thing: *We'll be all right, the five of us. We're together. We'll look after each other. The world is not as terrible as it appears right now. You'll see.*

Honour made up a lot of stories about Mama. She was not dead, she was a fairy, who had returned to her own kingdom, or transformed into the flowers she so loved. I didn't like the first excuse. I had seen her body, cold and stiff and *there*. But I did quite like the one about the flowers. Perhaps that's why I cared for her garden so. My sister is only two years older than I am, but I have always trusted her memories of Mama far more than my own, even when she was so clearly making them up. Mama was always magical in Honour's stories. She was perfection and light. I did not want to remember her any other way. According to Honour, Mama's touch could heal the common cold. She could predict the weather. She always knew when someone in the village was about to have a baby, and what it would be. Freedom once told me she always knew when someone was about to die, but I think he did that to scare me.

Remembering many long, sniffling colds, occasionally getting stuck with her during rainstorms, and knowing that she could not predict her own babies all the time, I had my doubts about her mystical abilities. But I clung to them nonetheless. It kept her close, and Beau always loved the stories. I would believe anything for him.

According to my time-keeping, today is Honour's birthday. Another event in her life I will miss. I will miss Hope's too, although I will be back for both my brothers'. My own birthday isn't too far away now. Ordinarily, I wouldn't be thinking of it just yet, but this is the first birthday I will be away from home. If I don't tell anyone, it will be like just another day.

Thorn would want to celebrate it, I'm sure, but I just can't imagine a birthday without my family, and songs round the piano, and Nanny's famous raspberry sponge cake.

I miss my family with a sharp pang. I don't want to make new traditions with Thorn. I don't want to make them with anyone.

The embroidery I've been working on loses its appeal. I abandon my project and go for a long walk instead, trying not to linger on the edge of the meadow, which looks much more grey than it did this morning.

When I return, it is past dinner time, but I do not seek out Thorn. I go to my room instead, light a candle for Honour, and write her another letter. It is less optimistic than the first, and a trifle miserable, although I do wish her many happy returns. I hear Thorn moving along the corridor not long after, pausing at the door, listening out for me. I pretend to be asleep, and after a few moments, he moves on.

Chapter Eight

A Birthday

Although it takes me a long time to sleep, I feel better the following morning. I get up early, finish my embroidery, and slip into my new dress. It's like I have sewn spring. I admire myself for a minute in the mirror. It is the finest gown I have ever owned, made more fine and more mine by the work I have put into it. I feel pretty, girlish, and dance down to breakfast with a little bit of a spring in my step.

Thorn is already there, sweeping the floor with some desperation.

"Good morning!" I say cheerily.

Clearly, my spring was a light one, for Thorn did not hear me come in. He drops the broom with a clatter. "Ah, morning!" he says.

"Why are you sweeping?"

"I was... trying to find something to occupy myself with," he admits. "I wasn't sure I would see much of you today. I was afraid that–"

"It doesn't matter," I say quickly. I am keen to avoid being angry with him today. "Let's put it aside."

Thorn looks grateful for this. We eat together pleasantly enough, and then head outside. He helps me re-plant a few larger bushes I've been struggling with. My little garden is blossoming with tame wilderness. What I really want now is a bench with an arbour; a cosy outside reading nook. I mumble this under my breath, trying to imagine where I would place it, and the next thing I know, Thorn is beside me with a stone slab slung easily over his shoulder.

"Will this do?" he asks.

I burst out laughing.

"What? Not appropriate?"

"I was thinking more of a small wooden seat, not something so heavy!"

"I can take it back–"

"No, no it's fine, just put it down in the corner."

Together, we manoeuvre it into the perfect place. Starting an arbour is a little more work than I fancy today, so we move onwards, down towards the lake. A greyness slithers in, and the surface of the water turns almost black.

Thorn wades in and tries to catch some fish for supper. I am glad of the disruption, for the lake is otherwise as still as a graveyard, and flashes of that face keep bubbling up to greet me. Who was she? What did she want? What *does* she want?

The thought gnaws at my mind for the rest of the day, and I spend much of it in contemplative silence. Thorn, thinking perhaps that I am still mad at him, doesn't press it. He is thankful for any crumb of company I throw at him.

The thought of the face occupies my mind for some time following. I keep jumping at shadows, certain I see things that aren't there, and I avoid anything reflective as much as I can for days. The feeling of being watched creeps under my skin. The weather imitates my mood, and it is too damp and grey and chilly for gardening. I turn instead to the library, but the books too do not provide any answers to my questions or distractions from my fears. I don't even know what I am looking for.

Thorn must notice a change in me, but he says nothing. The days creep by with the slowness of my first hours here. I look towards the end of my time in this place; my birthday will mark almost halfway through.

I wonder if Thorn is still counting the days. I wonder how he feels about the fact I will soon be gone. Well, not soon. Not quite yet.

"Rose," he asks me one evening, "are you... are you happy here?"

I swallow. "No," I reply quietly. "But... I'm not unhappy, either. And that part I think I owe entirely to you."

This is as good as I can manage, right now.

"Is... is there anything I can do to help you?"

Tell me the truth. Tell me who the face belongs to. But I am certain that even if he knew the truth, he would not tell me... and I do not want to wonder why he lies to me.

"Not right now," I reply. "But maybe one day."

He nods, and his eyes move past me to rest on the clock atop the mantle. It ticks a little too loudly that night.

We are eating a light lunch one afternoon beside my newly-erected arbour, when I turn quite suddenly to Thorn and tell him it's my birthday in two weeks.

"Your birthday?" his face lifts. "Well, we must celebrate!"

"We don't have to–"

"Of course we must! What else are we going to do? How do people celebrate birthdays again? I recall there's something about a cake–"

"You... don't know how people celebrate birthdays?"

"I've... I've read a little."

"But what about your own?"

"Well, I've had them, of course, but..." He looks around the room, his gaze finally settling on the mirror in the far corner. We look very small in it, very alone. "It has been a long time since I've had anyone to celebrate it with."

"Well, that settles it, then."

"Settles what?"

"You'll have to share mine."

"That's really not–"

"Well, it's my actual birthday, and I insist!"

Thorn tries to pretend he doesn't enjoy the idea, but he's grinning. It's a lot less frightening than it used to be.

Suddenly, I'm excited by the prospect. My mind starts to think about what I can give him as a present. I will have to make something, of course, seeing as I suppose he owns everything here. Something to wear, perhaps? No, I would never be able to make something without measuring him first, which would ruin the surprise. A book is out of the question; he has so many. What to make, what to make...

"What are you thinking about?" Thorn asks.

"Oh, just birthday plans."

The next two weeks pass relatively quickly. Our routine continues, but each day we try to do something party related. I teach Thorn how to make bunting. His hands are too large and lack the dexterity for sewing, but he can manage cutting well enough –if roughly– and is excellent at stringing things up. He leaps around the room we have selected for our festivities, looping string around lamps and frames, transforming the dull space into a festival of colour.

Thorn spirits a music box from somewhere that plays a variety of music, and pulls the harp into the parlour at my request. He doesn't know it yet but I am going to sing him happy birthday. We do not have enough people to play the games I am used to –musical chairs, yes/no, charades– but a pack of cards and a chess set suffice.

When we are not readying our room, we are both searching for gifts. I raid most of the rooms in the first few days looking for inspiration, before taking to the garden. I have no idea where Thorn goes during this time, but he is becoming increasingly secretive. I sense that he already has an idea that he is working on. I, however, am still clueless.

There's an uncomfortable itch, almost a sting, when I realise how little I still know of him, what he likes and dislikes. I am worried that his gift will be more thoughtful than mine, and he deserves a meaningful gift far more. He has never had a birthday party.

I stop beside a vacant rosebush. There are no roses yet, but there is greenery. I find a strange beauty in this plant as it is, coarse and bare. I have never stopped to notice the stem of a rose, or the way each thorn curves like a fang.

There is a stirring of inspiration inside me. I don't know if I can pull it off, if I have the skills and resources, but the more I think about it, the more I like it. I scramble about on the ground for a thick enough branch, and take it back to the castle.

The day of our birthday arrives. I am too excited by the thought of surprising Thorn that I don't have time to miss my family, or even think about how different the day has been in the past. I dress normally for breakfast –I have another gown I have been working on for the festivities– and join Thorn in the parlour. His face breaks into a wide smile when he sees me, and I cannot help but smile back.

"Happy birthday," he says, at the exact time I do. We both laugh. "So," says Thorn. "What first?"

"First, we breakfast," I tell him, "and then... we make cake."

It quickly transpires that Thorn has never made a cake in his life. In fact, he has never cooked anything, ever. He's never had to. He is, however, an eager pupil, if a messy one. The kitchen is half-coated in flour by the time he is finished, which is particularly impressive given its ridiculous size.

"Thorn!"

"What?"

"You've aged about thirty years."

"What?"

I gesture to the mirror out in the hall. White flour covers him from head to toe.

"Oh dear," he says, looking down sheepishly. "Am I hideous, Rose?"

"Very," I say, pulling his ear.

"Oh well," he shrugs, "guess I'll just have to make you hideous too."

He begins to shake fervently, showering me with flour. I shriek his name until he stops, beating him with a wooden spoon.

Icing the cake takes forever with Thorn's clumsy fingers, but he insists on doing it himself while I search for candles. Eventually, our wobbly masterpiece is complete. We transfer it to the party room and prepare the rest of the food. At lunch, I go back upstairs and change into a gown the colour of crushed sunset. I weave Thorn's ribbon through my hair.

His eyes light up when I enter the room, and linger a little longer on his token. "You look... lovely," he says. There is a slight pause, and I wonder if he wanted to say something else.

"Thank you," I return. He is wearing a new outfit too, a navy blue one with careful silver embroidery. It makes his eyes gleam in the light. "I like your new waistcoat. Who made it?"

"Oh, er, it was just something I found," he says, scratching the back of his neck. That seems a little odd to me, his size being so wide and tall, but I reason that he cannot be the only person with such a form to have walked these halls.

"It suits you," I say, twirling my hair around my finger. "Shall we eat?"

We dine on sandwiches, fruit, cheese and biscuits, followed by extremely generous helpings of cake and sweet wine. We blow out the candles together, and I sing him happy birthday with the harp. He repeats the song for me. I challenge him to a game of chess (he wins, being the far better player) and then teach him how to play 'beggar my neighbour'. It is a simple game that goes on for far too long, and ends in another victory for him. He is not remotely boastful and asks to play again.

"I think it's time for a dance now," I say, going over to the music box. A jaunty tune immediately springs to life.

"A dance?" Thorn sounds fearful. "Are you sure? I can't really..." He looks down at his feet awkwardly, at the long, padded paws.

"You were graceful enough on the ice," I say.

"Yes, but..." His voice trails off.

"Suit yourself."

I dance anyway. It has been a long time since I last danced. Not since I awkwardly roped James Saintclair into one after I impulsively kissed him. Perhaps I should feel awkward now, dancing on my own, but I do not.

All of a sudden, there is a presence beside me. I open my eyes, and Thorn is there.

"Changed your mind?"

He nods.

"Good."

I grab him by the hands and charge down the room with him. He is taken aback at first, but he quickly gets into it. He is much more coordinated than his awkwardness might have implied. He is almost as sure-footed here as he was on the ice, and we speed up, going faster and faster, spinning around, the two of us almost out of breath by the end of the song.

"There," I say, trying hard not to pant, "that wasn't too bad, was it?"

He shakes his head. "No."

"Were you afraid you'd step on my feet?"

"A little," he admits. "I... I've never danced with someone before."

"What, never?"

"No."

I am the first person he has ever danced with. I feel overwhelmingly sad and a little bit privileged as well, to have shared this with him. Something in my face leads to an awkward silence, and he says, "So, presents?"

"Presents," I smile.

"Close your eyes."

I do. I hear Thorn rustling about in his pocket. Gently, his hand brushes mine, opening it. Something small and cool drips into my outstretched palm, the size and weight of a pebble. I open my eyes. It is a round, amber pendant on a golden chain, with the smallest, tiniest rosebud preserved in the centre. I have seen perfect pearls, polished diamonds, gleaming jewels before. They all pale compared to the value of this gift.

"Do you like it?" asks Thorn, his eyes as gleaming as the necklace itself.

"Yes," I say. My voice is very faint. "It's beautiful. It's perfect."

"Then it suits you," he says. I brush my hair over my shoulder and gesture for him to fasten it around my neck. His fingers skim my skin, grazing it gingerly. "I– I can't..."

His face is as taut as his voice. I turn my hands to the back of my neck and do it myself, and take his hands before they can drop away. I hold them, not willing to let them slip from mine. I know he is ashamed. However stupidly, however needlessly, he is embarrassed that he cannot do a simple thing like attach a necklace. I worry about my gift; is it long enough?

The pendant rests coolly on my bosom. "Where did you

find it?" I ask.

"I, er, made it. With a little help."

"Thank you."

I do not know why I am so moved. Is it because of the time and effort he must have taken to craft it? Is it because it is simply so beautiful, and so clearly a thing I wanted, even when I didn't know it? Is it merely the swell of sympathy I feel for him?

Perhaps I am a little moved by how well it matches my gift. I pull a little black pouch out of my pocket and pry open the string, dropping the gift into his hands as he did mine. His eyes light up.

It is a polished piece of rosewood, on a leather string, fashioned in the shape of a thorn. It took me several attempts to get in just right, several mishaps, and a lot of whittling and sanding, all of which is worth it to see the look on his face.

"Rose, this is... this is lovely, thank you. Thank you so much."

I take the pendant and loop it over his chest. It rests against his heart, a perfect fit. I hold mine up to his.

"We match," I say teasingly.

A smile pours out of him. It is a real, genuine, true smile, and it suits him beautifully. He does not often smile, and if he does, not for long. Like he becomes self-conscious halfway through, and decides not to show me that part of him. Tonight, there is none of that. He is only and completely him.

Somewhere, in the distance, a wolf howls.

"What was that?" whispers Thorn, stepping back.

"A wolf, I think."

"A wolf," Thorn sighs. "It has been years since I have heard one."

"They were common enough back home," I say sadly. "I have always had a strange affinity for them."

"You like wolves?"

"They sound so beautiful when they howl," I reply. "Sad,

impossibly lonely, but beautiful too."

"I have never liked wolves particularly," Thorn says. "And you wouldn't either, if you'd ever fought with one. I wonder why they've returned."

The clock chimes seven. Thorn jolts. "It's getting late," he says quickly. "We should head to bed."

"To bed?" It's barely evening, as far as I'm concerned. It's not even dark. We haven't even had a proper dinner, only picked at the remains of our birthday lunch. How many nights have we stayed up until midnight, reading in blissful silence?

"I'm... I'm tired," he says, sounding anything but. "I wouldn't want to..."

"To what?"

"Nothing."

"Haven't you... did you not enjoy yourself?"

Thorn stills for the first time since the clock chimed. "Today has been... one of the very best days," he says calmly. "I think we should leave it like that."

"But—"

"You should stay in your room tonight."

"I doubt that the wolves are going to come into the castle."

"I mean it." He sounds fearful. "It's better... safe than sorry. Stay inside."

"All right," I say, concern rising within me. "I wasn't going to wander out anyway."

The festivities have reached an abrupt halt. I don't feel like continuing the party, and Thorn is clearly spooked. I wonder if the wolves here are like the wolves back home, if there is something worse about them. I can't imagine Thorn being scared of much. He offers more cake, as if to lighten the mood, but I refuse. I have no appetite. He insists on walking me back to my room. We say a brief goodbye and then he hurries off.

I had planned to have a nice bath, unwind with a book, maybe put my hair up in rags. None of this appeals to me any more. I hover in front of the fireplace, staring somewhere between the flames and mirror. For a second, I think I see something, a sharp flash of darkness in the glass. But the moment I turn around, there is nothing. Only shadow lies behind me.

"Happy birthday, Rose," I tell my reflection.

The sound of a low, throaty growl tears me from my reverie. I run to the window. Three grey shapes are moving in the trees. Wolves. What are they growling at?

It is still just light. I press myself against the glass, trying to expand my line of sight. There is something else there, too.

Thorn.

Thorn on all fours, staying perfectly still, trying, I think, to look like the fiercer predator. It should work. He is far larger than any of them. He has horns, fangs– claws too. He should be able to frighten them off.

He *should.*

I do not know what sets them off. I do not know if they notice his clothes, or sense something wanting in his growl, something human and vulnerable. Perhaps it is none of these things. Perhaps they reason that there are more of them, and he is a threat, and they are better off taking him down. I do not know how wolves think.

All I know is that when the first one launches at Thorn, the rest follow, and when one of them sinks its teeth into his back, I begin to run.

Chapter Nine

Wolves

It would be foolish to rush out into the open, utterly defenceless, so I race into the armoury first and grab a crossbow from the wall. It has been years since I have practised with moving targets; will it be any good against claw and fang?

I'm still attaching the quiver to my hip as I tear into the gardens. It is not hard to find them– I just follow the sounds of growling and snapping. One of the wolves is already downed by the time I reach them, but the other two are still circling around Thorn, and the forest behind them is moving. More are coming.

I load my first bolt, pull myself up on a nearby statue, and fire. It hits the ground beside the second wolf, but it does not seem to notice.

Thorn does.

I load another arrow, but he shakes his head wildly.

I fire again.

The second shot hits one of the wolves in the shoulder, but it is only a graze. The arrow strikes the floor. Now the wolves take notice. Instantly, both pairs of eyes are on me. I scramble frantically at the statue, trying to pull myself into its arms, but I have never been the best of climbers. I do not gain an inch above the pedestal, and the wolves scramble at my heels.

There is a terrific roar and Thorn's hand comes tearing out of nowhere. No, not a hand, not today. A paw, with fully-extended claws that sink into the wolf's back and drag it along the ground.

"*Run!*" he bellows.

I leap from the statue and stream back towards the castle, but slow when I realise that Thorn is not following. He is on the ground, wrestling with the two of them, a mass of fur and fang.

"Thorn!"

"Get to the castle!"

"But–"

He tears one of the wolves from his back and sends it flying into the statue where I stood, seconds ago. Dust and stone explode into the air. He grabs the other by the back of its throat and pins it against the ground. Its back legs flail wildly.

"I can handle a few wolves! Lock the door and don't come out–"

"And leave you here with them?"

"I'll be fine!" His words are less like words now, more like sounds. He stops for a minute, shuddering. Is he injured? Badly? The light is growing dim. It is difficult to tell.

More wolves howl in the distance.

"Go, Rose!"

I do not want to go. I do want to go. I want to flee for safety and I do not want to fight, but I also do not want to leave him here to face those monsters alone.

I mount another arrow and fire it at the wolf emerging from its slump at the bottom of the statue. This time, it hits its mark.

"Rose!" Thorn screams. "Leave!"

This time, the roar is directed at me. When he looks back,

he doesn't look like Thorn any more. His face is contorted, his fangs bared.

The rest of the wolves are nearly upon us, and I am shaking.

"*Go*," he hisses, and then charges towards them.

Somehow, I find the strength to move. I break back to the castle, his howls and the wolves' howls meshed together in a discordant cacophony that invades my very flesh. My ears scream, the breath inside me spiking against my heart. But I do not stop. I reach the castle, slam the doors shut behind me, and fly up the stairs.

Halfway up, I stop. An awful, monstrous, screeching howl slices straight to the stone. That was not a wolf. That was something else. And Thorn is still out there.

I swallow, lowering myself down, my crossbow raised. Any minute now, he'll be coming. I'll cover him when he does.

He doesn't.

Night penetrates the room, moonlight spilling across the marble. The beams cut themselves on the jagged fragments of glass. No Thorn comes. It grows colder.

The wolves continue to howl, but eventually, the wailing subsides. Are there fewer of them, or are they further away? Is Thorn trying to lead them away from the castle?

Is he trying to protect me? Did I make things worse by going to his rescue?

His rescue. What was he even doing out there in the first place?

A chill I have not felt in many weeks pervades the air. I light a candle, but it emits little warmth. The shadows crawl closer as I watch the wax slowly dribble into a stub.

Still no Thorn.

I cannot possibly sleep with him still out there, surely? But then it occurs to me that he told me to lock the door. He will not be coming back here. He has probably shut himself in one of the many outbuildings. I cannot hear anything anymore. That must mean that it's over.

I don't want to go upstairs. I want to go out and find him,

but I know that that is a foolish idea. I will not help anyone by putting myself in danger.

Finally, I return to my room, undressing slowly, carefully, still hoping that at any moment, I will hear him knocking at the foyer and have to dash out again. My hopes are met only with silence, and soon all of my clothes lie in a pile on the floor. I fold them away and sit by the very faint embers of the fire.

"Is anyone there?" I call out, hoping to see the faint little sparks again, the ones that scolded me for eavesdropping. I want them here now, even if they hiss at me for leaving him.

You did the right thing, says a voice.

Sure, for yourself, says another.

I am such a nasty, horrible person. I can't believe I left him there. He was hurt, too, of that I was sure—

The thought gives way to several tears, which swiftly turn into choking sobs, and I fall asleep on the rug, praying for home, hoping against hope that he is all right.

I wake painfully early, pale, bluish light trickling through the curtains, with a heart as heavy as lead. I grab my dressing-gown and head, wishfully, straight to Thorn's room.

"Thorn?" I knock loudly.

When all I am met with is stony silence, I open the handle and peer into the room.

No one is there. Not a hint of Thorn, not a whisper of anything living at all. His bed beside the hearth lies cold and untouched. The stillness is grave-like.

I go back to my room, pull on my boots and coat, and head into the gardens, taking my crossbow with me just in case. A cold fog lingers over the lawns, enveloping the trees. My voice echoes, bouncing back against the endless, white landscape.

I find a few dead wolves and a path spotted with blood, but it is impossible to tell who or what it belongs to. I feel no sympathy for the creatures now, no kinship with these things, though they look far more peaceful than they did last night.

He took down a number of them, which is promising. And he is surely too large to be dragged away if...

A shadow runs across my path.

"Thorn!" I call out desperately. "Where are you?"

I don't know how long I scream his name. I search the stables, the coach house, the graveyard, the ruined chapel, the boathouse. All the outbuildings I know of. All the places that could offer shelter. There is no sign of Thorn, but I continue searching until my voice is hoarse.

He can take care of himself, I reason, at the same time that my heart thumps wildly in my chest. *Be all right, be all right.*

All that is left is the woodlands, but I am acutely aware that that is where the wolves are likely hiding too, and the fog is getting thicker. I will not be able to search much longer.

My hands clench around my crossbow. I summon my courage and head for the trees, calling out as loudly as I dare. A few rabbits scuttle about the undergrowth, a couple of squirrels. No voice reaches me, and the fog grows denser still.

"Thorn?" I whisper.

I hear something else. A muffled, tiny whimper. Inhuman, but plaintive. Pitiful. It cannot be Thorn, surely? It sounds like a dog. On a whim, I whistle.

The whimper gets a little louder, turning into a bark.

I follow the noise to a wilder part of the woods. It is so overgrown it's virtually uninhabitable, unexplored thus far. As I go closer, I see something moving in a patch of brambles. I drop down. A pair of large, yellowy eyes stare back at me.

"Oh dear," I say softly, "we've gotten ourselves in a right pickle, haven't we?"

It is a young dog, more a puppy really, long-haired, and covered in mud. Its front paw is thoroughly tangled in the brambles. As I reach to pet it, it growls at me.

"None of that," I warn. "I'm trying to help you."

It makes a feeble snap, but I catch its muzzle with one

hand, trying to soothe with the other. I pat its head, rub its ear.

"I'm not going to hurt you..."

The creature continues to snap, and I realise that it's looking at my crossbow.

"This?" I gesture towards it. "This isn't for you."

It doesn't seem to believe me, but I unbuckle it and slide it out of view. It's a little more at ease as I try to free it. The brambles are still tangled in the poor thing's paw, but I need better light and probably a pair of tweezers to fix it. I can't help it here. Instead, I take off my coat and wrap it up. It struggles for a bit, but then simply shakes in my arms. It is quite heavy, and the walk back takes longer than ever. I cannot help Thorn right now, but I can help this little thing.

The fire is already going when I get back to my room, the bath already running. I lower the dog into shallow waters. It trembles as I wash away the dirt to try and see what I am dealing with.

Mud free, I gather him in a towel and place him on the hearth. He is shaking less now, in the warmth, as I dry him off. Finally, I get to the injured paw. He struggles as I pry the brambles away from his flesh, and I have to pin him down in order to do it safely. A couple of them are deep, and the floor is dotted with blood.

Eventually, the task is over. I leave him licking his wound by the fire whilst I hunt for food. Unsurprisingly, a meaty bone materialises on my table by the fire, but when I turn around, he's hiding under my bed. I coax him out with the bone and lure him back to the fireside, where he sits contently, gnawing. He is much happier now, but still jerks and growls when I try to stroke him. He is a grey, brownish colour, quite scrawny and pathetic-looking. Where did he come from?

The clock chimes two. Thorn has been missing all day. Where has he *gone*?

"I don't suppose you saw anyone today, did you little one?" I ask my new pet.

He blinks back at me.

Leaving him to get settled in, I try to eat myself, but I can only manage a few mouthfuls. The incident with the dog has been a welcome distraction, but there is nothing more that I can do for him now. My thoughts return to Thorn. I imagine him lying in a ditch, too hurt to call out.

What if... what if it's worse than that? What if he's dead, and I am alone here? What if it's my fault, and he would have been fine as long as I stayed inside?

Far off, the main door swings open.

Thorn.

I race towards the entrance hall, my heart leaping like some demented creature. I want to scream his name but I can barely breathe until I see him, standing at the threshold. He is dishevelled, his cloak muddy and torn, but he is alive.

I hurtle down the stairs, stopping a few feet short of him, and am just about to throw my arms around him when he speaks.

"I saw your crossbow in the woods," he says numbly. "There was some blood nearby. I thought–"

"I rescued a dog," I say quickly. "This morning. I locked myself in all night, just like you told me."

"Why were you out in the first place?" His voice sounds rough, even... even angry.

"Excuse me?" I say. "Why was I out there? You were getting attacked! Why were you out there?"

"It doesn't matter–"

"Of course it does! You can't put yourself in danger and be mad at me for trying to help you–"

"I can look after myself."

I gesture to the wounds seeping through his clothes. "Clearly!"

"It takes more than a few wolves to defeat a monster like me."

"You are not a monster!"

"Look at me!"

"I *am* looking at you!"

I close the space between us, reaching for one of his hands, but he jerks it out of reach. His nails are coated with blood.

"Do you know a man who can rip apart wolves with his bare hands?" he asks.

I know men who would like to, but I do not like them. And I do not think you are one of them.

"I didn't say you were a man," I snap shortly. "I said you weren't a monster."

Thorn scoffs. "You don't know what you say."

His tone is twisted and bitter and it makes my blood boil. *I* don't know what *I* say? As if I haven't been here long enough to know something of the person he is, however much he tries to keep from me. He may not be a monster but he is certainly infuriating.

"Neither do you!"

I was stupid to have worried about him. He clearly doesn't care. And there's not been one word of an apology for making me worry about him all day. I suppress the childish urge to stamp my foot and scream that I hate him. Instead, I turn on my heels. The whole way back to my room, I wait for him to stop me.

Why *was* he out in the gardens? I try to trace his actions back through the day. He knew the wolves were there; we heard them together. He seemed concerned about them, worried about their presence. But then why go out in the gardens at all? And why tell me to stay inside? The door should have been ample protection. And then, there was the howl I heard. The monstrous, inhuman roar.

With a shudder, I remember the monster I saw in the gardens, the night of the last full moon.

Was there a connection between the wolves and the monster? Or... or was he worried that the howls might be from the monster? I had sworn I heard it outside my door before. If it had got in once...

He *was* trying to protect me. But he was doing so by lying to me.

I run back to Thorn's room and hammer on the door.

"Yes?" His reply is groggy.

"Is there a monster in the grounds?" I demand.

There is a long pause.

"*Is there?*"

An even longer one follows. I swear I can almost hear Thorn breathing on the other side, trying to find the right words.

"*Thorn!*"

"Yes," he replies, with unexpected firmness. "There is."

"Why wouldn't you just tell me—"

The sound of his voice gets louder. "Oh, I don't know," he throws open the door. "Because maybe 'Oh, hello Rose, nice to meet you, I hope you enjoy your imprisonment here. I should mention, once a month the castle plays host to a ravenous monster that might eat you. Have a nice stay' is not the best way to welcome someone!"

He glares at me, waiting, no doubt, for some venomous reply. I did have one, too, up until when he opened the door. Now, all I can think of, all I can stare at, is the dozens of deep slashes across his bare arms and torso. My breath stills in my throat as though caught on a piece of glass. His cloak had hidden most of the damage, but his clothes are shredded to the point where they barely fulfil their function. There is blood all over his chest, gashes across his arms, his face, any exposed bit of skin. Freedom has bought kills into the kitchen in better states.

"What?" he barks.

"You... your... *Thorn*," I whisper desperately.

He looks down, suddenly conscious of his missing attire, his shredded flesh. "It's nothing," he says, trying to disappear behind the door. "I can manage."

All fury I had at him has been somehow magically flurried away and I march in after him. "Why didn't you say anything–"

"I didn't really see the point. You don't have to help–"

"You're right, I don't. But I want to."

"Why?"

I swallow. *Because I don't like seeing you in pain. Because I... I just want to.*

"You helped me," I say instead. "When I first came here, and cut my hands. And when I fell into the ice–"

"I had help," he says shortly.

"The little... remnants?"

He nods. That explains a few things, including how he managed to undress me.

"You helped me," I say. "Let me help you. Please."

He sighs reluctantly, and sits himself beside the fire. There is a little pot of water there already, bandages, cloths. His shredded shirt lies nearby. The lines are so deep...

"I'm still mad at you for not telling me about the monster," I whisper, trying to make my voice sound harder. I press a hot cloth to the first of his wounds, as gently as I can muster.

"I know," Thorn replies, equally quietly. "I'm just... I'm very conscious of scaring you."

"Because I have been so easily startled this far."

"That's just it. I keep thinking, *one more thing and it'll be too much for her. No one can shoulder all of this.* I don't want to frighten you away."

"Where exactly would I go?"

"Just... away." He swallows, and his eyes look downwards. "You see... I rather like the part of my day with you in it."

"Well, that's... sweet."

It's more than sweet. It is perhaps the nicest thing anyone has said about me, but then... he has not much to judge against.

"I'm still mad at you." I snip.

"Be mad then," he says. "But just... don't leave."

It is hard to stay mad at someone when they say things like that. I bite down anything I would say in return and I move on to a deeper set of slashes. He winces when I touch them.

"Sorry," I say. "It's been a while since I've doctored any wounds like this. Freedom stopped asking me to help because I was too rough with him. He said I did it on purpose."

"Did you?"

"Of course. He was being careless. Someone had to teach him a lesson." Not that he ever stopped getting into scrapes. Not that I stopped offering. Not that I ever stopped feeling just a little bit jealous whenever he asked Honour or Hope for help instead.

Thorn smiles a little, and I try to be a bit more gentle.

"What type of monster is it?" I ask gingerly.

Thorn's sigh is bone-deep. "It does not have a name. I only know that it comes once a month, during the full moon."

"Has it... always been here?"

He nods.

"And it attacks you?"

"Not usually. Usually it minds its own business."

It did nothing, I reason, for the first three months. What has changed? Me?

"Will it–"

"It will not hurt you," Thorn says sharply, as if he has any choice in the matter. "I will not let it."

"But–"

"Just... don't go anywhere near it. Promise me."

I have never heard him sound so serious before. Serious, and fearful.

"I... I promise."

Thorn exhales, very quietly, and all his muscles seem to relax. He doesn't even tense when I apply the water to a new set of bite marks. *Usually it minds its own business.* He endured these for my sake.

"What do you see?" he asks.

I blink. "I'm sorry?"

"You said that you were looking at me, earlier, in the hall. What do you see?"

There is a quiet urgency in his voice, as if he has been fixating on it for some time, and, for a moment, I do not know what to say.

"You." The answer is surprisingly easy. "Not a man, not a monster. Just you. Sure, you might have big hands and claws and teeth larger than most, but you are, most categorically, *not* a monster, as you seem to insist."

"Then what does a monster look like?"

"Like everyone else," I say quietly. "There is many a monster who wears the form of a man; it is better of the two to have the heart of a man and the form of a monster."

"You still find me ugly then?"

"I always said you were. Not everyone can be as beautiful as me."

This, at least, makes him laugh, which distracts him as I move onto the deeper of the cuts, cleaning the dried blood away from his matted hair.

"If you have always been a beast, why should the shape of men matter to you?"

"I'm sorry?"

"You seem to be quite bothered by the way you look. I'm trying to discover why."

"I have said this before; most people appear unhappy with their outward appearance."

"But I'm asking why *you* care."

Thorn sighs. He looks down at his hands. "I just feel as if my experiences are limited by my form... I want to be able to do the things that others take for granted. Write neatly. Paint. Ice a cake without it looking ridiculous. I don't... I don't even know what it feels like to have somebody's skin on mine..."

"You can still feel me, can't you?"

"Yes," he says, ever-so-quietly. "But not in the way I'd like to."

I'm not entirely sure what this means, but I know that he is sad, and I want to take some of that sadness away from him. Ever-so-slowly, I slide my free hand into his. I squeeze his fingers; he thumbs mine. I want to ask him what he feels, but I am afraid to, so I take my hand back, fetch the bandages, and tell him a story instead.

"When I was very little," I say, unravelling the bandage around his arm, "I used to be jealous of my sister, Honour. She is so beautiful, and people are drawn to her like flowers move towards the sun. I used to think that if I looked like her, people would be the same towards me. But then my mother said that people have this strange relationship with beauty; they always think it will bring them happiness. She said that that was not the case, and even if true love is fostered between beauty, true love happens but once, and it will find us regardless of how we appear. She said it did not matter if we were not loved by everyone, so long as we are loved by someone."

"I am not sure of what you are saying."

I move the bandage around his back. "Beauty is subjective, and it does not bring you happiness. Nor does it bring you understanding, companionship... love. It is a lesson I am glad I learnt young. I stopped... I stopped trying to get people to like me. I found enjoyment in being myself. I don't think I became rude or arrogant, but I stopped caring what others thought. If people don't like you for you, then they aren't worth your time. Somewhere, out there, your people are waiting. The ones who will love you unconditionally and irrevocably."

Thorn looks at me carefully for a long time, his head tilted to the side. "Is your friend, the one who kissed you at the party, one of these people?"

He does not let that one slide. I almost regret telling him. "First off," I reply, "*I* kissed *him*. And secondly... no, I don't think so. James is a dear friend, but... I have been here months and I have barely spared him a thought since I told you about him last. No, at the moment, those who love me unconditionally and irrevocably are limited to members of my immediate family, and Nanny."

"You are lucky."

"To have so many?"

"Yes. And to be so sure of yourself."

"Do you really care so much, about what others think of you?"

"I care about what you think."

I smile. Of course he does, as I'm his only company. But does he really think, after all this time together, that I think so little of him?

"Well, I rather like looking at your face."

"I'm... I'm sorry?"

"Well, like I said, it's definitely not pretty, but I still like looking at it."

"W-what? Why?"

"Because it's yours," I say. "The face of a person whose company I have come to enjoy. I mean, my father's pretty rough around the edges and I still like looking at him."

Thorn stares at me, utterly perplexed, unaware that I have finished bandaging him. I place my hand against his chest.

"Better?" I ask.

"Hmm? What?"

I tap my handiwork.

"Oh, yes, quite."

I do not remove my hand. He almost looks worse now, with the damage covered. It shows how much there was in the first place. I am still mad. He should not have lied. He should not have gone outside.

I am still thinking about all of these things when I lie my head against his chest.

"I am really glad you're all right," I whisper.

I remember falling into Thorn's arms the day I slipped off the dresser. Back then, he was just the Beast, not Thorn. I cringe at how I flinched, how I wanted him to let me go. Now he is the one flinching, and I don't want to let him go.

Slowly, carefully, Thorn's arms rise up and encase me. There is a little increase of breath against my ear, and for a minute, I am sure he is going to say something, but then his lips close. It is only when I inch myself away and turn towards

the door that he finds his voice.
　　"Thank you," is all he says.
　　I do not know what for.

Chapter Ten

The Hall of Mirrors

W hat a collection of secrets this place holds, what aged whispers haunt the corridors. Who is this creature that stalks the halls? Who is the face that haunts my nightmares? And why is Thorn, a person with a noble heart made to wear the form of a monster, condemned to live here shackled to the shadows and the stone?

My head spins with thoughts that stir me in and out of sleep. Who is Thorn indeed. He lies to me, or avoids telling the truth, and yet there is a goodness in him that far outweighs my own. Can a liar be a good person? Can I care for someone who keeps me in the dark?

That depends upon the reason.

But what reason could be good enough? That I care for him is certain. He has stitched his way into my skin with a finality that frightens me far more than the secrets of this place. But though I trust him to protect me, and trust that he cares for me, I do not trust that he is honest, and thus there is a limit to my affections.

Perhaps that is for the best, I reason. *It will make it all the easier when you leave in three months' time.*

Three months' time. I am halfway through.

The following morning, I introduce Thorn to the pup. I have decided to call him Bramble, much to Thorn's amusement.

"Because I found him in a bramble patch!" I insist.

"Of course. I suppose we'll have a cat called Briar, soon, maybe a bird called Fern... how about a fish called Petal?"

"I am not calling anything Petal," I hiss. "Least of all, a fish! And you're teasing me."

"I will admit it is swiftly becoming one of my favourite past times."

I punch him on the arm, and he winces, making my stomach twist guiltily. I turn back to Bramble.

The introduction is somewhat limited, as he is still refusing to come out from underneath my bed. We pass him bits of food which he snatches from our fingers before scuttling back to his den, whilst we flick through a book on canines, trying to identify his breed. We decided he is mixed, and no older than six months.

Bramble's arrival offers us a new pastime: house training. It is quite clear that wherever he has come from, he did not live with people. It takes a few days of passing him food under the bed before he accepts us as part of his pack, but convincing him of the difference between outside and in is trickier. As he sleeps with me, morning duty is mine, and Thorn takes him out in the evening. Sometimes, I watch them from my window, walking through the gardens in the low evening sun. Every so often, Thorn will drop down on all fours and the two will chase each other like puppies. Then Thorn will look up to my window, and see me sitting there. He'll stop and wave, and continue the game with renewed enthusiasm.

He looks up to my window a lot, I notice.

"Where do you think he came from?" I ask Thorn one day, as Bramble chases a bee through a bush.

"I don't know," replies Thorn. "It's possible he came through the gateway."

"I thought it only opened twice a year?"

"It usually does, but sometimes tiny holes can open up–small enough for birds, or insects..."

"Or a medium-sized puppy?"

"Precisely. Not large enough for a human, I fear."

It takes me a little while to realise what he is talking about. He is assuming I am thinking of escape. Wondering if Bramble managed to get in, I can get out.

I do not admit to him I have become less concerned with the days. Sometimes a week will pass before I remember to check it off. Although I am keeping track of the moon. Nineteen more days until the monster's return. I have asked Thorn little about it since he first admitted its existence, partly because I didn't want to have another argument, and partly because I am a little afraid of it. Everything else in the castle exists at all times. Even the wolves, I know, lurk in the woodlands during the day. But the monster seems to come out of nowhere.

Its likeness to Thorn has not escaped me. I think about the fairy stories of old, the idea of darkness and light. Is it some demonic cousin of his, his opposite? Are they the same species? I have read the Fey book now from back to front, but I can find nothing in its pages that resembles Thorn, nothing that comes close. The little snatches of his past I can gather shed little illumination. His parents are dead, but he remembers his mother. There have been visitors before me, but none of great importance. He has not always been alone here, and yet he feels as if he has.

I have the strangest urge to take his hand, whenever I remember these words of his. I want him to know that he is not alone now, that neither of us are, but I do not. This is but a respite from his loneliness, and soon I will vanish from his side.

I try not to think about this too often, but it haunts the shadows of thought at the back of my mind.

Rain comes to the castle. For a period of almost three days, we are caught in a torrential downpour. Rivers stream from the skies. Silver coats the garden.

I know I should be happy for the rain; the plants need it. But a coldness comes with this weather, and the sun is hidden behind a sheath of water. I miss the warmth, the smell of flowers, the long walks. The rain makes me restless.

I spend some time in the music room, trying to compose, but everything I create sounds angry or sad or melancholy. My fingers eke out only tragic notes, my voice struggles with joy.

I wander around the castle. There is little I haven't explored yet, but any change of scenery is welcome. I return to the hall of mirrors I visited during my first week. It is a strange place: thirteen mirrors wrap around the golden chamber, covering almost every surface of the room. The mirror at the end, larger and grander than any of the others, is obscured by a black sheet. The curious part of me longs to remove it, but when I approach, there is a cold hum behind the sheath that warns me to stay away.

I turn my attention to the other mirrors instead. I wonder what their purpose is. Was this some kind of vanity room, where nobles would come to see themselves reflected a thousand times from a thousand different angles? Was it some kind of status play, a symbol of wealth and privilege? I veer towards the one beside the black mirror. As I move closer, the glass ripples and my reflection fades away. In its place is water, deep and dark. It is like I am lying at the bottom of the lake. Tiny pinpricks of light glimmer far, far above me. I can almost feel the pressure of the water against my chest. Hard, aching, overwhelming.

I shudder.

The minute I step away, the image vanishes. I return to the frame. It is then I notice that the mirror is titled. Beneath the glass, in miniscule writing, is a single word. *Fear.* I call for Thorn.

"What?" he cries. "What is it?"

"The mirror," I stammer. "It... it doesn't show my face. It showed me–"

"They're working again?" Thorn's eyes light up. He looks around excitedly.

"They're *working*?"

"The Hall of Mirrors," he says, by way of explanation. "Each one has the ability to show you something different. What you desire most, who you really are, what you fear–"

"I'm acquainted with that one," I say, pointing numbly.

Thorn looks a little guilty. "I'm sorry. What did you see?"

"Water," I reply, "deep, deep water."

"The lake?"

I nod. "I've never liked deep water. I don't like... not knowing what's beneath the surface, or not having my feet on the ground, or being out of my depth." I stiffen just thinking about it. "What do you see?"

Thorn takes a step back, involuntarily, I think. "I'd rather not see it with my eyes," he says.

He must know exactly what it is already. I wonder if it shows you only one thing. There are so many things I fear, if I think hard enough. Water is relatively mild.

"Now this one," Thorn says much more jovially, pulling me to a different mirror, "I think you'll really enjoy. This mirror will show you anything in the world, anything real and living." He points to a little engraving at the top. *The present.* "It can show you your family, if you like."

There is nothing in the world I want more. "How does it work?"

"Just step up to the glass, and ask it. You have to ask this one– there is too much in the world for it to show you otherwise."

I move eagerly towards the frame. "Show me my father," I ask. The mirror swirls like ink, then suddenly there is a crystal-clear image of my father, sitting in his study. I gasp. It is like I am there. My fingers press against the glass. It is cold.

Papa looks older than I remember, but the study is just the same. The same faded books and weathered globe. The dried flowers that only I ever replaced. The same pipe. I can almost smell the tobacco. He coughs. I can hear him!

"Show me Beau."

The mirror swirls again. Beau is in the garden, surrounded by flowers, playing with his little toy soldiers. Hope is sitting on the swing nearby, and Freedom is in the background, target practising against a tree. They all look happy, carefree.

"Show me Honour." Honour is in a parlour I do not recognise, a little nicer than ours, just as cosy. I find our clock on the mantelpiece, and spot a vase on a nearby table that used to be Mama's. She is gazing out of the window, knitting contentedly. Just then, Charles comes into the room, leans down and kisses her, and sits down in the chair opposite. Golden wedding bands gleam on their fingers.

"She's married," I whisper.

"What's that?" Thorn is at my elbow.

"My sister, Honour, she's married."

Somehow, Thorn knows immediately where my mind has gone, and he sighs. "I'm sorry you missed it. Time does not always flow so perfectly between this world and that one; a part of me hoped you would be home before they missed you–"

"I'm sorry?" I startle incredulously. "Time flows differently between worlds, and you didn't think to mention it when I arrived?"

Thorn hangs his head. "I did think to mention it," he replies. "But with so little magic left in this place when you arrived, I knew that was highly unlikely to be the case this time.

123

It would have been a false hope I was giving you. I do like to limit the falsehoods between us."

There should be no falsehoods, I think bitterly, but I try to swallow my anger. He was right, after all.

"How do you know time flows differently?" I ask, as tonelessly as I can manage.

Thorn looks down. "I've been known to look in on my previous visitors, every now and again," he admits. "Just to see... that they're all right."

There is a guiltiness to this confession, more so than simply spying on them. "I can understand you wanting to make sure they returned home safely," I tell him.

"It's not that," he says. "I just want to know... that being here didn't hurt them."

It's then that I recall he was not friends with most of his previous visitors. Six months for them would be much more isolating, much more damaging, if they remained strangers all this time.

"It isn't your fault they come here," I say, but I struggle with making my words soft. My family has been so long without me. What have I put them through? Yet... my siblings all looked happy enough. And Papa... well, he did look older, but he has never really been happy. I hope he's all right.

Thorn seems to sense my distress. "Would you like to see something else?" he offers. "That one will show you whatever your heart desires, and that one will show you–"

"Why is that one covered?" I ask.

"It's broken," Thorn replies quickly. "'Tis bad luck to have a broken mirror uncovered."

"What did it used to show?"

He pauses. "Nothing worth seeing again."

A chill passes between us. Another restriction, I fear, but this one I feel I can live with. I do not want to know what lurks behind the surface of that glass. "A mirror of desires?" I pipe up. "Lost many hours in front of that?"

"Too many," Thorn admits.

"What did it show you?"

"A very personal question," he starts to smirk at me. "Why don't *you* step in front of it, and tell me what it shows *you*?"

"No!" I rush. I cannot help but wonder what it *would* show me, but I am too afraid to look myself, let alone have Thorn see it. I point to another. "And that one?"

"That is the Mirror of Remembrance– any one that's passed. Then there's the Mirror of Truth–"

"The Mirror of Truth?" I stop him. "What does that show?"

He swallows. "That one shows you for who you really are."

The thought intrigues me, so I immediately step in front of it. I am disappointed with the result; I look just the same. "Do I look any different to you?" I ask.

Thorn laughs lightly. "You always look the same to me."

"You have a go."

His face drops. "No," he says. "I cannot."

"You can't?"

"I do not wish to see it."

"Haven't you ever... aren't you curious?"

"I am not sure I would like what it would show me."

He thinks he will see a monster.

"Could you not step in front of it for my sake? You can close your eyes!"

Thorn sighs. "You know I would do anything, for your sake."

He closes his eyes obediently, and holds out his hands to be lead. Gently, I lead him forward, and place him next to me in the frame. Try as I might, a little gasp escapes me when I see our reflections, standing side by side, hand in hand.

"What?" asks Thorn.

"You should open your eyes."

He turns his head, just enough to face me, but still avoiding his reflection. "I would much rather see myself through yours," he says.

"I see what I already see." I lean up on the tips of my toes, pull his face to mine, and touch our noses together. Our breath mingles. "I see that you are beautiful."

I try my best to put Thorn's reflection out of mind, but it haunts me, thumbing the back of my mind for days afterwards. I do not look at any of the other mirrors, but I cannot help but feel that the Mirror of Desire would show me something similar, and I feel equally certain that the Mirror of Fear would now cast a very different image.

Why doesn't he want to see? Perhaps if he saw it, he would know, as I do, what he really is...

I do not think that I will visit the room again, although another niggling voice tells me eventually, the desire will be too strong. The mirrors can show me anything; my family, my home, my dreams, my fears, my heart. They can show me, me. Who could avoid that temptation?

They can even show me the past. My mother.

The one thing, Thorn explains, that they cannot show, is the future, which suddenly I find myself wanting to know more than anything else. What is to happen when I go home in ten weeks' time? How is the rest of my life to be changed by what has transpired here? I am no longer the person I was, and I fear trying to fit myself into the shape I once used to fill.

As the days pass, I put the Hall of Mirrors out of my mind, although I know that Thorn visits it frequently. I am constantly passing along the corridor and finding its door closed, and his absence is touchable. For the following week, Bramble is more my companion than Thorn is, rarely away from my side. He is a hopeless gardener and tends to howl at my music, and sometimes I get cross with Thorn for not looking after him more. But I understand his fascination with the mirrors. They must have been his doorway to the mortal realm long ago; his companions, entertainers and teachers long before me, and they will be with him long after I go.

My nights have been less lonely since Bramble's arrival. It is comforting, after all these dark hours alone, to have someone to share my room with, and, eventually, my bed. I felt swamped by all the space I had before. When I wake from nightmares of faces and shadows, of crying babies and blood-stained bed-sheets, his presence is soothing. The darkness no longer feels so absolute when tempered by his soft snores.

Yet my days do feel lonelier. I miss Thorn, but I cannot tell him. I reason that some time apart will be good for us, that it cannot be good for him to rely too closely on my company when I am to leave him, but at the same time... should we not be enjoying what time we have together?

Then, one day, Thorn emerges from the room, and we resume our old routine with renewed vigour. We dine together constantly, with Thorn even suggesting certain menus. Cuis-ines from countries I have longed to visit, exotic delicacies and foreign extravagances. Each meal becomes an exercise in flavour, a feast for the senses. Some days, he proposes eating elsewhere; picnic lunches beside the lake, breakfasts in the gar-dens, candlelit dinners out on the balcony. He makes his own additions to grounds, installing a rock garden filled with lav-ender and a rudimentary swing like the one I have at home. Knowing my wistfulness for Nanny's home-cooked pies, we harvest fruit together from the orchard and bake dozens of wonky, bursting monstrosities, which taste a lot better than they look and pair beautifully with sunsets, mulled wine and fine company.

Some nights, Thorn sets up the Hall of Mirrors with a cold, buffet-style supper, pulls in several rugs and cushions, and re-quests one of the mirrors shows us a play. It is a miraculous thing to behold, and we lose hours in front of it, soaking up our favourite stories coming to life, and discussing how we would have done it differently if we were directing.

I am still wary of its power, and wonder what Thorn was watching to come up with all these ideas.

"You didn't... you didn't spy on my childhood, did you?" I

ask him one evening.

"The mirrors would never show me what you would not allow me to see," he explains, seeming a little hurt. "Why? What gave you that impression?"

"The food I've always wanted to eat... the swing like the one I have at home... the plays I adore... I thought you might have got them from watching me."

"You've mentioned the swing before," he explains. "And I know you love the idea of travelling. I cannot take you to other places, but I thought the cuisine might appeal. As for the plays, you are very forthcoming with your preferences there–" he trails off, looking at me intensely. "What is it?"

It occurs to me I'm staring at him. In the other mirrors, I see an expression that does not convey the depth of the over-whelming pleasure and gratitude and affection that ought to be pouring out of me. He listened. He did all of this because he thought it would please me.

"That's... that's... thank you," I manage.

"You're welcome."

The intensity of his gaze does not waver. I swallow, and divert my eyes around the room. "What *were* you looking at then, if not my life?"

"Inspiration, mostly," he admits. "Things to do to... entertain you."

I wonder which mirror held the answer to that, and what questions he had to ask it. I also wonder if entertainment was truly what he had in mind.

I turn back to the performance playing in the mirror before us, and rest my head against Thorn's broad shoulder. "I've missed this," I say quietly.

"Watching plays?"

"Being close to someone." The soft confession glissades out of me. "You know," I add hurriedly, "being physically close to someone. Like my sisters, for instance."

While it's true that I do miss the physical contact my sisters and I used to share, physical contact with Thorn of any kind was entirely different. For a start, he would rarely touch me without me first touching him. I thought perhaps he was afraid of hurting me –he was so large, after all– but I was starting to feel it might be for gentlemanly reasons, too. James Saintclair was always so careful where he put his hands whenever we were together, always awkwardly conscious of wherever his limbs were. Thorn was not so awkward, but I felt he was restrained.

I wish he were not so. I miss the way my father used to hold me in his lap, the way my brothers would grab me in the kitchen, or dance with me around the room. I miss the feeling of being held, of having my hair stroked. That gentle link of family, the feeling of owning a little bit of that person, enough to hold them. Enough to know when they wanted to be held.

Thorn stares at me for a moment, and then laughs. "Ah, Rose, you truly know how to compliment a man!"

If he realises what he has just said, he does not acknowledge it. My mouth freezes in a smile; it takes me a moment too. Without really thinking, I lean forward and kiss his cheek, inhaling the scent of pine and wood smoke.

"What was that for?" He blinks, and I wonder if he is blushing. Can a beast blush?

A man can.

"If you have to ask, you shall never know," I smile, and pick myself off the floor. I cannot help but twirl as I head towards the door.

"But… where are you going?"

"An evening walk," I announce. "Are you coming?"

There are stars on my ceiling as I dream that night. They swirl above the gossamer, glittering, twinkling like bells. I dream the stars have voices.

"She kissed him!" says a high, young voice.

Another one groans. "That was not a kiss."

"He looked like he enjoyed it."

"He can enjoy it all he likes," a matronly one replies. "It's *her* we've got to worry about."

A silence passes between them.

"She still can't see us, can she? After everything we do for her!"

"She saw us outside of the chamber! I think she even felt Ariel kick her."

"But she hasn't noticed us since."

"I think she will surprise us. She certainly surprises him."

"He can't see us either."

"Not yet. But soon, I hope."

"I don't think we've ever been this close."

"I hope the shadows don't get her first."

There is one day left before the full moon arrives. Thorn tries his best to distract me, but he is visibly agitated all day, restless and lethargic all in one. Even Bramble seems to sense that something is amiss. He sticks closely beside me all day, and far from Thorn.

I take a long walk through the gardens to occupy myself, but the fog is massing once again, and all I can think about is *that's the statue I tried to climb, that's where I shot that wolf, that's where Thorn lay bleeding...*

I tend to the garden, but there is little to be done. I try to teach Bramble to fetch, but he prefers to horde the sticks I throw for him. I go back inside, fidget with a tablecloth I am making for our parlour, tidy and sweep even though the room could not be clearer. Thorn joins me, reading out passages from his latest book, and we make polite and awkward conversation.

I try to while away the remaining hours by remarking that this is the one month anniversary of Bramble's arrival. I tease that we should start measuring him; he is growing so fast. I can no longer pick him up. But my jokes that we should throw him a party fall on deaf ears.

We retire early to our chambers.

Thorn begs me to lock my door. I beg him not to go outside. He says he cannot promise me this.

"If I think you're in danger..." he says, "I may act rashly."

"And what if I think you're in danger?"

The face he gives me is impossible to read. "No more taking on monsters for my sake," he says. "You promised. Stay away from it, whatever you see. Whatever you hear."

I nod slowly, and close the door softly behind him.

One of the little sprites hovers over my mantelpiece. She – for I feel certain that it is a she– dips a little and makes a sound more like a hiss than a hum.

"What?" I say, a little more sharply than I mean to. She buzzes around my face and disappears under the door.

My evening routine takes longer than ever tonight. I linger in the bath, ears alert for any noises from outside. The darkness swirling against my window seems alive, and I shut the curtains with some vigour, like barring a door.

I am glad of Bramble's presence this night. I haul him up on the bed with me and bury him under the covers.

Chapter Eleven

The Beast Within

The shadows clash like the sound of steel, as if the darkness has become a tangible thing. I know I must have been dreaming, and for a moment, I think I still am. The room is filled with slippery smog, and yet the shadows have edges.

Bramble growls. Something hisses back. My breath stills in my chest.

"Hello?" I whisper, "Who's there?"

I pray for the quiet tinkling of the castle sprites, but there is nothing but gloom. Swallowing, I creep out of bed. I can hear something, a buzzing, scratching sound. Not a pleasant hum, like the touch of the sprites, something more mechanical.

A horrid scrape pieces the darkness, like a nail on glass. Bramble snarls.

That's when I see her. The monstrous, pale face, the cruel mouth, wide open and laughing. Her laugh splinters silence, splinters the air, splinters against my spine. Her red lips cackle from the mirror.

A scream rips through the castle.

Thorn.

I dash for the door. The sprites appear out of nowhere, furiously tapping my hands as I yank at the handle and spill out into the corridor. The laugh carries on. She is everywhere, in all the mirrors, in every gleaming surface. I have to get away from her. I have to find Thorn.

He is not in his room, but this does not surprise me. I can hear him in the gardens. I know I shouldn't be able to, but the noise he is making is so loud, so awful, that it reverberates through the stone.

"Thorn!"

I wrench open the castle door and flee into the darkness. Moonlight dusts the surface of every statue. The shadows are silvery.

"Thorn!"

The screaming is closer. Oh God, what is happening to him? He sounds as if he is being ripped apart. I am going to need a weapon. There is a crypt nearby, suits of armour with swords of steel. I pry one loose, desperately trying to remember everything Freed ever taught me about wielding a blade.

Newly armed, the weight of the rusted weapon tugging at my arm, I follow the noise back into the grounds.

"Thorn, where are you?"

There is a faint light from another tomb, one I have never been into. I think it used to be barred. I am drawn to it before he screams again.

It is not a tomb. It is a dungeon. Cells line the walls, filled with leaves, moss, tree roots. It has lain abandoned for some time. A glowing candlestick sits on a nearby table. Underneath it lies a pile of clothes in a heap. They are unmistakably Thorn's.

The screams sound more like howls now. I grab the candlestick and head off down the passageway, the noises growing louder and louder, more and more wretched. Finally, I see a cell at the end, wrapped in chains. Behind them, ever so faintly, I see a large, dark shape.

"Thorn?"

A low groan sounds back.

Who could have locked him in here? The monster? I do not stop to ask, I do not wait for a reply; I am already dropping the sword and tugging at the chains. The little sprites return, beating furiously against my chest with feeble strength. I swat them away.

"Leave me alone! I'm trying to help him!"

They do not stop. Their efforts increase as I see a set of keys lying nearby and slide them into the lock. Their buzzing gets louder.

I swing open the door and step into the cell. "Thorn?"

No reply. There is another candle nearby. I stoop to light it, adding a little more light to the chamber.

"Are you hurt?"

Slowly, the large form turns to face me. It is not Thorn. It is some monster, similar to him in size, shape. It has the same black fur, the same limbs, the same tail and teeth and claws. But its face belongs to a monster. Its face is twisted and ravenous, red-eyed. Hateful. It is not Thorn. It cannot be.

The monster emits a low growl, and lunges forwards.

I scream, throwing the candlestick in its face as I break towards the door. I kick the bars closed, gather up the sword, and hurtle back up the passageway. I gained a few seconds with the candle and the door. I gain a few more slamming the dungeon shut, but I cannot see a way to bar it. The castle is my only shelter, creature in the mirror or not.

I am still screaming for Thorn. He must have locked that thing away. He must be nearby. Why doesn't he answer me?

I reach the castle, the monster so close at my heels that when I turn around to slam the door, its arm gets trapped. In the commotion, I see something awful. Something impossible.

Spitting against the monster's chest is a rosewood thorn on a leather string.

No.

The sprites are back again, furiously pushing against the

door with me. One of them goes straight into its face, stabbing its tiny body against its eyes. I hear it yowl in pain.

Him. I hear *him* yowl in pain.

"I don't want to hurt you!" I cry.

He continues to wrestle against the door. I pick up the sword and swipe at his hand. Blood splatters the floor. He cries out again, withdrawing his hand. I use the moment to dash for the stairs.

I've just reached the top when the doors fling open. In three leaps, he is at the top, cutting across my path. I hurl the sword in his direction and stream down the one way still left to me, knocking over suits of armour, stone busts, whatever I can. A piece of debris catches my ankle and I slam against the floor, turning just in time to see him towering over me. Red eyes sink into skin. I raise my arms to cover the blow I'm sure is coming, when out of nowhere Bramble comes flying. His teeth clamp around his master's arm.

Thorn barely registers the pain, flinging our dog aside as if he were no more nuisance than a fly.

"Bramble!" I scream.

He is up again with barely a whimper, this time going for the leg. One of the sprites flies past my cheek, I scramble upright and race down the corridor, hitting the door of the forbidden chamber. It is locked. The sprite flees into the keyhole, the other two still trying to delay him. They cut down a chandelier. Glass explodes onto the floor. Bramble is lying whimpering in the corner.

The lock clicks open. I rush inside, slamming it shut. The little sprite dashes back through, locking it again.

Thorn pounds against the door. I am not sure it will hold him. A great big wardrobe stands a few feet away. It is leaden, but the sprites stream in and somehow the four of us manage to tip it. There's a table too. An armchair. I heave both across the room. The sprites are gone. The pounding gets lighter, quieter, less frequent. Perhaps they are distracting him. Perhaps he is getting tired. Perhaps I wounded him more than I thought.

Him.

Why didn't he tell me? Why didn't I *know*? I saw how similar they were, but the truth is as simple as it is shocking: I could not imagine Thorn as that thing. I stopped seeing him as anything but him a long time ago.

As my breath calms, and my heart subsides, I realise how cold it is in this chamber. There is an ice in the air, a frostiness that I had forgotten, that once inhabited every corner of the castle. I spot a hearth, unlit, and set to work making a fire. The embers only make the shadows more prominent, and I'm in no mood for shadows. I move around the room, lighting every candle I can find, vanquishing whatever darkness I can.

A luxurious suite peels out of the darkness, gold and white and marble. It is far grander than any of the other rooms in the castle. Far dustier, too. A large, full-length mirror stands beside the fireplace, and opposite is a painting of a beautiful woman. The brushwork is so exquisite that her gown almost ripples, and her dark hair shines as though caught in the sun. She is proud and flawless, but there is a kindness to her face. I have no doubt that this is the person Thorn was talking to several weeks ago, the person he claimed to have lost... but who is she? There is no name on the gilded frame.

There is one other curious thing about the room. Next to the bed is a broken cradle, one side of it completely torn away. The blankets, stiff with dust and age, have been ripped to shreds. What happened to this occupant? Is this... is this woman someone Thorn loved and lost, a long time ago? Was it... was it possible they had a child together? And the claw marks...

No, it didn't bear thinking about. I couldn't imagine Thorn as a father, and I always imagined him as little older than me. This crib had been abandoned for years.

I am not so sure my theory about the woman is incorrect, however. I have heard him talking to her image. What had he said?

I'm not sure I could survive losing you both.

Thorn is still prowling outside. He has stopped pounding, but I can still hear him growling, the hot, angry spurts of breath, the clinking of claw on marble. Beside the crib is a little music box. Not a magic one, like the one we used for our party, just a perfectly ordinary box. It plays a simple lullaby, one that reminds me of a tune my mother used to sing. I cannot quite remember the words. Something about home and the heart.

I place it on the table next to the fireplace. I am not sure I can hope to sleep, but the song is soothing. Even he sounds quieter than he was before.

I do not wish to disturb this bed, this shrine, more than I have already, so I find a blanket inside a dresser and wrap myself up in it.

The little sprites wander through the keyhole, skimming the floor like dying dragonflies. They are so faint, I can see them wavering. When I scoop them up, they are barely moving at all.

"Thank you," I whisper. "I know why you tried to stop me now. I'm sorry I didn't listen."

They are absolutely mute. I do not know what good it will do, but I lie them down on the rug beside the glowing fire. I wind up the music box again and douse the other lights before crawling onto the hearth beside them. I try to remember the words to the tune.

"Home is the sweetest of places..." I forget the next bit, forget most but the last line. I sing it to the darkness, praying that he can hear me too, wherever he is. *"You are safe, I am here, this is home."*

The stars are talking again.

"Six others have come before her, and not a single one has

ever ventured out of their room for any of the nights," the childlike voice squeaks.

"Which either makes her very brave, or very stupid." The matronly one retorts.

The third –my favourite– is succinct, matter-of-fact. "She left because she cared."

"Silly girl doesn't know what's good for her."

"Whose side are you on, exactly?"

"I'd just rather see her gone than dead."

"You know what will happen if she goes."

"It's never happened so far."

"He has never loved any of them before."

The door clicks open, and I awaken on the rug in front of the fire. I have no confusion about how I came here. I remember everything about the night with perfect, frightening clarity.

The furniture has already been pulled away, and I can see Thorn curled up right outside the door. Bramble is beside him, licking the wounds he inflicted the night before.

Thorn says nothing as I exit the room, does not move or even acknowledge me, until I am standing beside him. "Please tell me I didn't hurt you," he begs, not looking at me. "Just tell me that."

I take the blanket from my shoulders and drape it over him. He is completely naked. I know I should be angry at him. He has lied to me. He has unconsciously put me in danger. But in this moment, I completely understand. He was ashamed. He was afraid. I cannot do anything but pity him. I crouch down beside him and he stiffens at the closeness, then begins to tremble. He curls inwards, and I think he might be crying.

"I'm not hurt," I say, as solidly as I can. I touch the back of his hand, where last night's wound pulses angrily. "I am sorry about your hand. You'll have to let me bandage it."

"As long as you're all right–"

"I am not all right," I say firmly. "I said I was unhurt, not all right."

Thorn slowly moves into a sitting position. He still avoids my gaze, but I see his cheeks are damp. "I would sooner die than let any harm come to you."

"I know. I know you would."

"If you had only stayed in your room–"

"No! No, Thorn, I am not a child! You cannot shut me away! I came out looking for you because I did not *know*. If you had only told me–"

"I did not want you to know that I was a monster–"

"You are *not* a monster!"

"There is an equal measure of despair and delight I feel at your utterance of those words, but I assure you Rose, once a month I truly do shed any semblance of humanity."

"Well, once a month I'm not that much fun to be around either."

Thorn looks at me like he wants to laugh, but is either too exhausted or too frightened to. "Why... why did you come out last night?"

Now it is my turn to be frightened. "There... there was a face in the mirror," I admit. "The same face from the lake. The horrible, twisted face. I ran out to find you and... I heard you screaming."

"You can't possibly have heard me all the way–"

"But I did."

Thorn looks at me blankly, taking this in.

"This face I saw..." I continue. "She's the dark fairy, isn't she? The one who started the war, brought ruin on the fairy people, and was trapped here as a result."

Thorn prickles. "She ought to be dead by now," he says. "Or as powerless as a ghost. But somehow she still clings to life. A dark remnant of her former self, imprisoned in this castle. Just like me."

He whispers the last part, and suddenly I have a horrible idea. "Are you... are you like her?" The words cut against my throat. It cannot be. "Is that why you look–"

Thorn cannot look me in the eyes. "I am one of her creations," he admits. "A monster she made to inflict misery on her enemies. I should be... what you saw last night. That is the way I am supposed to be, but for the mercy of the fairy queen."

"The lady in the portrait," I realise, my eyes drifting back through the chamber door. I do not ask why I was not allowed to go in there, why he treats the place like a shrine. I am afraid to. "All right."

"You don't seem... surprised by all this."

"I live in an enchanted castle."

"Yes, quite. Well, the castle is under a curse."

"Oh my, do you really think so?"

Thorn glares. "I am trying to be serious here, Rose."

"Sorry."

"I told you once that this place was a prison," he continues. "I don't think I explained for whom. You see, after the great battle was fought, the Queen of the Fairies, fearing for the lives of her people, cast them out into the realm of men, and imprisoned those who fought against her within the walls of the castle. She then gave up her own life to ensure that was where they remained. But over the years, her endeavours drained all magic from all lands, and placed a curse upon the place she once called home."

"What... what happens when the curse is broken?"

"Life returns to the castle. The lights regain their forms. Magic is free to walk the world once more."

"And... the shadows?"

"They die, hopefully."

"And... you?"

"What about me?"

"You turn into a monster once a month," I say placidly. "We haven't yet talked about why that is."

Thorn sighs. "The Queen, she... she made me what I am. Human on the inside, save for one night a month when dark magic is at its peak."

"Why?"

"Sorry?"

"Why did she save you, if you were one of the dark fairy's creations?"

Thorn is very quiet for a moment. "You know, I've often asked myself the same question." His tone is bitter. "You've seen my true form now. Do you see now, why I told you I was a monster?"

I am petrified of my next question. "Have you ever hurt anyone?"

Thorn swallows. "Yes," he replies. "Never willingly, never wantingly, always apologetically... but I still did it. It never mattered to me that I had no choice, that I couldn't help it. Only a monster could do what I did."

"Only a monster could do that *and not care.*" My words do not seem to be enough to convince him that I cannot, will not, ever agree with him. He is no more monster than me. Most days. "How... how is the curse broken?" I ask, when Thorn says nothing in response.

"The details are a little... hazy. It was said that only a young woman, fierce in soul and fair of heart, could break it. Every time the gateway opens, it has pulled in another maiden."

"And... and what is she supposed to do?" I have read many a story about a curse before. My mind whirs with thoughts of blood-letting, frog-kissing, and virgin sacrifices. I'll happily kiss a frog, but sacrifice is not really my preference. And I cannot imagine it is something as simple as a kiss.

"I am unsure," he replies, although the tiny pause in his voice, the way he looks to the side slightly, makes me think that he knows a little more than he is saying. "But I am fairly sure you are doing something right."

"Because of... the garden?"

"The entire place. The mirrors, the magic, the light... Life returned to this place, once you came."

"Slowly though," I say quickly.

"I was once told all the best things happen slowly."

"I still... I still don't feel like I'm doing anything though."

"But you must be," Thorn says, with some desperation.

"*You must be.*"

The fervour of his gaze is alarming, and strikes me sense-less for a moment. What does he think that I am doing? Or is it more a desperate hope?

"When you transform, what's it like?" I ask, attempting to turn his attention to something –anything– else.

"Painful," he admits, after a pause. "It shouldn't be. My form doesn't change. The pain is all in my head. But it is... unpleasant."

"And... are you inside, the whole time?"

"I'm not... I'm not sure. The night after, I always seem to remember it, but like one does a dream. Hazy. You might have noticed I'm never myself the day after."

"You hurt yourself."

"Yes, usually trying to get out, if I'm caged. I don't... I don't usually bother with that, when it's just me here. When there's nothing else living about, I don't seem to be a danger. The first few full moons you were here for, I didn't lock myself away. I had forgotten what could happen until you told me that you'd heard me."

I stroke the scars on his arm. "These were for me, then."

"The lesser of two evils, I assure you."

Why does he think his pain is any less important than mine? He might be talking about how my death is worse than a few injuries on his behalf, but I am not convinced.

His hand is still bleeding from where I sliced it yesterday. Another injury he has endured for my sake. "Will you argue with me if I insist on doctoring you?"

"I am slowly learning that there is no point in arguing with you."

Part Three: Summer

Shall I compare thee to a summer's day?
Thou art more lovely and more temperate.
Rough winds do shake the darling buds of May,
And summer's lease hath all too short a date.
Sometime too hot the eye of heaven shines,
And often is his gold complexion dimmed;
And every fair from fair sometime declines,
By chance, or nature's changing course, untrimmed;
But thy eternal summer shall not fade,
Nor lose possession of that fair thou ow'st,
Nor shall death brag thou wand'rest in his shade,
When in eternal lines to Time thou grow'st.
So long as men can breathe, or eyes can see,
So long lives this, and this gives life to thee.

--William Shakespeare--

Chapter Twelve

The Rose Garden

Thorn and I reach an agreement: I will lock my door every night of the full moon and not come out, but I insist that I am the one to lock him in the crypt at night. It sounds strange to him at first, but I tell him that I will feel happier, knowing where he is, assuring myself that he is safe no matter how much he screams. He concedes to this, and I am satisfied. I know he still thinks I am afraid of him, but I am less afraid than I have been in months, now that I know what truly stalks these halls. Now that I know what secret he has been keeping.

Thorn rests for most of the day, recovering and also, I think, hiding his shame. Coming to terms with letting me see this ugliness inside him. I don't really want to be apart from him, but I do not think this is something I can fix. He needs to learn how to be at ease with this himself.

Bramble, thankfully, does not appear to be injured, and spends the day by his master's side. I busy myself with cleaning up the mess of last night's escapades. The little sprites help, and I am glad to see them unhurt.

They do not say anything however, even though I was sure I heard them this morning. The next day, I ask Thorn about his previous guests again.

"Did any of them come close to breaking the curse?"

"No," he returns instantly.

"How can you be so sure? Did the gardens not–"

"It took a long time for magic to vanish entirely from this place. The gardens were the last thing to start crumbling. They could not be used as an indication."

"Then how could you tell that they didn't come close?"

Thorn goes silent for a moment. "Quite frankly, most of them did not really care," he says eventually. "They did not engage with the castle –or me– in the way that you have."

"And... all of these girls... They all chose to return to their families when the time came?"

"Can you blame them?"

I realise before I speak that that is what I am planning to do. "Does the portal never open again in the same place?"

"It can do. It has several places it er, docks, as it were. It has opened in the same place before."

"Is... is there any way to control it?"

"Possibly," he replies. "Why do you ask?"

"Because... because I was thinking... perhaps... of coming back to see you, a couple of times a year. If... if I may?"

"You... you want to see me again?"

"Of course I want to see you again!" I snap.

Did none of the others feel the same? Did they all care for him so little, that they could abandon him to his isolation? That they were content to never speak to him again?

Thorn could not have looked more shocked if I had slapped him.

"Did... did none of them express a desire to do the same?" I ask gingerly.

"One or two of them promised to, but then a year passed, or two, and they forgot. Moved onwards, as they should."

"I cannot believe that not one looked back."

"Can you not?"

My chest feels tight. "Thorn, when..."

"Yes?"

I want to promise that I *will* return, when my time comes, but he has had that promise before, and I do not think he would believe me if I repeated it. I also realise that although I desperately, desperately want to see my family again... I do not want to leave here. I do not want to leave Thorn. Could I bear it, to be apart from him for so long? Could he bear it, to be apart from me?

He has born it with others. Why should I consider myself different?

I feel different. I feel different to me, if not to him.

"When I go," I say finally. "It won't be easy. I... I don't want it to be forever."

"It goes without saying, that I don't want it to be forever, either."

I wish I had another choice. I wish I could take him with me, or come back any time I pleased. Perhaps... perhaps I can spend six months with my family, and then another six here. Live my life between two worlds. But I know, somehow, that this will be impossible.

"I've grown quite fond of you, you know."

"And I, of you."

Fond does not really aptly explain it, and I know Thorn would give it another word too, if I let him, but I do not. Instead, I make up some task that requires my immediate attention and sweep swiftly out of the room.

I dream of the other girls. I see them, talking to Thorn, smiling at him, their faces flat and expressionless like paper. Was it so easy for them to leave? Why did not one return, just for a day? How could they leave him? How could they not love him like–

Like what? Why do I find it so hard to comprehend that no one has loved him? Lots of people are unloved through life, tragic though that truth is. Why was Thorn so different?

I find myself wondering about what people are. What makes us human, makes us special, makes us different. Because we are. There are no species quite like us, or at least none that I have known. What makes us so? What are we cut from, what spark makes our minds move?

Because whatever we are made from, Thorn is made from something else. I have never known his like before, and lack the words to give it shape.

If you care about him so much, Rose, you should just tell him. What harm can it do? But even if I could find the words, I wouldn't speak them. The price is far too high.

One morning, just before lunch time, Thorn races into the parlour, all excitement. "I have something magnificent to show you!" he squeals, "Come on!"

He is so excited that he quite forgets how to walk upright. He bounds out of the room, slipping and sliding, before scooting back in to check if I'm following.

"Come on!"

"What is it?"

"It's a surprise."

"You cannot top the library, Thorn."

"This might come close."

He leads me to the narrow set of stairs that wind up towards the barren roof garden with the fountain. Not really expecting much, I put on a smile and follow him up.

The first thing I notice is the aroma of flowers, the scent of honey and summer. Seconds later, I step into the sunlight and am enveloped in colour. Pink, white, red, purple, yellow, orange... roses in every shade, style and shape. Roses I never knew even existed. For a moment, I am struck speechless, rendered utterly incapable of shaping words to express this wonder.

"Roses have always been my favourite," Thorn says softly, "even before I met you."

When I turn around from admiring a particularly beautiful pink rose, Thorn is standing very close. It startles me so much that I prick my finger on the bush.

"Ouch!"

Thorn grabs my hand quickly, as if I will bleed out without immediate attention. "Over here."

He pulls me over to the gold-bottom fountain and dips my hand in the waters. The feeble pain vanishes almost immediately. I lift it out. There is nothing there.

"Healing waters?"

Thorn grins. "Healing waters. Blessed by the fairy queen herself."

"How convenient."

"Well, it won't heal any serious wound, but nicks and scrapes it can manage." He massages my finger. "You should be more careful when admiring roses," he says smugly. "I hear they can be dangerous."

"Personally, I've always rather enjoyed them for their thorns." My eyes fall to the pendant I gave him.

He laughs. "You are an odd creature."

"As are you." I tap his chest. "Luckily, we're rather of the same oddness, so I rather think we suit."

Thorn looks a bit awkward at this, and turns away. "I got your rosebud up here, for your necklace," he says swiftly.

"That was months ago!"

"They certainly took their time. I wasn't sure they would bloom at all. They were the last thing that dried up, you know. The last to come back. It is my favourite place in the entire castle."

I grin, because it is mine now, too.

"Let me show you why."

There is a ladder at the edge of the garden which leads to a small platform, almost like a gazebo. Thorn lets me go first. It is the highest point in the castle. I can see for miles, the ever-changing mountains, the blue skies, the streams and lakes and trees and meadows. I fancy I can even make out little villages, and I notice that the landscape is moving, shifting slightly every few seconds.

"I think we can say, quite certainly, that the magic has returned to this place," says Thorn, appearing beside me. He sounds in awe, but a little sad, too. "When the solstice comes, the gateway should be clear. You will have several hours with which to make your escape."

"What do you mean?"

"When you came here before, the way closed almost immediately. There was not enough magic to keep it open any longer. This time, I think it will be open for a while."

"Oh, good."

Thorn looks at me quizzically.

"I don't want to have to rush."

A hand slowly drifts across my cheek. It stays there, half in my hair, half on my skin. Thorn's eyes are tied to mine. They are such beautiful eyes, bright and blue and so wonderfully his in a way that is hard to put into words. I do not want to move. I want to press this moment between the pages of a book, preserve it like a flower. I want to take it out again, admire it, keep it close to me, like Thorn's snowdrops.

"Stay here," Thorn requests. He leaps off the platform and disappears behind the roses. "No peeking!"

The view is just as captivating without him, but a little less magical without him by my side, as if I need a second pair of eyes to fully soak up the sight, grasp every colour. I can see a deer grazing in the woodland, make out the rustle of life in every bush and every tree. We are certainly not alone here, any more.

149

I thumb my little amber necklace. A sudden thought occurs to me. "How did you make this, when you say your hands are so clumsy?" I call down.

"I had help," Thorn replies. "From our little fairy friends." He reappears at my side, and the lights are buzzing around his face.

"Oh, hello!" I say, "How nice to see you again!"

Thorn grins, and extends a hand to touch them. "It's been a while, old friends."

"How did they help you if you couldn't see them?"

"Just because we cannot see someone," he says, "doesn't mean they aren't there. They've been here my whole life, keeping me fed and the castle as upright as possible... fixing chains and tying ribbons." He holds out his other hand. It is filled with the most beautiful bouquet of roses and greenery, soft yellows and pinks and bright oranges, little pops of red, tied with a scarlet ribbon.

"Thank you," I breathe, clutching them to my chest, inhaling pure summer. "You truly have a talent when it comes to arranging flowers! You're extremely good with colour." I begin to wonder if his desire to paint may not be a bad ambition, and am struck with a sudden idea. "Wait here," I tell him.

It takes me a while to locate them, and even longer to haul them up the stairs, but I eventually emerge on the rooftop with an easel, paints, and a blank canvas.

Thorn frowns as he helps me set up the easel. "What... what are you doing?"

"Painting!"

"You want to paint?"

"Actually, I'm a terrible painter, but I can sketch well enough. You're doing the painting."

"Me?" Thorn steps back. "I'm not sure that's a good idea–"

"Well, how will you know until you try?"

Thorn exhales and silently concedes. He loads different paints into a tray whilst I sketch the outline of the garden. Carefully, gently, he picks up a brush and begins to mix the colours. Perfect shades begin to emerge.

I try not to spend too long on my outline. I'm really not much of an artist, especially compared to Freedom. I can just about manage to copy. He was the one with vision, perspective, creativity. He could disappear into his paintings the way I could a book, and I would be lying if I said I didn't envy his talent.

I push Thorn into my seat. He gulps nervously, holding up a shaking brush... It divides against the canvas, leaving a splurge of red on the page. He looks up at me hopelessly. I ease the brush out of his fingers.

"Try it without the brush," I suggest.

"Without the brush?" He looks at me like I'm mad.

I load my little finger with a small measure of red, lean over his shoulder, and press it against the white. I spread it out slowly, following my rough lines.

Thorn follows my example, coating his nails in various shades, dragging it along the canvas. He finds this easier. The roses begin to bloom. He layers the canvas with colour, oranges and reds. He spreads blue over the sky, rubs clouds into life. I help with some small, fiddly bits– tiny lines, little more. I adore the way the roses burst through my sketch, the way the colour leaps from the lines. Before long, not a spot of white remains. I step back to admire it.

"It's messy," Thorn says critically.

"Oh no, it's wonderful!" I declare. "It doesn't have to be perfect to be beautiful."

I have not seen anything of its ilk. It does not look realistic, by any means, but it is clearly a rose garden, a vibrant explosion of summer and colour.

"Do you really like it?" Thorn asks.

I turn my face to his, and nod.

"Do you want it?"

"More than anything."

We are both so close. Thorn has a spot of paint on his nose. I lean forward to rub it away, but keep my hand on his cheek, longer than I should. For a long moment, neither of us says anything. When Thorn eventually does, his voice is softer than the wind.

"I wish I was a human man, and had human lips, so that I might kiss you."

My first response –the one that runs to the tip of my tongue before I can think it– is, *if you were a human man, I'd let you.* I catch it just in time. I do not want those words spoken. I fear they would do more harm than good. I do not want Thorn to hear those words, "if you were a human man" not from me, not from anyone. Thorn is a human man. Or as good as one. Or better. *So much better.*

I push back my thoughts. "Who says I'd let you?" I say, and punch his arm, smiling at him like I might do Freedom, and then run for the steps.

Thorn pauses, ever-so-briefly, and follows, carrying the painting. He escorts me back to my room and excuses himself to wash up, saying nothing else. I hope he isn't thinking about... the not-kiss.

I take down the portrait of an unknown woman and hang Thorn's painting. It truly is wonderful, I said nothing merely to bolster his confidence. I absolutely adore it. I hope I can convince him to do more.

His bouquet sits on my dresser, his ribbon folded in my drawer, next to the snowdrops he presented me with, so long ago. I pressed them rather than watch them wilt. I wonder what he would think, if he knew I did that? I'm not sure I want him to know, and I'm not sure why.

I touch my lips, absent-mindedly at first. They feel softer than before, larger, more noticeable. I touched them like this after I kissed James Saintclair, too. They feel different now, moved by the mere thought of a kiss, the possibility of fireworks.

But that is not what would happen if I kissed Thorn. I drop my hand away. It does me no good to dwell on something like that, something that cannot be. My lips still sting, but now they feel as if I've picked at a wound that was starting to scab over.

It is the day before the funeral and I cannot sleep. There is not the slightest bit of weariness in me; each little corner of the room is awake. Moonlight spills in through the gaps in the curtains and I can see every line and edge of the room. The quietness is palpable. There is the slightest ruffling of bedsheets from my two sisters, the occasional, whispered sigh. An echo of noise. Nothing is still.

I want to climb into Mama's bed. I want to snuggle into her warm arms and press my forehead to her chest. But Mama's arms aren't warm any more. She is not in her bed.

She lies downstairs in a box, her face painted, dressed like a doll, her skin as white as porcelain. Mr Arnold, the village toymaker, has a beautiful doll, whose eyes open and close when she is picked up.

Nothing will open Mama's eyes now, and I am scared of the person in the box. I am scared because she looks like Mama, but isn't. Mama is a laugh, a smile, a pair of gentle hands and warm arms. Mama is bright and lovely.

So Mama is gone, leaving only a shell behind. I wish I knew where she had gone. I wish I knew when she'd be back. I know –or they tell me– that she "has gone to a better place" but what was wrong with this one? What was wrong with *us*?

I know Mama won't come back. I know that she is dead. I just wish I knew why. I push back the coverlet and swing my legs out of the bed, press my soles into my slippers. I creep across the floor, ignoring every creak, carefully slipping through the door and down the stairs.

Mama's shell is laid out in the dining room, in a box lined with red velvet. She is dressed in white, flowers twined in her hair.

This will be the last time I see her face.

I hear a noise from the corner of the room. It is Papa, sitting in his chair. He has an empty glass in his hand, and his face is red. He looks more like my grandpa than my father.

He puts down his glass and goes into the dining room. I am afraid, as if I have been caught doing something that I shouldn't, so I stay still, waiting on the steps, my little head pressed in between the bannisters.

Papa puts out his hands and places them on my Mama's cheeks. He pulls at her ringlets. His face crumples into something angry, and he tears out the blossoms in her hair and claws at her gaudy wrappings. Then he starts to choke. A guttural sound rises from his throat. Tears peel from his eyes.

He levers her into his arms. Her body is stiff, but he does not seem to notice. His fingers turn into twisted talons. He digs into her skin. His face disappears into her hair and sobbing fills the room. It echoes around each crevice of the house, like a ghost.

I am no longer scared of the person in the box. I am more scared of the man outside it.

Chapter Thirteen

Mirror of Grace and Darkness

I am sitting under a tree, humming the lullaby under my breath, struggling with the lyrics. Something about home amongst the fairies in the realm of dreams and love...

"That's a lovely tune."

I startle. Thorn is in the branches high above me. He drops down in a single bound. "Sorry," he says. "I was up there when you came and I wasn't sure whether to stay, or say something, and now I feel... mildly awkward."

"It's fine," I assure him, laughing. "I'm trying to figure out the words, I can't quite pin them down."

Thorn throws back his head. *"Home is here in the realm of dreams, home is here in your arms. The realm of the fairies is your home my dear, here I'll shelter you from harm."*

"You know it!" Delight bubbles inside me. "I thought it was a family thing. Mama used to sing it to us, but no one else in the village knew it."

"I think your mother was part fey," he says simply.

"Be serious."

"I am. When this place fell, many fairies escaped into the world. I imagine they disguised themselves as humans, and lived ordinary lives, only telling our tales to their offspring."

It makes a certain degree of sense, I admit. It explains a lot of Mama's songs and stories. I wonder if she ever knew that they were more than just that?

There you are, Rose! I was afraid the fairies had come and snatched you away...

Thorn touches my arm. "Rose?"

"Sorry," I laugh, throwing the memory away. "You might be right, you know. Do you remember the rest of the song?"

He sings the next line. *"Here you are safe and here you are loved, and here I will stay for all time. I'll always be here, my darling, my dear, in the stars, the sea and the shine."*

I sit a little in awe for a moment, surrounded by happy, bubbly memories. "You have a nice voice," I say.

"Thank you."

A soft breeze sways through the tree. I look up into the branches, examining the spot where Thorn sat.

"I have never been able to climb trees well," I admit sadly. "Freedom pushed me out of a tree once, and even though he apologised and offered to teach me later, I didn't trust him enough to get up in the branches again."

Thorn is quiet for a moment. "Do you... do you want me to teach you?"

"Yes."

"I... I'm not sure I can. I mean... I am so much larger than you, and..."

"Stronger?"

"Yes."

I am not annoyed. He *is* stronger than I am. I am not sure how much of a difference it will make.

"Will you try?"

"Of course, if that is what you wish."

I hitch up my skirts and tie them under my apron, trying to ignore the sudden shock of skin I've exposed. Thorn's eyes immediately leap to it, and then whirl upwards in an attempt to look somewhere –anywhere– else.

The first branch is far above my reach, so Thorn has to lift me up into that one. He follows me with ease.

"Put your hand on that one," Thorn instructs. "And your foot there. If you grab that branch with your other hand... can you pull yourself up?"

The first three instructions are easy, but the fourth is considerably harder. My immediate thought is that I am never going to manage this, that I have none of the muscle strength required to lever myself upwards. But then Thorn is beside me, whispering in my ear.

"You can manage. Keep going."

I feel his presence keenly, more real and definite than anything else. He hovers, inches away, ready to catch me, or support me. I have never felt safer. I am afraid of nothing, with him behind me. It takes a bit of time and several failed attempts, but I finally pull myself, ungracefully, onto the next branch.

Only about six more to go.

Finally, the lesson is over. Thorn leaps out of the tree and then looks up to see if I am following. Impulsively, seeing he is waiting, I let go and launch myself into his arms. He obviously isn't expecting this. He catches me perfectly, but is caught off balance, and we both go tumbling into the grass. I giggle as I roll on top of him.

"Sorry," I say.

I am thankful when he doesn't ask if I am all right. I am not a piece of pottery. Instead, he reaches up and pulls a bit of grass from my hair.

"A little warning, next time? My catching skills are usually much more impressive."

"I remember."

How much has changed since the first time he caught me? It is difficult to imagine me, us, back then. The time when we were strangers belongs to someone else.

It takes me a while to shuffle off him, and had I not had a sudden idea, I think I could have spent the rest of the afternoon lying there quite comfortably.

"Come on!" I say, leaping up.

"Where are we going?"

I run back to the castle, dragging him behind me, and pull him into the music room. A dozen sheets are thrown in his direction. "These are all the ones I know that I could find," I say. "Pick one."

I sit down at the piano while Thorn thumbs about awkwardly for one. Finally, he drops a song in front of me. A pleasant, rowdy tune that I must have sung a hundred times before. There was always singing in my house. Mama would sing her old ballads and folk songs, Nanny her country tunes as she kneaded the bread. I would sing whilst I was gardening, and Honour and Beau just sang perpetually. Even Freedom could frequently be heard humming an old favourite, or whistling whilst he polished his weapons or chopped wood in the garden.

After a few notes, a few lines, Thorn's voice starts to slip on top of mine. We merge together. He cannot know how much this means to me, to finally be singing with someone again. For a moment, it feels like home again. Honour and I are doing a duet. I would always take to the piano –less easy to be noticed– and back up Honour's beautiful voice. I loved singing with my sister.

Then, there is a strange moment, when I look up at Thorn, and I prefer this. I like singing with him more than with her. Is that right? Or am I just forgetting what it was like to be by her side? Perhaps Thorn and I are just better at harmonising. Perhaps it just sounds more lovely.

He does have a lovely voice...

The song draws to a close.

"Was that all right?" Thorn asks. "You look... peculiar."

"I just... I enjoyed that."

"We can do another."

We do. Afterwards, Thorn admits that he has never done this before, accompanied a woman on a piano. I think perhaps, he is as moved as I am. When I go to bed that night, my room feels different, and so do I. I can feel a shift inside, but I do not know what it is, and the words do not exist to explain it.

I have to break the curse. The thought keeps me up for several nights, twittering at the back of my mind, squirming into the snatches of slumber I'm able to steal. I have to find some way to free this castle from its cage, to free Thorn. The trouble is, I don't know where to begin. The library has been thoroughly unhelpful, and it's not like I have any other way of–

But I *do* have another way. I have the mirrors. Thorn told me that they couldn't show him anything of mine I wouldn't wish him to see, so I imagine there are limits to its power, but it is a much better starting place. I waste no time, disturbing Bramble as I leap from the bed, hastily pulling on my dressing-gown as I hurtle towards the chamber.

I am not entirely sure where to begin, but the Mirror of Memories is a good place to start. "Show me... the curse being cast."

The mirror ripples, like liquid silver. I see a figure cloaked in black moving towards the forbidden room. A fairy guard is stationed in front, but is immediately cut down. The figure slips inside, but then the image whirls again and disappears. I cry out in frustration; someone, or something, does not want me to know what happened in that room.

"Show me why it was cast."

The ballroom door blows open. Darkness swells, engulfs

the lights. The same dark figure swarms upon the floor. Her face sends shivers running through me. The face from the lake. She marches towards the throne, where she screams at the golden person seated there. Her voice crawls under my skin.

"How dare you close the way to the mortal realm!"

"It had to be done," the golden figure of the fairy queen replies.

"Our people were growing foolish, causing the humans harm–"

"You would choose them over us?" The dark fairy laughs. *"Of course you would. You love them. But they are not like us, they are weak and mortal–"* Her eyes dance to the portrait behind the throne, fully whole in this memory. The Queen stands beside a beautiful man, but he looks ordinary compared to her. Ordinary but... slightly familiar.

The queen rises, a pale, silent anger twitching in the corner of an otherwise flawless face. A wave of her wand sends the intruder flying. When she rights herself, she shoots the queen a look that could melt stone, and vanishes.

The mirror goes dark. "Show more," I demand, "show me what happened next–"

My own reflection argues back. I shout a little more, but nothing happens. Why won't the castle let me see? Doesn't it want the curse broken?

A cold chill runs through me. My eyes drift over to the covered mirror. Perhaps the castle *does* want the curse broken. Perhaps something else prevents me.

What am I to do? I cannot heal the wound I cannot see. A dozen Roses stand dumbstruck and helpless, and all but one of the images move to wipe their damp eyes with the back of their sleeves. The one image that does not move resides in the Mirror of Truth. She stands still, defiant, unblinking and unmoving. Is that really who I am?

I swallow, and this other Rose stares back bravely. "Can I even break this curse?" I ask her.

The reflection nods.

"Am I doing something to help break it right now?"

Nothing.

"Can I have a clue?"

She is as still and silent as ever.

"This is infuriating!" I turn back to the Mirror of Memories. "Show me the others!" I demand. "The others that came here before me– show them to me!"

What am I doing that they didn't?

A young girl swirls into view. She is small and slight, pretty and skittish as a kitten. I see Thorn watching her arrive at the castle, smaller and younger than he is now, and bubbling with excitement. He races out to meet her and–

Her face explodes into screams. Screams that carry on, reverberating around the room, shaking the castle to its core. The screaming seems to last for weeks, until her voice fades and she becomes a shadow in the corridors. Thorn too, learns to shrink away, damaged far more than she is by their meeting.

Was that the first time he thought he was a monster? When he saw himself through someone else's eyes?

The second girl has dewy skin, honey-coloured hair and a smile that could make most people melt. She wears it when she stands in the gardens, when she plays at the harp... but that smile vanishes whenever she catches sight of Thorn. Snippets of their time together unfold before my eyes. At one point, she laughs. *"Who could ever love a monster like you?"*

A rage boils inside of me. I want to reach right through the glass and strangle her, wipe this memory from existence. How dare she. But she is not the only one.

"Get away from me!"

"Hideous creature."

"Out of my way–"

"Disgusting–"

"Monster!"

There are some, some who do not shout or scream or rage. They offer kind words, nods of sympathy, whispers of understanding... but there is such coldness, reservation, distance. Where are the nights of fireflies by the lake, cosy evenings in the library?

I can barely watch. Is this why I am different from them? Is this how I am breaking the curse? By... by treating Thorn as he deserves to be treated? Or... or is it by accepting this place as my home? By being happy here?

I do not know. I look back at the mirror, hoping for more enlightenment on the subject, but instead, I see my mother. She is almost the spit of Honour, with her golden hair, shining complexion, bright smile. Only her eyes are more like mine than I remember, dark green and glorious. I have a touch of her curls, too. She is as young and fresh as a rosebud... this is Mama before she was a mother.

Have I made a mistake? Did I accidentally ask the mirror to show me her, instead? Or has it somehow read my mind, felt my need for something warm and pleasing?

She is sitting in a rose garden, tending to the bushes, humming under her breath. She drops a few stems into a basket by her side, and then looks about for her secateurs. A hand I know only too well dangles them above her head. She looks up, laughing.

"Oh, dear Beast, you do like to tease!"

Thorn smiles and hands them back to her. It is then that I realise where Mama is: she is in the garden. Our garden. Mama was here.

"Rose?" A sleepy voice sounds from behind me. "What are you doing up at this hour? Who are you..." His eyes sail over me to the baffling image within the frame. He breathes longingly. *"Grace!"*

A sharp silence stretches between us. I know what I've seen, I hear what he has said, and yet it takes me an age to understand. "You knew her," I say finally.

"Of course I knew her. She was one of the few I could have called a friend. Why are you–"

"Because she's my mother!" I rush. "You didn't know?"

Thorn's eyes widen. "She's your... your mother? No, no I didn't know–"

"How is this even possible? She died eight years ago and you're... you're not secretly really old, are you?"

"What? No, no. She was here only three years ago. I knew time ran differently, but it just never occurred to me..." He can barely take his eyes from the mirror, but he does, briefly, as if to check my face against hers. "I should have known," he whispers finally.

"We don't look alike."

"No, it's not that. It's more to do with how you look *at me*."

Of all the strange, bizarre and inexplicable things I have experienced in the past few months, this feels to me the most impossible. But then a million tiny details click into place. Mama's fairy stories. Her mystical wedding dress. The way she would stare fondly at the land behind the stream, but forbid us from crossing. She was not part fey, like Thorn had theorised earlier. She knew all about the fairy realm because she had visited it before. Because she knew him.

I think about what Thorn has just said. We were different from the others because of how we look at him. How many times had she told us not to judge by appearances? Was she thinking of him, every time?

"What was she like?" I ask him earnestly. "No one alive has fresher memories of her than you do."

"She was... kind," he says, as if this is the nicest word in the world. "A thoroughly beautiful soul. She was patient and sweet. It's a shame you don't take after her."

I elbow him in the side.

"She screamed, when she first saw me," he continues. "But it was a flustered sort of scream, as if she were trying to control it, knew that it was impolite to say anything. Then she ran into the next room, shutting the door behind her and blabbering. 'I'm so terribly sorry... terribly sorry. Just... just give me a minute, please! I really must apologise...' Her tone and her words were so unusual, that I began to laugh. Then she slowly crept out of the room, giggling nervously. By the end of the week she was calling me her dear friend."

I cannot help but smile. "That sounds like Mama."

Thorn and I share a look, not one we've had before. I don't know entirely what it means, but it is born out of this shared person we both knew, and loved. I feel he knows me even more through her, and vice versa. I am so glad she knew him.

"What do you remember of your mother?" I ask him.

He blinks at me.

"You knew my mother," I explain. "I should like to know a little more about yours."

"I remember very... very little. She was kind. Selfless. A fierce protector. I remember... I remember how she made me feel, even though I cannot remember her touch. I remember... I *know*... that she loved me."

I swallow painfully. "There's nothing greater than that, is there?"

"No, I suppose not."

"And nothing worse." Thorn senses I have slipped into a painful reverie.

"Come," he says, taking my hand. "I have something else to show you."

He takes me to a small gallery room in one of the towers. Faint dawn light is already spilling into it. I may have been in it before, but clearly paid it no heed, because now I see what Thorn has bought me up to see: a portrait of Mama.

"This appeared the day she left," he explains. "The last truly magical thing to happen, before your arrival. The castle started to decline not long after."

There are five other portraits in the room, each equally spaced. "The others," Thorn explains. "The visitors before you."

I take a moment to examine them now, side by side. Why have only women visited, I wonder? A name is printed beneath each one. That is all they are now, a name in this castle's history. There is a blank frame in the room. A seventh. Mine. Thorn sighs when he sees me looking at it.

"It arrived a few days ago," he said.

The wooden backing glares at me. It is getting ready.

When I finally sleep, I dream I am back at home, watching Mama's spirit dancing around her home. She kisses all of us goodnight, and then settles into the chair opposite Papa. He always kept that seat free, for her, and it is like she has never left.

Then the dream shifts. I am still at home, but bars are placed around my window. I am screaming, and my scream flies through the wind, all the way to a ruined castle, where my portrait hangs in a dusty chamber.

I will not become a portrait. I am not a part of this castle's history. I am not paint, or dust. I will not abandon Thorn. I will not.

Chapter Fourteen

Ariel

When the next full moon comes, Thorn and I walk down to the crypt together. Bramble comes too, warily. I sense that he knows something is amiss, that Thorn is less Thorn than he usually is.

We reach the door of the cell. Wordlessly, he slips inside. I close it behind him, place the candlestick on the ground, and wrap the chain around the lock.

"You don't have to stay," he says.

"I want to," I respond.

"At least until you're not... you anymore."

"It won't be pleasant to watch."

"I can't imagine it's pleasant to go through."

"I'll need to change."

"No peeking, I promise." I turn around to give him some privacy. He passes his clothes to me through the bars. I fold them neatly. The least I can do.

"Who used to let you out?" I ask, back still turned.

"Myself. Apparently, I don't know how to use keys when I'm

in that state."

The sky is darkening significantly by the time Thorn comes to sit beside the door, his back against mine. We have perhaps ten minutes until sunset.

"You can still–"

"I'm staying." I wiggle my hand through the bars until I find some part of him to hold. "You won't be alone tonight. Unless... unless you really want me to go?"

Thorn is quiet for a moment. "No," he says finally. "I don't want you to go."

We sit in silence for a few minutes more, me absentmindedly stroking his arm. Suddenly, Bramble starts to growl.

"Ssh, boy!"

Thorn tenses. He lets out a slight moan. "Rose... it's starting."

I turn around to face him. He is on all fours, his face contorted in pain, pressed against the bars. I press my forehead against his, grab his balled-up hands. He jerks away.

"I don't want to hurt you."

"Less concern about me, please, more concern about you."

"You are a far more pleasing topic."

"A joke. A joke is good."

"It wasn't... a joke..."

"I know." I reach forward and grab his hand. This time, he relents. He squeezes back, and I can tell from his stiffness just how much pain he's in. I can almost feel it falling into me, like he can't contain it. I touch his cheek. "You're going to be fine."

"I don't... I don't feel fine."

"That's all right. You don't have to feel fine all the time. I don't."

"Tell me... tell me something about yourself that I don't know."

"Oh, um. My favourite colour is blue–"

"Something serious."

"I love the colour of your eyes."

Thorn unscrunches his face, just for a second, to stare at

me. "Not... a good time... to tease..." he breathes.

"I really wish you'd believe me when I try to compliment you," I swallow. "That's another thing you don't know."

Thorn is shaking, vibrating, trembling so hard it is difficult to believe that something isn't about to break out of him. Difficult to believe this change isn't physical.

"I used to joke that you were hideous," I rush. "I was serious, at the time. But now I see you, now that I *see* you... I just wish that you could see yourself as I do."

"Even... like... this?"

"In all ways, in all lights, in all things."

I truly do believe, in that moment, that I have some kind of power. My eyes can see him like nobody else can, and if I hold onto him tightly enough, he will know it too. He will see what I see, believe what I believe.

"Rose," he cries out, his voice coarse and gravelly.

"I'm here."

"Thank you."

But then his voice turns into a roar. I wrench my hand free from his grip, and he leaps to the back of the cell. Red eyes glare at me. Thunder rumbles in his throat. Bramble barks.

I am not scared. A part of me wants to stay, right here by his side, until the night is over. I will sing him the lullaby that seemed to soothe him last time. But I made a promise, so I make good on it.

Before I head to my room, I go to the library, to see if there's anything left to find on curses. The fairies try to help, pulling out various tomes, but one of them keeps getting confused and loads the pile with romances. It makes me laugh a little, which I need at the moment.

I do not spend too long in the library. I feel like I am breaking his trust, lingering outside my room, so I hurry back there and lock my door. Bramble sits by my side all night as I scour through the volumes.

Thorn doesn't howl tonight. I like to imagine it's because he knows, this time, that he isn't alone.

First light wakes me, and I am up and dressed in an instant. I head down to the crypt with a blanket and a cup of tea. I unchain the door, envelope him in the blanket, and wait patiently for him to awaken, sipping the tea.

It doesn't take long for him to come around. The first thing he sees is me.

"Are you–"

"How are you?" I say over him.

He rubs his head. "I have been better, but... I've been worse."

"You didn't howl last night, I don't think."

"No, I didn't... I didn't feel as angry last night, as I usually do."

I do not ask him what he might feel angry about. I am not sure I would like the answer.

"Tea?" I offer. "It's cooled down, now. I didn't drink all of it, promise."

He accepts my cup, drinking carefully. I lean against him.

"It wasn't... it wasn't too horrible for you?" he asks.

"No." My answer is candid. "I think it would have been worse for me, not to see, and to stay up there and wonder."

He nods. "Thank you, for being there. It... it helped."

"I'm glad. I... I can stay next time, then?"

"Next time... will be the last time."

"Yes." I try not to think about that. I try not to think about how I will feel when I see a full moon without him, when I will know that somewhere in the world, he is alone, and hurting, and I will not be there.

I will not be there.

One more month. I have one more month left, before the solstice comes and I return to the mortal realm. I continue to read up on the Fey, not knowing what good it will do, hoping to come across some hint of what the curse truly is, and how to break it. Because if I do, and magic returns to the world, there is a chance, however slim, that I will get to see Thorn again. I do not have to say goodbye.

I do not tell Thorn what I am doing. I do not think he would try to stop me –surely he wants the curse broken as much as I do– but I do not want to give him any false hope. I conduct my searches at night instead, after I am certain he is sleeping.

The mirrors offer me little more insight, as I am never sure what question to ask, and am offered snippets at best before someone or something steals back the scenes. I do check in on my family, however. Honour knits in her new parlour every evening, and Charles brings her mulled wine and sits beside her, stroking the back of her hand affectionately. Nanny and Beau are invariably always tucked up in bed when I check in, and Papa has dozed off in his study. Hope is still up, reading at her desk, but sometimes if I catch them during the day, she's tending to my garden.

Freedom doesn't seem to sleep at all. He's either painting in his shed, or stalking the woods. I assume he's hunting, but one night he stops, sticks his torch in the ground, and sits on a grassy knoll. Slowly, my eyes eke details out of the gloom, and I catch the trickle of running water.

He's sitting beside the stream. If the image alone claws at my heart, his next words nearly shatter it. "Rose," he whispers, "where did you go?"

Oh, Freedom. My fingers leap to the glass before I can stop them. I want to fall right through it. "I'm here," I murmur back. As I do, a breath of wind flits through the woods and touches Freedom's hair. "I'll be home soon, soon, I promise."

I have to believe he has heard me, because the alternative is far too painful.

A soft tingle stirs me from my reverie. One of the sprites

is hovering beside me. It bobs up and down, darting forwards and then back. I sense it wants me to follow.

It rests in front of the Mirror of Truth. Illuminated behind the glass is a faint, shimmering image, shrouded in a soft, coloured mist. A figure rests within; a girl, my own age, I think, although there is a timeless quality to her flawless skin which is almost golden. She is wearing a ruffled dress of green and white, which floats against the glass as if it's filled with water. Her short, gold hair does the same too. I would think her a ghost if not for the keen, live green eyes that stare back at me.

I move closer. She is the person I saw when Thorn pulled me from the lake. The person who undressed me, no doubt. The person who keeps this place moving.

Her face breaks into a smile. "You can see me!" Her voice sounds strange, filtered, echoey. "I was so worried you wouldn't."

"I've seen you before," I say, "the night I fell into the lake."

"I thought you did, but it seemed so unlikely! I guess, you were near-death at the time, and I exist in an in-between place too, so..."

"Who... who are you?"

"I'm Ariel," she says, "I... I was a... a servant here, long ago."

"Are you a ghost?"

"No," she says quickly, but then pauses. "Yes. I suppose that term fits. I am no longer alive... but then not truly dead, as you see." She waves her arms, and the little dot begins to buzz furiously. "This mirror shows me for what I truly am."

"Are... are the other little sparks like you?"

She nods.

"Thorn... Thorn calls you remnants," I continue. "How... how did you come to be this way?"

She sighs, and it is the sigh of a hundred years, a long, endless, exhausted sigh. "I had a real form once," she explains. "And powers too; far beyond that of the simple summoning tricks you've witnessed before. But the castle was dying. If we didn't become one with it, it would crumble into nothingness

171

within a few years, and with it any hope we ever had of magic returning to the world once more. We became a part of it, losing our bodies and then our voices, only regaining these fragile containers when... when you came."

So she, like Thorn, believes that I am doing something to break the curse, but her voice sounds more uncertain than his.

"But... why *not* just leave?" I ask. "If the castle was going to die anyway– why not go through the gate the next time it opened?" She looks human enough, and with the magic she said she had, she could probably completely disguise herself. It would be easier, surely, than enduring this solitude. "There's nothing here to keep–" but suddenly, I know why. "Thorn. You were keeping this place alive for him."

She nods.

"But he said... he said he was one of that... that *face's* monsters. Why would you–"

"He is more than that," Ariel says quickly. "Yes, she made him what he is, but... it is hard to explain. He holds the key to restoring our world. To bringing back our people. And..."

"And what?"

"And we love him."

This news should make me happy, but for some reason it just emphasises his loneliness. He had people, all this time, people who were here but almost as gone as his mother.

"He acts as if you are dead," I whisper. "I should go and get him–"

"Wait, Rose–" She darts across my path, pulling my gaze back towards the mirror. "I need to tell you something. You're in danger."

I already know this. "The face in the lake," I say quietly. "The dark fairy, or whatever she is."

Thorn had tried to tell me that the shadows were harmless now, mere reflections of what they were. And perhaps that was true, before I came. But then I remember, with startling clarity, that awful face, both in the lake and in the mirror, the night Thorn almost killed me. She has been trying to hurt me for some time.

"Thorn wishes to believe she is gone, or weakened by her captivity." Ariel continues, as if reading my mind. "Because the alternative is far too frightening for him. And he can live in that ignorance, if it pleases him. But I would have you know otherwise. You are not one to run from a fight, I think."

A cold, dark chill claws through my bones. "Who... who is she?"

"A sorceress of immense power. The dark reflection of all that is light. We all hoped she was gone forever, but it appears she has been lingering here for some time, hoarding her power... She still has a little left, and she is growing desperate. She will come for you. You are far too great a threat."

"What... what do you mean?"

"You are the key to breaking the curse."

"But you said Thorn was–"

"It is both of you," she says shortly. "Your purpose is now entwined."

"But I'm not *doing* anything!"

"Yes," says Ariel, a little sadly, "you are. But if I tell you what you need to do, we may lose our only shot of ever being free. And I want the curse broken."

"You can't give me *any* clue?" She is little more use than the mirrors.

"If I am honest, none of us are completely sure of the required conditions. I will say this, however: speak your heart."

"Yes, wonderfully descriptive, thank you."

"There is so much at stake, Rose, you have no idea."

"Does Thorn know, that he can break the curse?"

"Yes, but, like you, he is a little in the dark. He has been trying for so long–"

Then how am I supposed to manage, in the time I have left? "Is there any chance you could be just a little more descriptive about what it is I am supposed to do–"

"You're running out of time," she rushes. "You must... you must tell him, before you go. Be brave. Don't be afraid."

A voice calls out in the dark, a scream cuts through me like a hard knife of wind. *Don't be afraid, Rose. Don't be frightened.*

"I'm not afraid!" I spit, more venomously than I mean to.

"Yes, you are," she says softly, "and it is killing him."

My mind churns over what Ariel said. Why couldn't she tell everything about the curse? Why must I "speak my heart"? What does that mean? Why should it matter? Aside from pumping fiercely against my chest, my heart is mute. My head, on the other hand, is loud and angry. Frustration rattles around inside.

"I'm so confused," I say aloud. "Just... tell me what you want me to do. Help me break the curse."

But the castle is silent, and my heart says nothing on the matter.

I tell Thorn about Ariel, but by the time he rushes back to the hall, she is gone, and does not come when he calls. I tell him she'll be back, but I wonder if her form is permanent. Maybe she isn't tangible all the time, like the sorceress' power.

I do not tell him what we spoke about, her final words brewing in my mind; *my fear is killing him*. My fear of what, exactly? Contrary to what I told Ariel, what I tell myself, I have so many. I don't see how any of them could hurt him any more than they would hurt me.

I return to the hall each night after he has gone to bed. I do not see Ariel, although I catch a few more snippets of the castle's history. I see it turning grey and lifeless. I see the fairy queen dismissing her subjects. The gardens lose their lustre, slowly begin to shrivel. The sun darkens. I see the fairy queen weeping over the ruined crib, and then...

Then she is gone, but the gardens begin to bloom again. What happened to her? Where did she go? Is she, like the shadows, still somewhere within the walls?

She was certainly the woman Thorn was talking to, but was he merely addressing her portrait, or something else?

I don't know what I'd do if I lost you both.

Who was she to him? If setting her free brings magic back, ensures that Thorn won't be alone when I leave, that we can see each other again... then I will gladly do it, if I know how. But... I will not deny the stab of jealousy I feel, at her being here in my stead, of her being Thorn's confidante, companion... whatever I am, whatever she was.

I want to ask Thorn more about her, but I'm afraid of his answer. I am afraid of who she was, and what we are becoming. I am afraid of what will happen when the magic runs out, if the curse is completed, if whatever lurks in the shadows is released, if she is free.

I think about what she said to the Queen, her clear disdain for mortals. I do not want to think about what she will do, but it haunts my thoughts.

Maybe I shouldn't leave. Maybe it's irresponsible of me now, now I know what I know. But what *do* I know? So many mysteries, so few absolutes. If life returned because of me, will it go when I do?

Perhaps it will take years, like it did the last time. Perhaps I will be able to find a way to break it back home. Perhaps it's not even me. Perhaps I can come back. #

Perhaps, perhaps, perhaps.

Sleep is impossible, so I turn to another mirror and check in on my family one more time. They are mostly all asleep. Hope and Beau are curled up in bed together. She has an open book against her chest. Papa is sleeping in his own bed for a change. Nanny is tucked up in bed, her hair in rags. I figure night time is not the best time to spy on Honour and Charles, so I skip to Freedom. He is still up, burning a candle in the tool shed he uses for painting. Red swirls around the canvas. The image is just as shocking as it is moving. Me. He is painting me. I press my fingers against the glass. A tear rolls down the painting's cheek. No, it is my own tear, my own reflection. I whisper his name, and an awful question rolls up inside of me.

I turn to the Mirror of the Past. "Show me... show me my family missing me."

I regret the words almost as quickly as they tumble out. I witness Honour sobbing in Charles' arms, the night of her wedding, still in her dress, crying that she should have waited. I see Freedom searching the woods, ten, fifty, a thousand times. I see Beau screaming to go too. I see Nanny coughing out tear-less sighs as she cooks, Hope sitting quietly in a snow-covered garden. Papa's is worse. He is crouched by Mama's grave. Snatches of awful conversation spasm about the room.

"Help us... guide her home... I failed you... I'm so sorry, Grace..."

And he wails, wails like he did that night over her coffin.

I go back to my room, horrified by what I have seen, what I have done, and know I cannot wait another six months. What-ever the cost, I have to go home.

Chapter Fifteen

A Flash of Lightning

I get so badly burned by the sudden burst of intense, summery heat over the next few days, that Thorn has to fetch a bucket of water from the fountain for me to bathe in. Ariel –or one of the other sprites– summons me an ointment made from aloe vera to soothe my raw skin. The following day I am flaky and brown. Thorn tries not to chuckle as I shed skin like a snake.

"You're enjoying this," I spit.

"I enjoy nothing that causes you pain," he returns. "But I do enjoy being the attractive one, for a change."

Attractive. Thorn thinks I'm attractive. I'm not sure he's ever said anything about my appearance before. I am not naïve; I have seen his eyes linger on me whenever I wear a particularly lovely dress. I have felt his gaze skim my bare flesh. But he has never said anything before, never really alluded to it.

You always look the same, to me. How do I look to him? Why should it even matter?

"Attractive, am I?" I poke.

"Well, compared to some," he teases. Perhaps something in my face changes, because he quickly adds, "You are very attractive, Rose, and well you know it."

My cheeks redden furiously, because until that moment, I hadn't really felt I was.

It has become so warm here, so hot, that the weather keeps me up at night. I twist and turn in my sheets, like a fish on land. The heat is suffocating. I have cycled around to that phase that must come once a year for all who live in countries with such defined seasons; I almost long for winter. I cannot remember why I hated the cold so. I can't even remember what it felt like to *be* cold. It cannot be as much of a hassle to get warm as it is to get cool. At least in winter, you can shelter under blankets, surround yourself with firelight, curl up beside your loved ones. Heat is inescapable.

It sounds foolish –and also impossible– but I like the idea of doing winter again with Thorn. Dozing beside the fire, my head in his lap. Our warmth pressed together. Our winter was over quickly, and we were not so close before. Things are different now, so different that I cannot imagine my winters – any seasons– without him. I will have others by my side, but they will not fill his shape. Wherever I go, whatever home I have, there shall always be a space beside my fire that Thorn is supposed to fill. That he *will* fill, for I shall feel his absence as solidly as a physical presence.

The heat also makes it difficult to concentrate. Despite the volumes at my bedside, I get through so little. I try to read whenever I can, try to fool myself into sleep by tiring my brain with words, but nothing sinks in. I will read pages only to realise I have read nothing; the words do not seep in, and the frustration tangles with the heat and makes me even more frustrated. I do not sleep properly, and I snap at Thorn in the mornings, which I think hurts me more than it hurts him, at this point. I am wasting my time with him. I have only two weeks left. I have not discovered anything new about the curse.

I think perhaps this is it. What more can I do? I try to spend more time with Thorn, enjoy the hours we have left, but all the minutes I spend with him are tinged with sadness, regret, annoyance. I could have done more. I should have tried harder. I should have been better to him. I should have cared more when I had the time.

One night, we sit together on the rooftop garden. It is breathtaking, illuminated by soft, shimmering candlelight. We are both trying to read, but neither of us are succeeding. It is too beautiful tonight to do anything but breathe and stare.

"Rose..." His voice is a whisper, and his eyes grow dark and serious. I can tell from the slight waver in his voice that he is nervous, but he does not turn away. Our gazes are fixed. "Are you happy here?"

I respond in an instant. "Why wouldn't I be?" I expect his expression to lighten, but the most I get is the twitch of a smile. He is still nervous.

"I know it is impossible for you to return the sentiment," he continues, "but... I'm very glad you came here."

For a moment, his words hang between us, while I unravel their meaning. Of course he is glad; I'm sure he was glad when the others came, too. A break in his solitude, his loneliness. But this is not what he is saying.

I smile, try to make light of it. "The experience has not been as awful as I first thought it would be." I play with the tassels on my shawl, trying to sound placid. I am not sure it works. I'm not sure I want it to. Despite myself, despite... my family... being here with Thorn is, is... "And... I'm very glad to have met you, too. I can't imagine ever not."

All pretence evaporates. I jump from my cushion and throw my arms around him, burying my face in his neck, fingers tight around his clothes. I want him to know, *need* him to know, just how much I mean it. I can't find the words. They don't exist. How to explain that even when torn from my home, my family, even when haunted, and miserable, I am *happy.* Happy to be with him, in whatever way I can.

Pressed up against Thorn's chest, I realise how broad he is.

I feel taut muscles under his shirt. His arms are big and strong, yet they hold me with such firm gentleness. No man I have ever known has touched me in such a way. Then I remember that Thorn is not a man, not exactly, although he is in all the ways that matter.

All the ways that matter, except one.

I inch back and place my head in his lap. A few precious moments tick by in harmonious silence. I am so comfortable, so sleepy, but I do not wish to sleep.

"Thorn?" I whisper.

"Yes, Rose?"

"I do desperately want to see my family again, but... I'm not exactly looking forward to saying goodbye."

Thorn strokes a lock of hair away from my face. Sad eyes gaze down at me. He murmurs something about missing me too. I can't quite make it out; I am virtually asleep. Thorn has to guide me back to my room. I half wish he would just scoop me up again. I do love being in his arms.

I know we have another ten nights together, but there is something about this one that feels like the last. When Thorn closes my door, he stops for a moment, and looks at me like he is afraid that this will be the last time we see one another.

"Rose," his voice sounds almost grave.

"Yes?"

"I know... I know my interaction with other people has been... limited, somewhat. But, I wish you to know that, of all the people I have ever met..."

"Yes?"

"I could meet every soul in the world, and you would still be my favourite."

For some reason, I cannot find the energy to tell him he is mine, too, and always will be. I kiss his hands instead, and slip back into my room.

I wake at first light, too early for breakfast. Knowing I am unlikely to fall asleep again, I decide to start penning a letter to Thorn, not knowing if I will ever give it to him. I think it is more an exercise in organising my thoughts.

Dear Thorn, I begin, then quickly scribble it out. No, *Dearest Thorn.*

I did not ask to come here, but now, I cannot imagine my life taking another route. I don't think I want to go. No, I know I want to go home. I do, so badly, but I am not ready to say goodbye to you.
I don't think I'll ever be ready.
In short, I cannot imagine my life without you. You are the greatest friend–

I stop. Friend is not right, too small a word. Companion? Too formal. Thorn walks this line between friend and family. He feels so much a part of me. I should have called him Stem or Root instead.

I leave the letter, scrunching it up and stuffing it furiously in my top drawer. I cannot say goodbye to him. I cannot.

I just want to be with him.

All right, says a voice, one that sounds much like my mother's, twinned, perhaps, with Honour's. They both used to speak like that, as if everything in the world were really quite simple. *Then do. Be with him.*

But that is not all I want. I want to be with him and *be with him.* Be with him in a way I can't. And that isn't just what I want, either. I want a way to be with him that means I can be with my family, too.

You can't have everything.

It isn't fair. Most people do not have to choose between their family and their... whatever Thorn is to me. Honour has both. But then, life isn't fair, and sometimes there is a choice that must be made.

I am not sure I can make this one.

I've read enough stories where a girl is placed in a similar predicament. I can't remember anywhere where she chooses her family. The story ends with her riding off into the sunset with the man of her dreams, and we are told it is a happy ending. But does the story truly end there? Why do we not get to see her two, three, five years later, when the ache of her loss has had time to broaden, and her passion lessen?

I do not miss my family as much as I did when I first came here, for certain, but I feel that is because the gap is closing. I know it won't be forever, that it won't even be long. If I could truly never see them again, that hole inside would widen until it engulfed me. What I feel for Thorn could not possibly fill it, could it?

Could it?

I would have said I could not have lived without my family, and yet I have. I have learned to live without them. I have even, miraculously, been happy.

So happy.

I can survive without them. There are moments, so many moments, where I am filled with wondrous, exalted bliss. I am sunbeams and clouds and cool, translucent waters. I am so many things I never was before. I know the shape and curve of my soul, here.

I can live without them.

I do not think I can live without him.

How did I manage all the years before? How will I manage all the years ahead?

Thorn doesn't come to breakfast. I find him in the ballroom instead. We rarely come in here, but it really is a beautiful room, especially with the blooms now cascading through the roof.

When he sees me, his face breaks into a smile. He races over and grabs my hands.

"Let's have a ball before you leave," he declares.

"A ball?"

"Yes. Fine dining, beautiful music, fabulous clothing, slightly clumsy dancing."

"I am not sure I have the time to create something fabulous to wear..."

"Anything you wear will be made fabulous by proximity."

"Oh, you–"

"So, what do you say?" He twirls me under his arm. Clumsy dancing indeed. Maybe from me.

"Yes," I say hurriedly. "I say yes."

I raid all of the wardrobes I can find in search of something beautiful, ball-worthy, and not completely uncomfortable and over the top. I find one –white– which might do, if I can cut away the ruffles. I would love to add some gold embroidery, but I am very conscious of time. So few days left. A lot of hours to waste on a project like this, when I have so little time left with him.

I put it away, deciding to focus on it when Thorn is in the dungeon during the next full moon. I will need something to pass the hours with. But today I want to spend with him.

It is a beautiful day, so, at lunchtime, we pack ourselves a picnic and head to the lake. It is humming with life, completely separate from that frozen wasteland it was when I arrived. A painter couldn't have made it any more perfect. After we eat, I glare at the still, shining water like one might a nemesis, and start unlacing my dress.

"What– what are you doing?" Thorn swallows nervously.

"Facing a fear," I declare, letting my loose layers drop to the ground until I am standing in nothing but my undergarments. "Would you like to join me?"

Thorn does not refuse. He doesn't deny me anything. He

pulls off his shirt and hurtles into the water fearlessly. I stay closer to the shallows. I am not a strong swimmer, and I have still not forgotten the face in the lake.

"You won't drown you know, if you go out of your depth," he says. "Not while I'm around."

"I know. I've just never been the best of swimmers."

"I'll teach you," Thorn declares.

We both ignore the fact that there is only so much he can do in the time we have left, and I let him pull me in. He holds me in his arms as we go further out. I am not afraid. Nothing bad can happen as long as he is here.

We spend several hours in the water, before lying down on the bank to dry. The evening rolls in, but I don't want to go back yet. Thorn catches a fish, which we fry on a fire we build ourselves, and dine on along with the remaining picnic.

That night, I pen a letter to Honour. I forget to mention anything about being home soon. My letter is filled with news of my swimming lessons, of Thorn and Bramble playing fetch in the shallows, of how it felt to stretch out in the sun beside them and feel like the warmth was coming from me. Time seemed to stop that afternoon.

It is moving exponentially now.

On the day of the full moon, Thorn and I pack enough food to last us an entire day and spend all of it outside. We eat breakfast in the orchard and read aloud summery poems. Then we head to the lake for another swimming session. I almost make it to the island in the centre, before I panic and have to turn back. Thorn doesn't tease me, this time.

We have a long, slow, hazy lunch, savouring every delectable morsel and crumb and treating ourselves to a delicate champagne. It pairs perfectly with everything.

We try to pretend this isn't likely the last time we'll do this, what with Thorn usually needing a day to recover from the change, and the ball to plan. We try to keep the conversation light. We discuss the books we are reading, what we will eat for dinner. We sing songs, and ignore anything about the future. Anything that sounds like goodbye.

The sun slithers behind the mountains. Darkness trails in, not far behind. Fireflies blossom along the surface of the lake. The moon, larger and more intrusive than ever, glares down.

"Rose–" he starts.

"Not yet," I reply, snuggling into his chest.

"It's time."

I nod silently, and pack up our things. There is no point in going back to the castle; we head straight for the crypt. I haven't told him yet, but I am not planning on leaving him tonight. I will wait, safely, by his side, all the way to morning. Just for a few more hours. I will bring down my sewing and a dozen candles and work by that pale light, whiling away the hours until Thorn returns to me.

A storm rumbles overhead. Bramble growls.

"Head back to the castle, boy," I rub his head.

Bramble looks up at the sky doubtfully, and then at Thorn, as if weighing up his options.

"Go on," I urge. "It's all right."

He soon scampers off, his head bowed slightly, as if he's ashamed of abandoning his mistress.

"Perhaps you should join him," suggests Thorn. "You don't want to get caught in a storm."

"I don't mind."

Thankfully, he says nothing else about leaving him tonight. I hope he was serious about me helping him. I hope he wants me there. I am more a lick-your-wounds-in-silence, type. I do not like to share my pain. That doesn't mean I don't want to help elevate others'. Specifically, his. I don't think I've ever felt another person's pain so keenly before.

Lightning splits through the sky, followed shortly by a downpour. The day has been so hot that it sizzles on the stone.

We are still five minutes or so from our destination.

"Quickly, over here–" Thorn pulls me into a little band-stand, sheltering me under his broard arms. I do not mind getting wet, but I do not mind being here, either. We do not have long. "It might blow over soon," he says assuredly.

I place my head against his chest. "I'm in no hurry."

We wait as long as we dare, the lightning and thunder growing closer and closer, and then finally we race out. Thorn holds my hand as we dash towards the graveyard.

I see the flash seconds before he does.

"Thorn!" I scream.

Lightning strikes a nearby tree, as straight and sure as an arrow. The whole thing comes crashing down. In an instant, Thorn's hand is yanked from mine. The whole of him vanishes, swallowed under branch and bark. I smell the smoke before I see the flames rising at the roots. My scream is lost under a roar of thunder. I dive into the foliage, hands searching madly for him, touching nothing but lifelessness.

"I'm... I'm all right–" comes his muffled reply. A hand reaches for me, a face. "I'm... I'm stuck. My leg–"

"Thorn, the tree is on fire."

"I know. Don't worry. I think I can get myself out–"

"It's really on fire!" I search desperately for the rest of him, breaking what I can. Finally, I find his leg. It is trapped firmly under the trunk of the tree, a thick branch is wedged right into it. Even in this light, I can see the blood pooling onto the ground.

"Oh, oh no..."

"Rose, Rose! It's all right." He fumbles desperately for my hand, clutching it closely. "In a few minutes, I'll change. I'm stronger then. I can get myself out. But listen– you cannot be here when that happens."

I can taste salt in my mouth. I think Thorn is shaking, but then I realise it's me. "I am not leaving you like this!"

"Rose, you have to."

"The tree is on fire and you're bleeding really badly–"

"I'm aware. It's fine, I can't feel it–"

"I can."

"Please," he groans. "Go back to the castle. I need to know you're safe."

"Thorn... you could die."

"*Please*, Rose!" His voice is becoming more taut. Suddenly, his face contorts. He curls inwards. "*Rose!*"

I nod because I cannot speak, and then I close my eyes, because there's no way I can move unless I can't see him. His barely-contained screams rip through the air between us as I run, and it feels like my bones are breaking.

Crash.

Another tree swerves in front of me, cutting my path. I turn left. I can get in through the kitchen.

Lightning strikes the steps before I can reach them. A chasm opens between me and the door. This cannot be happening–

I wheel back towards the graveyard. I can hide in the dungeon. I am mere inches from the door when the statue beside it explodes. I crush down on my knees and try to pull apart the wreckage. The stone is white hot.

Against the pounding wind, I hear something growling. A dark shape darts behind a tomb. Another flash of lightning illuminates a trail of blood. At least I know he's escaped.

There's a ruined chapel a few yards away. It has no door, nothing the lightning can attack. If I can get in there, I should be safe from this weather. I can barricade myself in the crypt there, wait it out till morning–

I make a dash for it. The storm is relentless. Each statue I pass explodes, rubble litters my way. This is not natural.

Thorn is following me, but I don't turn to look. I mustn't.

I dive into the chapel, cursing its lack of doors, and charge towards the crypt entrance. A window shatters. Pews skid. My foot hits a seat and I go flying, wrenching myself up just in time to see Thorn sailing over me. He lands in front of my escape. Not thinking, I move backwards, tripping into the debris.

My back hits wall. There is nowhere for me to go.

"Thorn–" I hold up my hands. "It's me, it's Rose. You know me, I know you do."

He does not appear to. He creeps towards me, his back leg dragging. Snarling, growling. No trace of the real him. Not a flicker of recognition.

"Thorn, you don't want to hurt me. You were willing to risk your life to keep me safe… I was willing to risk mine to save you." He does nothing but move closer. "Thorn, dearest, just listen–"

He is so close, I am running short of ideas. I am terrified. I can't let him hurt me. I don't want to die, but if given the choice, I would choose any death other than this. He will die if he kills me. I know, because I feel the same.

Do something. Anything!

When he was chasing me before, nothing stopped him. Not my screams, not the door, not even me slicing his arm. He continued his pursuit all the way to–

To the chamber. He stopped hammering against the door when the music box was playing. I do not have the music box now, but I remember the tune.

I start to hum.

He slows, but does not stop. I raise my voice against the crescendo of the storm, louder and louder with each crash of lightning. Another window shatters, then another. The wind tears at the building, howling, screaming, but he pays no attention. His eyes are fixed on me, like a sailor's might fix on a lighthouse.

There is the tiniest, faintest flicker. He pauses.

"Thorn?"

For a second, his eyes look blue. His mouth opens, not to snarl, but as if to speak.

I keep singing.

Thorn shakes his head, as if trying to wriggle the song out of his mind. He snorts, splutters. I call out his name.

He looks at me, somewhere between monster and man,

and then leaps out the window.

I sit in the dark, covered in tiny shards, the rain still battering relentlessly against the roof. I hear him howling in the distance, louder and more lonely than any storm.

Slowly, carefully, I have to get up. I shake the glass off my clothing. I am unhurt, bruised at most. There is no way I can risk returning to the castle, no way I can help him now.

As I walk towards the crypt, I feel like I am stepping into my own grave. When I close the gate, it makes a sound like a nail against a coffin.

Chapter Sixteen

The Solstice

Somehow, I grab a few hours of sleep, but it does not feel like rest. I half-wake continuously, treading the lines between sleeping and waking. I think I dream, but I cannot be sure. My thoughts are jumbled, but my heart is pounding, and my clothes coil around me.

I wake at dawn. A blue, watery light filters through the bars, swamping the flagstones. The minute it is light, I get up and leave my makeshift prison. The chapel is awash with glass, and dotted with dark droplets of blood. I follow the trail outside. It is a little hard in places, obscured by the gravel and glass. I know I should be relieved –this means he is not bleeding badly, right?– but fear still gnaws at my insides. I shall not be relieved until I find him.

I hear Bramble barking in the distance, and call out to him until he appears. He does not come to me, but continues to yelp until I follow him into the orchard. A dark shape lies slumped under one of the apple trees, in ragged, blood-streaked clothing. He moves a little, lifting up his head until his eyes rest on mine, but no relief comes.

"Oh, Thorn..."

He is still when I approach him, still when I reach out to touch his matted hair. His eyes are deep blue now, but they are far away and glazed over. He is damp, clammy, and completely unaware.

"Rose?" he croaks eventually. "W–what happened? Are you all right? Why am I–"

"I'm fine," I say quickly. *"You're* fine. You are going to be fine."

I wrap my arms around his neck and hug him gently. He does not hold me back. I am terrified of hurting him, but tug gingerly at his arm and pull him up. He follows my motion, rising to his feet, but collapses seconds later, whimpering. His leg is bloody and oozing. He cannot place any weight on it.

"Thorn!"

Bramble circles round to his other side, slips under his arm, and licks his cheek. Thorn lacks the energy to even acknowledge him. His eyes keep circling back into their sockets.

"Help, please!" I call out.

In a matter of seconds, the three little fairies appear out of nowhere. They buzz under his arms, and together, the four of us somehow pull him to his feet. It is a long, slow limp back to the castle, and several times Thorn stops, completely lost, as if he has forgotten I am even here.

I finally get him into his room and sit him down on the bed, where he goes limp, resting against the bedpost with a dazed, unfocused gaze. It is impossible to get him into the bath, but the little sprites summon a basin of hot water, presumably from the fountain. They hover uselessly by his side, while I pick out glass from his wounds with a pair of tweezers. Every so often, he makes a slight moan when I remove a particularly large piece. It is the only sound he makes.

I clean the wounds as best I can, smearing them with ointment provided by the fairies, and bandaging the worst of the ones. His leg is a horrible, pulsing mess. My basin is dark by the end of the process. He looks almost like a mummy, swathed in bandages.

He did this to himself for me. He is hurt because of me.

I reason that this is the lesser of two evils, that this is what Thorn would have wanted, that it is not my fault. But that does not change the fact that he is hurt. Because of me.

I take one of his hands in mine and kiss it. "Thorn," I whisper. "Thorn, my dearest, I am so sorry. If I had only–"

A finger reaches down and wipes a tear from my cheek. "You're safe," he says softly. "You are all that matters."

"You matter," I say. It hurts to speak. I'm going to start sobbing soon and if I do, I will not stop. *You matter so much.*

I put my head against his neck and breathe him in. A soft hand presses against my back. I refuse to let myself cry any more in front of him. He is in more pain than I am. My tears are useless.

"I'm just going to get something," I say, easing back. "I won't be long."

Thorn nods. I know he doesn't want me to leave, but I need to collect myself. I go back to my room, change my clothes, tidy myself up. I barely recognise the girl in the mirror, covered in dirt and dry blood, hopelessly pale. I take a minute to freshen up and erase any trace of my tears, before grabbing a book and heading back.

Thorn is still resting against the bedpost when I return, and I have been gone much longer than I expected. He startles when I walk in. Bramble is lying at his feet, head in his paws, looking incredibly helpless and forlorn. He is a perfect reflection of how I feel.

Thorn blinks. "You came back."

"Where else would I go?" I touch his cheek.

"Elsewhere," he mumbles. "I'm always... so scared... that you will go."

I'm not entirely sure what he means by this, so instead I pull back the covers and ease him towards the pillows. He says nothing, eyes circling up towards the ceiling. He is burning, and I know that means I should try and keep him warm.

When I turn around to grab an extra blanket from his nest beside the hearth, I see the fairies have brought in a tray of hot soup, enough for two, and a bone for Bramble. They hover cautiously around the bowl, faint in colour.

"Thank you," I say.

They move over to the mantelpiece, and I know they are watching him too. They always have been. I bring the tray over to Thorn's bedside and take a spoon towards his lips. He manages a few mouthfuls, but no more. I can only do a few myself.

Thorn slips into an uneasy sleep, shaking and muttering incoherently. All I can do is be here.

I read my book aloud, because I haven't the strength to read it silently, listening to him. This keeps me focused, distracted. It is *Tromeo and Lessida*, his favourite. I finished re-reading it months ago, but kept it beside my bed for some reason.

I wonder why it's his favourite? It's not a wholly remarkable story. Tromeo is a rich young nobleman, and Lessida is an intelligent healer. They are from very different worlds and are very different people, but despite this, find themselves falling in love. Then a war comes and separates them both for several years. Both believing the other to be dead or far out of reach, they attempt to move on with their lives, never forgetting each other despite the time and distance. They are only reunited with each other after several decades, when their other halves have died and their children have grown.

I suppose there might be something romantic in the longevity of their love, but it never sat well with me that they lost so much time together. Some time later –the minutes blur together– Thorn wakes with a start.

"What? What is it?"

Thorn is on the other side of the bed, pressed against the poster, breathing heavily. His eyes are wide in fear.

"Thorn?"

"You're all right," he breathes.

"Of course I am. Why wouldn't I be? It's you I'm worried

about."

The fear in Thorn's eyes slowly dissipates. His shoulders relax.

"I thought... I must have been dreaming..."

My heart a little tighter than it was a minute ago, I sit up and inch forward to place a hand on his hot cheek, stroking his hair. "I'm fine," I tell him. "You aren't. Lie back down again."

He makes no motion to move. His eyes are glazed over, his thoughts far off. It scares me, to see him so helpless, when I want so badly to help him. My heart feels like it's spread to every corner of my body, and each part of it aches.

I notice Thorn's hair is all stuck up, down one entire side of his body, the side that was pressed to mine.

I smile a little. "You have bed hair," I tell him, making a feeble attempt to pat it down. "It's sweet."

Thorn's eyes slowly, briefly, catch mine. "Why aren't you afraid of me?" he asks. "Why are you so sure I won't hurt you?"

I swallow. The question hurts me. I hate it when he hates himself. "Because I know you," I say, and this time, I lean forward and pull him carefully into my arms. I kiss the top of his cheek, smooth his hair. Slowly, he loosens, allowing me to lie him back down. He feels as small and weak as a child. I lie down next to him, a little apart, even though I desperately want to take him in my arms again. His hand reaches out and closes around mine feebly. "Rose?"

"Yes?"

"Please don't leave."

I stroke his face with my free hand. "I'm not going anywhere."

It is night time when I wake. The clock reads two in the morning. Thorn is still sleeping, although it looks far from peaceful. Having only had a bowl of soup in the past twenty-four hours, I find myself hungry. Luckily, there is more food laid out for us. A bit of cheese and bread. I couldn't handle much more.

I walk around the room to stretch my legs, then I sit by the window and wait for the dawn. Any more attempts at sleep would be fruitless. Black turns to blue, the night thins and pales, and faint, watery light falls from the heavens. Thorn wakes shortly after.

"Have you been there all night?"

I give him a smile almost as liquescent as the sun this grey morning. "I slept," I tell him. "Have no fear."

I cross the room to check his forehead, and pretend he feels a little cooler. "How do you feel?"

"A little better," he says, not all that convincingly.

"You seem a little more coherent today."

"I'm sorry if I worried you."

"You did," I say. "But I'm all right as long as you're all right."

I bring over the breakfast tray, and we eat a little together. Thorn can still only manage the smallest of amounts.

"My leg hurts," he tells me.

"I'll change your bandages for you."

A fresh set is summoned, along with more warm, tingly waters. I inspect some of his other injuries first, finding them healing to my satisfaction. The leg, if possible, looks worse.

"Does the fountain water heal infections?" I ask, trying to sound light-hearted.

"Usually," Thorn replies. "Why?"

"Just wondering if I should boil the water first, is all."

Thorn smiles a little at this, and I finish cleaning the wound as best I can. I wish there was more I could do for the pain.

"Any better?"

"A little, thank you."

"Is there anything I can do?"

"Just... stay with me."

"Well," I say breezily, crawling up onto the bed beside him. "That I can manage."

"Are you... planning on sitting there?"

"Unless you'd rather I sit somewhere else?"

"No," says Thorn quickly. "No where else."

I slip my hand into his and fold it around his middle, and he pretends to sleep, to spare me the pain of seeing his.

The next few days trickle by. Thorn does not improve. His appetite lessens, and he becomes cold and shivery. I barely leave his side, barely sleep, barely eat myself. I read to him, sew when he dozes, try and make light whenever I can. He does not say much, but at one point, around the third day, he turns to me.

"We may have to think of an alternative plan."

For a moment, I'm worried he's hallucinating. "Plan for what?"

"Our ball," he replies, matter-of-factly. "I'm not entirely sure I'll be up for dancing. I won't be nearly as charming and graceful as I usually am."

I smile at him from my seat by the window. "You must be feeling better, if you're making jokes."

"Jokes? I'm expressing extreme remorse. I was looking rather forward to the whole thing."

So was I.

"I will miss seeing you in your dress."

"I can still wear a dress. Shall I fetch it now?"

I do not fetch it. Instead, we talk and laugh for a little bit longer, and then Thorn drifts quietly into a deep sleep.

He appears to be improving, over the next day or two, and although his leg remains in a bad way, he eats a little more, and is chattier and more coherent. I don't relish the idea of leaving him injured, but at least he is getting better. On my last night, we make an effort to do something, anything. A decent meal arrives, we play board games in bed, and then lie there listening to beautiful music play on our music box. We talk until we run out of energy, both avoiding anything that sounds like goodbye.

"Rose?" Thorn asks tiredly. "You won't... you won't leave before I wake, will you?"

"Of course not," I tell him, almost crossly.

"Good," he relaxes a little more. "I have a few things to tell you, before you go."

"I might have a few things, too."

His eyes close, and I can feel sleep pulling at mine, too, but I don't want to sleep. I want to stay here, watching him, being with him. Planning how on earth I'll say goodbye.

I don't want to.

But sleep comes anyway, and all too soon dawn invades the room, and my eyes drift up to the window to a sight I have almost forgotten. A stream dividing a meadow, leading up a wood. Behind the wood, I can see the dim outline of a spire.

Home.

The clock on the mantle chimes 6. I let out a little sob. We have lost our final time together. I pry myself from Thorn's side and step towards the glass. *Go away.*

I look back to the bed. Thorn is shivering. How can I leave him like this? But he said the way would be open for hours. We still have time. Perhaps he just needs a little more rest, he'll wake up soon, a little tired and dozy, but clearly well enough. We can say a quick goodbye and then–

And then what? I leave this place forever? I promise to return in six months? How can I possibly leave him like this? How can I leave him at all?

I creep back to his bedside and put my hand against his head. He is burning up.

"Thorn?" There is a touch of desperation in my voice that I cannot hide.

He does not respond, does not give any indication that he notices me at all. I give him a shake. "Thorn! Wake up! *Please!*"

Still nothing. I race around to the other side of the bed and yank his leg out of the covers. He lets out a low, painful moan. The flesh under the wound is swollen beyond recognition.

"Oh, oh no..."

One of the sprites hovers overhead. It is Ariel, I am sure. I look at her, and her little form bobs. She knows what I do not say. I run to the Hall of Mirrors, arriving breathlessly at her frame.

"Oh Rose–" she flutters.

"Help me!"

"I don't know how–"

"There must be something here, some kind of pharmacy or something–"

"There is, but–"

"Take me there."

"But–"

"Now!"

Her little form dashes away down the corridor, almost too quick to follow. She leads me to a small study not far from the kitchen. It is in complete disarray. Books are everywhere, the shelves, the desk, the windowsill, the bed. Illustrations of herbs are pinned on the walls. The medicine cabinet is a mess, bottles of every size and colour, all of which have labels faded beyond recognition.

"Dammit!"

"I tried to tell you," Ariel hisses, "We've been raiding the supplies for days–"

"Then we'll make something!" I look around at the books. One of them must hold something helpful, but I do not have time to look through them all. Ariel buzzes around the room, scanning every spine.

"*This one, this one!*" she squeaks, tapping on a thick tome.

I haul it off the shelf and slam it onto the nearby desk. I head straight for the index, skimming for the word *infection*. I have never turned pages faster.

"*A salve to treat infection,*" I read aloud. I scan through the ingredients, only recognising what some of them are. "Ariel, I don't know most of these ingredients!"

"I do," she asserts, "and we have most of them."

"*Most* of them?"

"Enough. We have enough. If we brew it with the water from the fountain–" She heads towards the cabinet, pulling out various bottoms, unstoppering them. "This, and this, and this–" she flutters back towards the book. "Ah."

"Ah?"

"We need Aspira. It's a herb. It used to grow in the garden."

"*Used to?*"

"I haven't seen it in a while, but it might still be there–"

"What does it look like?"

She hovers around one of the illustrations on the wall. "Like this."

"Find the rest of the ingredients," I say, tearing it loose. "I'll be back."

How many hours have I spent out in these gardens? How many days? I do not know this plant. I've never seen it before, but I have to find it. I have to.

I race out into the grounds, heading immediately for the herb garden next to the kitchens. I clutch at every stem, every leaf, holding it against the image. Nothing matches.

Remembering the untamed things that clamber around the stone, I rush to the graveyard. Wild lavender taunts me. The ivy mocks me. Nothing tries to aid me, nothing at all. I have a faint memory of spasms of herb-looking things growing down by the banks in the river, and dash there next. Nothing but reeds and rushes. The woodlands turn up little better. Nothing grows wild in the maze, I know. And the rest of the gardens are so stiff and manicured I am sure I would have noticed something, anything.

If Thorn dies, I will die. I may continue to breathe, and my heart may continue to beat, but whatever made me, me, will be as cold as he is. I will not lose a part of myself, but all of it. I will be a shell without a soul.

I search the illustration for some other clue, anything. *Aspira,* says the faded grey writing at the bottom. *Often found growing among wild flowers.*

Wild flowers. The meadow.

My chest feels like it is breaking. I have never run so fast in my life. My sides are splitting, but I barely notice. I have no idea how much time I have. The warm, tall grass rushes up to greet me. I can hear the stream, see it even, peering through the gathering fog. So close to home.

I grab fistfuls of the meadow in my hands, pulling it up, frantically searching. I see poppies and buttercups and cow-slips and sorrel. I see nothing like the spidery leaves of this Aspira.

A voice calls to me through the fog. *"Rose!"*

Through the mist, on the other side of the stream, I see a tall, grey figure. My imagination, surely.

"Rose!" The voice is clearer now.

"Freed?" I can almost make out his face. "Freedom, I'm here!"

"Come here!" he calls. "Come *home!*"

"I'm coming!" I cry. "I'm coming, I promise! It just... it might take me a while. I'm safe, I promise! I'll be home soon!"

"Where are you?"

The fog swallows him up. I cannot stop for him now. My eyes fall onto a sparse patch of spidery leaves. They are so small... I gather up a fistful. Is this it? It looks so much like it, but there is so little...

It will have to be enough. It must be. I race back to the castle, straight into the pharmacy. Ariel has gathered all the in-gredients in a bowl. "Did you find it?" she asks.

I hold it up. "I think so. I hope it's enough."

"Me too."

I quickly wash and strip the herb, slamming it into the bowl and mashing it up frantically. Ariel gushes instructions as I add it to the pan of simmering water. The other two sprites appear to ferret it upstairs. I race back to join them, heart pounding against every inch of all that I am.

All three little forms hover over Thorn's immobile body, trying to tip a teacup of the liquid into his mouth. Ariel leaves the others to gesture towards a pot filled with the dregs.

"Quickly, Rose, apply the paste!"

I throw back the covers. There is the quietest of moans when I hold his leg. He is still alive.

Not needing to be told twice, I unravel the bandage and apply the medicine in thick clumps. I smear it over the wound, covering the whole of it. Thorn barely makes a sound, not even as I wrap the bandage tightly around him.

Something clinks behind me. The fairies are refilling the cup. "He won't drink!" one of them calls out desperately.

I snatch the whole teapot from mid-air and press it to his lips, prying them open. The liquid trickles down his cheeks.

"Thorn, you have to drink this." My voice is stretched. "*Please*, Thorn!"

"Tilt his head!"

This is no easy feat. He is so heavy. A dead weight. No, not dead, not yet. In the end, I scramble into the bed, stick my knees under his shoulders, and pull him into my arms. I tilt his head back in my lap and ram the spout into his mouth. Water creeps out of the corners. "Please!"

"It's not working."

"It has to!"

I need to get him to swallow. I need to get him to wake up. I barely know what I am doing when I wrench away the pot and cover his mouth with my own.

Wake up. Drink. Breathe.

Ariel gasps.

I breathe into Thorn, and I feel his own chest rise with my breath. His body moves under mine. I pull back, he splutters, coughs up most of the liquid, and then looks at me.

I wrap a hand around his neck, placing the pot back against his mouth.

"You need to drink," I tell him.

He nods, and slowly and carefully, he takes it.

Chapter Seventeen

A Bitter Kiss of Home

Thorn falls into the deepest of slumbers, but I stay where I am, holding him tightly. His chest rises and falls in the sweetest of rhythms, and his heartbeat plays the most beautiful of songs. My own is still lodged somewhere in my throat.

"I think it's working," says Ariel. "Thank you, Rose."

I stroke the hair from his face. "I couldn't let him die." I drag my eyes away from him to look at her impish, glowing form. "How... how is it that I can hear you now?"

"I have always been talking to you," she says promptly. "It is about time you heard me."

It certainly is. "I don't mean to sound ungrateful," I continue, "because you helped me save him, but couldn't you just have magicked the Aspira out of nowhere?"

Her little form shakes. "We can't actually summon things out of nowhere. All the food is placed in stores beneath the castle. It's preserved with magic, and we use magic to cook it, but we don't create it. You have to know where what you're summoning is."

This makes me feel guilty for all the food I've wasted, and I wonder how much food is left. Perhaps Thorn and I should attempt to refill the stores now that I... now that I am trapped here for another six months. The gateway must be closed by now, but I do not have the strength to check on it. I ask Ariel to go in my stead, and she flutters over to the window.

"I'm so sorry, Rose."

"It's all right," I lie. "It was worth it." This, at least, is the truth.

"You should tell him that, when he wakes."

The other two fairies drift down from the mantelpiece, where they have been loyally attached for some time. "We'll save introductions for tomorrow, bring up some food, and let you rest," Ariel decides. "It's been a long day."

I thank her, glad of the stillness, the quiet. It is just the two of us now. Minutes thumb by to the slow, steady sound of Thorn's breathing. I half-sleep, dozing by his side, more restful than I have felt in days.

"Rose...?" Thorn shudders awake, his eyelids half-open.

"I'm here."

"I wanted to tell you, before you went... I couldn't bear letting you go before you knew... you should know–"

"Ssh, it's all right, dearest. I'm here now. I'm not going anywhere. Rest. Just rest."

I take his hand in mine, and then, to ease him or myself, I begin to sing.

"She didn't say it. He was dying and she didn't say it. Why won't she say it?"

"It's so obvious she cares for him."

"Maybe not enough."

"She gave up going home for him. Also, did you see that kiss?"

"That was not a kiss."

"It looked like a kiss–"

"Did you see that man in the meadow? He was very attractive."

"Ariel! Priorities!"

"I haven't seen a man in a very long time, all right?"

"This is not the time–"

"She's trapped here for another six months. He's in no danger. We've got time."

"He's in no danger? Do you think that storm was a natural occurrence?"

I wake up to the three fairies chattering above a breakfast tray.

"I can hear you, you know."

Two of them hide behind a teapot in surprise. The remaining one giggles. I look back at Thorn, sleeping silently beside me. My arm is numb from holding him all night. I shuffle back and flex it.

"Thank you all, for your help last night. It's good to hear you, finally."

The one with the littlest voice emerges from behind a teacup. She hovers there, shyly. "I'm Ophelia," she says.

"Lovely to meet you."

"I'm Margaret," says the third, with the stiff, proper voice. "That was a very brave thing you did last night, my dear."

"Wouldn't you have stayed?"

There is a slight pause before she replies. "Yes," she says firmly, "I would have. But my reasons for saving him... might not be the same as yours."

"I don't know what you mean."

"By the time you do, it may be too late."

Thorn stirs.

"Well," Margaret says quickly. "We have plenty to be getting on with. Come on, girls..."

With a quick goodbye, all three of them vanish with a pop. Thorn yawns, opening his eyes. "Who are you talking to?"

"I believe they said their names were Ariel, Ophelia and Margaret."

"They can talk again?"

"Quite a bit, apparently."

"We'll never have a moment's peace now."

He leans back against the pillows, pretending he isn't thrilled. Suddenly, his brow tightens into a frown. "What... what day is it?" he asks.

I swallow. There is a hard lump in my throat. "The gateway opened yesterday," I say quickly.

"Oh Rose, I didn't know–"

"It's all right."

"You should have–"

"It's all right."

"I'm so sorry–"

"It's all right!"

But it doesn't feel all right. It doesn't feel right at all. Suddenly, my family's faces come rushing up in my head, and the thought of having to spend another day, let alone another six months, hits me like a punch to the gut. I double over, and begin to sob. Thorn puts his arms around me while I shake and my heart splinters everywhere.

I cry for what feels like hours, almost as erratically as I did when Mama died. Thorn says nothing while I sob. He holds me tightly, stroking my hair. I go completely limp. Eventually, my cries subside. A little bit of me creeps back.

"I think... I think I'm done now."

Thorn looks at me uncomfortably. "You... you should have gone."

"I couldn't."

"Why not?" His voice sounds like a child, asking a question when they are afraid of the answer.

"You shouldn't ask me that."

"I'm sorry," he says quietly. There is a long pause before he speaks again. "Is it because you promised me that you wouldn't leave, because I didn't mean–"

"What sort of person do you think I am?" I hiss, scuttling to my feet. "Do you think I am devoid of feeling? Do you think I am cold, heartless? That I have come to feel nothing for you? I was scared you were going to *die,* Thorn! I could never have left you! I didn't... the thought didn't even cross my mind, you know? All... all I could think about was you. If I could think at all."

There's more, so much more. Somewhere there are the words, *I don't want to live in a world without you in it.* I try to calm myself. Breathe. I am not mad at him. I am mad at the situation.

"Rose–" he says gingerly.

"It's all right," I tell him. It isn't. It can't be. But it will be soon. "I just... I need to..."

I sweep out of the room. I do not look back.

Did you see that kiss?

It didn't feel like a kiss, when I did it. It was more a... necessity. A way to shock him into waking, deliver the medicine. It didn't have the softness of the one and only other kiss of my life. It didn't feel romantic, just hard, and tasted only of the bitter leaves of the potion. No fireworks, no sunshine and starlight, which I feel should occur whenever you kiss someone that you...

I punch the pillow furiously, and my thoughts turn finally towards the storm. I knew, before I overheard the others talking, that it was far from natural. Something tried to kill Thorn. Tried to kill *me.*

And Freedom was in the meadow. Ariel saw him too. He was there, begging me to come home. It hurts more that it was him, the sibling I fought with the most. I am reminded of the portrait he was painting of me, as if he were afraid he might forget my face. If that is how Freedom feels about my departure... how must the rest of them feel? What if they are desperately missing me, frightened and worried every single day?

Inching forward, I lift my head to face the mirror in the far corner of the room. I half expect to see another face, pale and crowned with horns, but instead I see only an unremarkable young girl with reddish hair. The reflection does not show how much I am breaking.

I return to Thorn's side the following morning, sick of the silence and the thoughts of my family. I silently sweep into his room and deposit myself in the chair beside the hearth, tucking my legs underneath me and whipping out a book.

Thorn stares at me solidly for several moments. "Are you still cross with me?"

I raise my eyes from above the brim of my book. "You should know by now that I am rarely cross with you."

"I didn't know that." Thorn says, blinking. "What... what are you angry about, then?"

"It's difficult to explain."

"Could you–"

"Thorn," I say quietly, "please don't."

He nods and doesn't say anything at all for another few minutes. "The fairies have been in," he remarks off-handedly. "I never... I never thought to hear their voices again. I truly believed they were lost to this world."

"Who are they, to you?" I ask.

"My family," he replies. "Or as near as I had to one, until..."

"Until you met me?"

"Yes." Thorn swallows.

"It's all right," I say. "I feel the same."

Neither of us says what we both must be thinking: I already have a family, a family that is missing me. A family I long to return to.

Thorn is bedridden for another three days. He says it is because his leg needs more time to recover, but I can tell he is affected a little more than he lets on. Although he insists he is fine, he allows me to fuss over him a little, which I have to say I enjoy.

One night, I doze off in the chair in his room, reading *Tromeo and Lessida*. I know I should probably get up and go to my own room, but I prefer being by his side, and if he knows I am awake he might insist. Now that he no longer needs a nursemaid, it is not proper for me to sleep here with him.

A now-familiar buzz sounds from across the room.

"Hello again, Ariel," Thorn's voice is layered with warmth. "Where have you been, today?"

"Fixing the mess you two have made in the gardens. Ophelia is quite beside herself."

"I really am very sorry–"

She groans. "Rose is right. You apologise far too much."

"And how long have you been talking to Rose for, Ariel?"

"A while. She's a better listener than you. I like her."

The smile in Thorn's voice is palpable. "I'm glad. I like her too."

I know she has no real body, but I imagine her rolling her eyes. "Yes, we noticed. She's your *favourite soul in this whole wide world*."

"I did not say that."

"I'm fairly sure you did. It's a little over the top, don't you think?"

"No," Thorn says quietly, "it isn't."

"You two are impossible. Good night. Don't waste the next six months. Margaret is making a dress for this belated ball. PS

SAY SOMETHING TO HER."

"Goodnight, Ariel."

"Goodnight, sweet prince," she says mockingly. "Sleep well."

By the time Thorn is well enough to go outside again, the gardens have been transformed. They are more beautiful than ever. We wander down to the lake, and take a path we have never taken before. It was completely overgrown a week ago. The fairies have been busy.

The path stops just before the shore. There is a small stone building there, guarded by two statues of grand, regal fairies. It is clearly a tomb, but different from the others in the main graveyard. I have the strangest sense it wasn't built by tool. It has been crafted by some other means, for some other purpose.

I look to Thorn, and without waiting for any kind of permission, try the door. I expect to see something bleak, eerie, dismal. Instead, I find myself in a smooth, round chamber, filled with natural light. The roof, what is left of it, is glass, and ivy tumbles in and wraps around the opening of a shallow pool. It looks almost natural, but there is a clear, man-made incline, and a statue, sitting with its legs half in the water. A speck of light touches his half-hidden face.

"Incredible," I breathe.

"I had forgotten this," says Thorn, moving into the room. His voice has a strange, unearthly quality. He steps forward, a hand reaching towards the statue. At the last minute, just as his nails touch the stone, he pulls back. I am not sure if I imagine it, but I think his hand trembles.

"What is it?" I ask.

"Nothing," he replies, a little too quickly. He turns his back and looks up at the ceiling, admiring what, I don't know.

I move closer to the statue and pull the ivy from its face. It is male, I realise, as I work down. He is broad-shouldered, with long limbs, elegantly postured. He reminds me of a merman. There is something beautiful in the way he sits, so naturally although he is carved of stone. But it is his face I admire most. It is strong, with a straight nose, large eyes, cheekbones both soft and angular. At first, I think he is familiar, but the moment quickly scuttles away.

"Who is he?" I ask.

Thorn still does not turn around. "His name was Leo Valerdene," he says, after a pause so long I wonder if he will answer at all. "Or so the story says. He was a great lover of nature who one day, quite by accident, wandered into the realm of the fairies. The Queen of the Fairies found him bathing in the lake, and they were instantly smitten with each other. Now, the Queen of the Fairies had had many lovers in her lifetime, but none like him. They courted for many years, and, eventually, she decided to make him her husband. There was some outrage, of course. A human? In the court of fairies? For years he had been looked on as little more than a favoured pet, someone who would leave as soon as the Queen tired of him. But now, after centuries of life, she had finally chosen a husband, and a human no less. Would they even be able to have children, provide an heir for the throne? Fairies can live a long time, and as such, have never been the most fertile of creatures. But the Queen cared not for any of this. She loved him so. The court came to understand this."

"They accepted him?"

"They were married for ten years."

"What happened then?"

Thorn pauses. "He died," he says eventually. "The Queen built this place to mark his tomb, and remember the moment she had fallen in love with him."

"It is a beautiful tomb."

"I am told it is a beautiful story."

"You don't like it?"

"I don't like stories that end in death."

This, at least, I can understand. I reach out to touch Leo's face, imagining it when it was made of flesh. It feels a little wrong, touching someone else's lover, but there is something in this face that calls to me.

Thorn has turned around. "Do you find him handsome?" There is no note of jealousy in his voice, no note of anything.

"Yes," I say.

Thorn snorts, almost irritably, and sweeps out of the room.

That night, as I sleep, I dream I am down by the lake. It is high summer, the sky is golden, and the water shimmers in the evening light. I dream I am swimming with Leo Valerdene, not as the Fairy Queen, but as myself. He chases me, laughing, his hands skimming my bare flesh. His touch is pure sunlight.

I stop suddenly, treading water. Something isn't right.

"What's wrong?" asks Leo. His voice rumbles through me.

"This is wrong."

"Why?"

"You aren't... you're not him."

"Who?"

"Thorn. I shouldn't... I shouldn't be dreaming of you. It isn't right."

Leo laughs, and suddenly, his voice isn't foreign, his laugh is familiar. Thorn's laugh. "Rose," he says, pulling me towards him, "It's all right. It's me."

"What do you mean?"

"I'm Thorn, silly." He leans forward in the water, his hands sliding round my back. His face glistens, and his beautiful blue eyes sing into my very soul. "Can't you see?"

All at once, I *can* see, of course it's him, why couldn't I see it before? I place my hand against his cheek, and feel no surprise at feeling skin rather than fur, but when his fingers move

211

to wipe back my hair, my flesh sings. Before another word can be uttered between us, our mouths slide together and we are kissing. The kiss covers all of me. The warmth of his mouth spreads outwards, inwardly, pouring down into the tips of my fingers, the ends of my toes. I am undone, foldable, as malleable as clay. His kiss is a flame amongst the hay.

I awake hotly in my room, the weight of the phantom kiss still spreading through me.

"Did you sleep well, last night?" Thorn asks coyly at breakfast the next morning.

"W-what? Why? Why would you ask that?"

"Your hair is all over the place."

"Oh!" I furiously pat it down. "I just... I... never mind."

"You're very skittish this morning. Are you quite all right? You look flushed–"

"Well, the weather is getting awfully warm!"

I fan myself desperately, feeling the colour rise to my cheeks.

"All right," Thorn shrugs, and finally sits down to eat. He looks almost smug, as if he is inside my thoughts.

I cannot help but search his features for any trace of this strange man I saw last night, but it is no good. He simply looks like Thorn to me. And yet, I was so sure, in that moment, that this other person was Thorn. I eat my breakfast as quickly as I can, not feeling particularly hungry, and then go back upstairs and run myself a bath. I have *got* to calm down.

"You realise your bath is cold, right?" Ariel hovers at my shoulder.

"Quite aware."

"Your voice sounds strange."

"Does it?"

I suppose it does. It's high and quick, like I cannot say the words fast enough. Ariel helps me out of the dress and soon I am under the water. It is unpleasant, but I instantly feel better. Ariel adds some kind of oil, lavender, I think. The temperature heats up a little.

"I had a strange dream last night," I tell my tiny companion.

"What about?"

"I... I couldn't say." A few more minutes tick by. Ariel hums a dainty tune. "I often have dreams here, dreams that... are different, from the ones I had back home. Dreams that feel a little bit... real."

Ariel bobs, as if she is nodding. "You're asking if your dreams are real?"

"I'm asking if there's any truth to them, or if they're just... wishful thinking."

"A bit of both. Some of your dreams are just dreams... some a little more than that."

"Why is that? How can my dreams be anything other than just dreams?"

"You are... connected to this place," Ariel explains, "And the magic that sustains it. You are in the gardens and the walls and mirrors, in the old air that used to house the most powerful beings in the world. A little bit was bound to rub off on you, sooner or later."

I am not entirely sure what she means, but I think I understand. I *am* doing something to the castle, somehow. But I do not think I am doing it alone.

Chapter Eighteen

The Monsters in the Mirror

The following morning, I gather my courage and go to check on my family again, before Thorn wakes up. Nothing out of the ordinary appears to be happening with them. Nothing out of the ordinary ever really happens back home. Only my glance at Freedom unsettles me; he is walking in the woods again. Did he tell the others that he saw me there? Does he think he imagined the whole thing? Is he all right? His expression offers no clue. We are alike in that way, I think. Both of us can be hard to read unless we're furious.

I turn to the Mirror of Memories to show me the moment the garden started to bloom again. It shows me the first snowdrop emerging from the patch where I planted mine. I am nowhere to be seen.

"Show me what I was doing, at the same time." I am in the library with Thorn, turning a page. Neither one of us is doing anything remarkable. My eyes are rooted on my book, and Thorn is...

Well, Thorn keeps glancing at me, actually.

I try to convince myself that the book just isn't that interesting, but I know I am fooling myself. I think the garden started to bloom when he started to like me.

My eyes drift to the Mirror of Desire. I wonder if it would show me Thorn's, if I asked it. I wonder if my own would mirror his. Do I really want to open that door?

Next to it, the Mirror of Fear glistens. A part of me is less afraid of whatever this would reveal. I step in front of it once more.

I see my parents' bedroom. Papa is lying on the bed, older and obviously dying. My stomach churns. I know it's just a vision, that it isn't real, but it is still difficult to witness. Freedom, Honour, Hope and Beau all crowd around him. There are other people too, younger. Faces I don't recognise. Their children?

"Rose," Papa calls out, his voice raspy, "*where did you go?*"

This fear is hardly surprising. My family growing old without me. My father dying, never knowing what became of me. But this fear does not have to come to pass.

"*Rose!*"

The image swirls. This second vision is so much worse. Thorn is lying in the rose garden, our place, bleeding. The blood spreads across the stones like water against the riverbed. Unstoppable. He is calling my name, and I am not there. I am not there.

The unutterable reality of Thorn's death. The one death I could not bear. I came so close to it before, and I know now I could never watch him die. My soul could not survive it. But... but it could still happen, and, unlike my father dying without ever having seen me again, I will be powerless to stop it. The way he called my name cuts into me... like he knew I was never coming. The desperation in his voice was palpable.

"Rose..."

Another voice calls my name. I wheel around. The fairies are hovering in front of the Mirror of Truth. Eager to wipe the fears from my mind, I scurry over. Inside the mirror are three distinct figures. At the front is Ariel, more distinct and solid than she has ever been before, although she moves a little slowly, as if captured on a series of fast-moving portraits. To the left of her is a small, slight, pale-faced girl, with short, light green hair and eyes like chipped aquamarine. She is half the size of the other two, a child in stature. For a second, I think she is wearing a glittering cape made out shimmering gossamer, but then the cape wiggles. Not a cape– wings.

The other figure belongs to a stately woman. Of the three of them, she looks the most human, with her long, straight nose, proud neck, and brown hair piled on top of her hair. But her eyes are cool and golden, caught somewhere between a cat's and an owl's.

At this stage, I know it shouldn't surprise me, but I cannot help but gape in wonder at the three fairies in the mirror before me.

Ariel's lovely face breaks into a wide smile. "Hello!"

"Hurrah!" exclaims the little girl at the back. "You can see us!"

Ariel gives her a playful nudge. "Rose, I think it's time I introduced you officially to Margaret and Ophelia."

"I was thinking the exact same thing. I should have insisted days ago, but–"

"You were occupied," says Margaret pointedly. "We saw."

I feel a blush rise to my cheeks.

"Anyway, this is Ophelia," Ariel says, gesturing to the little green girl. "She minds the gardens, mostly. We get around a lot nowadays. And this–" she turns towards the stately woman, "is Margaret. You can blame her for all the dresses."

"Oh, er," I stifle an awkward blush. I had taken apart most the dresses I'd been given, not giving a thought to the one who made them.

Margaret sniffs. "I assure you, they were the height of fashion at one point," she says stiffly. "Your mother loved them. But not to worry. I will find something perfect for you in time."

"I loved the nightwear."

"Those were Ariel's."

"Oh, um, so—"

"Anyway," Ariel intervenes, "I thought you would like to meet the rest of the team. What's left of us."

"Is it just you? All three of you, for this entire castle?"

"I know," Margaret says proudly, "we do a good job, do we not?"

"What... what happened to the others? I've... I've heard the stories, of course. The war between light and dark, the queen dismissing her subjects, but... I feel like I'm missing something. Who is this dark fairy? What does she want? What can I *do*?"

The fairies sigh, casting furtive glances are cast between them, as if they are discussing something telepathically. Ophelia tugs on the corner of Ariel's sleeve. She leans up and whispers something in her ear. Ariel turns to Margaret, and all three of them hang there for a moment, conversing silently.

It is Margaret who responds. "We will show you, Rose," she says reluctantly. "Or show you what we can. It is not a short story, however. You may wish to sit down."

"Show me? What do you—"

Before anyone can answer, the Mirror of Memories bursts into life. Images and figures literally pour out of the frame, sunlight floods the room, birdsong crawls into the air. I have never seen it do this before, but then, I am not one of the Fey. The mirror's magic collides with that of the fairies' in beautiful and discordant harmony.

The meadow blossoms before me. Two dark-haired young girls are skipping about in it, little golden wings trailing behind them. They are so similar they could almost be twins, although the younger one has the smallest, sweetest set of horns protruding out of the top of her hair. A flower is tied to one of them.

"*Eila! Wait for me!*" she calls out to the older one.

Her sister stops and grins, holding out her hand for her to follow. I miss Honour and Hope with a sudden pang.

"*Come on!*" Eila calls.

The two run on, hand-in-hand, until they reach a river bank. My riverbank. They slow to a crawl, creeping through the long grass, spying on a group of very ordinary human children splashing around in the stream. They are dressed in very loose, very old-fashioned clothing.

"Boo!" Eila leaps out at them. I expect them to startle at the sight of a fairy child appearing out of nowhere, but they don't. Instead, they laugh joyously and start splashing them too.

The game continues for some time, until there is a sudden cry. Eila spins round, and her sister is standing over one of the human boys, who is clutching his cheek. His eyes well up.

"Monster!" he yells, and then he and the other boys turn on their heels and run.

"Moya!" Eila calls, racing to her side. *"Why did you do that?"*

"He pulled my horns and asked me if I was a goat," Moya sniffles. *"I'm not a goat!"*

"Of course you aren't," Eila replies, *"and I love your horns. But you shouldn't have slapped him. You know what humans are like."*

"Stupid."

"No, sacred. I know a lot of the grown-up ones are frightened of us."

"Why would they be frightened of us?"

"Because," Eila responds, *"we are not like them."*

The scene changes, morphing into the ballroom, now many years later. A ball is in progress, and the guests are as colourful as the surroundings. The entire fairy court must be present, plus many of their human neighbours. The sisters are adults now. Eila is dressed in soft yellow, and her golden wings float down her back like a cape. She reminds me of sunlight on a cloudy day; all of the beauty with none of the harshness. Moya looks a little different to her now, the moonlight to her sister's sun. Her horns are larger, and her wings more silver than gold.

By the table, two human adolescents are staring at the older sister. *"Isn't she beautiful?"* one gapes.

"For sure, but I've heard she can turn men to stone just by look-

ing at them."

"I heard that was the younger one."

"Oh, that makes sense, she looks the part after all." He mimes the curve of her horns with his fingers and the two of them snigger.

"Shall we test the theory?" Moya materialises behind them. They stumble back into the table, upsetting the punch bowl. *"Careful, boys,"* she sneers. *"Did you not hear? If you touch the food of the fairies', you will have to stay with us forever. Wouldn't want you to have to put up with me all of that time."*

One of the boys is trembling, but the other gathers some courage. *"Witch,"* he spits.

Moya puts on a face of delight, but it is not hard to see the hurt in her eyes. *"I could be,"* she hisses.

Another day, another scene. Moya is walking through a market, simple and ordinary. She stops to coo at a baby. The baby giggles, but the mother whirls around and snatches it away. *"Get away from my baby, fiend!"* she curses. *"I've heard what your kind do to them."*

A grand announcement, a royal procession. *"All hail Queen Eilinora!"*

Moya is in the Hall of Mirrors, what could be years or decades later, it is unclear. The sisters appear to have stopped aging. There are some differences in Moya's face, however. Her features are sharper, her skin sallower. Eila stands behind her, taller and grander and more beautiful than ever, a crown woven into her shining hair.

"Your majesty," Moya mock-curtsies.

"To you, I will always be Eila."

"If you say so," Moya turns back to face her reflection, her mouth turned up in a look of utter disdain. *"Tell me, dear sister, what is it that you see when you look in the Mirror of Truth? You probably look even more beautiful than you do now, don't you?"*

"You and I look virtually the same, dearest–"

"We used to," Moya says bitterly. *"Do you know what I see now?"*

"No."

"I see a monster."

Snippets of stories spanning decades. Reports to Eilinora, *"Your sister appears to be inciting violence against humans..."* *"There's been a rumour of..."* *"A fairy has been accused of stealing a child..."*

Eilinora's face grows tired and weary. She speaks to Moya. *"I just want to know why they might be saying these things, dearest."*

"Why do you think?" her sister screams. *"Because I look like a monster, that's why!"*

"But you aren't!"

"Well, maybe I want to be!"

"You... you don't mean that."

"Why not? If the crown fits..." Her eyes fall to Eila's. *"Not all crowns are made of silver and gold."*

The Queen meets Leo down by the lake. Their entire courtship plays out at lightning speed.

"When do you think you'll tire of this pet of yours?" Moya asks.

Her sister grimaces at the use of the word, 'pet'. *"Actually, I think I'm going to marry him."*

"Marry him? But– he's a human!"

"I know, which is why I think I must seize the precious time we have together. Mortal lives are so short, after all."

"But they hate us!"

"Leo doesn't."

"You wait," Moya spits. *"He'll never be happy as your husband."*

But they look wondrously, blissfully happy. Even though, in the scenes that follow, there are slight signs of Leo aging whilst Eilinora remains untouched by the years.

Then there is the day I've seen before: when the Queen closes the way to the mortal realm, where Moya fights her for the first time. Now I see her coming back, dozens of supporters behind her. They look like they used to be fairies, but now their skin is turning grey, their eyes dark. Moya's wings are the colour of pitch-black night.

"*Open the way again, Eilinora.*"

"*You know I will not. We are meant to be allies. If we cannot be that, then it is better that we live apart for now.*"

"*We were meant to rule them. And if you won't, I will.*"

"*Do not start this fight, sister. It is not one you can win.*"

Moya's face twists into a horrible smile, and for the first time, she is fully recognisable as the face in the lake. "*Who said anything about winning?*"

A series of battles unfold in the room. Lightning pervades the air. The castle is mutated into a war ground; bodies pile along the corridors. Leo vanishes from the picture; I do not see him fall. The next stark image is Moya bound in chains, being held in the Hall of Mirrors.

"*What have you done to him?*" Eilinora screams.

Moya just smiles, and the smile splits the scene. Only fragments of what follows are visible: Moya being dragged towards a mirror of liquid silver, shrieking with a strange, desperate delight. "*I will be free one day, and you... you will have lost everything!*"

Eilinora watches as her sister disappears, and a black cloth is fastened around the frame. "*I already have.*"

The next image is quieter, but by no means calmer. There is a defeated, tired quality to the entire room, as if the walls themselves are slouched. Eilinora sits by the remains of her throne, staring up at the scorched portrait.

"*Your Majesty,*" Margaret approaches her, flanked by Ariel and Ophelia. "*I beg you to reconsider. There must be another way–*"

"*This is the only way,*" she sighs. "*Moya is too strong to be contained forever. I must enter her prison too. I will fight her from within, and keep this place alive for as long as I can.*"

"*This could kill you.*"

"*It probably will,*" she says. "*Please... take care of him.*"

She vanishes in an eruption of light.

It is long past morning when the mirrors finally go quiet.

"They were sisters," I say eventually, turning back to the fairies. "They were sisters, and she..."

"We were there, Rose. We saw," Margaret responds. "I was present for all of it. They are my memories too. Three hundred years of it."

Three hundred years. A long time for dark thoughts to fester, for Moya to turn from the child to the monster. Could I ever grow to hate Honour or Hope in the way Moya hated Eilinora?

Not in a thousand years, Not in a million. I could never want anything of theirs so much.

"I still... I still don't know what the curse really is," I say numbly. "And... and where was Thorn in all of this?"

"Alas, dear, if we tell you, we may lose all hope of the curse ever being undone. We have made that mistake before."

"What do you mean?"

"One or two of the other girls figured it out, or were told," Ariel explains. "As you can see, it didn't help."

"But how do you know that I'm the same–"

"You're not the same," says Margaret tartly. "Which is why we cannot take any risks."

"This is... immensely frustrating, you know."

All three of the fairies sigh in unison. "No need to tell us, dear," Margaret titters. "We've been watching girls fail for a decade, now."

"Is there a reason we've all been girls?"

"Yes," says Ariel. The other two fairies glare at her, as if she's given too much away. "Well, there is."

My eyes drift towards the blackened mirror. It seems to rumble, thundering quietly. If the others notice it, they say nothing. "What... what would I see... if I tore down the cover?"

"With any luck, you would see nothing."

"What else could I see?"

"At worst?" says Ariel. "Her face, staring back at you."

An icicle shoots through me at the thought. "But... she's not contained to the mirror," I continue. "I've seen her face before. In the darkness, in other reflections..."

All three of the fairies shudder inwardly. "We know," they say. "We were there, too."

"How can she do that?"

"Trickery, magic," Ariel says. "I told you before, that she was hoarding it. Waiting for a chance to break free, originally. Now waiting for the chance to hurt you."

She had tricked me into falling through the ice, and then terrified me into going out after Thorn, putting myself in danger. The storm had to be the worst of it. Were her powers growing? I share my thoughts with the fairies.

"I imagine, after an attack like that, she needs some time to recover," Margaret surmises. "But we shall have to take precautions during the next full moon. If you haven't managed to break the curse by then, of course."

I swallow. *No pressure, Rose.*

"It has to be you now," says Margaret sternly. "And if you fail... all will be lost forever."

Chapter Nineteen

Memories of Winter

I ask the fairies to give me some time alone, to process what I have just seen. In reality, I am sick of them: sick of the well-meaning lies and the frustration they bring. I need to see something good. Checking in on my family is out of the question, so I step back towards the Mirror of Memories instead.

"Show me a moment in Thorn's childhood, when he was happy."

I am certain he will not mind me seeing this, that it will not show me anything I should not see. But I am desperate to know his story, whatever pieces I can.

The library flickers into view. Thorn is there, a mere sniff of the size he is now. He is so tiny. How old can he possibly be? His back is pressed up against a wall, an oversized book open on his lap. He is reading aloud.

"Once upon a time, in a land far away, there lived a beautiful girl in a quiet village..." He stops, grappling at the corner. "I can't turn the pages."

"You'll learn, little one." A voice sounds from somewhere, but I cannot see its owner. It is a lovely voice. Soft and deep, but also... sad. She sounds like she's in pain. Thorn, I think, is too little to pick up on this. "Try again. Be gentle. Take your time."

Thorn struggles, screwing up his face, trying to force his nail under the paper. "I did it!" he exclaims eventually.

"I knew you would, dearheart," the voice says proudly. "You can do anything you wish, if you try hard enough, for long enough. Remember that. Whatever happens. And remember... you are never alone. Never, ever, ever." The voice trickles away.

"Mother?" says Thorn. "Mother!"

The mirror swirls back to normal, and I know why. That memory is no longer a happy one. I ask for other moments. I see him playing out in the gardens with Ariel and Ophelia, back when they had forms. Margaret is laying out a picnic. Thorn dashes into the lake and comes out with a fish in his mouth. Ariel and Ophelia both fall apart laughing whilst Margaret sighs. Once the fish is liberated, she wrestles him into her arms and begins to dry him off furiously.

"How will you ever find yourself a wife if you don't behave at least a *little* bit like a gentleman?"

Thorn scowls. "I don't want a wife. I like being me!"

As if to prove his point, he leaps away from her and bounds back into the lake. She is knocked off her feet with the force of this, which makes him laugh even harder.

"You can still be you with a wife!" she yells.

At one point, he was happy being him. When did this change? When the others came, from outside? When people screamed at him? When the fairies faded, and he became alone in the world? At what point did he look in the mirror and decide he was a monster?

This, I think, is too personal to ask.

"Show me another happy moment."

There are more moments with the fairies, but they soon trickle out. They must have vanished early in his life. Soon, they appear only as talking sprites, then little lights, then...

nothing. Thorn grows older without them. The happy moments I am shown now are limited to him buried inside a book.
A feeling I know well. That's how I first eked out happiness
after Mama died.

There are a few moments of happiness with the other visitors of the castle. Only a handful. Six visitors before me, and
only a handful of pleasant memories.

I startle when Mama is there. The two of them are eating
dinner, laughing pleasantly. Mama sings a song on the harp. He
nods along. He hands her flowers that she sews onto a dress...
her wedding dress.

I was sure, from the way he spoke about her, that there
were more. A few happy memories in so many months.

"Another happy memory, please."

White bursts across the glass. I remember this scene well;
the first day we played in the snow. Our snowman. It is so
strange, watching myself from afar, watching Thorn watching
me. His eyes follow wherever I go.

The mirror shows me giving Thorn his birthday present.
His face is so much more beautiful than it was the first time I
saw this scene. It melts when I put it around his neck. His voice
is barely a whisper when he thanks me.

Thorn and I dancing. Thorn helping me in the garden. The
two of us reading together. Me bandaging Thorn's arm. How
can this be a happy memory? Then I see the way he looks down
at the bandages after I am done, touches what I touched. Is it
because I wasn't afraid of him, or because I helped him? Because he knew I cared?

Teaching me how to climb a tree. Falling on top of him.
Singing in the music room. Us in the rose garden. Us by the
lake, me snuggled in his arms during the thunderstorm.

There are so many memories of me. Are these truly the
only happy memories he has? Is the rest of his life so clearly
eclipsed by his time with me? I do not feel surprised, but I do
feel something. Honoured, strange, sympathetic, awful, glowing.

"Rose?"

I startle at his presence, so far wrapped up in our memories. Thankfully, the mirror has returned to normal.

"Are you all right?"

"Fine," I say, quickly dabbing at my hot, damp cheeks. "Come and sit beside me."

Thorn does so. "What are we looking at?"

I turn back towards the mirror. "Show us *my* happiest memories."

I have so many more, compared to him, but I share them all. I can tell he loves seeing the ones I have of Mama, playing with us, reading to us, being so happy and being so her. I was not expecting so many after she died, but there are still dozens. So many beautiful days spent in the woods with my siblings, or singing around a piano. So many spent teaching Beau how to do things. I am surprised at how few there are of me reading. I have always felt that that was when I was happiest, but apparently not.

I am thankful the mirror does not include my kiss with James Saintclair. It does include a lot of moments with Thorn, though. Here, our memories match. A perfect mirror.

He says almost nothing until the montage of my life is over, and when he does speak, all he says is, "Thank you."

Thorn and I settle on a new date for our ball: three week's time, a few days after the next full moon. It is the first one that I am really, truly dreading. What if something tries to stop us again? I have not seen the shadows since the last one, but I wonder if this doesn't just mean that Moya is biding her time, gathering her strength for the next attack.

The ball is a welcome distraction, both for ourselves, and our fairy companions. They are quite dedicated to the cause. Margaret has ferreted away my dress and refuses to tell me anything about it. She says it will be her masterpiece. Ophelia, meanwhile, is determined to secure the best flowers to decorate the ballroom with. Ariel dithers between the music room, apparently composing, and the kitchen, where she plans to cook us the finest food we have ever eaten.

We are absolutely forbidden to help.

Thorn takes me back to the lake and we continue our climbing and swimming lessons. Inspired by our previous success, he decides to take up painting. I get several more canvases from this endeavour, and when I feel I'm almost running out of space, I suggest he turns his attention to the task of calligraphy; I know he is self-conscious about his handwriting.

Thorn is usually the far more patient out of the two of us, but after a while of practising his letters and still having little more than a few, untidy scrawls, he grows frustrated. One evening, he picks up his paper, crushes it into as much of a ball shape as he can manage, and hurls it towards the fireplace. It falls a little short. I can still make out the occasional, shaky letter. R, S, E, O...

"This is hopeless!" Thorn cries.

I hurry over before he spills his ink. "You're doing fi–"

"I'm not, Rose!" He thumps his hands against the table. "These ridiculous paws– nobody can write with them!"

I take his hand and imprison it in mine. I wait until he looks at me, which takes some time. I can still feel his shame. "I love these hands," I assure him. "They are by far the most gentle that I have ever held."

The rage in his face softens as he holds my gaze, and somehow, I find the courage to ask him something I have been longing to for some time now. An impossible request, but one I must have his answer to.

"Thorn," I start, swallowing a lump in my throat, "when the gate opens, and I go home again... would you come with me?"

Thorn's silence makes my heart beat faster. The weight of what I have just asked is crushing. I cannot breathe until he speaks.

"No, Rose, I cannot."

His hand slips from mine, and he gets up, moving closer to the window.

"But why not?" I knew this would be the answer. I even know why, and yet... and yet I wanted to be wrong. I was not expecting the misery the answer would bring me.

"Well, I admit I know little of the outside world, but I am sure I am right in guessing that it knows little of magic, and thus might be a little hard to explain... me." He gestures to his body.

"I wouldn't mind explaining," I say quietly, and truthfully, because I feel that I wouldn't mind anything in the world, if he were there too.

"I would," he responds, almost as quietly. "That's even if I lived long enough for you to begin explaining."

"Don't talk like that."

"You know it's the truth. The outside world is not a place for me. They would kill me or put me in a cage... one much smaller than this."

I want to tell him that I would never let that happen. I want to tell him that they would have to get through me first, that I would fight and scream and tear them apart if they even tried. I know I would want to. But he is right, they would put him in a cage, and try as I might, I would never be able to stop them. How can it be that there is no place for him in the outside world –my world– when he is so very much a part of mine?

I have heard the saying so many times before, "you are a part of me" but I had never understood it, until him. He is more than a part. He is some intangible force that both surrounds me and lives in me. Greater than my skin, my flesh, my heart. Sometimes, I found it impossible to tell where I ended and he began.

And other times, it was all so very clear.

A coldness settles in the air between us. I stare at his back for a long time, before I gain enough strength to continue. How to express something, but not too much?

"I... I'm not sure, if I go back, and I never see you again," I start, somewhat lamely, "that I will ever be... truly happy again."

Thorn's laugh is hollow. "A touch dramatic, I fear."

"Will you be happy, without me?"

Thorn pauses for a while. "No," he says, "but that is because I will be alone. You shall have your family to distract you from any immediate loneliness, and I've no doubt, after some time, you shall move on from this experience."

Now it is my turn to laugh. "Move on? How can you think such a thing?"

"All the others did."

"Well, I'm not all the others, am I?"

"No," says Thorn, a little sadly, "you certainly aren't."

I do not know why he looks at me this way. It is not the first time either of us have insinuated this, this fact, this idea. I am different from the others. This is the first time I want to hear why.

"Why am I so different?"

Thorn looks at me for such an age that for a while, I do not expect I will receive an answer. Finally, he says, "You always treated me like a person. And then, very quickly, like a friend."

This is not the whole truth. "My mother did the same," I add, "and you said one or two others you might have called friends. I am more than a friend, whatever we are. Why?"

Thorn's silence is once more deafening. "I do not know," he says eventually. "I wish I did. Perhaps then, it might be easier to explain while I shall not move on, but expect you will. I never... I never knew what it was like, to truly be myself with another person, until I knew you, and your soul slipped so easily into mine that I so quickly forgot what life without you was like. If only it were so easily expressed, if I could squeeze it into numbers rather than words. If it were logical, rather than akin to madness. You *are* more than a friend. You are more myself than I am."

I cannot think of what to say to this. I agree with him unutterably. It's like he said– my soul slipped so easily into his. They cannot be so easily separated. He is with me always.

"I'm going to come back," I tell him, "on the next solstice." I'm not prepared to say goodbye forever. I won't ever be.

Thorn exhales deeply. "It won't be enough, Rose."

"Enough for what?"

"Either of us. I don't think I could bear to see you only for a few hours every year. The rest of my existence would be suspended, waiting for those few moments. I would be like an unfurled flower, all year long, waiting for those few moments in the sunlight with you. I don't... I don't presume to imagine your feelings, but... you will have a life outside of this place, a life that shouldn't be held back by a promise you made to me, when you were lonely and had no one else."

I *do* have no one else. Logic wrestles in the back of my mind. I have a family. A family who loves me. And yet... no one, not even Honour, understands me in the way Thorn does. I mean to tell him that it won't be just a few hours, that I was thinking of spending my year between two homes, but I see the future he is suggesting for himself mirrored in my own. I will live for those months with him, and live as he will, like a flower unfurled, awaiting the sunlight his presence brings to my life. The days without him will be cast into shadow. I feel my soul will shatter the minute I splinter from Thorn's side, and all the love my family could ever heap on me would not plug up that wound. I will bleed inwardly for the rest of my days.

Thorn says nothing more. It is probably my turn to speak, but I cannot. I move towards the door. My fingers clasps around the handle, my throat just as tight. "I was always lonely, until I met you," I say softly, and then slip away to my room.

Chapter Twenty

The Shadow and the Soul

Anything that passed between us last night is ignored when dawn comes around. We fall back into our routine and pretend the question I asked was never ushered, and Thorn never told me that his life would be spent waiting for just a few brief moments with me. The weight of both is shouldered, shelved, or ignored.

A few days later, I am walking down to breakfast when I hear Thorn talking to Ariel. Neither has noticed me, and for reasons I cannot explain, I find myself slowing and coming to a stop. Perhaps I don't want them to think I am eavesdropping, or perhaps it is precisely the opposite.

"You two are killing me," Ariel buzzes.

"Not as much as it will kill me, I'm sure."

There is a long pause between the two of them. "I'm sorry," says Ariel, unusually seriously. "I didn't mean–"

"I know, Ariel."

"Can you... can you feel it? Your heart?"

"No. Yes. Sometimes."

"I don't think she's as fey as some of the others, you know. She doesn't seem to feel her heart at all."

"She was fey enough to bring the castle back to life."

Ariel pauses.

"Ariel?"

"I think," she says carefully, "that we might have to accept the possibility that it may not have been her, not completely."

"What do you mean?"

"You are fey as well."

Thorn exhales. "You think it might not be her at all."

"I am certain that she cares for you."

"But not enough."

Not enough? *Not enough?* The word 'care' barely scratches the surface of how I feel for Thorn– but what does that have to do with the castle? I chew on this thought for a while before I remember Thorn's other words: *She was fey enough to bring the castle back to life.*

Part-fey. I don't have any powers that I am aware of, but that might explain the dreams, and maybe it does explain the castle coming back to life. It might explain why I saw the gateway in the first place. Thorn had theorised as much before, that I was descendant of one of the fairies who escaped from the war. It makes sense, but I fail to see what difference it makes, especially if, like Ariel suspects, it might not be me bringing life back to the castle at all. It might be Thorn, who is clearly completely fey.

I try to put it out of mind, ashamed of my eavesdropping, and of the pain in Thorn's voice when questioned about my affections.

I head along to the parlour. Bramble is already there, waiting under my chair for any scraps, even though he is far too large to manage to get more than a nose under it now. I lean down to kiss him, guilt dancing about my insides.

Thorn enters the room almost immediately after. His voice is unusually bright; I think he is trying to hide what has just transpired. "Little creature gets more kisses than I do," he moans, sitting down on the settee.

"Don't grumble," I say, equally cheerfully. "You sound like my father."

"I am quite sure I do not wish to sound like your father. I am equally sure I would wish for a few more of your kisses."

I throw a nearby pillow at him, and he throws it back, so I seize it, sit on his lap, and hit him with it again. Then I relax my hands a little, kiss his forehead, then both cheeks, and stop. The pillow slides from my grip. I look at Thorn's eyes, and the patches of his face I've kissed seem to stick out, shining, a triangle of kisses that should be a diamond.

I am unfinished.

I slide my fingers onto his lips and I kiss his nose with my own.

I care enough.

That night, I turn and twist in the darkness, and think of Thorn's lips. What would they feel like, pressed against my own? Should felt and fang touch flesh? I only see Thorn in his face, I only hold Thorn in my arms– will I feel Thorn in his kiss? Would I attempt to cross that bridge, and risk getting stranded in the centre, unable to cross? Unable to go back?

Thorn has wormed his way into my thoughts, inflicting himself on every passing moment. Even my dreams offer no escape. He is there, always, his presence heavy. His face taunts me, and his voice rumbles my soul like thunder.

I have another dream of phantom kisses, another tantalising fantasy of sunbeams and fire, deep inside me. It rouses me from my slumber, and sleeping again would be pointless. I tiptoe along to the chamber of mirrors, bringing a pillow and a blanket with me. I will not move until I am completely exhausted.

"Show me the moment my mother and father met."

My mother and father grew up in the same village. They first passed each other in the marketplace. My mother was in a pram, my father a scrawny ten-year-old with no interest in babies. He rolled his eyes when his mother stopped to coo at her.

"Show me the moment when they first noticed each other."

Time moves forward. My father is playing with his friends in the woods, and they come across Mama having a tea party with her friends. One of my father's group decides to throw a snail at them, and pretty soon, all the other boys are joining in, pelting the beautiful tea party with sticks and slugs and anything then can get their hands on. Even Papa joins in, although he looks guilty about it.

The other girls burst into tears, and the boys laugh and start to run away. My mother, who can only be about six at the time, runs after them. She picks up a pebble and throws it at them. It hits my father squarely in the jaw. I have never seen my mother angry, and by the looks of things, neither has he.

He stops, startled, rubbing the side of his jaw, while she yells at him.

"Show me the first time they liked each other."

It is at a village fête, some ten years later. Mama is dancing with her friends. A lot of boys are looking at her now, including Papa, who is now a man. Mama's eyes, however, keep looking back at a young girl sitting by herself on a bench. Her loneliness is palpable, as is Mama's desire to help her. She carefully breaks away from the rest of her friends, but before she reaches her side, Papa is there, asking the girl to dance. She is so happy.

That night, my parents dance together for the first time.

"Show me when they fell in love."

The screen flickers, as though searching through a great deal of memories. It gives me nothing. It takes me a while to realise why; there is no moment, not one. Falling in love is a collection of moments.

"Show me the moment when my mother knew that she loved him."

The mirror shows her to me in what must have been her

old bedroom. She is reading a collection of fairy tales in a little seat much like the one I have, back home. All of a sudden, she puts down her book, and her eyes gaze towards the window. That's it, that's all. There's no fireworks, no flash of lightning, not so much as a sigh. She just knows.

"Show me when he asked her to marry him."

They are walking through the woods. My father is speaking, though I cannot hear the words. He looks incredibly nervous, his eyes serious, his mouth thin. All of a sudden, my mother puts out her hand and stops him in his tracks. She is nodding fervently. Then, she puts her arms around his head, lifts herself up, and kisses him. The gesture catches him so off-guard that they both fall into a nearby bush and emerge a few moments later, covered in leaves and laughing giddily.

I could waste hours in front of this mirror, asking for a lifetime of moments. Mama telling him she was expecting Freedom, was expecting each one of us. The look in their eyes when they held us for the first time. I could ask to see the dozens of family picnics, winter parties, birthdays. But those memories are already mine. I have seen all I need to of their past.

I am in a curious mood the next day, lighter than I have been in a while. There is little to be done in the garden, so I spend most of my day in the music room, playing old romantic ballads that seem to make sense in a way I didn't fully grasp before. I tell Thorn what I saw come evening.

"I didn't realise they didn't like each other at first," I admit. "Papa was so besotted with Mama, it seemed inconceivable to imagine it hadn't always been that way."

"And your mother," asks Thorn, "was she besotted with your father?"

"Yes," I say slowly, "but not quite in the same way. You could see the devotion pouring out of Papa in every glance he gave her. Mama was more subtle in her affections towards him. She showed her affections in what she did, not what she said. No wonder he looked so nervous when he proposed!" I smile fondly at this remembrance, then a thought occurs to me. "Have you ever looked at your parents' lives?"

Thorn nods.

"What were they like?"

"Oh, utterly besotted. It quite poured out of them as well."

I wonder what Thorn's parents looked like, if he would show them to me if I asked, but his past always seems to be a sad memory for him. Whatever happened to them, their early deaths, clearly weigh heavily on his shoulders still.

"Do you miss them?" I ask.

Thorn contemplates this for a long while. "It is difficult to miss a person you never met," he says eventually. "But yes, I do. I cannot hope but imagine what my father was like, what we would have been like, how different my life might have been if he had lived. My mother... yes, I miss her. I feel her presence, and her absence, almost every day."

I nod, because I know this feeling all too well. "I felt Mama's absence so keenly for so long," I tell him. "I was so angry that she wasn't here with us. I was angry at the rest of my family when they looked happy without her. That feeling faded, in time. I was less angry when people started talking about her again. It was like she was still there."

Then I look at Thorn guiltily, because he has no one who remembers his mother, except–

"Do the fairies remember your parents?"

Thorn smiles. "Yes," he says, "and I must admit, it is good to have someone who knows them, back in my life."

"I should like to know them," I say.

"And I should like to show them to you, one day."

"But not yet?"

"No, not yet, Rose. Someday, I hope."

I wish to know why that day cannot come sooner, for I am sure in my heart that he trusts me, but perhaps this is a matter of privacy. There are things about me that I have not shared, do not wish to... not because I do not trust him, but because I do not want them spoken. How can I expect him to share everything with me when I will not return in kind?

Although, a strange thought occurs to me: if Thorn was a creation of Moya's, how does he have parents? Parents that could love, could be remembered fondly by the fairies? What is it that I'm missing– that everyone is keeping from me?

I have wondered time and time again if Thorn was secretly Leo Valerdene, made into another shape by Moya's magic. The dream I had in which the two of them were muddled up... and the faint remembrance of Thorn's reflection in the mirror of truth. But this didn't marry up with the knowledge that he had always been this way.

Later that night, I ask Ariel as she runs me a bath. "Ariel, do you think that Thorn trusts me?"

Ariel pauses for a moment, and I realise this isn't as straightforward a question as I thought. "With all but one thing," she says eventually. She stresses the "all" but all I hear is the one thing he doesn't.

"And what thing is that?"

"The thing that matters most. The thing you have yet to trust him with, either."

For some reason, this irks me. "I trust him with everything."

Ariel sighs. "You really think that, don't you?"

I try to put it out of my mind. What does Thorn not trust me with? Why does it matter so much?

The days creep closer together. Five more till the full moon.

Thorn and I are sitting in the library. Bramble is at my feet, basking in the warm glow of the embers. It is getting late, but neither of us are in the mood for sleep just yet. Thorn is reading a story aloud. I enjoy his readings. He always does different voices for the different characters.

He reaches the end. "*And their happiness, as it was founded on virtue, was complete.*" He sighs a little. "Another happy ending. I'm glad."

I laugh. Thorn always treats the characters in books like real people. He is affronted whenever they are wronged and devastated when tragedy befalls them, as if they were friends of his. It is utterly endearing.

"You are smiling at me, Rose."

"That is because you are very sweet," I reply.

"They deserved their happy ending," Thorn says testily, "after everything they've been through–"

"I am not disputing that in the slightest."

"Oh. Excellent. For a moment, I thought you were teasing me."

"Whenever I say you are sweet, I am not teasing you." I reach up and tug his ear. "Other times, however–"

"Oh, Rose!" He pulls my hand away, but then he holds it, his thumb gently caressing my palm. "Rose," he says again, softly.

I have a feeling he is going to say something, but then he doesn't speak. "You say my name a lot, do you realise?"

"Do I?" Thorn looks genuinely surprised. "I didn't realise. I suppose I just like the way it sounds."

"So do I," I return, and then he looks at me, and my cheeks feel oddly hot. "On your lips," I add, and my face feels even hotter.

I get up from my seat beside him and move towards the writing desk. I barely know what I am doing, but it was too hot where I was before, and here, beside the window, is a semblance of coolness. I can see a heap of papers in the corner; he has been trying to practise, with fair degrees of success. One page contains a full poem.

"What's this?" I ask, holding it up.

Thorn rushes to his feet. His tail twitches nervously. "Ah, that, yes, um, no–"

I begin to read. *"Like flames, my heart has flickered, felt before–"*

"It's just a work in progress–" He moves to snatch it from me, but I dive under his arm and dart to the other side of the room.

"Yet never till those eyes held mine
Did it move, and beat, like unfurling wings
To fall in rhythm with each breath she took.
O, that I have lived to feel such joy,
And weather each hard pain it brings.
Endure her closeness, heart I beg thee,
For each step she takes from me is hell,
And each moment with her bliss, heaven-kissed.
Such sweetness turns my withered heart to spring.
Whenever I should die, cut it from my chest
It lies there in my breast, my heart, rose-shaped."

I look up from the page, and my eyes hold Thorn's. It is as if our gazes have been threaded together. In the fireplace behind him, a log collapses. Sparks flutter up the chimney while ash spills onto the grate. Neither of us speaks.

"It's just a... writing exercise." Thorn says. His voice is feather soft, and deep as darkness. "A silly thing–"

"It was beautiful," I breathe. "Where... where did those words come from? How... how long did that take you–"

"It was just there..." he replies. "Written. In the space between..."

"The space between?"

He comes closer. "In the space between. In the only between that matters."

The clock on the wall chimes two. Two? I look at Thorn in shock, and his face mirrors mine. "Good lord, it's late!" I laugh. "What would my Nanny say? Up until two with a man after dark... I do hope he declares his intentions!"

Thorn looks at me and opens his mouth. It hangs there for a while, unspeaking, frozen.

"Will you marry me, Rose?"

"What?"

That is quite possibly one of the worst things you can ever say to someone who has just asked to marry you, but I am sure, at first, that I must have misheard. He cannot be serious. Thorn looks as shocked as I am.

"Forgive me," he says after an age. "That just... slipped out. But... I should like an answer. Yes or no, without fear."

I smile. "As if I could ever fear you, dearest."

His eyes light up. "Is that a–"

"No, Thorn."

All at once, the light that has been there vanishes, extinguished in an instant.

"For a start," I say breezily, "there is no priest to marry us, and what would my family say, if I did not invite them to the wedding? I do like to do things properly."

Thorn laughs.

"What amuses you so?"

"Your answer. I have never imagined such a pleasant rejection."

"I am sorry it was a rejection."

"Do not be sorry," he says, and for a minute, I almost believe he means it. "Goodnight, Rose."

"Goodnight, Thorn."

Part Four: Autumn

When reeds are dead and a straw to thatch the marshes,
And feathered pampas-grass rides into the wind
Like aged warriors westward, tragic, thinned
Of half their tribe, and over the flattened rushes,
Stripped of its secret, open, stark and bleak,
Blackens afar the half-forgotten creek,—
Then leans on me the weight of the year, and crushes
My heart. I know that Beauty must ail and die,
And will be born again,—but ah, to see
Beauty stiffened, staring up at the sky!
Oh, Autumn! Autumn!—What is the Spring to me?

--Edna St Vincent Millay--

Chapter Twenty-One

The Consequences

I lie awake in bed that night with Thorn's question playing over in my head. What did he mean, when he asked me that? More than anything, my own answer confuses me. I was so quick to refuse his offer, but I did not wish to reject him. Nor did I wish to do so simply to spare him pain.

It was simply such a strange question, phrased so oddly, as if he were asking me on a walk. Yet his pain at my refusal seemed genuine.

Perhaps he does not see marriage as I do. Perhaps he does not understand. Perhaps he has been here alone so long... perhaps he does not know what it means to be man and wife. He may only know what he has read, and believes marriage to be simple companionship. Is that all he requires from me? Is that not what we already have?

And that poem. Those *words*. Were they... were they aimed at me? Were those words mine? He did not say as much, and yet he did, in every word, in every look and gesture.

It takes me many hours to sleep, and when I finally do, it is fitful. I dream I am in the meadow with Thorn, and a cold dark mist rips him away from me. Seconds later I wake in my bed, shaking so uncontrollably, it is all I can do to stop myself from calling for him in the dark.

Although we spend the next few days in each other's company, we do a terrific job of ignoring each other in the politest way possible. We converse about the weather, we report factually what is happening in the books we are engrossed in. We compliment the food, the flowers, the gardens. Not a personal word is uttered. We barely speak each other's names.

We mention nothing about the proposal, if indeed that's what it was. I am too afraid to ask the fairies if they saw it, or if they know what Thorn was thinking when he asked me. What answer scares me more? Thorn knowing full well what the question meant, or having no idea at all?

Do I regret my answer?

The night of the full moon comes. Thorn is surprised to hear that I will be coming with him again, but he appears pleased considering the distance between us the last few days. We go down to the dungeon early, hoping to avoid the disaster that befell us last month. Bramble and the fairies come with us, our personal guard. Any last minute pleas for me to stay in the castle are ignored.

In any case, the concern is not necessary. Nothing happens. Perhaps Moya hasn't recovered from her last attack. Perhaps the magic of the castle is too strong for her now. I do not think of it too much. I count my blessings and look to Thorn.

There is no need to lock him in immediately. All of us sit in the lighted corridor. We play games, chat, elevate the tension. I have never spoken with Ophelia or Margaret at any great length, but I learn more about them here. Margaret is a syren. She is somewhat miffed when I believe this is a type of mer creature that sits on rocks and lures men to their doom.

"I am part owl!" she declares stiffly. "And the luring men to their doom part is exaggerated!"

She used to be mistress of the robes, and, when required, the castle governess. She was clearly a respected member of this ancient court, used to being obeyed. Ophelia, I sense, is a little afraid of her.

She tells me she is a pixie, a small winged humanoid creature, but her grandmother was a nymph, and therein lay her love of the outdoors and gardening.

"I hope you don't mind me pottering around the flower-beds–"

"Oh no, not at all!" she says. "They are meant to be shared!"

Ariel, as I suspected, is a full-on fairy. She has little magical talent "apart from the ordinary" but tells us all that her "wit" is her true power. Everyone else groans at this.

"I don't know why you're all laughing. The Queen herself said, 'Ariel, thou beist the most talented and most skilful of all of my domain, but thy wit biest thy greatest trait.' True story."

"I find this very difficult to believe," says Thorn.

"The great thing about my wit is it doesn't need to be believed to be real."

When the hour approaches, the fairies vanish, promising to return to escort me back to the castle. Bramble stays by my side as Thorn climbs into the cell.

"I haven't seen a shadow in a while," I tell him.

"Me neither," he admits. "Not since the last full moon. I wonder what changed?"

I feel like a lot has changed since then, but I don't have the words or the courage to explain it.

I turn around as Thorn sheds his clothes. We sit together in the silence for a little while, our backs to each other. We still have a few minutes.

"Rose, if you could... if you could go back now –or today, or tomorrow– would you?" he asks trepidatiously.

"But I can't go back."

"If you could. Would you go back?"

"I... I have to see them again," I tell him. "They have to know that I'm all right. And I miss them. I miss them *so much*."

But I might not go tomorrow. And I would not go unless I knew I could come back.

I try to banish that old fear from my mind. It is another five months until I have to make that impossible decision. What was I hoping would change in the extra time I was given? Things have changed, but not for the better, not here. The changes will only make the decision worse.

Because I have to go home. I *have* to.

"I would not go home tomorrow," I say. It is all that I can manage.

"Why not?" I feel him tense behind me. The change is not far off.

"I'm not done here," I say. "I've still got to break the curse, remember?"

Thorn snorts. "Is that all?" he asks.

"No," I reply truthfully, even though I want to say, *'Isn't that enough?'*

His body pulses. I wheel around, stick my hands through the bars, rub the back of his neck. His forehead presses against mine.

"Why... why do you want to stay?"

"I told you before; I don't want to leave you."

Despite the pain, Thorn manages to smile. "You didn't say that before."

"Didn't I?"

"No. You... you implied... you... needed to... not... wanted."

"They're the same thing, where you're concerned."

When I open my eyes, when they're finished with flushing out tears, it is clear that Thorn is gone for the night. I do not know if he heard me.

The following morning, when we go to pick him up, it's clear that he has had a rough night. He is a bit scratched up – nothing that a quick trip to the fountain doesn't fix– and obviously exhausted. We manage to have breakfast together, but then I insist he goes to bed. It is a testament to how tired he is that he accepts this without question.

I spend a few hours by myself, but am hardly better off. I did not sleep much either, huddled under my covers, trying not to imagine Thorn in the dungeon, prowling the stones, howling, claws tearing at the walls. Covering my ears did nothing to block out the sound of his voice rattling in my head.

Eventually, I give up trying to fight the sleep. I tiptoe back to Thorn's room. He is sleeping on his side, half under a quilt, most of his limbs spread out in front of him. His ears prick up as I enter, and he sleepily opens his eyes.

"Rose?" he says in a daze.

"Ssh," I hush him, creeping across to the bed. I press my knees into the mattress and slip under the coverlet. Our knees knock together. I put my hand on his cheek, gently thumb his lip. "Don't say anything." I turn around, bend my back into the hollow of his torso, and lay my head against his arm. "Are you comfortable, with me like this?"

He nods, and lays his own head next to mine. His hair brushes the back of my neck. He pulls it away, and his fingers skim my skin. I feel his breath there, hot and full.

He pulls the covers up to my shoulders, and then gingerly drapes his arm around my middle, unsure of where to put himself. I grab it securely, wrapping it tightly in my own, and clutch it to my chest.

Two hot tears ease out of my eyes. I pray he cannot feel them. I swallow, kiss his hand, and wriggle more firmly into him. It takes a little time, but his body relaxes.

For a few hours, I sleep soundly. Blissfully. Then I dream.

I cannot remember what it is about, but I wake aching on the inside. My stomach feels hollow, my throat parched and raw. I lie awake for several hours, listening to him breathing, and hope that his dreams are sweeter than mine.

I leave before he wakes up, and finish the rest of my day alone. Next morning, he is considerably brighter, but says nothing about

me coming to his room. I wish so badly to crawl into his arms again, to lie beside him in that way, but I cannot. It is not right, not allowed, not proper. It is too much, and not enough, not enough at all.

The following evening, we are sitting together in stony silence. Thorn asks me if he's done something wrong.

"No, not you," I reply, as softly as I can manage. I don't think it works.

"Then... you?"

"It isn't that simple."

"Could you try to explain it?"

"No."

Thorn falls silent for a while. "Do you... are you missing your family?"

Yes. No. Not all the time. Sometimes more than ever and sometimes I don't even think of them. I'm forgetting what they feel like. I want to speak to Honour. I want to curl up in my little nook and shut away the rest of the world and just–

Just not be the me that I am now. Not be the me that you have made me.

"Yes," I say, not caring if it hurts him. "Yes, I miss them."

Thorn nods, but says nothing else. I am glad he doesn't try to comfort me, I would push him away.

I pick up the next book in my pile. It is one of my least

favourite books. It is about a boy and a girl, young, vain, vapid, who fall in love one "magical" night and pledge to love each other always. Unfortunately, she is engaged to another man, and he is due to fight in a war. Nothing much happens between them, as he is sent off to battle the very next day. Less than a week later, she kills herself rather than marry another. Her lover, hearing of her death, dies in the fray.

I hated the characters, their sudden, unbelievable love story, their unbearably over-dramatic ends. If they had really known each other, I reasoned, I would have felt more pity for them. If they had known each other for years –or even months– I would have found it more believable. If they had corresponded throughout the war, if you could see the slow descent into hopelessness, I would have cared, rooted for them.

It was one of my mother's favourites. She found it romantic. I never did. Not remotely. But now there exists in me the smallest twinge of pity. The slightest inch of understanding. For now I know what it is like, not to want to live without someone.

I snap the book closed and throw it on the fire. The pages blacken in seconds, edges curling, flames tightening around the cover.

"Rose!" Thorn leaps off his seat, "What are you doing?"

I stare at the title as it is licked away by the flames. "It's a bad book," I say coldly. "I didn't like the ending."

Then I turn away and rush upstairs, only half-knowing why I want to cry.

"I never thought that I could be driven crazy by any individual person," says a voice, "but that was before I met you."

I do not look up, but I can feel Ariel hovering nearby. I do not want to speak to her right now. I do not want to speak to anyone.

"You and him. You are driving me insane. Just. Tell. Him. How. You. Feel."

"It's not that simple–" I snap.

"Three little words—"

"It would never be three," I say firmly. "And you act like... like explaining it would be the conclusion of it all. Like it would solve everything."

"It would. Believe me."

"No, it wouldn't. It would be the beginning and end of everything."

"Are you apprehensive because he's... you know... a beast?"

"He is *not* a beast."

"So you keep saying. So what's the issue?"

"The fact that there are some... fundamental biological differences between the two of us is... potentially problematic."

"I'm sensing that's not the only reason."

"There's my family," I say pointedly. "I can't have both, and yet... I think I have to. I cannot choose between them and him. I cannot choose between two parts of myself."

Ariel cannot think of anything to say to this. She goes away. A few minutes later, there's scratching at the door. It clicks open of its own accord, and Bramble jumps up on the bed. He whimpers a little bit, and presses his nose to my face. I can deal with a dog, it's just people and voices –including my own– that I cannot process. I wrap my arms around him and cry into his fur.

We speak to each other less and less. I spend longer in my room, shut up with Bramble, doing anything I can think of to pass the time. I emerge at meal times, just to let people know that I'm all right. I am polite and courteous in every exchange, but avoid spending too much time alone with Thorn. I've taken to walking around the gardens a great deal, which is sometimes awkward because Thorn has taken up this habit too and we occasionally bump into each other and have to feign an excuse to separate. This is difficult when you live together; the lies are harder. Neither one of us can say we said we were going to call on our dear friend for tea and mustn't be late.

The gardens are cooler now. A light coat is required to explore them comfortably. The leaves are beginning to brown, the flowers are drying, wilting. There is a slight chill in the air that I have almost forgotten. Autumn is finally upon us.

I have never really enjoyed autumn. It is the precursor to winter, that blank, cold, dead time of year, a reminder that the days in the sun are over. Freedom would always try and appease my dislike by pointing out the myriad of colours coating the forests, but all I saw was the death and decay, how the season stole away the flowers, coated the landscape with ice, and stole the vibrancy of the summer.

I do not relish autumn, but I do not miss the summer, either. Not now. The impossible, baking heat. The endless days. It was good that they were gone. Nothing was built to last forever.

Thorn asks me what I am thinking one evening when he catches me staring at the trees.

"I am thinking that all things have their time," I reply earnestly. "And that everything must die."

I wake to the sound of shouting. *Thorn.* He is screaming, almost as if the change is upon him. Bramble whimpers.

"It's all right, boy," I tell him, "stay here. I'll find out what's wrong."

I pick up a candlestick and follow the sounds down the corridor, slowly, as if waiting for the noises to stop. Praying they will. A part of me doesn't want to move. He sounds desperate, angry, a howl that any other person would stray away from. Hairs creep up along the back of my neck. A small voice tells me to turn back.

But he is in pain, and so I must go.

The door to the Hall of Mirrors is ajar. Inside, Thorn has thrown a chair at one of the mirrors– the Mirror of Truth. Glass litters the floor, spotted with blood.

"Thorn! What are you doing?"

Thorn carries on as if I am a ghost, throwing his fists into another pane. The Mirror of Desire. Shards of glass glitter around his feet.

"THORN!" I throw down my candlestick and topple the others. The flames quickly flicker and die. Only a dim, sliver of light pools into the room from the open door. Reflections turn to shadow. Slowly, Thorn's howls die out, and I creep beside him.

"Thorn?"

"I am sick of seeing."

"Seeing what?" It is a stupid question, I know. I know what he was sick of, it just always takes me a little while to remember.

He looks at me in utmost despair. I grab his face and force his gaze to stay on mine. "Listen to me," I demand, "I know what you are! I know *exactly* who you are."

I do know, although I can't explain it. I could give you a list of his traits, a list of all the reasons I love him so, but none of these come close to explaining what he is. My mind struggles with all the poetic verse it knows, scrambling about for something that perfectly encapsulates my feelings. It finds nothing. Nothing exists that could express this, that could even contain it.

Thorn looks at me, and seizes my wrists roughly. "Then what am I, Rose?" His voice is hoarse, hard, almost monstrous.

Gingerly, I pull my hand away from his grip and place a palm against his cheek. My other slides over his chest, until it feels the soft beat of his heart.

"You are just like me," I say. For in whatever way we are different, there is one absolute, one thing we share. "Your soul is shaped like mine." And if the rest of him were shaped like me, I know that in that moment I would have kissed him.

Chapter Twenty-Two

The Ball

Thorn refuses to let me bandage his hands. He marches up to the roof terrace, alone, while I sit the remnants of what had become one of my favourite parts of this strange, beautiful place. A large shard of glass sits at my feet. I pick it up, and the image flickers. The Mirror of Desire. In the little fragment, I see myself, and Thorn, and my family. All of us, together. All of us happy and smiling. A future that can never be.

Suddenly, I want the image smashed also.

The fairies arrive to clean up the mess, but I hiss them away. They say nothing to me. I go back to my room and wait for morning. At first light, I walk down to the meadow, and I imagine Freedom's voice again. I should have taken his hand. It would have spared me this.

But then Thorn would probably be dead, and my life would not be any easier.

I go to breakfast.

"Nice walk?" asks Thorn. It sounds almost mean, as if he hopes it wasn't.

"I went to the meadow." I make my words sound like an insult too. *I went to the meadow because I wanted to get away from you.*

This stops any conversation. We eat in silence. Eventually, it gets so awkward, that the fairies trickle in and try to generate pleasantries.

"So, the ball tomorrow!" Ophelia chimes. "I'm very excited. Are you excited?"

Neither one of us replies.

"I'm looking forward to it," Ariel says loudly. "I've prepared some divine music."

"And you will positively *die* when you see my ball gown!" Margaret beams.

Thorn growls –actually growls– at her. They hush immediately. I drop my spoon with a clatter and walk away, running to my room as soon as I am out of sight. I slam the door and throw myself down on the bed, expecting to cry. But I do not. Instead, I punch my pillow, tear at the sheets, and sit there shaking. Anger and misery claw continuously at my insides.

Later, he knocks at the door.

"Yes?" I bark.

There is a long pause before he speaks. When he does, his voice is quiet. Still. Measured. "Do you still want to have this ball?"

I wait a little while before replying too. "The others have worked so hard."

"Do *you* still want it?"

Another pause. "Yes."

He does not speak, and for a moment, I think he must have slunk away. I get off the mattress and cross the room, but I know he is still there before I reach the door, before I hear his breath, before I feel his body pressed against the other side of the barrier. Something of him seems to burst out of the corridor, suffuse the air between us. I can feel it as keenly as temperature when I reach out to touch the door.

"Thorn… I have… I have almost another five months here. I don't think we can continue being mad at each other."

He exhales softly, almost as if he's in pain. "I'm not mad at you."

"I'm not mad at you, either."

There does not seem to be anything else we can say to each other. Nothing we say will fix the mess we're in and yet...

Nothing will change.

In the hours leading up to the ball, the fairies are all a-flutter, moving swiftly between my room and Thorn's. Even Bramble is caught up in the excitement; he cannot decide who he wants to be with, and keeps dashing back from one room to the next.

I am bathed and anointed with perfumes and oils. My hair is cleaned and combed and curled. I am scrubbed within an inch of my life. My nails are tidied. It is hard not to feel a little excited by the fairies' enthusiasm.

Finally, I stand in my undergarments in front of a screen. All the fairies are here for this part.

"Are you ready?" asks Margaret.

I nod. The screen is pulled back, and behind it is the most beautiful gown I have ever beheld. It is white and gold, simple and extravagant, billowing and dainty, made with shimmering thread and layers of soft white gossamer.

"Do you like it?" I see a flash of Ariel in the mirror, surrounded by Ophelia, and Margaret.

"It's perfect." My voice sounds like a ghost's. "Thank you."

I slide into it easily, the laces pulled by their feathery touch. The dress has a beautiful weight, and yet it fits like a second skin. It could be made of clouds, I am so sure I am floating.

I stare at myself in the mirror as invisible fingers weave pearl beads and flowers through my hair. I am like a stranger. No, not a stranger, not at all, almost the opposite. I am myself, but a part I have never seen before. The more I am done up, the more I am revealed. Hello me, where have you been?

No one presses on me any adornments, any jewellery. The dress is decoration enough. The only thing that stays is Thorn's necklace, which matches perfectly, not that I would remove it if it didn't.

I glide towards the ballroom with my heart thumping wildly in my chest. I have rarely cared about how other people perceive my outward appearance. Why does it matter to me, how Thorn sees me?

When he startles as I enter the room, when he gets up, knocking the chair slightly, mouth agape, I know why.

He is the only one who sees me. His eyes alone, are the only ones that matter. The only eyes I care for.

"You... you look..." He gulps nervously. "You look beautiful, Rose. Otherworldly."

The word is a thousand times more powerful, more real, coming from him. I must be blushing furiously. "A statement that applies to us both."

He chuckles. "Which one?"

"Both."

He is dressed in a dark blue suit with gold adornments. His hair has been clipped, and he smells faintly of cinnamon. His eyes are brighter than ever. Soft music plays as we sit down to dine through five courses of the most exquisite food I have ever eaten. The conversation is light, slow but not uncomfortable. I am intimately aware of everything I am doing, everything around me.

"Ophelia's flowers are magnificent," I declare, looking at the garlands strung from the ceiling, wrapped around the pillars. I have never seen such a display.

"She has worked hard on them," says Thorn.

After dessert, we step out onto the balcony for a minute. There are a few final rays of sunset left. The nights are getting longer, I realise with a pang. There is a sharp change in the landscape. Browns and reds dominate where blues and greens used to be.

"A fine evening," I declare. "Reminds me of the one that Tromeo and Lessida spent together, before..."

Before he went off to war, and they were separated for years.

Thorn leans against the railing, his gaze on me. "You've read that many times."

"I wanted to know why you liked it so."

"And? Have you worked it out?"

"I think you're a romantic. I think you like the selflessness of their love, and the endurance of it."

He tilts his head at me, and I can read so little in his gaze. It's like we're going backwards, like we're becoming strangers again. I hate it, but I don't know how to make it stop.

"And you?" he asks. "What do you think of it?"

"I... I'm not a romantic."

He snorts.

"I'm not," I continue. "I... I might enjoy reading the occasional romance, but I don't... I don't *feel* it like you do."

I love words, but I can't create them like he does. I don't feel everything the characters feel. And I don't believe it, not really. It's a painting, an imitation of life.

"Rose," he asks carefully, "what do you think of love?"

My reply shoots out of me. "It makes a fine story." Because it's safer as a story. Neater. Happy endings are not for real life.

"And for yourself?"

"I'm..." I hesitate. "I'm not sure that romance is to be a part of my story." How can it be? How can I ever have a happy ending? How can there ever be a romance in my future when...

When Thorn is here. When he is not beside me.

"My future," I finish, avoiding his gaze.

"Why... why not?" His voice is very quiet.

"I'm not sure I have it in me."

There is no space for anything, anyone else. There was barely any space for him to crawl into in the first place, and yet he did, and when he's wrenched from my side, when I am gone from his...

They'll be nothing left of me but a shell.

Music stirs from inside. I turn to Thorn. "Can you dance with me?" I need to banish the darkness.

"Of course," says Thorn, and then, a little sadly, "I can deny you nothing."

I try to ignore his sadness, not knowing where it comes from. Tonight, I want us to be happy.

When the music sings, it breathes. Veins pump through invisible strings. Piano keys transform into bone. The room lifts, sways, moves with us, transforms from stone and marble and glass into living flesh. I am heavy and light at the same time, a puppet on a string and utterly free. The music exists like an extension of my soul, of our souls. I can feel it flowing in and out, like the ebb of a tide. I do not know where it begins and I end. The colours of the room swirl together, more vibrant and more beautiful in their proximity to each other. I cannot tell the floor from the ceiling. Starlight floods the room on the curling shadow of night. I am caught in a shimmering, glittering bubble of gold and silver and blue and white.

There is a moment, a split second, where I almost feel as if I have left my own body. I am somewhere else in the room, beholding this scene, wanting to capture and preserve every sliver of it. But there are sights that can never be painted, too majestic to be forged from paper and ink. This is one of them.

The music ends. I am in Thorn's arms, my head resting against his chest, my eyes tightly shut. I can almost feel the colour trickling away. The music slithers off like a snake. There is no starlight now, only shadow.

It is not enough. I want to hold him tighter, faster. It is impossible to believe that we are two separate people at all. There should be no space between us. I can hear his heart beating, and for a moment, forget that it is his at all. It is my heart that I feel in his chest. I feel that if I keep holding him, our two hearts will press together into one, and this emptiness I feel at not being able to have him in the way I want to will cease.

"Rose." My name eases past his lips, part sigh, part question. He wraps his arms around me until I am cocooned inside his embrace.

I wish for words to explain this to him, but there are none. I ease back, for fear this longing will break me. I feel as if I am standing on the precipice of a pool. I want so badly to dive in, but I cannot. I am held back, I am barred. I know I will never even touch those waters, and suddenly I am dying of thirst. A clock chimes, echoing round the chamber like a drum.

"It is late," I say. I edge towards the doors. I cannot take my eyes from him, from his. They are mirrors of my own. I turn with poisonous reluctance.

I have not stepped one foot across the threshold before a hand fastens around my wrist. I hear my name, murmured breathlessly, and a second later I am up in his arms again, my face against his neck, arms fastened around him.

He knows, he knows how I feel.

Oh God, moving away, disentangling myself is so hard. I cannot look at him this time, I cannot. I race up to my room, not daring to look back, and slam the door shut behind me. I want to lock the door, but what against? Not him; I would never shut him out. What I want to shut out is the injustice. I want him in here, by my side, as always, and I want to throw away the world that makes *us* impossible. How can I dissociate him from our problem? They are one in the same. But it does not feel that way. He is he and I am me and the simple fact that he is what he is does not change–

Does not change. Cannot be changed. However much that does not stop me feeling the way I do, it does not change.

The fairies have set up a bath for me by the fireplace. I am glad of their absence, of their hovering, sad forms. I cannot deal with others right now. There is nothing I can say to them.

I shed my clothes, ripping away the fabric and hurling it to the floor. If only we could change ourselves so easily.

I sink into the waters, break the surface with my mouth and let the salt spoil the water. I hear Thorn prowling the corridors, pausing ever-so-slightly at my door. I pray he cannot hear me cry.

I crawl damply into my bed, pressing my face deep into the pillow. I bite the feathers and do not scream. I remember his heartbeat. I feel mine.

Nothing changes.

I want to say I hate him. I want to scream it. It feels –in that moment– like the biggest truth I know. *I hate him I hate him I hate him.* But I don't hate him. The opposite is true. What I hate, what I truly cannot stand, is what I cannot change.

That's what he hates, too.

It has been a while now since I have thought of home, but tonight, I can think of nothing else but how much I long to be there, and be the person I was before I came to this cruel, enchanted place.

Chapter Twenty-Three

The Sacrifice and the Gift

I do not leave my room the next day, or the day after that. Thorn comes to talk to me three times, but I ignore him. His voice alternates between concerned, hurt, sad, and then even angry. He begs me to let me in. To talk to him. To tell him what's wrong.

You know. You know what's wrong. You must know.

I wonder what I would do, if he said it. Would I be able to ignore him then? Would I be able to lie to him, to spare us further pain?

I don't think I can ever lie to him. I would have to tell him the truth, and then where would we be?

I want to be with you, but we cannot be. I must leave you, because this is killing me. I think I need to hate you if I am to survive this.

I whisper for him to leave, because I lack the strength to speak. He does not hear me, but eventually he gives up. Perhaps he will give up entirely if I leave it long enough. Then the fairies wander in. They try to convince me to eat, to get up, to talk to him.

"I'm sure you'll feel better once you do..."

"Just tell us what's wrong Rose, we'll help!"

"This is hurting him, too, you know..."

I do not listen. I do not care if this is hurting him. I need to find my own remedy. If I can stay away from him, perhaps it will feel less. Perhaps this is best for both of us.

But I can still feel him, I can feel him everywhere, whether he is standing outside my door or in some other part of the castle. I can feel him in my soul and in my skin and I need him gone if I'm to survive knowing, and leaving him.

On the third day, Thorn comes again to my door. "You know I would do anything to make you happy. Anything within my power."

I know you would. I would do the same.

"Tell me what you want, Rose."

I cannot.

He sighs. Pain personified. "Do you want me to leave?"

No, never.

"Do you want to go home?"

This is easy to answer, in this moment. "Yes."

But this is my home. My home is wherever you are.

If Thorn exhales, he manages to control it. I hear the buzzing of the fairies as his footsteps slope away from my door. The others wait until they think they're out of ear shot.

"You better not be doing what I think you're going to–"

Thorn does not reply.

Another two days pass. Thorn does not come back, neither do the others. I fill the days with silence, and I sit and watch the garden wilt. Leaves crumble from the trees in fists of burnt orange and red. I only open my door to let Bramble in and out. His is the only face I can stand.

My dreams are fitful. I see Moya laughing. The shadows dance around the castle. I hear someone screaming, a woman.

"No, no, please! Please, don't go! Stay!"

Who is she talking to?

I wake one morning to Ariel and Thorn talking in the hallway. I pretend to be asleep. I do not want to be a part of anything.

"Don't do this!" Ariel sounds frantic, even angry.

"I must."

"Just give it more time–"

"I've given it time enough. The garden is beginning to wilt. If I don't do it now, she may not get another chance–"

"She can go back in five months. *She will wait.*"

"She is not happy. You know that."

"You don't know the reason–"

"Do you?"

I sigh, push Bramble off me, and cross to the door. "Do you two mind?" I hiss. "I'm trying to sleep!"

There is silence on the other side. Ariel, I think, has vanished.

"Rose," says Thorn, his voice serious, "can you get dressed, and meet me in the foyer as soon as you are ready?" His voice sounds solemn. The closest I can compare it to is Nanny's voice, the day of mother's funeral, asking me to come downstairs. It is not a pleasant comparison.

"Yes," I say, just as seriously, "I'll be down soon."

I do not dress as quickly as I perhaps should. I am frightened of what Thorn has to show me. When I do meet him, his face is as taut as the skin of a drum. His clothes are crumpled, like he's been sleeping in them.

"Are you ready?" he asks. His voice is sharp.

"For what?"

"Follow me."

When I do not, he comes back and grabs my wrist. He has never been so rough with me before. He is not hurting me, but this is not like him. What is wrong?

He marches me to the edge of the grounds then stops suddenly. He points at the meadow.

"What? What is it?"

He says nothing but gestures again.

"It's just the meadow."

Still, he does not reply. I follow his hand, past the waving wheat, past the stream–

The stream. The stream is there. *My* stream. And beyond that, my fields, my woods, my *home*.

It cannot be true. It's an illusion, crafted by wishful thinking. I've been wanting to escape so much recently, my mind is making it up.

"The stream," I say dumbly, "it's not... How is this even... It's... it's not possible."

"Yes, it is."

I tear my eyes away from the sight to look at him, assess the meaning behind the heaviness in his voice. But his eyes avoid me completely. A horrible, sinking feeling catapults inside.

"You? You... you can open it?"

"Yes."

I stare at him. It cannot be. He would not have done this to me. He would not have–

"Ask the question, Rose."

"Have you... have you always known?"

"That I could open it? Yes. The entire time you were here."

"No. *No.*" It's not true. It isn't possible. He saw how much I missed my family. He knew how much I wanted to return. He wouldn't have kept me here, he... he couldn't have... "I don't believe you," I say stubbornly. "You've... you've just figured it out, or... or something–"

"Why would I lie to help you hate me?"

"I don't know!" He is lying. He has to be. "Ariel!" I scream. "Where are you?"

"She won't come."

But she does.

"Tell me," I beg her. "Tell me he's lying. Tell me he hasn't known this the whole time."

Ariel is silent. Her little form shrivels. "He has always known," she says quietly.

Thorn's eyes drop away from mine. *No.*

"Ever since your mother," she continues.

"My... what?"

"Your mother was only here for a few weeks," she says. "It was the day of her wedding, when she came here. Thorn felt so terrible that she was to be trapped here away from your father, that he began to look for a way to open the gate prematurely."

"How... how can he do that?"

"A gift," Thorn says hollowly, "from the fairy queen. I am a fey creature too, after all. I have a magic of my own."

"It can't... it can't be as easy as that."

"It isn't," Ariel interjects.

"Ariel–" Thorn growls warningly.

"A sacrifice of sorts needs to be made."

"What... what sort of sacrifice?" I eye Thorn, who still avoids my gaze. My first thought is that he will have to pay with his life, and that is why he hasn't let me go, because that is the only good reason he could possibly have kept me in the dark like this.

But then, he let my mother go, and he is still here.

"The garden," he says quietly. "I drained the life of it to open the gateway for her."

Flowers. A few flowers could have been spared to let me go home. He could have let me go the moment I–

No, not the moment I came. The garden was lifeless then.

"How... how long have you been able to send me home?"

His eyes raise a little; he is surprised I have worked it out. Why did he want me to believe that he always had the power?

"Since a little before it opened of its own accord," he admits. "It did not seem to matter, then. You were going home anyway. I told myself that a few more weeks with you was worth the lie, was worth the garden..."

"But then I lost my chance." Six weeks. He has kept my family waiting for six weeks. Lied to me, all that time. "But... why?"

"Because I was selfish," Thorn says quietly. "Because I did not want to be alone again, and because I tried to convince myself that you wanted to stay."

Would you go home tomorrow, if you could?

"Maybe I did want to!" I spit. "Maybe, if you'd just told me... I could have gone home, let my family know I was safe, and come back here! Maybe that's exactly what I wanted!" I throw up my arms. "Why does everyone here *lie*?"

Ariel hovers closer. "Rose–"

"Go back to the castle, Ariel." Thorn barks.

"There's more–"

"Ariel. Return."

Ariel's little form shrivels, as if she cannot believe what he has just said. "Fine," she snaps, and promptly disappears.

"I don't want to hear the rest," I whisper.

"You... you would have stayed?" Thorn's voice is hoarse. "You would have come back?"

"Maybe," I say, knowing that that is exactly what I would have done. Gone home, let everyone know that I was safe and happy, and come back here. Because I was happy. Wondrously so. But can I ever be happy here again, knowing what I know now?

"But... why?" Thorn's voice is desperate, but I do not care.

"It doesn't matter now," I say stonily. I turn to stare at the meadow. The stream trickles by. The fog is growing thicker. I do not think we have much time.

Stop me, I beg, as I take three very slow steps forward. Say something. *Anything. Make me understand.*

Am I honestly going to do this, walk away in anger, never to see him again? Once this door is slammed, it may be slammed for good. But how can I stay, when he has lied to me? And I've been saying for days that I want to go, that I need to go, that this is the only way to survive.

Why then, does walking through it seem like a death sentence?

I cannot think of anything to say. All niceness is beyond me. Hurt dominates affection, betrayal triumphs over friendship. The mists call to me.

"Goodbye, Thorn," I whisper.

I race off through the meadow, not looking back as the grass whips my skin, snatching at my clothes. I reach the stream and slide down the bank, tearing across the stones and up the other side, where I hit the ground with such force that I roll over, and stop, just for a second, catching my breath.

A horrible, fearful howl hollows out the wind, and I glance back at nothingness.

Was that him? No, it cannot be him. The sound is beyond that of any living creature, any man or beast. It is monstrous, unearthly, a spirit raked through stone. It clings to the air, splits through my spine. My heart stills in my chest.

I scream his name, but there is no reply. I am all alone.

For the longest of times, I sit on the bank, watching the blank slab of grass on the other side where my home should be. No, the *castle* should be. This is my home. This is where I'm supposed to be.

I didn't say goodbye to the fairies. I didn't even think of Bramble. I didn't stop to pack, to gather my books, my ribbons, my dried flowers... all the little things I'd planned to take with me. How could I have just left? How could I have just left *him*?

"Rose," the ghost of a voice calls to me. Tentative, awed, familiar. It's him. He's followed me through, he's–

The voice is coming from behind me. I turn with both joy and dread. Freedom is standing there, hand clasped to his mouth, looking as if Mama herself has returned from the dead. He races towards me with such force that he stumbles getting to my level, and his arms spasm as if he's afraid to reach out and touch me.

"I'm here," I say quietly.

Within seconds I am folded inside his embrace, and Freedom –who hasn't cried since the day of Mama's funeral– is choking sobs into my hair and shaking like a kite in a storm. It seems to go on for hours.

When he eventually pulls back, his mouth is caught in a trembling smile. "Dear God, Rose, where have you been?"

"I accidentally wandered into a fairy realm." There is no other excuse I can come up with. "I'm back now."

Freedom laughs. "Of course you did."

"I did." There is very little proof I can offer him, of course. I have nothing with me, and he will surely think any of my fantastic tales a product of my imagination, except– "I saw you, in one of the magic mirrors there," I tell him. "Painting."

"The entire family knows I paint, Rose."

"You were painting *me*."

At last, I see some flicker of belief.

"You were using lots of red," I continue. "And I'm really not that pretty."

Freedom smiles, an exhausted, relieved, shocked kind of smile, and then he hugs me again.

Chapter Twenty-Four

Home Is Where the Heart Is

We walk home slowly, arm in arm, saying very little. I feel numb, like my legs could barely carry me unless I was latched onto Freedom. I am a child again, a little girl with skinned knees, being escorted home through the woods by her big brother.

Some energy returns when our house creeps into view, right on the edge of the village. It looks completely unchanged. There is washing on the line. I see Papa's jacket, and a dress that could be mine although it is probably Hope's. The beautiful aroma of baking bread wafts from the kitchen window. I had forgotten the scent, living in the castle, separated from the smells of the kitchen.

There is a cool, pleasant chill in the air today. A few rays of sun shimmer down on a fair-haired boy rocking back and forth on the swing under the apple tree, singing at the top of his lungs.

"I'm swinging, I'm swinging, on a tree, tree, tree, yesiree, my tree, tree, tree–"

His dark-haired companion tutters, looking up from the book in her lap. Neither one has seen me yet. "Beau, can't you sing something else?"

"I could... but I don't want to," he says matter-of-factly.

I want to say something. I want to open my mouth, sing a song from childhood, say something smart and witty that will make them laugh. But no words come. I hover by the garden gate, just watching them.

It is Beau who looks up first. There is a tiny, unfathomably long moment when his eyes fall to my face with a frown, as if I were a stranger. Then his gaze widens, his mouth opens, and my name escapes his lips in a half-whisper, half-scream. "Rose?"

Hope turns around gradually, as if it takes her a long time to process the word, but then she screams my name. Softly at first, and then louder and louder, and she is running towards me, Beau following, and I can't even move. When they reach me, we all sink to the ground, a mass of arms and hands and tears. There are no words, save my name, and a scream for, *"Papa! Papa!"*

Hope's voice is wretched and scratchy, almost like she's in pain, but she keeps screaming it as she clings to me and touches my face and Beau joins and paws me like a frantic puppy. There's a numbness in me, even though I am laughing and hugging them back. My flesh buzzes, overwhelmed, and the buzzing stretches to my temples.

Somewhere, in the corner of my eye, I register another presence. Papa is standing in the doorway. He is older than I have ever seen him. Beau and Hope are taller and ganglier than I remember, but he looks as if he has aged ten years. He leans against the door frame, rooted to the spot. Unable to move.

I shake off Hope and Beau, and make my way towards him.

"Papa," I say, and that is the only word I can manage, before we both dissolve into tears, and sob right there on the kitchen step.

Before long, I am seated in the kitchen, a bowl of porridge forced into my lap, and the questions start. I tell them the truth, mainly. I want them to know that I have been safe the whole time I've been away. So I tell them about the fairy realm, about being trapped until the doorway opened again, that it was a beautiful place, and that I wasn't alone.

I even tell them a little about Thorn, although I leave out the part where it turns out he was the one trapping me there. I still can't process that. I expect some resistance, particularly from Papa, but he just nods throughout. When I get to the part about Mama's portrait, I understand why. She has told him this story, at least in part. Nanny similarly does not take much convincing, and I wager she has heard the story first hand before as well.

Beau and Hope are, oddly, my biggest sceptics, and I am only half-sure Beau believes me when I reach the end of my tale. He keeps saying, "that's impossible!" over and over. Hope is quiet, impossible to read. I wonder how Honour will react when I see her.

"We'll bring her over first thing tomorrow," they witter.

"Why can't we just go over there now–"

"No!" say all the adults at once.

I blink at them.

"You should just rest today," Nanny says. "Let's not rush things."

"And we wouldn't want to shock your sister. Freedom will go over and break the news to her slowly."

This is a trifle odd to me, as everyone is bound to be shocked, but perhaps they are trying to avoid taking me through the town, and all the prying questions that would come with such an undertaking. Or perhaps they don't want me to leave the house just yet, which is understandable, given what happened the last time I left it.

Nevertheless, I long to see her. My heart is swollen with joy to see everyone else, but I am already craving the silence of my sister's knowing mind. There are things I need to talk to her about, things I've been unable to tell anyone else.

Nanny makes dinner, but we all abandon it, too excited and overwhelmed and exhausted to eat. At first, we share stories –what has happened to everyone in the time that I've been gone– but then the conversation shimmers down. Beau shows me something he's drawn while Hope gushes about her new favourite book. Nanny busies herself with tidying up, her face quietly streaming with tears.

Papa sits in his chair by the hearth, smoking his pipe, his gaze tight on me. It hasn't moved since we met at the doorstep. There is a greyness in the rest of his skin, a dullness in his eyes. He looks almost ill. *Yes*, I tell myself. *You had to come home. You had to.*

Beau puts his head in my lap and fastens his arms around me. His fingers tangle into my clothes, and I wonder if he ever plans on letting go. "I'm so glad you're home," he whispers.

I kiss his hair, inhaling the smell of sunflowers and peppermint. "Me too, dearheart."

I am home, I am home, I am home.

The next morning, I awake to the weak, warm light squirming through the flimsy curtains. The threadbare coverlet is twisted around me, bunched up around Hope, who is sleeping soundlessly by my side, her arm still wrapped around my middle as if she was afraid I'd vanish in the night.

I lean down and kiss her cheek as I wriggle carefully out of the bed. I pull back the curtains, just a crack, slip into my slippers, and lower myself into my reading spot.

My slippers! I put them on automatically, and there they

were– right where I had left them. I stare, marvelling the ratty old things. The room of my childhood is utterly unchanged in the months I've been away, apart from the spotless corner Honour used to inhabit. Perhaps Hope has different clothes strewn over the chair in the corner, and perhaps that is a new vase of dried flowers, but nothing else is different.

My old books are piled up exactly how I left them. They are weather-worn, and the paper smells unfamiliar. I thumb through the first one. A classic tale of mystery and adventure, a journey of self-discovery and impossible places. I set it quickly aside; the book is the same, but it doesn't provoke any wanderlust. Perhaps I have seen enough of wonder, these past few months.

Downstairs, Nanny gasps when she sees me, and Beau runs over to squeeze me, as though he was afraid I was a dream of yesterday. I pull him up and spin him around, which is no easy task. He is so much bigger than he was.

I pat Fifine and Azor and grab a bowl of porridge. The whole family trickles in, one by one, all bar Freedom, who is already out. It is a quiet meal, and everyone keeps staring at me.

"You're very brown, Rose," says Hope eventually.

"I've spent a lot of time in the sun. The gardens, Hope, they're so beautiful, if only–"

I stop, because Hope will never see the gardens, no matter how much I might wish it. Spoons scrape bowls. Nanny remarks about the weather. Papa asks Hope what she has planned for today, quizzes Beau on his latest school work. I wish Freedom were here, even to annoy me.

Suddenly, I hear his voice. "You should slow down–"

"I can't believe you didn't come straight to me last night–"

"We didn't want to shock–"

"She is my *sister*, Freedom!"

Honour. Honour is here. I've barely managed to get out of my seat before the door is flung open and she is there, standing on the threshold, her eyes wide and her hair wild.

She takes one look at me and bursts into tears, and we are

running towards each other, arms extended. We sink to the floor the second we are together, sob each other's names, and sit there on the floor until everyone else starts moving around us.

Nanny whips out a chair. "You really shouldn't sit on the floor, Honour love—"

"Here, take a pillow—"

"I'll get some tea!"

It is only when Honour has been properly sat down and everyone else has moved away that I see my sister fully for the first time, and realise what everyone is fussing about, something that should have been apparent the minute I clasped eyes on her.

Honour is very, very pregnant.

Everybody suddenly finds themselves something to do, and Honour and I are alone together for the first time in months. She wails that she's so sorry she got married without me. I gush that I'm so sorry I left her.

I can't believe she's going to have a baby; no wonder she was always knitting whenever I checked in with her. I wish I'd been there when she told everyone she was expecting. At least, I suppose, I will be here to support her now... although at what cost? *I will not be there for Thorn.*

I fill her in on where I've been, and she doesn't seem at all shocked or surprised.

"I knew you were alive," she says, beaming through her tears. "I just... felt it. The night before my wedding, I swear I almost heard you call to me, saying that you were all right and not to worry."

The night before her wedding. The night I wrote to her for the first time. Perhaps the magic of the castle could reach the outside after all.

"I'm not sure anyone believed me," she carries on. "Nanny and Papa wanted to, I think... Freedom never did, of course. He never listens."

"He's stubborn, like that," I mumble, knowing very well it's a trait we both share. Honour knows it too, and smiles knowingly at me.

"You look different," she says.

"As do you!"

She laughs, placing a hand on her massive belly. She must have conceived straight after the wedding; she cannot be any less than six months. I've seen full-term women with smaller bumps. The look suits her though, and she reminds me of Mama, all round and soft and devoid of sharp edges. She looks stronger than Mama ever did though, thankfully.

"I mean it," she regards me carefully. "Something's changed in you."

"I feel different," I tell her. "But I don't know why."

Honour tilts her head disbelievingly.

"I met someone," I conclude.

"Ah, yes, your mysterious companion. What was he like?"

I tell her the absolute truth, about who –or what– he is. She sits there in silence for a moment, not stunned, not shocked, just... silent.

Finally, she says, "But what is he *like*?"

Unfathomable relief washes over me. There is no judgement in my sister, not a sliver. Just pure understanding, unquestionable clarity. Honour indeed.

Talking about Thorn is difficult, but somehow, with her beside me, I manage it. "He is intelligent, witty, compassionate and kind... at least, I thought he was. I thought..." *I thought he was everything.* "I thought he was the most gentle soul that I had ever met." A lump is rising in my throat. "But... he lied to me."

I tell her, with some difficulty, about terms of my entrapment and release. This makes her quieter for even longer.

"I see," she says, "and... how does that make you feel?"

275

"Furious," I whisper. "Betrayed. I never thought... there were always things he was keeping secret, but I had my secrets too. Not like this, though. I couldn't... I honestly couldn't believe he would do something like this. Even though I completely understand why."

Even just a day's perspective has given me that much. *Of course* he didn't want to be alone. *Of course* he wanted more time with me.

I wanted more time too.

But the deception eats into me: he should have told me, and trusted that I would not leave.

"And does it change the way you feel about him?"

It should. It did, in that moment. But already my old feelings are sliding back into place. I shake my head. "I think those are somewhat firmly fixed," I admit.

But he kept you prisoner.

Was I a prisoner? I did not feel like one. I was not treated like one. And... and I still cannot shake the feeling that there was another reason he didn't let me go. Ariel was trying to tell me something before Thorn sent her away.

"There's more." She had said. What had she been prevented from revealing?

"Did you tell him, this gentleman of yours?" asks Honour. "How you felt about him?"

"He knows."

Honour groans, and her whole body seems to groan with her. "Oh, Rosie..."

"What?"

"You didn't tell him."

"I... I've told him lots of ways!" I argue. "I've told him that... that I like his face. And that... his soul is like mine! I... I assure you, I made my feelings perfectly obvious."

"I assure you sister, the poor boy probably thinks you're just friends."

I bite my lip. "You can't know that."

"No, but I do know you. You really aren't... the easiest of

people to read."

"I... you've always found me easy to read!"

"I knew you before you had expressions. I've picked up on your subtle ways. But honestly, dearest sister, you are very good at keeping things locked up. You have been ever since..."

She doesn't need to finish that sentence. We both know how it would end. And, as usual, of course, my sister is right.

Could Thorn honestly not have known I would have stayed, anyway? Did he honestly think, after all this time, that I didn't care? That I would walk away without a single glance over my shoulder?

But you did. You did exactly that.

It is after Honour leaves that it hits me for the first time, hits me with such a force that I have to clutch the mantelpiece for fear of falling.

"Rose?" Hope asks, walking back into the room, "What's wrong?"

"I'm never going to see him again!"

What have I done?

Chapter Twenty-Five

Letters From the Past

T ry as I might, I am sure my family can see my distress the following morning. I try to busy myself by helping Beau with his school work. Hope, of course, requires no such assistance. She's been smarter than me for years.

Honour comes round for lunch. I offer to visit her tomorrow, but this idea is quickly rebuffed. Either no one wants me to leave the house ever again, or they're still trying to think of a plausible reason for my absence that doesn't sound so truly remarkable before all the villagers learn of my return.

After Honour departs for her abode in the mid-afternoon, I find myself alone. Hope and Beau are at school, Nanny has gone to the market. Freedom, I suspect, has gone hunting. He is clearly trying to avoid me, having barely spoken a word since our reunion. It makes me long for the days when he used to tease me and push me out of trees.

I wander into Papa's study. This is usually the forbidden room, but today the door is wide open, and I sense I am welcome anywhere right now.

"Ah, Rosebud." Papa's face flutters into his almost-smile,

the nearest semblance of happiness he has managed since Mama's death.

I give him a hug which he gladly returns, and I stay there for a little longer than I planned to.

"I have a gift for you," he says.

"A gift?"

"It was... for your birthday," he says quietly. "It belonged to your mother. She wanted you to have it."

He opens his top drawer and pulls out an old, weather-beaten package, thick and dusty.

"From Mama?"

"Yes."

"Why... why me?"

"From your infancy, she had set aside gifts to give you all once you turned eighteen. Lord knows what I'll do for Beau's, poor boy. But this is most assuredly for you."

Gingerly, I peel open the wrapping. It is, unsurprisingly, a book. *The Fey Collection,* I read, and then open the cover.

My darling Rose,

You will know most of these stories already, but I have them here, written down for you, just in case. These are the stories of our ancestors. My mother gave this to me on my eighteenth birthday, and her mother gave it to her. Share these stories with your brothers and sisters, my little fairy. Be adventurous. Be afraid. Be brave. Above all, love fearlessly, for as long and hard as you can.

All the love in the world, Mama

A lump wells in my throat. I know she did. I turn the first page, and begin to read. The first few I am familiar with, particularly the one about the dark fairy, who the queen trapped at great cost.

There is another story I've not heard before, at least not from her. It talks about the castle the evil fairy is trapped in, how her magic weakens it with every passing day. How one day, she may break free, and wreak havoc on the world once more. It says she is guarded by a terrifying monster, but a neat line crosses through that part. Another hand has written over it, *"the castle is protected by a beautiful creature."* In the margin, in such clear writing, she has added, *"He is not a monster!"*

Mama. She is talking about Thorn. I left him alone with this evil creature still prowling the walls.

I pray that he is safe. I curl my hands around my little amber rose, and hope that he can feel the warmth of me through his thorn pendant.

There are other stories in the volume, ones she never got a chance to tell us. They are about what happened after the fairies fled their homeland, shed their wings, became human in almost every way. *"These are the stories of your ancestors."*

Thorn was right. Mama was descended from the Fey.

There is something else amongst the wrappings of the book, a tiny hand mirror of delicate design. At first, I am entirely confused as to why she would have included this in a gift to me, the least of her daughters to treasure such an item. Then I pick it up, feeling its heavy weightlessness, and notice the flawless etchings. This is a fairy mirror. She took it from the castle. I have seen so many like it.

Clutching it to my chest, I try not to cry. It is all I have left of that place.

For the next few days, I exist in some kind of dream. Nothing feels real, nothing feels right. It is akin to the numbness I felt after Mama's death. I am moving, but not breathing. I don't feel fully alive.

I try to put on a brave face for my family, eating and chatting with as much energy as I can muster. They must notice something amiss, but probably put it down to me trying to re-adjust to my old life. I make light of it, where I can, jokingly complaining about my narrow bed and lack of feathery pillows.

My family keeps me busy. Nanny always appears to be needing help with the laundry and the cooking, tasks I am more than willing to help with as they occupy my mind, and I'm worried I've grown idle living in such luxury. Hope and Beau always seem to need help with school work, even though Hope works out problems so quickly with just a little assistance from me, that it's quite clear her problems were invented. Honour visits whenever she can, which spares me from Freedom's attempts to busy me– namely, assisting him with skinning his kills while he stares at me stonily.

"I'd prefer to model for you, if I have the option," I tell him, which earns me a dirty rag in the face.

When I am left alone, the thoughts come as quickly and darkly as a winter's night. Thorn, Thorn alone in that castle, thinking I did not care for him, thinking I was gone for good. What can I do? Wait until the next Solstice, and pray it opens in the same place? Do I have another option? What if I can wait, and it doesn't open? Or even...

What if he can't wait? What if I do go back, and Thorn is not there waiting for me?

The next day, I share the book with Honour. "Why do you think she gave it to me?" I ask.

Honour shrugs. "She left me her best linens for my eighteenth, and a set of exquisite spoons. Sometimes... sometimes I think Mama knew that she was never going to live to see us grow up."

She had not been well for a while before Beau came. It might have been logic, rather than instinct, but somehow, I am inclined to agree. Her note, her advice to live bravely, is the sort of thing one would write if they weren't planning to say it in person. "Did she leave you a note too?"

Honour nods. "She told me that I was the most caring person she knew, but that I should look out for myself, and not be afraid of asking for things," she smiles shyly. "I told Charles to dance with me the very next day."

"I wonder what she told Freedom."

"She told him that he would always look after us, that he would never fail us, and that he should be careful when shooting." I stare at her. "She gave him a crossbow," she says, by way of explanation.

"How... how do you know what she told him?"

Honour looks about guiltily. "After you left–" she starts, but is interrupted by Freedom marching from the study out into the cool evening air. He looks at me darkly as he passes.

"Is Freedom angry with me?" I ask.

Honour wriggles about uncomfortably. "Mad at himself, I fear."

"How so?" Honour sighs and re-adjusts her seat. I still can't stop looking at her. She is so *large*. I've missed so much. I find it difficult to concentrate on her words, even when I've asked for them. "When you went missing, we were naturally all distraught, but Freed... he was out there in the forests every day, every hour, searching for you. That first week he barely ate or slept. One day, I found him in his room, clutching the note that mother had left him. He was just seething with rage. It... it almost got to the stage where I thought about trying to convince him that you were dead, that there was no point searching. But then he stopped of his own accord. I think he's wishing he carried on."

Except, he didn't stop. He just started being more secretive about it. I had seen him in the mirror, walking the woods day after day. "It wasn't his fault," I mumble.

"Try telling him that," Honour advises. "Because he's not listening to anyone else right now."

I step outside and find him there, leaning against the wall. I know at once that he has heard the conversation. "I should have searched harder."

"What part of *trapped in a fairy realm* don't you understand?"

"I could have found you. If I'd been quick enough. If I'd realised you were missing– I could have found that stupid gateway and made it give you back to us." He is shaking. "You heard what Mama wrote to me. She said that I would always protect you, never let you down. But I did. I really, really did."

"Freedom, no one is to blame for this but me."

"But–"

"I am sorry for what I put you through. Don't do this to yourself. I'm safe, I'm unhurt, I'm here."

"I saw you, you know. A few weeks ago."

"I... I know."

"You were standing in this meadow, across the stream, flanked by fog. I thought you were a ghost or a vision... but I called out to you, and you called back. Why... why didn't you come to me?"

"Somebody was hurt," I answer. "I couldn't let them–"

Freedom grabs me roughly and pulls me into his arms. "Don't leave us again, Rose. Don't you dare."

I want to make some sort of joke, to tease him, to push him away and make light of it, but I don't, I can't. For a few, rare moments, I am just a girl who loves that her big brother loves her, and never, ever wants to leave him.

Except, of course, I do.

"I missed you," I say earnestly, burying my face in his chest. "Also, I learnt to climb trees."

At this, Freedom laughs. He holds me at arm's length. "You did?"

"It's a lot easier when your teacher doesn't push you out."

"You are never going to forgive me for that, are you?"

"I'm your little sister. I don't have to forgive you for anything. That's my speciality."

"I thought that that was winding me up?"

"That too. I have lots of specialties. Also, I shot a wolf."

"You did?" Freedom's face breaks into a proud smile. "Well done! Did you– wait. What were you doing hunting wolves? I thought you said it was safe where you were?"

"It was... mostly."

I think of the shadows, of Moya in the glass, which makes me worry about Thorn again.

"Mostly?" Freedom is not impressed. "What... what else was in that castle, Rose? Apart from your companion?"

"It doesn't matter now," I say quickly, only to appease him. It matters now more than ever.

I couldn't let him die. At the time, I convinced myself that anyone would have done the same. Perhaps most people would. But what had Margaret said? She would have stayed... but not for the same reasons.

At the time, I didn't know what she meant, or ignored it if I did. I did not stay to save his life. I stayed to save mine. Because I have no heart if his ceases to beat. No life without his. His death would have destroyed me, reduced me to a ruin of whoever I was before. I would have been a shell for the rest of my days.

I remember similar sentiments were expressed in *Tromeo and Lessida*, when they both realised the other was safe, but far beyond their reach. They admit –separately to themselves and not to each other– that this will do. That they can continue to live so long as the other one does. It will be enough. This is why it's Thorn's favourite book. It is why Thorn let me go. He told himself that it would be enough, that I was alive and happy. He did not know that I would not be happy without him.

And Tromeo and Lessida find their way back to each other. Despite everything, despite years, despite wasted decades, they are reunited. They come back to one another.

I need to go back to Thorn. I just need to wait until the next solstice, and pray that it opens in the same place. I don't even know what I will say to him–

A sharp pain burns in my chest, so sudden and so strong

that I cry out, clutching the bedpost to steady myself. Hope murmurs in her sleep, but doesn't wake.

As soon as it started, it's over.

What was that? I clutch the little fairy mirror, as if I can fall right through the glass and reach him.

Be all right, I pray, *I am here. I will come back soon...*

Knowing that sleep isn't coming easy tonight, I light a candle, conscious of not disturbing Hope, and begin to write.

My Dearest Thorn,

I cannot stop thinking about how I left, and how I long to take back the way we ended things. I worry about you. I think of you constantly. I miss you, like one misses a part of their heart. It feels impossible that I can live without you.

I should be mad at you. Your deceptions cut me deeply, but your absence cuts me worse. I think I understand why you did what you did. You did not trust that I would stay with you anyway. I did not give you reason to trust me, and for that I am most sorry.

I never told you quite so plainly what you meant to me, even though I felt it so keenly it should have poured out of me.

You are my everything.

Please stay safe, until I can see you again.

All my love, Rose

I fold the letter, take it to the window, and burn it with my candle. The blackened wisps float away on the breeze. Let them reach him, like my words reached Honour. Let him know that I am coming home.

I dream that I am inside the Mirror of Moments, watching Thorn. He sits in front of the ruined Mirror of Truth, a dozen

Ophelias, Ariels and Margarets reflected in the shards.

"I am truly sorry," he says.

"There's no need to be sorry," says Margaret, her voice softer than I have ever heard it. "It couldn't be helped. You tried."

"Couldn't be helped?" The fury in Ariel's voice is palpable. "You should not have let her go!"

"I had to. I should have tried to long ago. It was selfish of me to keep her here."

"I do not think she minded," Ophelia offers quietly. "She was happy to leave."

"That is not what I saw," Ariel persists. "I saw you practically throw her out! Didn't even let us say goodbye–"

"You would have stopped her."

"I would have told her the truth! Do you think she would have left if she knew why you hadn't let her go–"

"She might have done."

The fairies go quiet.

"Oh, my dear boy," says Margaret softly, and a hundred hands reach out towards him. "You actually still fear that, don't you? Even after everything?"

"If she stayed," replies Thorn tautly, "it would not have been for the right reasons."

"I don't know," adds Ophelia, smiling weakly, "she was very reluctant to go, even after you told her that you were keeping her here. I am sure she'll be back, if... if you can wait."

Thorn shakes his head. "I watched her reunite with her family. She will not return. This is as it should be."

"This is not as it should be!" Ariel hisses venomously. "How could you just– she should be here! You need her and she–"

"Ariel, calm down. There's nothing to be done now."

"I'm sorry." Her voice cracks. A dozen tears slide into shards. "I just... I really liked her, and I like here, and I like the idea of having a body again, and I like you. This isn't fair!"

"We're still here," says Ophelia hopefully. "For now, at least. It isn't over yet."

Thorn moans quietly. Is he hurt? He looks like he is. "Yes, it is."

In the reflections, I see a dozen hands reach out to touch his shoulder, a dozen faces almost as sad as his. The reflections flicker, dim like firelight.

"You... might..."

"Ariel?" The reflections are fading. "No–"

"It's... right... here... still... won't... leave..."

"Margaret! Ophelia!"

Then they are gone, and he is alone once more.

I call out to him, bang against the glass. For a second, I am sure he has heard me. His ears turn in my direction.

Say my name. Say it.

"Rose," he whispers, "I know I am only imagining you, but will you stay, regardless?"

I will stay with you forever.

Thorn sits alone in the Hall of Mirrors, looking up at the covered glass. It hums, as if alive.

"You can come now, Moya," he says. "There is nothing left for you to destroy now."

Chapter Twenty-Six

The Emptiness Inside

Every mealtime when we came together, I would sit with my family, watch them talk and laugh and talk and laugh with them, but in the way a puppeteer moves a puppet. I was frightfully, inexplicably, impossibly lonely. I could not understand it. I had never been lonely in my life before I left home. I liked solitude. I liked stillness and quiet. I liked the way the rest of the world could melt away whenever I dreamed.

But the world was more present than ever. I couldn't make it stop or stand still, and I had lost the ability to take pleasure in the things I once loved to do.

I wanted to cry out. I wanted to tell anyone that would listen, that I felt lost and filled with sorrow, but I could not. I could not hurt them, and they would not have understood.

Thorn would. Not a thing I had kept from him, not a thought or secret. Was this simply because there had been no one else around?

No. No, I had never been one to divulge thoughts easily, not before.

Life before Thorn. I look around the room of my childhood. I was happy here, wondrously happy. These walls contain the scars of my life, but a haze surrounds them. Life before Thorn does not seem to exist.

Not a thing had I kept from him.

There was one thing. And, in the end, it was the only thing that mattered.

The next day, I declare my intention of going for a walk. As I expect, this declaration is met with stony looks and pale faces. I am getting ready for an argument when Nanny says, "Well, you can't stay inside forever!" and turns to my father to have a discussion about mentioning my return off-handedly to the neighbours.

Freedom looks like I've stabbed him. Beau pulls at my elbow. "Can we come?" he asks.

I want so desperately for a few minutes to myself, but it is hard to refuse that little face. I agree readily, which appeases Freedom somewhat. He insists he come as well, but walks several feet behind us the entire way. The dogs are better conversationalists.

We are gone for several hours. Beau keeps us entertained by spouting off all the new names he's learnt for things. Hope fills me in on the latest stories I might have missed. I, however, am unusually silent. When I walked with them before, I would fill their heads with fairy tales, but this is now a forbidden word amongst us.

The walk back takes us within distance of the meadow. Beau wanders on ahead, chasing a toad I think, whilst I pause, my eyes fixated on the bank of green beyond the stream. A touch of fog, thin as frost, brushes the damp grass.

Somewhere, behind, between, close by, Thorn is. He is there, and I am here, and the space between us might as well be an ocean.

"That's where it is, isn't it?" Hope stops at my shoulder. "The gateway that took you. Across the stream."

"Yes," I reply, not knowing what else she expects me to say.

"Did you miss us, while you were gone?"

I turn to face her. How can she ask me that? "I thought about you almost every single day."

"So why are you thinking of going back?"

I startle. Hope is fourteen. When I left, she was more of a bookworm than I was. She detested parties, abhorred crowds, hated looking people in the eye. When did she become so observant? Her expression is as clear as glass, the pain, the fear, the disappointment, the honesty and the clarity. I cannot lie to her.

"I love you, you know that, right?"

She nods, although she looks a little surprised. "I assumed so. You don't say it much."

"No," I admit, "I suppose I don't. But I think it all the time, and more than ever when I was away. But there is this beautiful thing about families. Even when we're apart, we're still as close as ever. Our families are a part of us."

"Like Mama," she says. "How she's still with us, even though she's not."

"Yes," I say, even though I have not felt that way, not until recently. "The point is, Hope, family is easy to carry around. If we're lucky, we meet other people in life who become a part of us too. But... they are not so easily carted around. The bonds between us are just as strong, but when we are apart, those stretched bonds begin to hurt, and we feel like we will break if we cannot return to them." I point out towards the meadow. "Somewhere out there, somebody is waiting for me to return, hurting just as much as I am now."

"How do you know?"

"I'm sorry?"

"How do you know that they feel the same way?"

How *do* I know? Thorn has always been more open with his

feelings than I have, but he has never expressed himself explicitly... and yet, he has. In every word and gesture he has cast in my direction, for almost every day. I know him better than I know myself.

"It sounds impossible, but... his heart speaks a language that mine can understand, more precisely and more perfectly than any words."

"So... he hasn't told you?"

I almost want to laugh. "He didn't have to."

But I should have told him. I really, really should have. I do not tell Hope this. Instead, I put my arm around her, ask her to keep my secret, and feel a little better for sharing it.

When we return, Nanny greets us at the back door, her face white and taut. For a second, panic floods me. Papa's been taken ill. Honour is having the baby. Something is wrong, something awful–

"You have a visitor, dear," she says uneasily, and steps away to reveal James Saintclair standing in the kitchen.

Nanny quickly steers the others away, and I am left alone with him.

This is one reunion I have not been looking forward to. I have not been fair to James. He has never acknowledged it, perhaps is even unaware of it, but I did not treat him as I should have done. I knew he liked me, I kissed him knowing that, and I never discouraged his affections even when I knew I did not feel the same. I knew I would never love him, and that was safer. He could never hurt me. That was wrong of me, but I didn't know better.

I know so much more than I did then.

"Er, hello," he says, awkwardly stepping towards me with a slightly dazzled look of stark bewilderment. "I... I heard you were back. They're saying... well, it's a strange tale–"

"That it is," I nod.

"You're... you're all right, though?"

A fondness stirs within me. He has always been so kind. No wonder he was one of the few I considered a friend. No wonder he was easy to play pretend with.

"I'm fine," I reply, taking a seat. "It was not a difficult place to be trapped in."

"I'm... I'm glad," he says. He moves towards a stool, but doesn't sit. He wrings his fingers. "I'm glad that you weren't scared, that you were safe. Your family missed you terribly."

I notice he does not include himself in his number, and something in my face must show it.

"I... I missed you too," he says quickly. "Although..."

"James?"

He looks down at his palms, wiping them together, tapping his fingers against the table. His eyes look everywhere but at me. "I... I told Delphine Bardot that I would marry her," he spits out eventually.

"Delly?" I don't think I've ever seen them together, and it takes my mind a little time to imagine it. But the more time I spend on the image, the more I see it clearly. Delly, polite, sweet, lovely Delly from the bakery. They will make a splendid couple. "Well, well done Delly! Well done *you*."

James stops trembling. His eyes stop darting about. "You aren't... you aren't put out? I know that there was never a formal arrangement between us, but–"

"No, James, not at all. I am delighted for you both."

He breathes a sigh of relief. "I would have waited, if I'd known," he adds, more out of politeness, I think. Then he stiffens. "No... I think, once I spoke to her –once I knew her– that I might have been stolen from your affections even if you were right by my side. That sounds awful, I know, and I'm terribly sorry–"

"You love her."

James' face breaks into the first real smile I've seen in a long time. "Yes," he says proudly. "A great deal."

"We would never have made a good match," I tell him.

"No," agrees James, "I don't think we would have been precisely miserable together, but–"

"We would not have been entirely happy, either."

"Exactly." At last, he comes towards me, holding out his arms. He squeezes my hands and places the lightest kiss on my cheek. "It really is good to see you, Rose," he says, beaming. He pats my hand, says his farewell, and departs for Delly's.

It is easy to wish him well.

That evening, after everyone else has gone to bed, I stay up with my father, staring into the fire as he thumbs through his newspaper. I sit on the hearth with the dogs, near his feet, the position I occupied as a child.

"Papa..." I start, "Do... do you ever regret marrying Mama?"

Papa folds down his newspaper and stares at me incredulously. "Why on earth would you ask that?"

"Because I know just how much it hurt you when she died."

"It did," he says, a whole lot of emotion tied up in those two words. "But she left behind five precious jewels that helped plug up the wound."

"But... what if you didn't have us?" I probe. "What if you'd married her, and she'd died within the year? If there were no children? Nothing to remember her by? Would you have regretted it then?"

"No." He says. How can he speak so simply?

"No? But you wouldn't have had anyone–"

"I would have had her," he continues. "And I would have taken a day with her over a lifetime with anyone else. And we had more than a day. We had years. If I have to live another ten, twenty, thirty years without her... it would still have been worth it."

My throat feels very tight. Papa reaches out, touches my hand.

"There are so many awful things in this world, my dear. And yes, death is one of them. But love is the only thing that makes any of the darkness worthwhile."

I rest my head against his knee so that he cannot see my tears.

"Why do you ask this now, Rosebud? Afraid you've missed your chance with Mr Saintclair?" He strokes my hair. Silence drifts by. He knows that that is not the reason. "If there ever was such a fellow, that you felt that way for... that you felt you had to be with, no matter what... you should know that whatever makes you happy, will make me happy."

For a long time, I cannot speak. It is only after the candles are nearly all burnt out that find my voice again, wiping my eyes on my sleeve. "Thank you, Papa."

I climb up the stairs and pick up Mama's book. I understand what she wrote, what she said to me the day she died. *Don't be afraid. Live fearlessly.*

I have not been living fearlessly. I have been living in fear, terrified at the thought of letting anyone get close for the fear they would be taken from me. Did Mama know this? Is that what she meant, when she spoke to me that last time? Had she known, all along, the path my life was to take?

The mirrors could not see the future, but perhaps... perhaps Mama could. Perhaps that was her power all along. I wonder if I have one, too.

I turn to the hand mirror, tiny blackened little glass that it is. I wonder if Thorn is watching me through his. I wish I could see him, so badly.

"Thorn," I whisper, "I want to come home to you. I'm not afraid anymore. I'm not afraid of anything apart from never seeing you again. Let me come back. Let me find a way to you."

For the merest of seconds, I swear I can see Thorn in the glass, looking back at me in utter disbelief, but after the moment has passed, I know I must have imagined it. Thorn has never been so thin. Am I already forgetting what he looks like?

Soon, my dearest. Soon.

Chapter Twenty-Seven

The Return

My heart feels heavy when I wake the next morning. Heavy and tight and painful. I dreamt of Thorn again, Thorn sitting in my room with Bramble at his feet, looking gaunt and grey, a plate of untouched food at his side. Was he ill?

Some of your dreams are just dreams... some a little more than that.

The castle is still trying to speak to me, and I am listening. I have to go back, I have to go back now.

Straight after breakfast, I march over to Honour's with very little but a casual word to the rest of my family. People stare at me as I walk by, turning to gossip with their companions. No one is brave enough to speak to me.

Charles is the perfect picture of politeness when I arrive at his front door, but even he watches me cautiously, as if he expects me to disappear into smoke. Honour has to dismiss him with claims that he is making her nervous, which is not good for the baby.

The minute he is gone, I unload my bag. It is full of every

fairytale volume I could find, and the mirror.

"What's all this?" asks Honour.

"Research," I declare. "I want to find a way to open the gateway early. I cannot wait another four or five months. I need to return to Thorn now."

Honour's smile radiates. "Because you love him," she says.

"Yes," I admit. I might as well get used to saying it.

Honour claps her hands gleefully. "Oh, hurrah! I'm so pleased." She pushes the books aside. "You won't need these."

"What? Why not?"

"Because you have true love on your side!" she says. "That will conquer any spell."

"It cannot be that easy."

Honour pouts. "True love isn't easy..."

"So your advice is to go back to the gate, and ask it to open nicely?"

"Have you tried that?"

"No–"

"Well, then! Off you go!" She half-pushes me towards the door, but then her arms fall away. A hand drops to her middle, and she breathes strangely. Her face goes white.

"Honour?" "On second thought, could you just wait a while? And... and ask Charles to fetch Nanny. I think the baby is coming."

I relay Honour's message to Charles and help Honour into bed.

"You can't be having the baby," I stammer, dumbstruck. *It's too soon. It's too soon and I have to go.* "It's too early."

Honour swallows guiltily. "No," she wheezes. "It isn't."

"But... but... you've... you've not been married nine months!"

The shame in her face reddens. "Charles and I–"

"Honour," I say, halfway between appalled and delighted, "You didn't."

"We did," she says. "That's why we couldn't wait for–"

She doubles over in pain. I rub her back gently. Shortly after, Nanny arrives, a picture of cool, calm serenity. She sends me to boil water while she unpacks linens. "First babies always take a while," she tells me matter-of-factly. "I'm sure it's in no rush."

But I really, really need this baby to rush. The need to return to Thorn is consuming. I can almost see him, sitting in the meadow, each minute seeming an hour, each moment consumed by the fear that I have deserted him.

Never, never, never...

A few more hours tick painfully by. The baby still isn't here. I go outside to catch some air. Charles is pacing the garden, Papa sitting on a bench nearby, smoking a pipe with some irregularity. His knuckles are as white as Charles' face.

"It's taking a long time."

"She'll be fine, boy."

"Is it supposed to take this long?"

"Rose!" Honour calls me back. Screams for my return. Her voice cuts through me like ice. But for a minute, it is another voice that I imagine, calling out to me in pain.

The clock ticks. The sun shifts. I am still here.

Honour begins to push and strain. I boil endless pots of water, ferry all the towels I can find upstairs, grab the scissors.

"I might need your help, Rose," Nanny says. "Stay close to me."

Nanny hasn't attended a birth since Beau's. No wonder she is worried. Honour looks terrible. Her face is contorted into a horrible, ghastly shape. She looks like she's breaking apart. She holds my hand with such ferocity that I could not leave if I wanted to. I am a rabbit in a snare.

"If anything happens to me, you'll be there for my baby, right?"

I feel the blood rush from my face, my heart tightens. Not

just with the thought of losing my sister, but the thought of making this promise. I cannot stay. Even if something happens. Even to look after this child. I cannot stay. I cannot.

Honour looks panicked. "Rose!"

"You're going to be fine, Honour."

"But if–"

"Your baby will be loved. Loved by everyone in their life. But most especially by you."

This seems to give her some ease, and she asks no more from me, whilst I offer silent prayers to anyone who might be listening.

The baby still isn't here yet. It's mid-afternoon. How many hours left till sunset? I shudder to think.

I'm coming, I'm coming, wait for me!

I nip out of the room to tell everyone that she is doing fine, even though I have no idea what that even means. Nanny just told me to say it. Beau and Hope have now arrived. Everyone is white-faced. They bolt upwards the minute I open the back door.

"Is she–"

"She's all right. No baby just yet. Nanny doesn't think it will be much longer."

Beau's voice is very quiet. "Is she going to die?"

"No, sweetheart, she's doing splendidly."

I wonder when Nanny and the midwife knew Mama wasn't going to live through Beau's birth. It was always a risky pregnancy, they said, Mama not being well beforehand. I do not think the birth took long. Mama had been fine all day, laughing and chatting. It was only towards the end she felt the baby coming. By morning, he was here, and she wasn't.

She lived long enough to name him, hold him, kiss his face and hands and feet. Nanny said –because Papa couldn't– that she poured a lot of love into his tiny body in the fraction of moments she had with him.

I seize both of my siblings in my arms and kiss them forcefully. Neither one recoils, struggles, or wipes away my kisses.

"What was that for?" Beau asks.

"Because I love you both very much, and I need you to know that."

They stare at me solidly for quite some time. Have I scared them?

"We love you too, Rose," Hope says. "Please–"

There is a scream so loud from upstairs that it shakes the birds from the trees. I race back into the house, and for a moment, I forget the dying of the sun.

An hour later, Honour is wrapped up in bed with a little wriggling bundle, better than she has ever been in her life. Her face is glowing, love pours out of her, and she holds her baby with such tenderness and devotion that I realise that she has become exactly who she was always meant to be. She was meant to be a mother.

She looks like ours now, more than ever, which makes it all the harder when I step outside "for some fresh air" knowing that I will not step back inside.

Charles sits stiffly on the step, Beau and Hope beside Papa on the bench. All eyes snap round when the door opens, their faces pale as moonlight. They have not yet heard the crying. I give them a wide grin.

"It's a little boy," I declare. "She's calling him Edward, after grandpa. He's absolutely perfect. You can go up and see him now."

Their faces break into the biggest, most relieved smiles that I have ever seen. They immediately barge past me, running up the stairs with such vigour it's a wonder they don't break.

I am an aunt now. Even if I never see him grow up, I'll still be his aunt.

I'll come again, I hope, on the next solstice. I shall see him a handful of times. I'll be the strange, mysterious aunt who appears just a couple of times a year with gifts for all the birthdays and holidays and then vanishes into thin air. His magic Aunt Rose.

I am walking before I realise it, picking up the pace the second I am clear of the village. In my heart, I am already home. My arms are around Thorn's and everything is perfect and wonderful and–

A vision as clear and painful as glass hits me. I am back in the rose garden, but the roses have turned to ash. I see Thorn lying on the ground, doubled over in pain. He is screaming, and I can feel his heart shattering like a mirror.

Something falls to the ground in front of me with a lead-like thud. My necklace. The chain has snapped clean in two. Since the day Thorn gave it to me, I have never taken it off. I fidget about trying to force the chain back together, but it's no good. The stubborn metal refuses to bend. It feels foolish, but I want to cry.

It's just a chain.

It doesn't feel like just a chain. It feels like an ill-omen, a warning.

"Rose!"

Freedom is running towards me, shirt untucked, looking frantic and breathless. I didn't even notice him. He skids to a halt in front of me.

"Honour," he gasps, "Honour, I heard she was... is she all right?"

"Fine," I say, as lightly as I can manage. "A little boy. Edward. They're both fine."

"Oh, thank the–" He straightens up, running both hands through his hair. His face breaks into an awkward smile. "Well, I'm an uncle."

"Congratulations."

"I suppose I should... I should go and meet him!" He takes a few steps, looking back only once. "See you at supper!"

No, you won't.

"Goodbye, Freed," I say, and watch the space where he was as he vanishes from sight.

I run with a speed I never knew I possessed. My sides tear, my lungs burn, and my heart... there is a pain inside it not caused by exertion. There is sickness, spreading, growing. And I know what it means. *I know what it means.*

"I'm coming!" I call out. "Hold on, I'm coming!"

There are only a few feeble rays of sunlight left when I burst out of the woods and into the meadow. I am so close, so close–

A grey-green stretch of darkness stares unblinking from behind the stream. No meadow, no castle, only a whisper of fog. No hint of the gateway, but it must open. *It must.*

Lightning fills me. The pain in my sides dissipates. I cannot, will not, stop. I throw myself down the hill, leap into the stream, scramble up the other side.

The fog gets thicker. I keep running, but I don't seem to reach anywhere.

"Please!" I scream. "Let me in! Let me get to him! *Thorn!*"

I scramble blindly through the swirling mists, terrified that any second, the mist will clear, and I will be standing by myself, nowhere and alone.

"Please," I beg, "I have to be with him. I'm here to set him free."

To set us both free.

The outline of the castle emerges through the smog. I am filled with blissful, wondrous expectation. I am already in Thorn's arms. I am tucked neatly under his chin. We are in our garden, and I am promising to stay with him for the rest of my life. We are starting our forever.

And then that second is over.

At first, I think I am in the wrong place, that the portal has spat me out elsewhere. This is not my home. This is a barren, desolate place. There is a castle up ahead, but it is not *my* castle. It looks almost like a ruin.

Except… it is the castle. It has all its turrets, towers, doors and windows. It has the sweeping steps up to the entrance and the fountain in the courtyard, though it spews naught but dust and air.

I do not stand long and stare, wondering if I've been transported back in time. I start to move, charging up the steps and flinging open the door.

It is cold inside, so cold. I expect to find the floor covered in dust, like when I first arrived, but it is not. Just fragments of dirt from the remnants of the garden.

"Thorn!" I cry. My words echo, but no returning voice cries out my name. I charge into the parlour, calling his name, then into the next room. I expect to see him, any second, stretched out in front of the fire, curled up in the window seat. Or he will come running in from the outside, scooping me up in his arms and calling out my name like it's the sweetest word in the world.

But I do not see him, he does not come.

I run into his room, flinging back the curtains around his bed. It is empty, empty and desperately cold.

My room? If Thorn were the one who had vanished, I would have haunted his room until his return, searching for any trace of him, any scent.

For a moment I am so sure I will find him there, that when I open the room, I think I see him, lying beside the hollow grate. A shape resides there, but it is not him. It is too small, grey in colour, and horribly still.

It is Bramble, and he has been turned to stone.

I crawl to his side and reach out to touch him. Nothing

touches back, nothing breathes. He is rock and nothing more. I kiss his forehead, and run my fingers over his stone skin, searching for fur to wind my fingers through.

"I will fix you," I promise, "I just need to find Thorn. Then I'll come back."

There is more I want to say, but I have to find Thorn. He will not be stone. Not him. No power on Earth will still the life in him, not while my heart beats.

I run through the corridors, flinging open any door I find, screaming any name I can.

"Ariel! Margaret! Ophelia! Where are you?"

Only the walls call back. *Where are you? Where are you? Where are you?*

Be safe, Thorn. Be alive. I've come back for you.

Where would he go? I feel like I have searched every room. I am about to head outside and search the gardens, when I remember.

The roof terrace. The roses. What had Thorn told me once– that they were the last things to die, before? If there was any, any trace of life, that is where it would be.

I stop calling. I stop breathing. There is no room for air in my lungs with my heart lodged firmly in my throat. I pick up my skirts and flee, along the corridors, right to the door and all the way up the narrow steps. I fall over as I reach the top.

That is where I see him, lying under the rosebush, covered in dried petals. They splatter the stones around him like drops of blood.

"Thorn!"

I am at his side, frantically brushing away the petals. He has a rose clenched in his palm. I tear myself on the thorns pulling it out of his grip. His palm is punctured. I kiss it fervently.

"No, no, *no*..." Was this the true price of opening the gateway? Was this why he didn't want to let me go? "Wake up, please!"

I throw my head against his chest. A tiny, fragile thump

beats beneath my cheek. He is alive.

I race to the fountain, scoop up the waters in my hands and sprinkle droplets over his face, into his mouth. "Thorn, please!"

Slowly, miraculously, he begins to stir. His beautiful eyes open.

"Rose," he says softly, "am I dreaming still?"

I cry with relief. "You most certainly are not!" I say, curling my hands around his clothes.

"Am I dead then?"

"Dead? No! You're as alive as I am!"

Thorn blinks wretchedly, and I shift backwards as he pushes himself up on his elbows. "You're... you're actually here."

"Clearly," I swallow breathlessly, brushing tears from my eyes.

"You came back. But, but the gateway—"

He rises up suddenly, and although the light is nearly all gone, it is still possible to see the mists dissolving. The way is still open.

"It isn't possible," he mutters. "I didn't open it—"

"You didn't?" I frown. "But then who—"

"What did you do?"

"Me? I just... I just asked it to. Prayed that it would."

"But... why?"

I open my mouth to tell him exactly why in four simple words, but before I can, Thorn's legs buckle underneath him. I slide my arms under him and we go to the floor together.

"Careful," I whisper, after a moment of holding him tightly. He is so much thinner than before. "What... happened here? What happened to you?"

Thorn sighs, inching out of my arms. "I told you that a sacrifice was required to open the gate—"

"The flowers," I said.

"It wasn't enough. I wasn't strong enough to open the gate and leave enough magic here to keep her at bay. Within days, almost all the magic was drained from this place."

"Bramble?"

"The fairies turned him to stone, rather than watch him wither and die like the rest of his place."

"And... you?"

"I thought you were gone from me forever," he says. "The fairies tried to convince me otherwise, but when they went... when... when I lost all hope that you cared for me, my heart broke. That's a very dangerous thing, for a creature like me."

I swallow carefully. "That's what Ariel was trying to tell me, wasn't it? That my leaving would cost you your life."

Thorn nods. The words, still unspoken, hang between us. *Because I love you.*

"You are an idiot, you know that, right?" I hiss, my eyes shut tight against the tears. "I would never, ever have gone if you'd told me that–"

"Precisely," Thorn interrupts. "You would have stayed out of guilt, wasting away for–"

"*Guilt?* You think I've come back out of *guilt*?"

"Didn't you?"

"No, Thorn! I came back because I–"

There is a rumble deep within the castle. Something shatters. The sound claws its way through the stone, splinters through the air. A triumphant scream sears into the sky and the clouds turn dark and cold.

"Oh, oh no..." Thorn's eyes are wide. He pulls himself up with great difficulty, and I cling to him.

"What is it?"

"Moya," he whispers, "she's escaped."

Chapter Twenty-Eight

The Dark Fairy

Lightning splits the sky. The mist turns dark and rolls towards us. We both stare, dumbstruck.

"The village," says Thorn abruptly, "you must escape, warn them–"

"I can't leave you! She doesn't want them–"

"On the contrary, she wants everything. Everything that has been denied to her all these years. Your family–"

What can I do? Leaving Thorn at the mercy of her and whatever shadows have crawled out of the dark will almost certainly result in his death, and will deserting him really help my family? Honour can hardly run; she's just had a baby– and will I reach the village before Moya, if that is her heading? I cannot run as fast as a shadow.

"No," I say. "My place is with you."

"You don't know what she can do–"

"I know I'm going to stop her."

"Rose–"

I fly from his side and bolt down the stairs, slamming the

door behind me and turning the lock. How long it will keep him there, I do not know. He is too weak to fight. Hopefully he is too weak to break down the door.

What am I thinking? The truth is that I am not. All I know is that I am not going to sit back and let her come for me, let her take Thorn away. Any thoughts of imminent death are pushed back.

I grab a sword from a nearby suit of armour and head to the Hall of Mirrors. She is standing there in the shards, surrounded by robes of swirling black. As the smoke clears, I see her fully. The years in the mirror have twisted her appearance beyond all kinship with her sister, turning her frame bony, shrivelling and shredding her wings to ruin. Her skin is utterly devoid of colour, her eyes black and bottomless as pitch. Her face is just as awful as I remember, just as bitter, just as cruel.

She sees me standing behind her in the reflection.

"Ah!" She wheels around. I am rooted to the spot. My weapon feels dull and useless in my hand. "My little beauty! My hero!"

"What... what do you mean?"

"My saviour! Honestly, I was worried there for a moment. You were so close to breaking the spell, but then dear old little Thorn had to be all noble and let you go. Used up any magic keeping me prisoner to open the gate. I must admit, your return was a surprise, for him as much as for me. He was so sure you weren't coming, and the minute he lost all hope was the minute I knew I would be free. So thank you, little beauty. Thank you for finally crushing him. I am free of my container and my miserable sister– well, I don't see her around anywhere, do you?" She laughs. "All she did to save that boy... all for naught, really. She just prolonged his pain. My end for him would have been much swifter."

"Leave... leave him alone."

"He will die soon enough," she says. She snaps her fingers. Two nearby suits of armour spring to life, grab me and pin me against the wall. I struggle against them, but it's like struggling against stone.

Moya only laughs, but she massages her hand, as though the motion has damaged her. When she catches me looking, she drops her hand.

"What do you want?" I cry.

In the space of a clap, her face is pressed against mine. "Everything," she hisses. "Everything my sister would have denied me. I want power and freedom and joy. I want to walk amongst the humans... and have them kneel at my feet."

I cannot imagine Freedom kneeling to her. I cannot imagine the village won't fight back. Perhaps they can defeat her, after all–

But then, her own sister had to give her life just to trap her.

Freedom doesn't stand a chance. I have to stop her, or, failing that, just delay her–

"You said your sister did this to save Thorn," I rush frantically. "What do you mean by that?"

At this, Moya throws back her head and laughs until she's almost hoarse. "You truly have no idea, do you? You really are stupid, even for a human. The droplets of fey blood in you really haven't helped much at all."

"I don't know... what you mean."

"The curse. *My* curse. It's not on the castle. It's on the *boy*. And you were *so close* to breaking it... I was *so pleased* when he let you go. For a moment I was sure–"

"You... you stopped me from leaving before," I argue. "When you conjured that lightning. You could have just let me go a few days later–"

Moya pulls a face. "I might have acted rashly, but watching the two of you that day down by the lake... I was certain you were about to break the curse. With his ridiculous plan for a ball and those stupid fairies' machinations... I was forced to act."

"But I stayed because of what you did–"

"Because I didn't manage to kill him! Or *you*. Either would have doomed this place, broken the seal on my prison. I used up so much magic in my efforts, infecting his wound when my first attempt failed..." She pauses, lifting up a fist filled with purple lightning. There is another tiny flicker in her face, a faint ripple of pain. "No matter," she continues. "Neither one of you can stop me now. And thank you for opening the gateway for me. That's going to make everything much easier for me."

"But I didn't open the gateway." I try to smile at her, rattle her. "And neither did Thorn."

Her eyes narrow, but there is the slightest waver in her voice. "You lie."

"Look at me. Do I really look like I have that kind of power?"

There is only one person who does, aside from Thorn, and she knows it. Her face betrays her fears.

An enormous crash sounds not far off. Shouts rally against the corridors. Moya forgets me in an instant and sweeps from the room. I see her reflection in the remaining mirrors. She glides down the corridors, clicking her fingers, bringing statues to life and pulling strange, grey, misshapen creatures out of the walls. The shadows are back again.

I have to get out. I scream for the fairies, but I know they are not coming back. Because of me, because of what Thorn did to save me, because I couldn't tell him that I loved him.

He will not die for this. He will not.

I still have movement in my legs. I press them against the back of the wall, trying to push myself up. It does no good. The surface is too smooth. I am, I realise, pressed against a mirror.

There is crashing as the rest of Moya's army breaks free of the castle. How many can there possibly be? I hear shouting, hissing, the clash of steel. What are they fighting against?

The reflections show light coming my way. A stout grey creature bursts into the room. A troll, I think. It is short and knobbly, with a face as tough as bark. It gurgles when it sees me, raises its axe—

A bolt shoots clean through the side of its neck. It drops to the floor in a second.

"Rose!" shouts Freedom, his hands immediately flying to

my face.

I have never in my life been happier to see my brother. "Freed! What are you doing here?"

Freedom immediately begins to dismantle my captors. Helmets and chest pieces clatter to the floor. They must need Moya to animate them; they are nothing more than metal now.

"This little creature brought me up here..." He gestures to the little glowing ball of light beside him.

"Ariel!" I do not know how I can tell who she is, but it is clearly her. She buzzes around my head affectionately as I struggle out of my bonds. "I thought you were gone–"

"Ariel, is it?" Freedom nods approvingly. "Thank you."

I grab my brother's arm and move out into the corridor. The place is awash with shadows, but also with men from the village. My brother has brought a small army of his own. "Freed," I say, much more seriously, "why are you here in the first place?"

"I came to save you! You're welcome, by the way–"

"It's not safe–"

"Yes, I can see that. I didn't come alone though, did I?" He pats his crossbow proudly. "What made you think–"

"After I got to Honour's, it struck me as strange, the direction you were running in. Towards the woods. I thought, at first, you were coming to get me, but when I replayed it in my head... you looked so surprised to see me. You must have been coming back here. Wasn't sure what to expect, so I rounded up a few reinforcements and–"

A bolt of black smoke hits the wall next to us. A bust explodes into dust.

"All right, I admit it, your timing has been worse," I tell him. "I need to get something from down the hall. Can you watch the staircase? Shoot anything... grey."

"Roger," he says. "You'll get somewhere safe?"

"Of course," I say, with no intention of keeping this promise. "And don't hit Thorn!"

I return to the hall to collect my sword, whatever good I

think it will do. I do not think I can defeat Moya with weapons, or surely the fairy queen would not have had so much trouble defeating her in the first place. Then again...

The look in her face when she enchanted the objects, as if she were in pain. She said she had used up a lot of magic, that night with the storm... how much magic had she used to free herself? She had been in there for years, and the magic of this castle, until recently, had been flourishing, and if Ariel was here... it wasn't all gone, or my return was bringing it back... If Moya wasn't at full strength–

Dodging whatever fray I can, and occasionally hitting what I cannot, I stream through the corridors in search of her. I pass by the door to the roof terrace on my way. It is open. Thorn is gone.

"Oh no..."

I pray he is somewhere safe, keeping out of the fighting. He is not strong enough. If Ariel is back, perhaps the others are too. Perhaps they are with him.

I cannot look for him now. Moya is an easier target. I just keep following the signs of battle.

The ball room. The *throne* room. Of course that is where she is.

She stands in the centre of the floor Thorn and I danced on just a few weeks ago, her head thrown back, laughing maniacally. Servants twirl about her, jeering and cackling as they beat back the villagers.

I know these men. They are my neighbours, my friends. James Saintclair is here. And, almost worse, Charles is too. He became a father just a few hours ago. If he dies here–

No, no, I cannot think like that.

Moya raises her hands to the chandelier. Purple lightning rises from her fists.

"Look out!"

I smash into Charles and knock him to the floor. Moya glares at me, but her pause gives James time to shoot at her. The arrow skids past her cheek. I hear her curse before sweeping onto the balcony.

Charles rushes to his feet, dusting off debris. "Rose!" he says. "You're all right! Thank heavens."

"What are you doing here, Charles?"

"Um... rescuing you?"

"You just had a baby! You should be with him and Honour–"

"Honour would never forgive me if I let–"

"Does she know you're here?"

"Well, no, I didn't want to upset her–"

I groan. Honour would never have let him come. She knew there was no danger here, well... she thought there wasn't. She was going to kill him.

James reaches our side. The rest of the creatures in the room are all dead. The fight is moving into the gardens. Good.

"Rose, are you–"

"I'm fine," I snap. I hurry out onto the balcony. Tiny droplets of blood dot the stones. "She's bleeding."

"Well, I did shoot at her–"

If she is bleeding, she can be killed by a mortal weapon. That is my hope.

Down by the lake, lightning crackles along the banks. "Follow it," I say. "Be careful. Try to get her to use her magic before attacking. She's weakest then." I think. *I hope.*

"Her magic, yes," says Charles numbly. I keep forgetting this must be strange to them.

The villagers stream into the garden. I turn back into the hall. From the shadows, a monster stares at me. It is at least eight feet tall, broad as a bear, with arms so long they almost graze the floor. Despite the width of its shoulders, it is skeletal, each and every one of its bones pushing out against its ash-grey skin. There is a horrible smell of decaying flesh.

I raise my sword seconds before it begins to charge. A black shape comes soaring out of nowhere, slamming into its side and knocking it clean against a pillar.

"Thorn!"

The monster is up again in no time. Thorn is on his feet, his hair standing upright, shoulders hunched. He is still not at full strength. He should not be fighting.

The monster raises its arms and Thorn meets both of them with his. I can see him straining, struggling to hold his footing, losing inches of ground.

I skid towards them, sword held firmly overhead, and slice the monster's belly. Blood spurts across the marble. It howls, releasing Thorn and darting backwards to assess its injuries. It is merely a flesh wound.

Thorn is bent over, but he clambers upright before I can assist him, panting hard. He cannot take much more of this, but I know nothing I can say will convince him to leave.

The monster readies itself again, but Thorn is quicker. He leaps into the air, soaring over its head, and grabs it by the throat. It struggles in his grip, clawing at his face, but before it can do any real damage I sprint towards it and plunge my sword under its exposed ribcage.

More blood pools out of it as I tug the weapon free. Thorn drops the creature. It lies there, jerking and bleeding, while Thorn and I stare at each other, trying to catch our breath.

The snap of a bolt comes whistling through the air. It hits Thorn squarely in the side, and my heart goes crushing to the floor with him.

"No!"

Thorn slumps into my arms. His weight takes us both to the ground. I hold him there. *He is fine, he is fine, he's going to be fine. It's all right, it's all right.*

I stare wildly over him at Freedom, standing in the doorway with a crossbow in his grip.

"What have you done?"

"He was... he was attacking you!"

"He would never–"

"Rose..." Thorn says faintly.

"He... he can talk."

"Of course he can talk!" I snap at him, before turning my attention to Thorn. I take his hand.

"But, but he's a..."

"He's *mine*."

If I could kill Freedom with a look in this moment, he would already be on the ground, beside Thorn, beside my heart. I do not care if he is my brother. I want to destroy him like he has destroyed me.

Freedom stands there numbly. "I didn't... I didn't know. How could I? I–"

"Leave us alone."

"I'm... I'm sorry–"

"Go away!"

Thorn squeezes my hand. "I'm all right," he says. "Just a flesh wound, I'm sure."

Tears run freely down my face. "You always say you're fine when you're not."

"So do you."

"Well, I'm not all right now."

Freedom crouches down, gingerly examining the wound in Thorn's side. Not touching him. Not daring. "I might... I might be able to fix that," he offers.

Thorn looks at him, and they share some quiet understanding. There is no fury in his face. How can he forgive him so easily? Then he looks back at me. "Moya?"

"She's bleeding," I tell him, even though this is wildly unimportant right now. "I think that maybe–"

He nods. "Her time in the mirror... it has weakened her."

"The others are fighting her–"

"It may not be enough," he breathes. The action hurts him. "But perhaps... the mirror." He looks at me. I can read his thoughts like a book. "You know what to do?"

"I think so, but–"

"Go, Rose. You have to. It might be the only way."

"But–"

"I'll wait for you."

I kiss his forehead fervently, closing my eyes, shutting out the world for just a second.

"I'll take care of him," Freedom insists. He does not try and convince me to stay, does not try to fight in my place. He knows what he has done, knows what he must do.

"You better," I say. "If he dies, I die."

Then I have to run.

He will be all right. He has to be.

There is only one thing worse than turning away from him in this moment. That is the thought of watching him die. But I cannot think of that right now. I have to think of stopping her. I have to save the castle, save the town, save him, save us. I have to make sure that Honour isn't a widow by tomorrow, though what good that will do me if I am without him. My soul will sink into the abyss with his, and I will pull the world down with me.

I burst into the hall and pick up a shard from the mirror that was Moya's prison all this time. It digs into my flesh. Will it be enough? Will I be able to hold onto it with enough strength? I have never stabbed anyone with a shard of glass before...

I have never killed anything remotely human before.

If Thorn wasn't dying, perhaps I would worry more about what that would be like, to take another's life. But I do not care. Somehow, I feel like stopping her will save him, and I know I would do anything, commit any evil, to keep him here with me.

Blood trickles down my palm. I am holding the shard too tightly. I rip sections out of my petticoat and bind it around both hands. It will have to do. No time to waste.

Before I leave, I have a sudden idea. I pray the extra seconds do not cost me deeply.

The garden is flooded with light. Several of the trees are on fire. Their leaves spasm frantically against the inky backdrop, their skeletal branches twitching. I can almost feel Ophelia crying.

Lightning still rages against the sky. Statues and tombs explode around me. I dropped my sword after Thorn was shot. All I have now is my mirror-dagger. It is too small to fight with, and I cannot risk it breaking. It is far, far too precious.

Moya is raising hell on the bank. She is surrounded by her supporters, withered, stout, pale, grey shadowy creatures. Many are trolls and goblins, but a few look like fairies. Fairies whose skin has turned to charcoal, whose faces are as twisted as hers.

Statues fight at her behest as well, but they crumble more easily than the others. Helmets and breastplates litter the shoreline, slivers of silver in the shallows.

Her cheek is bleeding where the bolt cut her. She looks dishevelled, but her appearance only adds to her madness. It is hard to tell if she is mad with power or mad with exhaustion. Her hair is all over the place, her eyes white and wild. Purple sparks hiss from her fingers. She looks up when she sees me approaching.

"What a lovely little welcome party you've brought me, my beauty!" she cackles. Her voice is like ice. "I am sure they will make welcome additions to my army!"

She grabs a fistful of blue energy in her palm and tosses it at James. It hits him squarely in the chest and he falls into the shallows. I plunge after him, pulling him to the surface. He splutters and coughs and then pushes me away. His eyes are not his own.

"James–"

He raises his sword towards me, but it misses and he falls into the water. I grab the back of his shirt, wrenching him towards the bank. His hand dives for his weapon, but I hit him with the back of my hand. Hard.

He spits blood in the sand. "R-Rose?" He looks at me dumbly.

I turn back to Moya. Her expression drops.

"Magic not working as well as it used to?" I ask.

Moya glares. She claps her hands, and the entire garden is engulfed in a thick, tangible darkness.

"The lake!" I scream to my companions. "Get in the lake!"

It will be harder for Moya to find them there, I reason. She won't be able to sense their movements too much. They'll be able to hide, even if she can see through this smog as well.

I do not need to see. This is my home. I know it in any light.

There is a scramble in the water. Crying, shouting, flailing. I sense I only have a few minutes before the darkness begins to falter, like all of her magic. A few minutes is all I need.

Gradually, eventually, visibility returns. My heart clenches in my chest. From my hiding place, the devastation is clear. The gardens have been transformed into a wasteland, a battleground. The trees lying in flaming, crumpled heaps. The statues have been chewed up. Between the ruin of the landscape and the decimation of the shore, bodies are piled. My home is barely recognisable. I pray that the bodies I see are not my friends'.

Where are the villagers? I cannot see anything moving in the water. Not a splash, not a glimmer–

When I lock eyes on James, I see that he and the others have been tied up in weeds, held with their heads just above the surface. They are completely trapped.

"Where are you, little beauty?" Moya croons. "Come out. You cannot hide forever. I'll burn this place to the ground, eventually. Burning to death is not pleasant, so I hear. I can give you a quicker death than that. I'll even let you see your beloved beast again."

Thorn. How long does he have left?

"Although, I notice he is mysteriously absent from our little soiree. Could it be that the dear old beast isn't even with us any more?"

No. No, he is still here.

"I tell you what, beauty. Surrender yourself to me, and I will let your friends live. I might even spare the whole village. What is one little village when the world will be mine? You still have a family, don't you?"

I keep to my hiding place.

"I see, I see. How about this? I will even spare *him*, if he still lives. I have no need of the boy's destruction now that I am free. You, on the other hand, you are far too troublesome. But if I can save him, I will. Fairy's promise."

She might be the only thing, the *only* thing, that can save him. But would Thorn ever forgive me, if I surrendered to her? If I left him alone? He would never hate me, I am sure of that, but if there is a life after this one, how could I bear to watch him shoulder this world –or Moya's version of it– alone? His death would destroy me, and mine would obliterate him. It is simple; we cannot live without each other. This is not a matter of saving someone's life, but saving their soul. It is mine that I am sacrificing when I leap out of the tree and plunge the shard of mirror into Moya's back.

I am hurled into the shallows. Moya is cackling still, but blood fills her mouth. She spits it onto the stones, and then reaches round and pulls the shard from her flesh.

"This little shard... did you think... that this could contain me? Did you see the last prison that was built for me?"

She tosses it into the water. I go after it, but her hand fastens around my ankle and yanks me back to the bank. Weeds wrap around my feet. She towers over me, grabbing my fists in hers.

"What a sad attempt, beauty," she grins. "Much like your attempt to love that silly creature."

Thorn. Thorn, I'm sorry. I'll be with you soon–

"No last words?"

She releases one of my hands, moving to grab a fallen weapon. Why doesn't she finish me off with magic? Has she run out?

"How about these ones?" she laughs. "True love will never set you free–"

My free hand reaches into my apron pocket. Before she can turn, before she can raise her own weapon, I plunge mine into her chest.

For one long, awful minute, Moya just stands there, still, her sword in her hand... then she turns her face towards the shard of mirror resting against her heart. I can almost feel it, struggling to continue beating, with the Mirror of Truth lodged inside it.

"See what you really are," I say.

The bonds around my feet shrivel away. The villagers are dropped into the water. Her remaining supporters freeze, paralysed.

"You are darkness, and dust, and poison," I say, rising above her.

Her white face begins to crumple. Her whole body seems to cave in, twitching like a spider in the flame. The clouds begin to part.

"Try surviving in the light."

In a flash, she is gone. Her supporters vanish into shadow. The skies open, the rain begins to pour. All fires are extinguished. I barely have time to look and see if the others are all right before I begin tearing towards the castle.

Thorn.

Chapter Twenty-Nine

The Transformation

Through the chaos and the debris, I race back to the castle, back to him. The others are not far behind, stopping only to free their friends or help people up. By the time I arrive, a crowd has already gathered in the ballroom, being kept at bay only by Freedom.

Three familiar lights hover wordlessly by Thorn's side. Freedom has made a pillow for his head, and covered him with a cloak. The dark stain at his side is growing bigger, and I wonder why Freedom hasn't tried to fix him. Then I remember; this was Freedom. He always knows when an arrow has hit its mark.

I look back at him, his face grey and grave.

"Rose–"

"No."

"I'm so–"

"No!"

Thorn calls out my name, and holds up his hand. I crush down on my knees, wrap my fingers around his and kiss them.

His grip is frail, kitten-weak and shaking.

I do not need to tell Freedom to leave, he is already moving. Somewhere in the corner of my eye I see him go towards the door, to usher people away. There are faces, faces I don't know, don't care about, have no right to be here. *Go away*, I think. There is only one person I want to be with, only one face I want to see.

"I was afraid... I would go... before you returned."

"I will always come for you," I assure him. I stroke his cheek. "I defeated Moya. She's gone."

"I'm glad," he says. His voice is hard and laboured, and digs into me like broken glass. "The castle, at least, will be free of her..."

"Thorn," I whisper.

"Speaking of terrible relatives," he continues, "your brother has impeccable aim..."

"Free–"

"Forgive him, Rose. He did not know... what I am..."

I lean forward, holding his hand ever-more-tightly. There are only inches between us, no space at all. "I have always known," I say desperately. It is so important he understands this. "Always."

He reaches up his spare hand and strokes my hair. "Bring him here. Bring your family. The castle is yours. Use it however you will."

"I won't... *I can't*... not without you. This is our home, do you hear? Yours and mine..."

"I am glad to hear you say that." His grip tightens, and his body jerks. I have seen this in animals, kills of Freedom's. I know he has seconds, seconds left. *I* have seconds left.

"Thorn, you don't have permission to die. I won't let you. I refuse."

"Thank you..."

I graze my fingers against his temple. He moves slightly under my touch. He is still here. He can feel me. He is here and so am I.

"What for?" I ask.

"For wanting me."

I open my mouth, shake my head, and my tears slide out like venom. "*Wanting you*? Of course you are wanted. How can you even... how can you even suggest otherwise? Do you not realise what you are? I need you, Thorn. I need you to stay with me. I just... I just got you back. We're ready for our happy ending."

"Could there... ever have been... a happy ending... for us?"

I close my eyes and swallow back my tears, leaning in a little closer. I run my thumb along his lips. "Any ending when I am with you is happy."

His fingers wind through my hair, his palm presses against my cheek. He clutches me close to him and whispers in my ear. "I love you, Rose," he says. "I have always, always... *Rose*..."

My name is the last thing he says. His eyes glaze over. He is falling away from me.

I throw myself against his chest, clutching him closely. He cannot leave. I will not let him. I wind myself tightly into his body. I will not let him go.

"I love you, Thorn. I love you. I love..."

I want to tell him how much. I want to explain to him just how seriously I cannot be without him, but the words are as lost to me as he is.

There is a little flicker of something in his eyes, a little flash of recognition, acknowledgement.

And then he goes limp, and his hand slides to the ground. I pick it up, kiss it, putting it around my neck and willing him, begging him, to wake up. To squeeze back. To say those words again, those words I have always known but never heard aloud.

"Thorn? Did you hear me? I love you. You know that, right? You have to know that. You need to know. I love you, I love you, I..."

I forget time. I forget the room, the faces, the battle. I forget everything but Thorn. I cling to him, hands holding fistfuls of whatever I can grab. I cannot let him go. This can't be it. This cannot be happening.

"Rose..." There is a hand on my shoulder. Freedom's.

I try to swat him away, but that would mean separating myself from Thorn, which cannot happen. I tell him to leave, or try to. I can't stop screaming.

"You have to move."

I can't...

"Let go of him."

I won't.

"Rose!"

His hands are wrenching me away. I flail against him, striking out with my fists. I scream, I beat him. I want to hurt him, to pull out his hair, to hate him. I struggle, fighting. Why can't he just leave me?

"Get away from me! Killer! How could you, how could you?"

"Something's happening..."

I force myself to look back at Thorn. I do not want to see him dead. I just want to curl up beside him and pretend that he is holding me back.

But I can barely see Thorn's body. He is covered in golden mist, and his fur shimmers like moonlight. The mist spreads across the floor, vanishing into the corners of the room. When it hits the grand portrait at the edge of the hall, a sheet of light springs out onto the floor. There is a sound like a gong, and bits of light come spitting out into the room like fireworks.

A golden figure steps out of the portrait and crosses the room to where I last saw Thorn. She has dark hair flowing down her back, and a gown of pale gold that drifts across the flagstones like smoke.

Queen Eilinora.

The mist clears, and I cry out. Thorn is gone. In his place is a young man about Freedom's age. A beautiful young man, with a slightly crooked nose, and dark mane of hair the exact same colour as Thorn's fur. I have seen this face before, in my dreams, in the mirrors.

Thorn.

The woman bows down beside him, and places her long, elegant fingers over his wound. Bright light shimmers all around, and Thorn's chest begins to rise.

A scream of relief escapes me as his eyes flicker open. The same, wonderful eyes. He blinks up at the woman by his side, and all my questions about who she was –and the shrine he kept to her– are immediately answered.

"Mother?" He frowns.

The tears falling down her face are given free passage, and her smile lights up the room. "Hello, dear." She touches his cheek. "You've grown."

They embrace there on the floor, in the dust and the ruin. She sobs into his hair and kisses his cheeks, over and over. He clings to her like a child, and I cannot move.

Freedom's hands dig into my shoulders. "Mercy me..."

Eventually, the two of them part. Thorn's mother turns to me, rushes forward, and clasps my hands in hers. She looks at me as if I'm the miraculous one. "Thank you," she says, "for saving my son."

Thorn looks up at me with his strange, wondrous face. He looks as baffled to be here as I am to see him in his new, fleshy body. "Rose–" he starts.

I do not let him finish. He barely has time to hold out his arms before I launch myself into them. My arms wrap around the back of his neck and he wraps himself around me. I breathe him in. He smells just the same, but the bare skin of his cheek touches mine in a way it never did before, and lightning shoots through me of a new and alarming kind.

"Rose," he says breathlessly.

"Don't talk."

I inch myself back and plant my hands firmly on his face. His mouth is open, too shocked to smile. He is alive. Alive and well and more beautiful than ever.

His fingers wind into my hair. I feel his hand cup the back of my neck. The other slides around my waist. I know he is feeling me differently too. It is as if I have gained another sense.

Our faces slide together. Our noses touch. Our mouths collide. I am kissing Thorn, pulling him into me. My insides burn, my flesh trembles, and I feel like we will split into starlight.

Breathless, we part, see each other, and laugh. I hold his face again.

"I probably owe you an explanation," he says.

"It can wait," I say. Then I kiss him again.

Chapter Thirty

Two Hearts

"When my son was little more than a babe, my sister placed a powerful curse on him, transforming him into a beast." Eilinora explains. "She hoped, I've no doubt, that I would slay him myself, not seeing him for what he was. But, much like you, I saw him from the start. Despite how wild he was. A mindless creature, at first. Her magic was so strong that even I could not undo it. I managed to soften the curse, bringing back his mind, save for one night every month when dark magic was at its peak. I searched desperately for a cure and finally, Moya gave me one: my son would be restored when a true beauty, fierce in soul and fair of heart, could love him for who he truly was. However, if he loved her, and she left him and broke his heart, he would surely perish."

"And that would be the end of every drop of good magic here," Thorn adds. His voice is ever-so-slightly different now, less rough. Still his. "Any magic containing Moya would snap. She would be free again."

"It would have broken my heart, too," the Queen says softly, gazing at her son. "I could not have kept her away from a world without you in it."

I stare at this new Thorn, almost lost for words. "But... I did leave you."

"It took a little while for me to lose all hope," he explains. "I saw you in the mirror. I dreamt of you, and dared to dream that you desired to return. That hope kept me alive for a little longer, but it could never have lasted until the next solstice."

"But," I continue, "it says you just have to find someone who loves you. I have loved you for a long time!"

Thorn smiles, and I can tell he had not known that this was the case. "Apparently, you had to say it."

"I *did* say it!" I retort. "Just not... to you. Or in so few words. And in any case, you didn't say anything either!"

"I did! Just in more words than you!"

"Well, I wasn't going to say it first!"

"I asked you to marry me, Rose!"

"You didn't say it was because you loved me!"

"It was implied!"

"You should say you love someone before you marry them. It's rather integral to the whole business."

Behind Thorn, next to Freedom, I see Ariel, not as a sprite, but as a full, whole person. She nods approvingly. Margaret and Ophelia join her. All whole. Ophelia's wings flicker with nervous energy. A minute later, Bramble comes splintering down the stairs. He crashes into Thorn and licks us fervently. We squeeze him between the two of us, the three of us together again. Bramble, Rose and Thorn.

"What's your real name?" I ask him. It is about time that I knew it.

He grins sheepishly. "Keane," he admits. "Not that anyone other than Mother ever really used it. It never quite suited."

"It means handsome, in our language," the Queen explains.

"Of course it does."

"But I really do prefer Thorn."

I look up at the man beside me. I am still not quite used to his appearance, but there is still the beast I loved in his eyes, in the bump in his nose, in the colour of his hair.

"Why did you not tell me who –what– you really were?"

"It would not have helped. If I had told you the truth–"

"I would have–" *I would have told you a lot sooner.*

"You would have pitied me. You cannot love through pity. I have told others, before. They tried, oh, they tried so hard, but knowing what they knew, they were trying to love me for who I could be, and not who I was." He places a hand against my cheek. "I could not risk that with you."

"This is your secret, I take it?" I ask. "Just to be sure. There's nothing else?"

He laughs. "No, this is it. No more secrets, I assure you."

The Queen touches his shoulder. "There are a few things you and I need to discuss."

I sense that the two of them need some time alone, and even though being away from his side is the last place I want to be right now, I let her lead him away. They deserve this time more than I do. Thorn glances in my direction as he disappears, smiling nervously. We have a lot to discuss too.

I walk back to the meadow with Freedom and the rest of his party. Bramble accompanies us. Dawn is spreading across the castle, and the sudden burst of magic has quietly brought life back into the garden. It sleeps, softly, like the day before the first snowdrops of spring. Closed buds hum in the bushes.

Everything is so perfectly still, that the gentle trickle of the stream seems voluminous. A delicate silver bridge arches over the widest part. Freedom stops, half-shrugging, half-laughing. Everyone else totters over, as if in a dream. Nothing else can surprise them today.

"I imagine this means you are remaining put, for the present," he says, one hand on the railing. He gazes out at the mountains. "I need to go," he continues, as if I didn't expect this. "The rest of the village should be told– wouldn't want them to worry, or do something stupid. You know, like I did."

I cannot think of something to say in response to this. I am still angry with him. I will never forget the terror of almost losing Thorn, the fear of being split in two. It is a mark, a brand against my heart. My anger at Freedom will fade much quicker.

"You are a strange couple," he says eventually.

I knot my brows together. "We're not," I say resolutely. "We are both very similar. I never knew myself, until I knew him."

Now it is Freedom's turn to frown. "You have always been yourself."

"Not with other people."

"Well, that's embarrassing– my little sister being wiser than me."

"It's not the first time, Freed."

"No, I guess not. I hope I know what it's like, some day." He pauses for a moment. "The willowy fairy girl, with the lovely eyes–"

"Ariel?"

"Yes. Is she–"

"Don't."

"Right. Well. One more question."

"Yes?"

"Why do you have a wolf for a pet?"

I frown. "Bramble's not–" I glance back at my large, yellow-eyed companion. "Oh. *OH*! He... he didn't look like that when we got him! Oh... this explains a few things..."

Freedom laughs, already over the bridge. "That'll teach you not to judge by appearances," he scoffs.

Back in the castle, I find the whole place lit with a strange, luminous glow, as if someone has washed away a film of dust I never noticed before. Ariel, Ophelia and Margaret are already sweeping up the debris by the time I return.

"Don't you three ever rest?"

"No," they say in synchronise.

Ophelia drops her broom and literally flies into me. "Look, Rose, hands! I have real hands again, and wings!"

"They suit you."

"I know!"

Ariel casts a cursory glance over me. "Hmm, not the outfit I would have chosen to meet the mother-in-law in..."

I look down. My dress is ripped to shreds, covered in mud, spots of blood, and pond weed. My skin is splattered with scratches. I can only imagine what my face looks like. Another part of me giggles. *She called the queen my mother-in-law.*

"Rose garden," she suggests. "I'll lay out some clothes for you."

"You don't have to–"

"Rose garden!" the fairies snap.

I think it is best to listen to them, and slowly make my way upstairs. Thorn and his mother are conversing in our parlour. The door is wide open, and their voices far from hushed. I cannot help but overhear them.

"About Rose, dearheart–"

"Please mother, don't say anything about her not being royal, because–"

"I like her."

"Oh. Good. Because I was just about to demand you turn me back into a beast. I have no intention of being human without her."

"I like her," says the Queen more fervently, "and I look forward to getting to know her better. Although, I think I should leave the two of you alone for a while."

"Alone? Mother, where will you go–"

"I wish to search for the remainder of our court, the ones I cast out to protect. If any still live, I would have them return, if they wish."

"I... I never thanked you," says Thorn, "I never even *wanted* to thank you, not till now. For what you did. What you sacrificed to save me."

The Queen reaches out a hand to touch his cheek. "A

mother will do anything to save her child."

She looks up, and notices me standing there. "Go and clean yourself up," she suggests to her son. "I should like to talk with Rose for a moment."

His eyes follow hers, and his face breaks into a giddy, awkward smile when he sees me. "Please don't frighten her off."

"She is not one to scare easily."

Thorn leaves the room, brushing the back of my hand with his as he does so. There is a strange nervousness between us now. Before either of us can utter a word, Ophelia comes flying straight down the corridor, accompanied by the other fairies. They swamp him and immediately drag him off down the corridor.

The Queen calls to me. "Did you hear all that?" she asks.

I nod. "I should warn you, I'm a terrible eavesdropper."

She holds up her hand dismissively. "I counted roughly three times. There's plenty you missed."

That is one of my theories confirmed. "You've been here then, the entire time?"

"More or less."

It must have been awful, watching her son in such pain, unable to help him. For a minute, I wonder if she resents me, for not freeing him sooner, but I don't sense anything like that from her. I believed her when she said she liked me.

"You will never be queen, you know," she says.

"Thank heavens for that. I would make a very awkward one. It might even have to turn him down because of it."

The Queen does not smile. "My son is only half-fey. He has inherited some magic from me, but he has his father's mortality. I will outlive him by centuries."

My mind flashes back to a conversation I had with Thorn, ages ago, when I first arrived at the castle. "Being here is not *my* punishment." The curse placed on him was Eilinora's punishment, and although her son survived, she has nevertheless endured the worst of it. She had lost him: lost his childhood, lost his future, and now, lost him to me.

"He has so many years left, though," I remind her. "So many still for you to spend with him–"

"So many for *you* to spend with him," she interrupts. "I like you, Rose. I may envy the years you will have with him that I will not, not truly, but I like you nonetheless. I could not have chosen better."

"But you did choose me." I realise. "It was you who conjured the flowers that lured me here in the first place, and the rain that made me go into the castle."

The Queen falls silent. It was not Moya's magic that trapped me here. Moya wanted me gone.

"The castle had maybe a year's worth of magic left," she admits quietly. "We were running out of time. I knew the gateway was open, I felt the presence of a young girl nearby. I took a risk. Do you blame me?"

I should, perhaps, but how can I, when I have Thorn because of it? "And... and you opened the way to let me back in, didn't you?" She nods.

"Most of my magic was always focused on keeping Moya locked away. I had to... I had to vanish completely from Thorn's life when he was still very little, in order to preserve my power. I kept some for emergencies; that was certainly one of them."

"Did you... did you send me the dreams? Were you the one who let me know he was in trouble?"

At this, the Queen startles slightly. "No," she responds slyly, "that... that I think was all you."

"Is that... my power, do you think?" I ask finally. "I know I'm supposed to have one. My mother could sense the future, I think, but I–"

"Have you not worked it out yet?"

I shake my head.

"You see the truth of things," she says. "Or the potential of it. The gardens, the weather, mimic your feelings. It would not have been so strong, in your realm, but I imagine you kept a lovely garden. You imagine a thing as beautiful, and so it becomes so. It was you who brought life back to this place, and your connection alone that brought about any dreams you had."

"That's it?"

"It's no small thing, to see a thing as beautiful."

"I just... I thought it would be more important, is all."

The Queen smiles, and reaches out to touch my cheek. All the queenly pretence evaporates with that touch. She reminds me of my own mother. "It was very important to me," she finishes, and sweeps across the threshold, down the long hall, to the gilded chamber where Thorn's ruined cradle lies.

I cannot tell you precisely what happens during the rest of the day; minutes and hours pass in a blur, short on substance but long in length. The castle is swept and tidied and primped, food is laid out in the old-fashioned way, though I have no appetite for it. Murmurs of preparing it for guests flitter about. I see little of Thorn during this time, and the fairies seemed to have multiplied, appearing everywhere all at once and creating a bustling hive of energy. I grow tired. I long for the solace of our empty castle, and realise, with odd longing, that it will never be empty again.

It feels like it will be days until Thorn and I are alone again, and eventually, defeatedly, I drift off to my room.

The candles are all lit, the bathtub filled with hot, soapy water. A basket of roses sits on the table, and Ariel is darting about the room, making the bed and laying out the clothes. She grins when I come in, flopping down on the bed she's half-made.

"I'm your lady's maid!" she announces.

"Says who?" I pretend to be annoyed, even though I am secretly overjoyed. I am going to like getting to know Ariel better.

"Me," she declares cheerfully, and then leaps off the bed to help me unlace what remains of my dress. "In unrelated news, does your brother have a–"

"Please don't finish that sentence."

She sighs dramatically. "I haven't had a body for so long, I think I deserve a little–"

"Stop, please, I beg you."

Ariel pushes me into the bath and dumps a jug of water on my head. I make a joke about missing her fairy form and she splashes me before pouring in a heaped measure of something soft and calming into the waters. This is by far the best bath I have ever taken. I soak for hours.

Eventually, Ariel helps me out of the bath and finishes scrubbing me dry. I slip into my dressing gown. There's a warm tray of soup on the table. I realise how long it's been since I've eaten.

"I'll leave you alone now," she says, and turns to go.

It is blissfully quiet, dark and warm. I finish the soup, licking the plate clean. I have never been so famished in my life.

There is a knock at my door and I smile. I do not need to answer it. A second later I turn around and Thorn is there. I leap into him with such force that it knocks him into the wall. I have forgotten that he is not as strong as he once was.

"Careful," he whispers huskily. "I'm struggling with my balance slightly. I have to admit, I'm missing the tail."

I grin up at him. "Does it feel right though, this body?" It certainly feels right to *me*.

His smile is slight, but erupts out of him when he slides his hand across my bare shoulder, stopping right before my nightdress begins. "Like everything I imagined and more."

Our lips are together again, and my skin explodes under the sensation of his. We wheel around, and end up in the chair beside the hearth, barely breaking for air.

When we do finally pull back, breathless and giddy, I run my fingers over his features, learning every new inch of him. How can he still look so much like his beastly self? I curl my fingers into his hair and kiss him some more, while his fingers explore the inches of my uncovered skin with new skill. The feel of his flesh against mine sends fire down my spine. I place my hands on his neck, brushing against his collar, and desperately wish the rest of his clothes would just melt away. I wonder what he would say if I asked him to remove them.

For minutes, moments, hours, we sit in perfect silence, breaking only to giggle. There is no need to talk for that time, there is nothing to say. Eventually though, Thorn speaks. His soft fingers are wrapped around my hair while I stroke the smoothness of his chin.

"Better?" he asks.

"I almost miss the hair."

Thorn laughs. "I suppose I could grow a beard."

I tug on the tiny cleft in his chin. "I don't know. I like you this way, too."

"You are so difficult to please."

I press the tips of my fingers to his lips, and his palm brushes my cheek. Neither one of us dares look away.

"I like you this way, too," he says.

I tilt my head, catching his hand against my shoulder. "What way?"

"All the ways." Thorn's mouth twitches crookedly. He leans down and kisses me with it, just briefly, eyes open, as if he doesn't want to stop looking.

My hands return to his features. "If all that it took to break the spell was for me to say I loved you," I ask, "why would you not say it first?"

"I didn't know you had to say it," Thorn tells me. "All the curse said was that I had to find someone to love me. I didn't know if she just had to fall for me, act on those feelings, or announce them. Ariel suspected that the latter was the case, but we couldn't be sure. I convinced myself that whatever you felt for me, it didn't quite match the level of my affections. I mean, I hoped, desperately. You gave me plenty of reason to hope. Your desire to return if you ever left, your insistence that you wouldn't forget me... when you lost your chance to go home to save me. But I thought your feelings might have strayed into the realm of familial. Whenever I questioned you about them, you seemed to suggest that anyone would have done what you did. I thought perhaps that, although you cared for me, your actions were motivated by morals rather than love. Then... the gardens started to die. I knew that somehow they were tied up in your feelings, and I took it as a sign. Either you didn't love me, you had fallen out of love with me, or you didn't love me enough."

My heart aches with the pain I must have put him through. I thought my feelings, confused as they were, were plain to see. I was worried my heart was too visible, I should have been afraid it was too hidden.

"You still should have told me," I say quietly.

Thorn groans but does not pull away. "I did, Rose! At least, I tried–"

"Well, you did an appalling job–"

"Did you not *hear* my poem–"

"Had you actually said it, of course I would have said it back–"

"I didn't know that!"

"How could you not know that? It practically sung from my skin."

"I hoped, Rose. I really did. I so desperately wanted to tell you, but I was... afraid. Afraid in the way a normal, mortal man would have been."

"Well," I say softly, playing with the folds of his shirt, "I can understand that. I was terrified in a normal, mortal way too. It had so little to do with you being a beast," I explain, desperately hoping he understands this, "and so much to do with me being afraid of the hurt."

"I would never hurt you."

"You would if you died. Which, by the way, you come close to a lot. No more of that, please."

"I will do my very best."

I lie down against his chest, and stay there for a while, listening to the beautiful beat of his heart. *My heart.* "When... did you fall in love with me?"

Thorn smiles, his heart beating a little faster. "I cannot put a time or date to it," he replies. "But early, very early. I was quite taken when you didn't scream at me."

"Be serious!"

"I am. I may look quite the dashing fellow now–"

"You have *always* been a dashing fellow–"

"And I would hate to be accused of having low standards, but I do prefer it when my prospective companion does not scream in terror at the sight of me."

I snicker a bit at his dripping tone, and snuggle back against him.

"Your laugh," he says quietly.

"What?"

"I loved the first time you laughed at me, when I teased you about your snort. My life has not had much laughter in it, and I saw a different side to you then. But I knew I truly loved you the night after you tried to take down a pack of wolves for me. I dared to dream, then, that you cared for me. I never stopped dreaming, after that night. You were my salvation and my doom, and every day afterwards was an ecstasy of agony, wondering which you would be."

"I knew I loved you when I thought that you were going to die," I whisper, and then clarify. "The first time, when I stayed. I knew then. But I loved you that day before, down by the lake. I loved you the night on the rooftop, when I almost fell asleep in your arms. I loved you when we made music together, when I fell from the tree, and didn't want to move. I think I even loved you that first day in the roof garden, when you wanted to kiss me, because I wanted to kiss you too."

Thorn leans across and kisses me again. His mouth crinkles into a smile. "Say that again."

"Um... I wanted to kiss you too."

"No," he whispers, "just the part when..."

"Oh," I say, "oh. I love you."

He kisses my neck. "Again."

"I love you. I love you, I love you..."

I want to call out, *forever, always, for eternity.* I want to tell him until the words lose meaning, but I do not. Those words will never lose their meaning, nor the shape they bear being so long in the making.

Firelight dances around the chamber and flames give way to ashes. Outside, the wind howls, and the rains come crashing down. The world moves and shifts and changes. I pull Thorn gently towards the bed and sit down, arching backwards. I take his hand, place it on my shoulder, and guide his fingers. Slowly, gently, we peel back the layers of cloth dividing the two of us. The slightest touch of Thorn's flesh on mine makes my insides sing. I am bursting with bubbling, liquid gold.

We do not discuss it, we are passed words now. We are both breathlessly, wordlessly eager to eclipse the one gap between us. He may, at one point, ask me if I'm sure. I say yes.

Thorn's lips touch my neck. His warmth spreads through me. The kisses descend. My fingers graze his back, glide down the shape of him, feel him in places I never knew existed. I pull his face back to mine and tug his body so that it covers me completely, and then I kiss him so deeply I could drown.

I don't want his face anywhere but here. I want his kiss to merge with mine, I want to press our bodies together until not a cell remains of me that isn't anchored to him.

We do not sleep. Afterwards, we lie in the candlelight, tracing new parts of our bodies. We whisper to each other, holding each other until the candles have worn away to stubs and faint traces of dawn glitter along the horizon. I lie my head on Thorn's chest and count every heartbeat. And then, at the exact same time, our eyes link together, and we ask each other the exact same question.

"Will you marry me?"

Epilogue

We are married within the month. Our wedding is a relatively intimate affair, by the standards of the fairy court, as much of it is still at large. Thorn does insist on inviting the entirety of the village, in thanks for flocking to my rescue, which raises the numbers substantially. He also insists that his mother uses both of his names for the ceremony.

It takes a while for Freedom to work his way back into my affections, and it isn't until the day of our wedding that I thoroughly forgive him, when he thrusts a clumsily wrapped book into my hands.

"A book, Freedom?" I say snootily, "I'm afraid I already have all of the books."

"Trust me," he says, "you don't have this one."

I slowly, carefully, pull back the wrapping. It is a thick leather-bound book, with a large golden title. *Beauty and the Beast.*

I peel back the first page. There is a beautiful illustration of a girl in a long red cloak, a basket of berries at her hip, staring out over a frosty landscape at a field of flowers.

"Freedom..." I flick through the other images. The detail, the artistry is incredible. I feel a little lump rising in my throat.

"Ariel helped me with some of the finer details," he admits. "I hope she didn't exaggerate too much."

"You've been spending a lot of time with her."

"We've been working on this!"

"Is that the only reason?" "No," he admits cautiously. Then, "Do you like it?"

"I didn't even know you could read!"

He punches me in the arm, and he knows that he is forgiven.

Not long after the wedding, Eilinora leaves the castle to search for the remainder of her court. Her visits home are not frequent at first, and Thorn and I spend many years more or less alone.

We travel, visiting places we both thought we would never see outside of an image. We barely spend one day apart.

Some years after Thorn and I marry, we welcome our first child, Briar. The day she is born, Thorn takes her in his arms and cries, admitting that he was sure he could never love another girl as much as he loves me, and yet he manages to spread his love not just between us both, but the next three children that follow; Grace, Leo and Liberty.

After the birth of her first grandchild, Eilinora's visits become much more frequent. She looks forward to the days, I think, that she can take them with her. I always sense a sadness in her that is never to be appeased. She mourns Leo, and mourns the time she should have spent with Thorn, time that is never to be hers again. She really did sacrifice her life to save him. She treasures every moment she has with her grandchildren, but she is always a little afraid. They too will be snatched from her before their time.

Papa, Beau, Hope, Honour and Charles, and their many children, often come to visit us, strolling across the gateway as if it is no more than a door. The time will come, I know, long after I am dead, when Eilinora will close it again, and we will be forgotten by the world of men, but I try not to think about this. It is unimportant to our present.

Freedom is not a visitor– he moves into the castle within weeks of our wedding. Officially, he is Captain of the Guard. Unofficially, he serves as court painter, and Ariel's favourite person to tease. So much so, that they eventually marry. Although fairies and humans are not known to be the most fertile of pairings, in time they have two daughters, who cause just as much chaos in Freed's life as I believe he deserves.

His book rarely ever sits on a bookshelf, it is too often read. To this day, it is still the story our children ask for most. We tuck them all up in our bed, Thorn one side, me another, with Bramble at our feet. I open the pages of my favourite book and begin to read.

"Once upon a time, in the midst of the longest winter that any man or beast has ever known, a Thorn fell in love with a Rose..."

And, you will be very glad to know, they are living happily ever after.

--The End--

If you enjoyed this story, please consider leaving a review on Amazon/Goodreads. Many thanks!

Coming Soon:

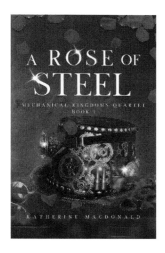

Head to Booksprout to score yourself a
FREE Advanced Reader Copy!

https://booksprout.co/arc/72719/a-rose-of-steel-
a-steampunk-beauty-and-the-beast-retelling

Now Out...

Read Thorn's side of the story in the companion tale

Afterword

To anyone who has ever dreamt of fairytales and true love, may you find the path in life you were meant to walk. Be bold, be daring, be afraid-- but never give up on your dreams.

I dreamt all my life of being a writer. I will probably die with stories still in my head. But until that day, I shall continue to craft stories of fierce heroines and gentle heroes, of real love and true magic, of fairies and families and triumph in the face of evil.

For latest updates and the chance to receive Free Advanced Reader Copies of my latest work, please subscribe to my newsletter at www.katherinemacdonaldauthor.com.

Other Books by this Author:

The Phoenix Project Trilogy

Book I: Flight
Book II: Resurrection
Book III: Rebirth

In the "Fey Collection" series:

The Rose and the Thorn: A Beauty and the Beast Retelling
Kingdom of Thorns: A Sleeping Beauty Retelling
A Tale of Ice and Ash: A Snow White Retelling
A Song of Sea and Shore: A Little Mermaid Retelling
Heart of Thorns: A Beauty and the Beast Retelling
Of Snow and Scarlet: A Little Red Riding Hood Retelling

Standalones:

The Barnyard Princess: A Frog Prince Retelling

In the "Faeries of the Underworld" Duology:

Thief of Spring: A Hades and Persephone Retelling (Part One)
Queen of Night: A Hades and Persephone Retelling (Part Two)
Heart of Hades: A collection of bonus scenes (subscribers only)

The Mechanical Kingdoms Quartet:

A Rose of Steel

Coming Soon:

A Slipper in the Smoke

About The Author

Katherine Macdonald

Born and raised in Redditch, Worcester-shire, to a couple of kick-ass parents, Katherine "Kate" Macdonald often bemoaned the fact that she would never be a successful author as "the key to good writing is an unhappy childhood".

Since her youth, Macdonald has always been a storyteller, inventing fantastically long and complicated tales to entertain her younger sister with on long drives. Some of these were written down, and others have been lost to the ethers of time somewhere along the A303.

With a degree in creative writing and eight years of teaching English under her belt, Macdonald thinks there's a slight possibility she might actually be able to write. She may be very wrong.

She lives in Devon with her manic toddler.

The Rose and the Thorn is her debut novel. A pseudo-prequel, "Kingdom of Thorns" was released in August 2020.

You can follow her at @KateMacAuthor or subscribe to her website www.katherinemacdonaldauthor.com for further updates.